Belonging

A Regent Vampire Lords Novel

By

K.L. Kreig

Published by K.L. Kreig

ISBN-10: 1505915953
ISBN-13: 978-1505915952

Dedication

To my sister, Tara. I would be lost without you, my Irish twin.

Prologue

Three Months Earlier…
Xavier

The look on Devon's face was priceless. He could barely contain his laughter. Xavier had Devon's mate in a stronghold, one arm around her neck, another around her midsection. Her slim, sleek neck was nicely bared for his teeth. One little twist and her spinal column would be permanently severed.

He mentally patted himself on the back. The power-extracting amulet his witch provided operated brilliantly. Since it only worked when he was touching another vampire, his plan was to draw Devon closer to him, and he had just the plan to do that. He also knew it would easily control any power Devon's mate had obtained so far.

He was confused with the power he could feel coursing through her. Since their bonding only recently occurred, she shouldn't be this potent this fast. But he didn't have the time right now to figure out this conundrum, he had more important things to do. Like capture Devon Fallinsworth.

"You broke our deal, brother," Xavier sneered. Devon wouldn't look at him, focusing solely on his mate.

"If you're trying to talk to your luscious mate, I'm afraid Katherine can't really communicate at the moment. You see I have some tricks up my sleeve, too, *brother*. I've spent the last five hundred years fantasizing about the day I would end your life, Devon. The same way you effectively ended mine when you ratted me out like the slimy traitor you are."

Devon remained silent, but Xavier continued anyway. "We could have ruled the world together, Devon. We are among the strongest, oldest and most powerful vampires alive. We could have had it all. We could have been kings! But you had to have a fucking conscience. How can you stomach living side by side with humans? They are animals! They are our food! They are not our fucking equals!"

Devon foolishly told his mate, "It's going to be okay, love."

"Hmmm, I'm not so sure it *is* going to be okay, my sweet," Xavier whispered in her ear. Licking her cheek, he studied Devon the entire time.

He noted every nuance on Devon's face, relishing his anger. Devon made a slight move toward Kate and Xavier jerked her back toward him more firmly, making her wince.

"You'll never make it in time before I snap her neck. And I'm not sure how much fun I would have fucking a vegetable. Never tried it before, but it could definitely be worthwhile. But I really do like my bitches to put up a fight."

Devon's mate started sobbing softly.

"You are one sick motherfucker."

Devon was trying to keep his cool, but was failing miserably. Christ this felt *gooooood*.

"Yes. I am."

"Me for her. That was the deal," Devon demanded. Like he had any leverage in this situation. Xavier was holding all the leverage he needed.

"Me for her, Xavier," Devon begged. Now *that* felt better than he'd thought it would.

"Yes," Xavier sighed. "That was the original deal. Until you broke it by trying to sabotage me. Now I'm afraid there is a new deal on the table. Well ... the *only* deal, really."

"And what might that be?" Devon's jaw ticked back and forth.

"I have been forced to spend the last five hundred years living underground like a lowly sewer rat. All thanks to you. My body has been ravaged beyond any repair, also thanks to you. I have spent the last half a millennia waiting, plotting, anticipating my revenge. And I couldn't have written a better ending to our rivalry if I'd tried. I am going to relish watching you suffer as I fuck and bleed your mate right in front of your eyes. I will let my men line up and use her over and over again. You will watch the life slowly leave her body, unable to save her. And when her body finally gives out and you watch her die, I will enjoy torturing you to the brink of death, only to bring you back again so you can suffer her loss in perpetuity. I will show you no mercy."

Xavier unleashed a tad bit of power, pushing it toward his enemy. But ... *nothing happened*.

What.

The.

Fuck.

Was.

Going.

On?

Not wasting time trying to solve the puzzle of why his powers wouldn't work on Devon, he sunk his fangs into Katherine's neck, and with the first pull of blood, white-hot acid burned his mouth, his esophagus, continuing its way down into his gut.

Poison.

Her blood was poison.

He threw her across the room, clawing at his throat. More concerned about his mate, Devon turned his back toward Xavier, which was a fatal mistake for him. Putting his agony aside, Xavier lunged across the room grabbing for the one vampire he'd waited centuries to capture. Only, instead of securing his nemesis, his hands slipped silently through the hologram in front of him.

Devon wasn't there and neither was Katherine; it only appeared they were. Seconds later the vision disappeared into thin air.

Xavier roared, the deafening sound destroying the rest of his already ruined compound. Fucking Devon and his goddamned illusionary power! But the distraction worked.

Devon had gained the precious time he'd needed to grab his mate and run.

ꕥ

Xavier flashed to his lair on the far outskirts of Buffalo. That was one lesson he'd learned so many years ago, courtesy of the lords. He no longer had just one lair. He had multiple, spread out all over the country. Girls were sprinkled everywhere and their children safely tucked away, only a handful of those closest to him knew where to find them.

As he nursed his scotch, which further burned his already scorched throat, he thought back to what he'd discovered just a short time ago. That dreamwalker, Katherine Martin, was his flesh and blood. She was his daughter. *How could that possibly be?*

Since he had a fucking genetic anomaly that only allowed him to produce females and female vampires couldn't reproduce, his offspring were supposed to have been eliminated. The last thing he'd needed was a constant reminder of his inadequacies roaming the earth.

He'd been duped by that beady-eyed doctor. That was the only explanation. He'd foolishly trusted him to get rid of the evidence so his army would be none the wiser. Show no weakness. Marcus had assured him they were taken care of. Xavier was absolutely furious with himself and his misjudgment. He knew better than to trust a lowly human and yet he'd done it anyway.

He'd lost so many vampires tonight. It was a complete blow and it definitely put a dent in his army. He'd also lost a large chunk of his medical staff, although he had several others spread throughout the other facilities. He'd lost many of his records, but he had backups. And backups to back those up. But the problem now was they were also in his fucking enemies' hands and they would quickly figure out what he was up to. Fortunately, he had another little trick up his sleeve even those physicians weren't aware of. *Never put all of your eggs in one basket.*

Thinking about this new predicament, he remembered the other information he'd discovered when he bit into Devon's mate ... his *daughter*. She was with child. Devon's child. His grandchild.

The more he thought about it, the more he decided how wonderful this little twist of events was. This could be used to his advantage. He had to build reinforcements. He needed to take a step back. Regroup. Rebuild. And maybe it'd be nice to start a little 'family' business.

As he finished his scotch, an idea started blossoming. Yes. Yes ... this was a far better plan than the one he'd had before anyway.

Chapter 1

Present day ...
Analise

"Order up!"

Analise sighed. Her feet hurt. Her back hurt. She had the mother of all headaches. And she had three hours left on her shift.

"Order up, Analise!"

"Effing hold your horses," she mumbled under her breath. Just her luck the prick of a night manager, Henry, walked by at that exact moment.

"Is there a problem, Ana?"

She'd asked him repeatedly not to call her Ana.

"No, sir." She smiled sweetly when all she wanted to do was kick him in his pint-sized balls. Not that she knew from experience they were pint-sized ... *eww.* Scrubbing her eyeballs was the first priority when she got home.

"Good. Then pick up the pace. Table seven has been waiting twenty minutes for their order. Table eighteen needs a refill on their drinks. And you were two minutes late tonight, so you'll make that up on the back end of your shift."

"Yes, sir." What she really meant was, shove your cock up your ass and fuck yourself with it. Unfortunately, she didn't dare say it. She needed this job, as lousy as the hours, the pay and the management were.

She turned to fetch table seven's order when she felt his hand on her ass. It was a full-on grab this time, with an almost painful tightening of his fingers around her curves. She gritted her teeth, moving to get the order. He'd done this repeatedly, getting bolder every time. First a nudge, then a brush, next a pat. Whenever he worked, after her shift she'd ask one of the other waitresses to walk her to her car. She wouldn't be surprised to see his face blaze across the evening news with the caption, *"Flashing suspect arrested. Full story at ten."* He seriously gave her the creeps.

"You okay, my dear?" Cara was a sweet little old waitress that had worked at Ollie's Diner for the last thirty years. They would have to drag her out of here dead. Even then, she would probably haunt the place. How she loved this job so much, doing it day in and day out for thirty years, Analise would never know.

Analise forced a smile. "Just living the dream, Cara." *You need this job, you need this job, you need this job*. She kept repeating those hollow words to herself.

She had exactly one-hundred-thirty-five dollars and forty-two cents in her checking account, her four-hundred-dollar rent was due in ten days, and the book for her class would set her back another one hundred fifty dollars. She wasn't sure where she would come up with *that* money. Upon checking her apron pockets, she counted fifty-two dollars in tips from her last eight hours. *Super*.

Screw it. She didn't need this job that bad. There were plenty of shitty waitress jobs available and she'd just get another one tomorrow. Maybe at a nicer place where the patrons tipped more than fifty cents on a fifty-dollar bill.

She stormed back toward Henry, punching him in the face before throwing a hard knee to his boys. He doubled over; howling in pain, blood gushing from his nose onto the white cracked linoleum floor.

"Keep your fucking hands off me, asshole! This"—gesturing to her body—"is not your playground!"

Her pulse skyrocketed; her heart almost beat out of her chest. She felt like her head might explode. And at the same time, she couldn't be more relieved. As she turned to gather her things she noticed the entire diner had quieted, watching the melee ensue. Cara stood by the register, mouth agape. Analise rushed past her, grabbed her purse and coat, and quickly left through the back entrance.

Getting into her 1979 Chevy Chevette, Analise gave her a little pep talk before turning the key. "Come on, baby girl. Don't make my grand exit turn to shit now." Luck was on her side, for she started on the second try. Her baby may be old, rusted and only have AM radio, but she was still pretty reliable. And most importantly, she was paid for.

Analise drove the six miles to her small rented duplex on the outskirts of Eau Clare. She parked on the dimly lit street, careful to look around before exiting her car. This wasn't exactly the nicest part of town, but it was all she could afford.

She made her way safely to her side of the duplex. Thank Jesus the other half was dark. She did not need to deal with her pervy neighbor, Johnny, on top of Henry tonight. He continually hit on her, making up one excuse after another to talk to her.

The most classic was when he asked to borrow a cup of sugar. *A cup of sugar?* The guy didn't even cook, let alone bake. She wasn't even sure he knew how to operate a microwave. He had empty fast food bags, pizza boxes and beer bottles strewn all over his place. She knew that, not because she had been in his apartment—*that would never happen*—but because he never shut his damn blinds. He was always trying to catch her coming and going.

It took her a minute to open the several locks and deadbolts, breathing a sigh of relief when she finally walked through the door. *Home.* After depositing her keys on the entry table, she kicked off her shoes and removed her coat as she made her way to the bathroom. She needed to wash the stench of the diner away. And her boss's hands.

Starting the bath, she deposited her stinky clothes in the hamper, taking care to retrieve the cash first. While the tub filled, she poured herself a glass of Two Buck Chuck, turned on her favorite playlist from her iPhone—her one splurge outside of her bi-monthly highlights—and recounted her tips. Yep. She was the proud owner of not quite two hundred dollars. Total. *Shit.*

She eased into the hot water as Sia belted out one of her favorite songs: "Chandelier". Relaxing against the cool porcelain, emotions overwhelmed her.

Relief.

Guilt.

Panic. She had actually quit her job. A job she couldn't afford to quit. What the *hell* was she thinking? She wasn't ... as usual. Being a waitress, especially at the shithole where she worked, was barely a living wage, but at least it *was* a wage. Now, she was jobless and practically penniless. *Go me.*

How apt that Sia was singing about holding on for dear life and keeping her glass full until the morning light. She felt exactly the same way as she filled up her now empty wine glass from the cheap bottle she'd brought into the bathroom. In wine, you definitely got what you paid for, but beggars couldn't be choosers.

Analise could admit she was a bit impulsive. At twenty-six years old, she *was* trying to get her life on track, but it was a long slow grind. She'd lived a hard life on the streets since fifteen, but at eighteen, she'd started getting her shit together. With her GED equivalent behind her, she began studies at the University of Wisconsin, but with a whole year left, her sociology degree still felt far out of reach. She had bills to pay and couldn't afford to be a full-time student. Thank

God for her grants or she'd have to give up her dreams of a college degree altogether.

Her thoughts strayed to Beth. They were actually never far from Beth, especially in the three weeks she'd been missing, without a word, without a trace. They'd met on the streets when they were teenagers. She was fifteen and Beth was sixteen. They'd quickly formed a unique bond that Analise never had with another living soul. Beth was her best friend in the whole wide world. Her only friend, really. She accepted Analise for who she was, flaws and all. Hell, she had the same ones. Most of them anyway. Beth knew *most* of her deep, dark secrets and loved her regardless.

Living on the streets was dangerous, especially for two teenage girls. They'd both lived in foster care, which had taken away much of their naiveté, but they were nowhere near prepared for the life they'd ended up living. Some of the things they had to do to survive made her physically ill to remember. She'd lost parts of herself that could never be replaced.

As Starset's "My Demons" played, she thought about how great of a friend Beth was and how much she'd helped save Analise from her own demons. The memories of her past circled her like a flock of vultures, waiting for her complete and utter demise so they could pick at her meager remains. She tried not to think of those days much, choosing to look forward instead. But some days, like today, it was so very hard to do and the vultures seemed ever closer. She could feel their rancid breath slithering over her. On these down days, Beth was the only person who could save her from her self-imposed quicksand, but she couldn't now. Not today.

This past winter, Beth had taken a job as a sous chef in an up-and-coming new restaurant on the lower west side of downtown. Like Analise, Beth couldn't afford much in the way of housing and also lived in a rough, run-down, gang-infested part of town. There were multiple shootings every day. But Beth had taken self-defense classes and carried mace.

Last week in a desperate attempt to find her, Analise had taken two days off and driven to Chicago. Analise had convinced the super to let her into Beth's apartment, but there were no clues. She'd simply vanished. The police had no leads and they weren't doing jack shit. At least that's the way she felt. The detective assigned to the case had even stopped calling her back. It could be because she left a dozen messages a day, each with progressively more curse words, but whatever. If Analise didn't advocate for Beth, no one would.

The worst part of all was she'd *known* something was off the day Beth went missing, but as usual she couldn't pinpoint exactly *what* was off. She'd only known Beth was in danger. It was frustrating. That morning, she'd begged her to be extra careful. Beth had come to rely on Analise's weird instincts just as much as she had and she promised she would take extra care.

In the early years, Analise had ignored these *feelings*. And bad things happened. Living on the streets, she quickly learned to take action when she felt a premonition surface. Did she avoid harm or was she just ultra paranoid? She never really knew, but she was done taking chances. Every time she'd ignored the feeling, things ended badly.

She unconsciously touched the scar on her stomach. It couldn't have ended worse for her *that* night. But she was not that person anymore and wouldn't be again. She was a survivor. She would make a difference in people's lives. She would help others like her. Eventually.

As her skin pruned, the water cooled and her wine ran dry, her conversation with Smitty resurfaced. One good thing to come of her time on the streets was that she knew people. People like Smitty. She had connections ... who had connections ... who knew other people. And those people knew very interesting things.

She'd been thinking about what he'd said all week long, running through a litany of excuses on why she should stay here. She needed her job, she had classes to attend, leave the detective work to the trained. She shouldn't get involved and step into harm's way. But none of those excuses really held water. She'd quit her job, classes could wait and she had a lead that she couldn't very well pass along to the detective. Like where to find a certain Vampire Lord, for example. *Thank you, Smitty.*

Yes, vampires were real. They did, in fact, suck your blood ... and a girl could sign up for that shit at certain places if she wanted. Analise never wanted, even in her most desperate days. And she'd never run across a vampire that she knew of, but she wasn't afraid to either.

And why would a puny, weak human purposely seek out a powerful Vampire Lord, one may ask? Because Analise *knew* a vampire was responsible for Beth's disappearance. In her premonition about Beth she saw darkness, malevolence, evil. She'd heard that the Vampire Lord she sought was extremely powerful, terrifyingly dangerous, but also fair and benevolent.

And while she was shitting her pants at the thought of actually confronting a vampire—okay, maybe she was a little afraid—if that gave her a lead on what happened to Beth, she'd do it. But how far would she go? Could she let someone take her blood and, God forbid, touch her? And wasn't it ironic that she worried more about someone touching her than taking her blood? Just the idea of someone, a man in particular, touching her body was akin to an arachnophobe being covered in spiders. She was hyperventilating just thinking about it.

But she'd do it. She'd do anything necessary to find Beth, even let a man put his hands on her. She'd survive. She had before. Mind made up, tomorrow she would head south to Milwaukee.

To Dragonfly. Lord Devon Fallinsworth's new nightclub.

Chapter 2

Damian

Stepping into Dragonfly, Damian was quite impressed. Looked like he may learn a few things from the Lord of the Midwest, after all. And fuck if that didn't sting, just a little. He decided to come through the main entrance so he could check out the entire club at its height of busyness.

He'd been anxious all day that something radical was about to happen. He blamed it on the premonition he'd had about Xavier, but he wasn't entirely sure that was it. His life was about to tilt on its axis, he just didn't know how yet. Most of his premonitions were more like a gut feeling, intuition some would call it, but it was more than that for him. Every one of them came to fruition. Occasionally he had actual visions, but that wasn't the norm.

The sound of the bass thrummed through his body, pulling him to the present. He fucking loved it. Rhianna's "Don't Stop the Music" blared through the speakers and the dance floor was packed to capacity, humans dry humping each other in the dim lighting. He could smell the pheromones oozing from them, making him hard.

Tearing his gaze from the dance floor, he took in the rest of the place. Walls were painted a deep, blood red. *Subtle.* A long walnut bar spanned the entire right side of the open space. Bartenders frantically tried keeping up, serving fruity concoctions and dry martinis to males lined three deep, hoping to score.

Tables, chairs and black leather couches surrounded the dance floor. A black iron staircase graced both sides of the room, leading to an open upper level that overlooked the main floor. Scanning from down here, Damian could see more of the same decor upstairs. There was a small bar to the left side, also very busy. Since there was no room on the dance floor itself, many people upstairs were bumping and grinding around the railing. The place was hopping for sure.

He made his way toward the back, enjoying the scantily clad females along the way. At six foot six, Damian knew he was imposing and good-looking. It wasn't ego; it was just a fact. He loved sex; he exuded sex, and women knew he would give them immense pleasure. And he never failed to please. They regularly, and willingly, opened their legs for him. Tonight he would enjoy sampling some of the goods, but the darkness was starting to surface and demanded to be fed by particular needs. He could dabble in vanilla, sometimes even enjoyed it, but his preference tended to be darker and it took a particular type of woman to handle those needs. He hoped he would find just the right one tonight.

After stopping several times to interact with beautiful women, he reached the back, greeting the main club manager, Frankie.

"How are things this evening, Frankie?"

"Just fine, my lord."

Frankie seemed nervous. As Vampire Lord of the East, Damian was imposing and intimidating and it's normal that humans felt like a predator was in their midst. But Frankie knew their little *secret*, of course, so he should also know they were fair. He wondered if it was just him or if he was like that with Dev also.

"Place seems to be doing well." Damian flagged the bartender for a drink. Not surprisingly, he was served right away. Patrón, neat, was his drink of choice.

"Yes, sir. Very well."

Damian laughed to himself. Frankie didn't seem to be very well spoken. He must have excellent management skills instead.

Damian threw his drink back in one gulp, shaking his glass at the bartender to indicate another. When he had it in hand, he turned back to Frankie.

"Why don't you show me the underground."

Beads of sweat dotted Frankie's brow. Priceless. Guy better grow a pair or he was going to end up vampire bait. If he were Damian's club manager, he'd be fired on the spot. Maybe Dev needed some help after all.

"Y-Yes sir. Right this way, my lord."

Damian followed him through the back, across the small kitchen to a steel reinforced door that looked like it would lead to a meat locker. Clearly it wasn't, as to the right was a sophisticated security panel. No one's meat was that precious. Well ... except *his*.

Damian knew the code, but let Frankie fumble around a bit, trying twice to get the code right before the door finally clicked open.

"That will be all."

"Thank you, sir," Frankie said as he turned and scurried away like a rat who'd been kicked.

Damian descended toward the underground portion of Dragonfly. At the bottom was another steel door, a duplicate of the one at the top. This one had a different set of codes, which he didn't believe Frankie knew. They all took these precautions to provide the utmost protection from unsuspecting humans accidentally stumbling across their underground clubs. Or from humans who were very much aware, but weren't welcome.

Damian changed his codes daily, sometimes more than once.

He couldn't hear a thing before the door clicked open, proving how soundproof Dev had made the place. It was an important feature to maintain secrecy. Walking into the club, the first thing he noticed was the music was a bit harder down here. In his, he vacillated between harder rock music and erotic, sensual music. Both suited his crowds' tastes. No matter the part of the country, most vampires had similar tastes in music. Country didn't tend to top the list. At least no self-respecting vampire would admit that it did.

Disturbed's "Inside the Fire" thrummed through him. This scene was similar to the one upstairs, with bodies writhing like snakes on the heavily packed dance floor. Of course, upstairs everyone was clothed, some questionably so, but down here ... down here clothing was definitely optional. Everywhere he looked people were coupling, in threesomes or more. All were in various states of undress. All were in various stages of fornication. If he thought the pheromones upstairs were thick, down here they were downright intoxicating.

The décor was a bit edgier than upstairs, Goth being the evident theme. The large open space boasted black walls and ceilings. The dance floor a smooth black marble. The long bar top was dark granite with fluorescent blue flecks peeking through, adding just a touch of color. Chairs and couches were all covered in inky black leather. Medieval sconces hung on the walls, dim red uplighting glowed from each one. *Nice touch*. It was all very sensual, very erotic.

The suggestive scene, coupled with the pheromones bombarding him, made his dick painfully hard. He needed to get laid. And since it had been over a week since he'd last fed, he was starved.

He spotted whom he assumed was Ronson, the underground club manager, rushing toward him. "My lord, glad you could make it. I'm Ronson, Dragonfly's manager." They shook hands.

"Nice to meet you, Ronson. I'd like to see the entire club."

"My pleasure, my lord."

Ronson gave him the grand tour, vamps moving quickly out of his way and females following his every move, even in the throes of sex.

The power rolling off him scared most vamps and attracted most females. Well ... *all* females, really.

What Damian couldn't see from his previous vantage point was there were several alcoves around the edge of the space. The alcoves contained large, circular plush beds, each with a ledge on one side, which he assumed was for drinks. Or leverage. All were occupied and had curtains that could be pulled for privacy, but only one was. It appeared most human females working here weren't self-conscious either. Note to self.

They made their way to a hallway in the back, leading to the private rooms Dev mentioned. He'd just finished gutting, renovating and opening the newest club he'd purchased and a portion catered to tastes leaning toward the darker side. He was anxious to see how Dev's place compared.

In addition to the office, there were a dozen small rooms in total, six lining each side of the short hallway. Each had a window and shades, but the shade could be left open so a couple could be watched if they chose. There was only one room open to tour, but Ronson said all rooms were similar in style and contained implements for pleasure, or pain ... whatever your poison.

This appeared to be almost double the size of his operations. While Damian definitely wasn't hurting for cash, if he'd put half as much effort into actually managing his clubs as he did frequenting them, he had no doubt he could trump even Dev's success. He resolved to pay as much attention to his businesses as he did his investments. After tonight, of course.

"I'd like an introduction."

"Of course, my lord." While Ronson was very respectful of Damian, it was clear he still feared him. As he should. Although Damian was very powerful and had a very short temper, he wasn't prone to violence for violence sake. He was more of a lover than a fighter. Not to mean that he didn't enjoy a good, bloody battle occasionally, because he absolutely fucking did.

Ronson took him to the last room directly at the end of the hallway. There were about a dozen women of all shapes, sizes and nationalities. Damian believed in diversity and inclusion, and he offered the same type of menu in his clubs. Who wanted to bang skin and bones every night? Who wanted only French vanilla on the menu? Most of his customers didn't.

He noticed a particularly beautiful African-American woman in the corner, with very luscious curves. She looked a little nervous, but he could sense a darkness lurking in her as well.

Ronson followed his line of sight, adding, "She's new. Tonight's her first night." While he loved to break in newbies, they weren't always into his style, but he approached her anyway.

"Care for a drink, gorgeous?" He liked to woo a woman just a bit before falling into bed with them. Call him old-fashioned or maybe just not a complete bastard.

"We may be a little mismatched." Over a foot shorter than him, she had to crane her neck to meet his eyes.

"Don't worry about it, doll. Our parts will still fit together nicely, regardless. What's your name?" It was painfully clear she wanted him. He could smell her excitement from across the room. Her blood smelled clean, which was good. He didn't do druggies. All of his girls were regularly tested for drugs and if they were positive, they were kicked out on their asses. He wouldn't stand for that.

"Ah ... it's Angel. Okay, sure."

For the next half hour they chatted while she sipped on a cosmo, loosening up considerably. He leaned down, whispering in her ear, "What do you like, baby?"

"Whatever pleases you, my lord," she whispered breathlessly.

"That leaves the door pretty wide open, Angel. And the things I want to do to your body are most certainly not heavenly."

She sucked in a breath but didn't respond.

"Come. What I want should be done in private." He'd asked Ronson to reserve one of the rooms for him while he was in Milwaukee. He hoped Angel would help exorcise the darkness from him tonight because he didn't have the desire to start all over with another female at this point.

Turned out he had nothing to worry about, as Angel certainly didn't live up to her name, but her friend Star who'd joined them later, sure did. She sucked cock like a champ. Hours later, sated in the pleasures of the flesh, he returned to Dev's estate to grab a couple hours of shuteye. Tomorrow night Rom would arrive and they would begin their search for Kate's two sisters. And, with any luck, secure them safe and sound before Dev and Kate returned from their honeymoon in four weeks.

It was a tall order, but Damian was definitely up for the challenge.

Chapter 3

Mike

"Fucking pick up the fucking phone!" he screamed futilely into his cell at the incessant ringing on the other end.

He'd alternated between calling Dev and Ren the entire day. He'd even tried Kate twice. Not one person answered their goddamned phones. If he did that to them, they'd have his ass fileted and fried for dinner before he could blink. These last three months, he'd been constantly at their beck and call, but fuck no ... when he needed them they were nowhere to be found. Bloodsucking bastards.

He'd been in absolute emotional agony. Jamie was alive. She was living in the shelter that Kate had graciously opened, helping the women recover from their trauma before returning home. They were all allowed to stay indefinitely. All had returned to their homes, except Sarah, Jamie and four others. The guilt he lived with every day was almost unbearable. He drank far too much, but it was the only thing that numbed the pain.

He'd taken a leave of absence from the MPD to work exclusively for Devon, trying to find the psychopath that had taken his Jamie away from him. No matter that she was still alive and she wasn't *his Jamie* any longer. The fires of hell now fueled his vengeance. He wouldn't rest until this motherfucker was completely destroyed.

And Giselle. He was twisted in knots over her. They'd spent weeks together investigating before everything went to hell and all their lives turned upside down. It was both pure heaven and tortuous hell. He had an unnatural attraction to Giselle and it disgusted him but made his heart race at the same time. She was a damned vampire, for God's sake. Vampires had kidnapped and done heinous, unspeakable things to Jamie and others. He wasn't sure how he could ever overlook the fact that Giselle was a bloodsucker.

But the more time he spent with Giselle and with the other vamps, the more doubt seeped its way into his head. Could he have possibly been wrong all this time about vampires? Were not *all* vampires evil and self-absorbed? Not one of them even looked at him with harmful intent during the time he'd spent at Dev's estate. Well ... except when Ren threatened to cut out his shriveled up heart if he hurt Giselle. Without a doubt, the guy meant it.

Goddamn it! He needed an update on Jamie. And Giselle. No one would fucking talk to him! The last update from Kate over a week ago was that Jamie was finally going to some counseling sessions, but she still spent most of her time in self-imposed isolation. And Giselle still hadn't spoken a word about what happened that night she was taken by Xavier, although Kate said she was starting to get back to her bitchy self. And she was so sorry, but both still refused to see him.

That sickly sweet Sam Smith song they played ad nauseam on the radio, "Stay With Me", popped into his head. One line about being emotional and gaining self-control repeated on a loop. Yeah, he needed to gain some self-control all right. He was a fucking basket case.

This is what he'd been reduced to. Thinking of a goddamned Sam Smith song. And the fact that he even knew the words, let alone the artist, made him a complete pussy. He was definitely growing a vagina. He obviously could never let this get out. Jesus, pretty soon he'd be looking up Backstreet Boys songs, trying to find lyrics that fit his fragile emotional state. He was a disgrace to real men everywhere. That was it ... he needed to do something manly. *Very* manly.

He had a small weight room in the basement of his house. He didn't get to spend as much time there as he wanted, but there was no better way to prove your manhood than benching a couple hundred pounds. Well ... the other way involved his cock, but he couldn't think about that now.

Over an hour later as sweat poured down his body, the chorus of that pussy song still rattled around in his brain.

The bitch of it was ... he wasn't sure to which woman it now applied.

Chapter 4

Xavier

Devon and his mate had disappeared. Again. And all Xavier could do was sit on his fucking hands and wait. Wait for information. Wait for answers. Wait for clues. And he was fucking tired of waiting.

He felt murderous. If he could've afforded additional losses, he would've gone on a rampage by now. But he couldn't. He'd already suffered catastrophic casualties at the hands of the lords several months ago and he simply couldn't afford to slaughter at will because his temper burned out of control.

And it raged.

Constantly.

By now, Devon Fallinsworth should be suffering endlessly at his hand, his mate dead and world domination within his grasp. Instead, he'd taken a gigantic step backward. Immense thirst for revenge had driven him for the last five hundred years, but after March's events ... it had quadrupled.

Since he couldn't locate Devon, or his daughter, he'd recently decided to change tactics. Go a different route to see if perhaps he could lure out Devon and the other lords. If he couldn't have Devon, he'd take one of the others in his stead. For the moment.

Xavier couldn't remember how many females he'd sired over the years. Quite frankly, he'd tried to forget. Who could have predicted that would become his most important problem now ... or his most important strategy?

Did he have other daughters alive? If so, how many? Had Marcus managed to keep all of them alive, or only a few? He had no fucking clue since the lords had also taken Marcus, his traitorous scientist.

He'd fucked so many females he had absolutely no idea which one bore the dreamwalker, Katherine. He obviously had no clue her mother was one or she would have been used for other purposes. Not that any one of the dreamwalkers in his possession had been useful so far, mind you. If he didn't have firsthand knowledge, he'd think the whole rare ability was utter bullshit. The dreamwalker gene was passed down only from female to female, so the chances any other daughters alive were also gifted was slim to none.

Still, leave no stone unturned. Unfortunately trying to find them was like finding a lost treasure at sea. Nearly futile. He thought back to a conversation he'd had last month with his now lead researcher.

"My lord, I believe I have found some useful information regarding at least one of your offspring."

"Go on."

"It appears that perhaps a female infant was dropped off to a potential adoptive family twenty-

six years ago in the Eau Claire, Wisconsin, area. December fifteenth."

"And how can you be sure this female was mine? Could be anyone's."

"I asked some of your minions in the local PD's to check their records for anything that may be useful relative to an infant child. A man matching Marcus's description knocked on a couple's door claiming to be from the adoption agency. They'd been on the list for some time, but they were suspicious. He came very late in the evening, told them he didn't have any papers or birth certificate and that the adoption agency would be in contact with them shortly to sort everything out. They called the police and the man fled, leaving the baby. They filed a report and turned the child over to protective services."

"What happened to the female?"

"We need to do some more research on that, my lord. Last we knew she was in the social services system, so we need to track her down. I didn't want to waste any time letting you know until we had a solid lead."

"About fucking time. Hurry up and find her. I'm done waiting."

"Yes, of course, my lord."

Whimpering brought him out of his musing. Now, where were his manners? How could he forget about the delicious young female tied to his bed, waiting for his cock? And his bite. He liked to think of himself as a gracious host and daydreaming about his revenge while in the presence of such a fine piece of ass was just plain rude. The female released a shrill scream as he slowly crawled across the bed toward her.

He'd just have to make it up to her.

Chapter 5

Damian

"Rom, my friend, good to see you." They did the "guy hug" thing, pounding it out. Since they all had their separate Regents, they rarely saw each other, but Damian kept in regular contact with Romaric, his friend, his mentor. And Lord of the West Regent.

"And you, Damian." Rom was always so formal. He made note to take him to Dragonfly while he was here. Rom was a workaholic and needed to loosen up a bit. Angel could definitely help with that. The females could only work two nights a week at most, given the fact they also donated their blood. And even that varied dependent on how many vampires they'd served in a shift. There could be serious health issues if too much blood were taken any more frequently. He made a mental note to check with Ronson on her availability.

"Did Circo accompany you?"

"Of course."

Damian had much respect for Rom, he really did, but the guy could use a serious personality transplant.

"Great. So why don't we get everyone together and look at what we have so far."

"Sounds like a plan."

Fifteen minutes later, Damian, Marco, T, Rom, Circo, Thane and Giselle were gathered in Dev's office. He'd sent Thane to retrieve Giselle. He thought Thane would have better luck and he did. They would loop in the local detective after their meeting, once they decided what they would share with him.

"So," Damian started. "We need to bring everyone up to speed. And for now, this information stays in this room." He looked pointedly at Giselle and Thane. "T, let's get everyone up to speed on the facts and then get into the new stuff."

T was insanely brilliant and, like most vampires, also insanely handsome. His almost translucent green eyes were the perfect complement to thick blonde wavy locks always tightly pulled back at the nape of his neck. But unlike most other vampires, T seemed more fascinated with research than fucking. He'd been in more than one situation with T where a beautiful naked woman would climb into his lap and he'd politely ask her to get the fuck off. So he implicitly trusted any intelligence T uncovered.

"Yes, my lord. We've been able to determine Xavier has indeed been somewhat successfully running a baby farm. He kidnaps young women of prime childbearing age and attempts to impregnate them after the doctors first prepare the female with a concoction they've developed, which helps with the fertilization process absent a mate. Success rate is about five percent.

"Unfortunately we don't know where the babies are taken, and neither do the humans we captured. There are no leads in the records we confiscated either. Looks like Xavier got a little smarter after we invaded him a century ago and he's spread his operations around the country. Hell, maybe even the world. At this point, we don't have a fucking clue.

"Our attack on Xavier several decades ago, though, set him back significantly. We took out a good part of the army, which took him almost a century to rebuild. We also know this latest attack wiped out over fifty rogues. However, since they've had more success recently, he's stepped up his aggressiveness. Dr. Shelton didn't know how many dreamwalkers Xavier had in his possession, but he did say he believed it was several."

T looked at Damian, who indicated he should continue.

"Dr. Marcus Shelton is Xavier's lead physician and researcher. He revealed to me that Xavier is only able to sire female offspring. According to the doctor, it's a genetic anomaly. No one apparently knows this besides Xavier and the doctor. They've even hidden it from his men. Dr. Shelton had been tasked by Xavier to find a cure, but has been unsuccessful. In addition, Dr. Shelton was given the task of eliminating unwanted female babies. Female vampire babies that were sired by Xavier himself."

Giselle popped up violently out of her chair, sending it flying, a murderous look in her eyes.

"Are you fucking kidding me? I'll kill the bastard!" She was already halfway to the door when Damian intervened. He pulled her aside, talking to her softly.

"Giselle, sit down. This is disturbing to all of us, especially you. I get it, but we need the doctor alive. For now." She was silent, hatred emanating from her in endless waves. "Please, Giselle."

She turned, sitting back down without a word. *Daaamn* ... he'd handled that pretty well. Dev would be proud.

Damian nodded for T to resume.

"Shelton indicated Xavier sired at least a dozen females in the time he'd been with him, but none within the last twenty-two years. At first, the doctor disposed of the babies as told. Then he grew a supposed conscience and was able to save three of the females by placing them with families who were on adoption registries but had no children placed with them yet." T paused.

"We all know Kate, Lord Devon's mate, is one of the three, but we need to find the other two before Xavier finds them first. For obvious reasons, Lord Devon does not know there are possibly two more female vampires out there, Kate's half-sisters at minimum. We don't know if either is still alive and we're hoping to find them before Lord Devon and Kate return from their honeymoon, when, of course, we will bring him up to speed."

At that little piece of news, Giselle's eyes snapped to Damian's. He knew she would be less than happy keeping any news from Dev, as loyal as she was to him.

T continued, "Unfortunately we have little information to go on, as the doctor doesn't remember the exact addresses where he dropped them, but he remembered one was in Eau Claire, Wisconsin, and the other somewhere in northern Wisconsin. He did say that the Eau Claire female was left with the family in the winter months, December or January timeframe. That one was a debacle and the adoptive parents called the cops on him, so he left the baby and ran. We don't know whether the parents kept that baby or not. The other female was dropped off to a family around July Fourth."

"And their birth mothers? Don't suppose they're still alive?" Thane asked.

"No," T replied.

Damian added, "One tactic we thought of taking was to check out the families that dropped themselves off the adoption registries. Kate mentioned her parents had done that, so maybe the others did as well.

"Giselle, we could really use the detective's resources to help with this part, especially where the cops were called on the Eau Claire baby. But I don't trust him to do it on his own. If we're going to involve him, I need you to shadow his six. But first, do *you* think we can trust him enough to involve him in this?"

"Yes." No hesitation. Good.

"And *you* will help?"

Silence.

"Giselle, please." Christ, he *never* said please and he'd uttered the pained word twice already. Dev owed him big time for this. "You already have a relationship with him and I need T to continue the interrogation of the recovered human medical staff. We need you." Not a lie, but it hurt to say it anyway. This was the ice queen after all.

After several beats of silence, she nodded. He returned it. Enough with the *pleases* and *thank yous* for fuck's sake.

"One more thing. Xavier knows we have his scientists and his records. We also are in possession of the one person who knows his flaw. Even with all of his faults, Xavier is a smart bastard and surely he's worked out the puzzle by now. He probably knows Kate is his child. And if he doesn't know, he has enough minions that he will find out soon enough. Since he bit her, he certainly has to know she's pregnant. And that puts her and her baby, in more danger. We can expect Xavier to come with guns blazing. The question is when.

"So, we need to find these two females and Xavier's other lairs, which should lead us to the babies and the remaining missing girls. Let's get to work."

And since they'd been trying to do that for centuries, this was a piece o' cake, he thought snidely.

Chapter 6

Analise

This toilet could use a good scrubbing. She was in the bathroom stall, head hanging over the white porcelain. She always felt nauseous before taking the stage, even though this was what she loved to do most in the world. Waitressing paid the bills and was steadier employment, but singing ... singing was her passion. Music was her first and only real love. If she could make a decent living from music, she would do it in a heartbeat. As it was, she had to settle for the side gigs she could get, supplementing her main waitressing income.

She'd arrived in Milwaukee just a little over a week ago and, since she didn't know how long she'd be here, was living in an Economy Lodge paying rent week to week. She'd packed only the bare necessities in her Chevette, leaving the rest at her shitty duplex. She'd called the landlord telling him her mom was very ill and that she needed to leave for a few weeks to care for her. She was the only child, the only one her mom had. He bought it hook, line and sinker, and it got her rent deferred for a month. She had no idea how she'd come up with two months' rent, but that problem was for another day. Sure, she felt bad lying but had no other option at this point.

In her bones, she knew she was Beth's only hope, so she needed to pull her shit together. She was due to perform in less than five minutes and needed this job. In *this* particular club. She was fortunate enough to get both a waitressing and small entertainment gig at Dragonfly and she couldn't blow it now. The pay was actually decent and the job provided her a valuable in, which she desperately needed.

She was to sing a two-hour set from eight to ten on Mondays and Wednesdays and was scheduled to waitress five nights a week, including one of the nights she sang. The house band or DJ came on at 10:30 p.m., so she provided the early evening entertainment. She had one day off a week, not that she cared. She'd work seven days a week until she got what she came for.

The club manager, Frankie, seemed nice and a lot less pervy than her old manager. In this particular case, that didn't work to her advantage. Analise was a very humble person, but even she knew she was attractive, and when it served her purpose, she didn't hesitate to use that beauty to her advantage.

And she was using it at every opportunity to get close to Frankie. She'd even resorted to touching him! It made her nearly physically sick every single time, not because he was *fugly* or anything, but she simply hated being touched, or touching anyone. But she did it anyway. A little brush here, a pat on the arm there, a laugh at the appropriate time at his awful jokes. She was a master at reeling in a guy. She just generally chose not to. *You're better on your own* was her mission statement.

But Frankie was only a means to an end and she needed to remember that. The person she really needed to get to was Devon Fallinsworth, Vampire Lord of the Midwest. And what a more perfect place to find him than at his new nightclub? Now she needed to find a way to the lower level as she didn't think he probably lowered himself by hanging up here too often. Once she'd reeled Frankie in all the way, she was hopeful he'd be able to help.

The thought made bile rise, but she continually reminded herself it was all in the vein of finding Beth. That was her sole focus. She would do anything for Beth. *Anything*. Analise didn't have a mother. Or a father. Or aunts, uncles and cousins. Or a sibling ... except Beth. Regardless of the fact they shared no actual DNA, she was and always would be her sister. That was why she'd made the decision to come here.

Banging on the stall door made her jump.

"Analise, you're on!"

Ugh, Amy. One of the other waitresses. She couldn't stand to listen to or look at her. Amy's high-pitched, whiny voice grated on her nerves like nails on a chalkboard and her DDD silicone boobs constantly spilled over the top of her low-cut blouse, courtesy of her push-up bra. Hey, Victoria's Secret ... don't sell push-up bras in DDD. Please. It's just not necessary.

"Coming! Jesus, a little privacy, please."

"Sorry, babe, but you're late. Frankie's freakin' the fuck out. Wanted to come in here after you himself."

"Christ. I'm coming." She heard the restroom door close, indicating Amy had left. Analise pulled herself together, left the stall and gave one last cursory look in the mirror. She didn't *look* green, so there was that at least.

On the way out of the restroom, she bumped into Frankie. She took a slight step back, cursing herself for her queasiness when it came to touching people.

"You okay, Ana?"

Eff me. Could *no one* remember her goddamned name?

"I'm just fine, Frankie. Sorry for worrying you. I apologize for starting my set late." She tried to scoot by him, but he reached out, cupping her cheek in his clammy hand. Her stomach rolled.

"No problem, Ana. I was more concerned about you. You've been in there quite a while."

She didn't think she'd been in the restroom *that* long. Guess time got away from her. She forced herself not to recoil from his touch, even though it made her skin crawl. He was standing a bit too close for her comfort, but this was what she'd wanted. If he tried to kiss her, she wasn't sure she'd be able to refrain from vomiting, especially since her stomach was still doing somersaults.

"Thank you. I appreciate your concern. I'll be sure to play a few minutes late." She waited a beat before stepping back. Surely that was an appropriate amount of time to keep suspicions at bay, avoiding the undoing of the work she'd put into him for the last several days.

"Well, I'd best get started." He let her go without protest, calling *good luck* behind her.

As Analise made her way to the stage for her second night, she couldn't help the feeling of foreboding that rolled over her. It was the same one she felt the last three nights she'd stepped foot in Dragonfly. It was unlike any other feeling she'd had. This time, something in her life was about to monumentally change.

She just wasn't sure if it was going to be good ... or bad.

Chapter 7

Damian

He'd arrived at the club much earlier in the evening than anticipated. Rom tagged along, albeit reluctantly. Damian was bound and determined to get the guy laid. Although he wasn't quite sure why, once again he came in through the main entrance versus the private entrance at the back of the building.

He'd no sooner set foot in the building when the most sensuous sound he'd ever heard caressed every single nerve ending in his body like a gentle lover. *What was that?* Or better yet ... *who* was that?

Taking a few steps forward, he searched for the voice that set his blood on fire. After just moments, his eyes landed on the incredibly gorgeous creature on center stage.

Fuck me. She's *mine*.

His heart raced as he drank in her exquisite beauty. Her straight, shoulder length chocolate hair swung loosely around her perfect oval-shaped face. Her eyes were closed tightly as she poured her heart and soul into the song. And it pissed him off. He wanted to see their color. He wanted to gaze into her soul.

She wore a curve-hugging, but conservative, short black dress with matching heels. But all he could think about was what lay underneath. He wanted to rip the somber dress from her body and uncover her secrets.

It was *her*. The one woman who just the other day he'd thought he wasn't ready for. The one woman he'd foolishly and selfishly told himself he didn't want to find yet.

Everything now made perfect sense. Since stepping foot in Milwaukee months ago, a hazy premonition had fallen over him that a life-altering event was about to happen. He'd thought it was just this mess they were in with Xavier, but he couldn't have been more wrong.

It was about her.

His Moira.

His Destiny.

His *Mate*.

MINE.

The ethereal vision standing before him was *his*. A plethora of feelings bombarded him at once, almost buckling his knees.

Joy.

Lust.

Excitement.

Lust.

Possessiveness.

Lust.

Completeness.

She sang with such emotion; her pain became his. He could feel it radiating from her and he wanted to take it away. He wanted her to smile. He wanted her to be happy. Her darkness called to his. But her light ... her light filled every tiny dark, desolate corner of his heart. Cracks he was aware of and those he wasn't.

She was full of pain. He would replace it with joy.

She had so many holes in her soul it looked like Swiss cheese. He would get out a fucking shovel and pack them so tight nothing would penetrate them ever again.

Every woman he'd ever met or been with in his entire life just fell away. He couldn't remember a one of them. He couldn't remember their faces. He couldn't remember their names. It was like they never existed. The only woman that existed now and forever would be *her*.

He forgot his entire reason for even coming to the club tonight. She'd clouded his mind. She already owned him, body and soul, and she had no goddamn clue.

He was aware of someone shaking him, but he couldn't—*wouldn't*—take his eyes off his Moira. She'd moved into singing "Broken Pieces" by Apocalyptica. Her sadness bled into him as she belted the chorus.

"Damian, are we just going to stand here all night staring at the singer?"

He shook of this nuisance. "Fuck off."

Suddenly something—*no someone*—blocked the vision of his mate. Rom. He looked into his friend's face and bared his teeth, barely holding back his rage. "Get the fuck out of my way, Rom, or I'll remove you myself."

Rom's brows drew together. Damian had never spoken to his mentor in such a manner. Rom was very old and the most powerful vampire he knew. Damian wasn't sure he could take him if it came to blows, but at this point, he didn't fucking care. Rom needed to get out of his way.

"What has gotten into you, D?"

"Not now, Rom. Move." His mate's voice had wrapped around his heart, her vocal fingers sensuously caressing it. Bringing it back to life. He wanted to watch every nuance on her face as she performed.

Rom moved, following Damian's line of sight and was unusually quiet as she finished her song.

"Congratulations, D."

Damian briefly glanced at Rom but quickly returned his gaze to his Moira. Rom was a smart guy. Damian knew it wouldn't take him long to figure out why he'd turned into a raving lunatic who'd just verbally challenged the most powerful vampire in the world. Very uncool and undoubtedly suicidal.

What was her name? He suddenly had an intense desire to get her off the stage. He didn't want to share her with anyone, let alone a bunch of drunk humans. Looking around the club, every single human male was as enthralled with her as he was. She had them entranced in her erotic web. They all thought they stood a chance with her, that they would be allowed inside her temple of a body.

Raging jealousy and possessiveness swept through him. *No one* should look upon her, but him. *No one* should worship her, but him. Her angelic voice belonged to *no one else,* but him.

He started toward her, but Rom firmly grabbed his arm, holding him back. Unbridled fury raged. No one, including Rom, would keep him from claiming his fated.

Right.

Fucking.

Now.

"Patience, young grasshopper. Now's not the time to make a scene."

Scene? The only scene he was going to make if Rom didn't get his hands off him was a bloodbath when he tore his mentor apart. Piece by piece. He had tunnel vision, his sole objective to get his Moira off that stage. *Now*. He began to turn toward Rom, when she looked right at him and their gazes locked.

His world narrowed to only her. He heard her sharp intake of breath. Her sweet voice faltered, then stopped. He ached for her to continue, never wanting her to stop. Except when she was underneath him, moaning his name as he made her come repeatedly.

Then his world crashed around him as he saw her sway and her eyelids close. To his horror, his Moira was no longer standing.

He stood helpless as the scene unfolded before him in slow motion. Her legs gave out and she crumpled to the stage floor, lying in a still heap.

Chapter 8

Analise

She'd had goose bumps over her entire body for a solid fifteen minutes, about the time the vibe in the room became intense. She'd tried to block it out and finish her set strong. The sense of both danger and excitement were almost too much to ignore. The desire to seek out what caused this reaction in her was strong, but she needed to focus on her music. Three more songs to go and she'd be done.

Earlier she'd thought about sticking around to snoop a little since she hadn't had a chance to do that yet. That was the sole reason she was here, after all. But now all she wanted to do was go back to the motel, take a bath and go to bed. She worked again tomorrow night and would find some time to sneak off and look for the entrance to the lower level. The *vampire* part of Dragonfly.

She'd just finished "Broken Pieces" and started a Halestorm favorite of hers when she spotted *him* standing just inside the entrance. Their gazes locked and she couldn't have torn hers away if her life depended on it.

Analise's childhood had been difficult. Some people got breaks in life, some didn't. She didn't. And she accepted it for what it was. She wasn't bitter. She didn't carry around a grudge the size of Texas. She wasn't resentful of the people who'd had it better than she. Envious perhaps. Resentful no.

But with her difficulties growing up, also came in the inability to form bonds with other people. Beth was the only exception. Maybe inability was a strong word; she just didn't *care* to form bonds with people. It was certainly a better way to protect her heart from the crushing loss and despair that inevitably happened when they disappointed you—or hurt you.

So the powerful feelings of desire and belonging she felt as she stared into this beautiful stranger's dark eyes were completely foreign and most unwelcome. Her breath caught and her voice faltered. She couldn't remember the words to the song. She couldn't even remember where she was. There was only him. His gaze was so intense it was frightening. He looked directly into her soul, seeing the darkness and sadness lurking inside. It was unnerving.

Suddenly she felt light-headed. Black spots swam in her vision. Her ears began to ring. Noises faded away as if her head were stuffed with cotton. Her knees gave way and she dimly registered she was falling.

The last thing she remembered was the look of horror on *his* face. Then the darkness consumed her.

Chapter 9

Analise

"Analise, you need to wake now, my child."

"No." She didn't want to wake. She wanted to stay in the comfort and safety of her dream world with her guardian angel. In the real world, she was weak, but in her dreams she was powerful. As powerful as Mara. She could manipulate the elements. Rain fire with a thought. Dig a hole with nothing but her mind. Pop a lock by blinking.

"I'll be waiting for you as always, child. But now you need to wake. Analise, your destiny awaits."

Destiny? What destiny?

That was her last thought before consciousness grabbed her again.

And she wished it hadn't. Her head hurt like a mother. It felt like someone was playing the drums on the inside of her skull. She moaned, reaching up to touch the offending wound. *What happened?*

A rough hand gently stroked her cheek and she vaguely registered someone talking. Muffled music played in the background.

"She's coming around," someone said.

"Thank fucking Christ." *Whose deep, sensuous voice was that?*

Her eyelids cracked open, vision slightly blurry. She blinked several times to clear it.

When she'd lived on the streets, one of her favorite escapes was window-shopping. She'd lose herself in a dream that she could afford the luxurious clothing mocking her from behind the thick glass. And that once her day of self-indulgence was over, she would have a loving home to return to. On one such day, she saw the most beautiful man she'd ever laid eyes on. He was tall, handsome, clearly fit. He oozed masculinity and sexuality. She often wondered if she'd dreamt him up for she'd never seen anything like him before or since.

Until now. The man staring into her eyes—*the same man from the club*—made window guy seem like Weird Al Yankovic.

He had piercing dark eyes, almost like onyx. Thick, dark waves framed his face, almost hanging in his eyes a bit as he looked down at her. And his face ... how could she possibly describe to anyone the most perfectly exquisite face she'd ever seen?

His eyebrows were textbook manly, dark and thick. Sharp, high symmetrical cheekbones framed a perfect, masculine nose. His lips were full and plump, with a cupids bow gracing the top one. They were completely kissable. A five o'clock shadow rounded out the sexy package. He was the most flawless thing she'd ever seen. He was an angel. Or the devil in disguise.

"Are you okay, princess?" The Adonis was speaking. *To her*.

"Ummm ..." *Was she okay?* She needed an aspirin, badly.

"What's your name, princess?"

"It's Ana." *Frankie?* In looking around, she was in an office of some sort, lying on a soft leather couch. Frankie, Adonis and another extremely attractive, but very scary-looking man were all watching her intently. She moved to sit up, feeling extremely vulnerable in her prone position.

"Whoa there. You hit your head pretty hard. You should lie still," Adonis said.

She ignored him, pushing herself up anyway. Bad idea. Her head throbbed and her vision blurred again. *Were there now two Adonises?* Hell, she could live with blurry vision if that were the case.

"Ana, are you okay? What happened?"

She was suddenly very angry. "My name is Analise. Not Ana. Not princess. And I'm fine. I just need a minute here. And possibly an aspirin." Or twelve.

"Analise. That's a lovely name." The reverent way her name rolled off Adonis's tongue almost made her orgasm. *Oh my God.* What was wrong with her? She'd never reacted like this to a man. She had to get the hell away from him immediately.

"Uh. On second thought, I'm fine. I'll just be going now." Just as soon as the spots in her vision cleared. She tried to stand and was gently pushed back down by Adonis.

"You're not going anywhere, kitten. I have a doctor coming to look at you and he's still a good ten minutes out."

She couldn't believe her ears. He'd called a doctor? She couldn't afford a damn doctor. *And kitten?* She should be furious! Instead, she was oddly turned on by the endearment. And she *loathed* endearments. In the past, when uttered by another man they seemed nothing but demeaning, but out of his mouth it was like a hot breath between her legs.

"Look ..." she realized she didn't even know his name. Even if she did, it would always be Adonis.

"Damian. Damian DiStephano," he offered, a slight smirk upturning his lips in the most deliciously erotic way.

Wow, even his name was supremely sexy. *Stop it Analise!*

"Damian. Look, Damian, I appreciate the concern, but I don't need a doctor. I must have locked my knees and passed out. That's all. I'm perfectly fine." Not exactly true, but she would be. She just needed some meds and a good night's sleep. And the way she was beginning to ache between her thighs, maybe some self-relief.

"I'm not letting you leave, kitten. End of." She'd thought it intimidating when he'd stood over her, but once he took a seat beside her—so close he was touching—she was completely overwhelmed, her brain short-circuiting.

Her body tingled where his leg connected with hers. Her breaths became choppy and shallow. She ached in a place she hadn't in, well ... *ever*. She was both captivated and scared shitless. Until she saw the smug look on his face, then anger reared her ugly head once again. A quick temper was just one of her many personality flaws.

She stood and quickly regretted it as the room began to tilt. Adonis—*Damian* —caught her before she fell and settled them back on the couch, but now she was cradled in his lap—*on his lap!*—his strong arms surrounding her.

"What the hell are you doing?" She tried pushing away, albeit her effort was weak given the head-splitting sensation threatening to make her brain explode.

"I'm protecting you from yourself, kitten. I told you that you needed medical attention and you can do it the easy way or the hard way. Your choice." He lowered his voice, lips brushing the shell of her ear as he whispered, "And personally I hope it's the hard way, because I've never felt as good as I do now with you in my arms."

Holy panty-dropping, Batman. He did *not* just say that, did he?

She scrambled off his lap, taking a seat at the end of the couch, needing to put as much distance between them as possible. His knowing smile lit up the entire room. His smile had effectively morphed him into a *super-sized* Adonis.

His smile was like the sun.

Warm.

Inviting.

Intense.

Dangerous.

And that was bad. *Super* bad. He stirred feelings in her she never knew existed. She wasn't a virgin, sadly, but she also couldn't remember feeling passionate desire like this ever in her life. And that's what scared her the most. She didn't let anyone under her armor. But somehow, he was a chink. A small chink that she needed reinforcements against. Quickly.

Mara's parting words tumbled in her head like clothes in a dryer. *"Your destiny awaits."* Surely she didn't mean this man ... did she?

"Fine. I'll let the doctor take a look." She wouldn't win the argument against him so she'd just figure out later how to pay the two hundred-dollar bill. Maybe the club would pay it so they didn't worry about her suing them. Not that she would do that.

"Frankie, why don't you take Rom on a tour of the club? Introduce him to Angel. We'll be just fine in here until the doc arrives." Damian never looked away from her, even though he spoke to Frankie.

"Uh ... I should probably stay here with Ana. I mean, Analise," he stuttered.

That got Damian's attention right quick. He stood and next to Frankie she realized just how tall and intimidating he really was. He was at least six and a half feet tall.

He was huge. He was broad. He was muscled.

He was *perfection.*

Her mouth was suddenly very dry. What she wouldn't give to run her hands all over his perfectly honed body. Where the hell that errant thought came from, she had no clue.

"That's not necessary, Frankie. Analise will be just fine with me. Go." Frankie scrambled for the door, clearly intimidated by Damian. Who wouldn't be? She had no shame in admitting she was ... just a little.

"Rom, I'll meet you back at the house. Enjoy your evening."

Good-looking, scary guy number two simply nodded. Had he said a word the entire time he'd been in here? She didn't think so.

They both left and, as Damian turned back to face her, the air was sucked out of the room. She could hardly breathe as she shamelessly raked her gaze over his sinewy body. Dark denim molded powerful thighs. Rolled sleeves on his black-and-gray-striped button-down revealed tan, tattooed skin. The top two buttons of his shirt were left undone and the smooth skin of his chest nearly made her weep. *Oh my lord*.

When they locked eyes, he stared at her with such intensity, such desire, she felt like his next meal. She swallowed, unable to speak. *Busted*. He knew the effect he was having on her. She watched him deftly walk back over to the couch, sitting right beside her ... again.

"So, kitten, how are you feeling?"

"Why do you keep calling me that?" It did funny things to her insides and she wanted that to stop. *Right*? Yes, absolutely. And next time she'd say it with much more conviction.

Another panty-dropping smile showed his perfectly straight white teeth. "You've got some claws on you, kitten. I like it."

She sat there with her mouth open but, not knowing how to respond, closed it. *Was that a compliment?* She wasn't sure but decided to let it go. After tonight, she wouldn't see him again, so no reason to start a verbal war.

She needed something else to do besides ogle him and fantasize, so her gaze fell on the expansive office. She hadn't remembered seeing an office like this upstairs. "Where are we?"

"We're in the owner's office."

The owner? Devon Fallinsworth. He knew Devon? Did that mean he was a vampire too? Was this a stroke of luck or what? Maybe she needed to be just a bit nicer to Damian so she could get some information.

"You know Mr. Fallinsworth?" She tried not to sound too curious as to not arouse suspicion.

His lips drew into a thin line, glaring at her for several uncomfortable seconds before responding. "Do *you* know *Mr. Fallinsworth*?"

Was it her imagination or did his question drip with sarcasm? "No. I just thought maybe I'd get to meet him since he owns the club. I just started a couple of nights ago."

"Well, I'm sorry, kitten. Dev is on his honeymoon. I'm watching the club in his absence." Heavy emphasis was placed on the word honeymoon.

Honeymoon? *Shit.* And if he was watching the club that meant he probably was a vampire also, as she couldn't imagine a Vampire Lord would leave his club under the watch of just anyone. Now what was she going to do?

"You look a little distraught, kitten. Have your sights set on him, did you?" His voice dripped with disdain, which only served to fuel her anger.

"Fuck you. Of course not. I simply wanted to meet the owner of this great night club, that's all." So what if it was only the partial truth? She was so out of here. She stood to leave and was halfway to the door when he grabbed her arm, twirling her to face him. His face was full of anger ... *and lust.* Butterflies took flight low in her belly and the warmth between her legs intensified.

"Let. Go."

He didn't say a word, walking them backward until her back was flush against the door, arms held overhead by her wrists. She was trapped. She started to panic, twisting to get away.

He held fast, leaning down to run his nose along her cheek before nibbling her ear. "Do you know what he is, kitten? Does that turn you on?"

"W-What are y-you talking about?" She *was* turned on, but not for the reasons he was thinking. It was because of him and him alone. She couldn't catch her breath as he continued to run his nose along her ultra-sensitive skin.

"Did you want him to fuck you? Is that why you wanted to meet him, Analise?" He nipped her earlobe hard, then soothed the hurt. *Oh God.* Her core went liquid. She wanted to kick him in the balls almost as much as she wanted him to ravage her.

"You're an asshole," she managed to say, pretty convincingly even. He pulled back, his eyes flitting between hers and her lips.

She had met him only minutes ago. Why was she so irrationally attracted to this man? Or vampire? Why didn't the fact that he *was* a vampire scare the shit out of her? *Because he'd woken something inside me I'd thought long dead.*

Your destiny awaits.

"So I've been told." He leaned down, slowly. Oh, so achingly slowly. He was going to kiss her. She should turn her head. She should bite his lip.

But she did neither; every last vestige of common sense had simply evaporated. Instead, she wet her lips in preparation as she watched him bring his mouth to hers.

The kiss started out soft, slow, gentle. Hot breath teased her skin as his skilled mouth took her upper lip first, paying equal attention to its mate. His tongue ran along the seam of her mouth, demanding entry, which involuntarily opened for him. Now her whole body was in on the treachery.

As soon as their tongues met, the kiss turned wild, passionate. His hold tightened on her, almost painfully so. He ravaged her mouth, exploring every nook, every cranny. She couldn't get enough. She wanted to crawl inside him and live there forever.

He tasted like danger.

Sex.

Sin.

His free hand ran up her side, cupping her breast. He kneaded its fullness, plucking her aching nipple to a hard point under the thin fabric of her dress. They both moaned in pleasure. His pelvis ground into her stomach and she felt the evidence of how much he wanted her. Her lower body moved in time with him and she rose on her tiptoes to align them better.

A knock on the door scared the crap out of her and the moment evaporated. While Damian had stopped kissing her, he hadn't given her any quarter. Bodies still touching, breathing erratic, he leaned his forehead against hers. His jaw ticked; his body was strung tight as a bow; blatant lust was barely checked. His sinewy body holding her firmly in place, he stared intently into her eyes, a faint glow in his. Definitely vampire. This man—*vampire*—wanted her. *Her*. It was a heady feeling.

He was commanding, yet gentle. She felt safe physically, but in danger emotionally. He exuded darkness, but his light shone brilliantly. The dichotomies made her head spin so fast she couldn't latch onto a coherent thought.

"Coming," he thickly answered when another knock sounded. He slowly moved away from her body, the loss of warmth chilling her to the bone. While he'd let her arms go, he linked their fingers, eyes boring into hers. She tugged to get free, but his grasp tightened.

"Big D." He nodded in greeting to the interloper as he opened the door.

Big D? What kind of a name was that?

Damian led her to the couch again, gesturing that she should sit. Refusal sat on her tongue. She'd never been good at following directions. Instead, she did his bidding, all the while berating herself. He took a seat beside her, thigh to thigh, *of course*. The doctor came to sit in front of her, bag in hand. He was classically handsome, but didn't hold a candle to Damian. No, he was one of a kind.

She tried not to reflect too much on what just happened or she just might go into a full-blown meltdown. How far would she have let her hot and heavy make out session go if they hadn't been interrupted? Would she have stopped herself at second base? God ... she'd just let a complete stranger feel her up against a door. At her workplace! *Uh, Analise ... what in the hell were you thinking?*

"How are you feeling, Analise?"

"Um, I'm fine. Thank you. Really, I'm a lot better now. Just a slight headache." Slight was an understatement. Someone had inserted a pickaxe inside her skull and it was trying to get out.

"That's good. If you don't mind, though, I'm going to do an exam. You did lose consciousness for a brief period and that could mean a slight concussion."

Oh crap. She hadn't thought of that.

"Do you have someone at home to watch you in the event of a concussion?" He asked as he dug into his bag for the necessary supplies.

No. No, she did not. "Uh ...."

"I'll take responsibility for her," Damian quipped. She couldn't believe what she was hearing. She whipped her head in his direction. Bad idea in retrospect as the black spots returned and Damian's face looked like it'd been splattered with paint.

"What? Hell, no." Oh, hell to the *n-o*!

"Oh hell, yes, kitten. You can't be left alone with a concussion. It's the rule."

Was he even listening to himself? "Rule? Whose rule? Yours?"

"No, kitten. It's a medical fact." Damian had a most serious look on his stunning face. He truly believed the bullshit he was spouting.

"Stop. Calling. Me. That. And, no. You will *not* stay with me."

"Why don't we do the exam first before we argue about this, okay?" Finally. The voice of reason by the only medical professional in the room.

"Yes, okay." Analise calmed slightly. They were quiet as the doctor checked her pupils and the tender bump on her head. He then asked a bunch of questions.

Did she have a headache? Yes.

Did she remember hitting her head? No.

Were her ears ringing? Slightly.

Was she tired? Um, yes. It was probably close to eleven by now, right?

Was she confused? Did letting a stranger feel her up count? Good, she'd used her inside voice. Her outside voice replied no, she wasn't confused.

Did she know what caused her to black out? No way in hell was she admitting the truth to that question, what with Mr. I-Have-The-Biggest-Ego-Ever sitting right next to her, so she stuck with the lie she'd told earlier. Yep, locked knees.

Finally, he took her blood pressure. Which was high. Go figure. Was it anger or lust fueled? Probably both. The second time was closer to normal.

"So, what's the conclusion, doc?" Damian asked, breaking the silence.

"I'm sorry, Analise, but you do have a slight concussion. Your pupils are not responding as quickly as they should. You'll need someone to stay with you for the next twenty-four hours at least, waking you every couple of hours this evening to ensure you don't have any issues doing so."

She looked at Damian, who had a big smirk upturning his full, sexy lips. With great surprise, she suddenly realized she hadn't cringed *once* at his multiple touches. *Huh?*

Well ... *shit.*

Chapter 10

Xavier

"Come in," he barked when someone knocked.

In walked a tall, lanky human male wearing a white lab coat. Next to Marcus, he was the smartest scientist Xavier owned. And now, the only other one to know of his genetic deficiency. That was one of the reasons this search was taking so fucking long. Discretion was essential.

"What the fuck do you want, Philip?"

"Sire, I believe we may have found your daughter. Or who we think is your daughter. Of course, we can't be sure until there is DNA testing. Her name is Analise Aster."

A malevolent smile crossed his scarred face.

"Really? And where is this female?"

"She's working at a newly opened club in Milwaukee called the Dragonfly. Just started there two nights ago. Sings a couple nights a week and waitresses as well."

"And she's the same female as the Eau Claire baby?"

"Yes, sire. She's the same one."

"Any word on the others?"

The human paled. Xavier detested being disappointed and that was all his servants had done lately ... disappoint. "Not yet, sire. I'm following another lead, but so far it hasn't panned out."

"Keep fucking working on it. I want every last one of my children found and brought to me. Do you understand?"

"Yes, my lord. Of course." Purplish bags framed the doctor's eyes. Looked like he hadn't slept in a month. Oh well.

"That will be all."

"Yes, sire." He scurried as fast as he could out the door, leaving Xavier alone.

"Geoffrey, in my office. Now."

Within seconds, his lieutenant stood in front of him, at the ready.

"How may I serve you, my lord?" Such a loyal servant.

"I need you to go to a club called Dragonfly in Milwaukee and find a singer named Analise Aster. I don't know what she looks like, but it shouldn't be too hard to track her down. Bring her to me, by force if necessary. But do not harm her. You hurt a single hair follicle on her head and I'll gut you. Do you understand?"

"Of course, my lord." Geoffrey nodded in respect and disappeared.

"Analise Aster. It's time to meet your daddy," he whispered.

Chapter 11

Damian

She didn't have a concussion at all, but there was no way in hell he was letting her out of his sight and the concussion story was just the excuse he needed to stay by her side.

"Thanks, Doc."

"My pleasure, my—" He stopped just short of using his title, finally getting the gist of the look on Damian's face. He wasn't quite ready to let his Moira know who he was yet.

He could not get her taste out of his mouth, or off his mind. He needed to savor every single creamy inch of her body. What would it be like to sink his cock into her warmth? What would it be like to sink his teeth into her tender flesh? Nirvana, no doubt. How would she look bound to his bed? Like a goddess, guaranteed. He hadn't ejaculated prematurely since he'd been a teenager, but at the first taste of her he was ready to come in his pants. He could still feel the warmth of her perfect breast in his palm. His body tingled where hers had been pressed against his. The smell of her arousal caused his incisors to drop. She wanted him. She was made for him. *Only him.*

He'd been insanely jealous when she'd mentioned Dev. The thought of her wanting to fuck Dev made him shake with fury. He was quite sure his kitten was up to something and it hadn't better be that. He would find out, though. If she knew about Dev, then she most certainly knew Dev was vampire. That may actually work in his favor, since his nature shouldn't surprise her. He could avoid a similar fiasco between Dev and Kate when she accidentally found out he was a vampire.

In a dare of sorts, he'd let his eyes glow with desire, but she hadn't mentioned it so neither would he. He was anxious to see how she was going to play this little charade.

"Let's get your stuff, kitten. You're coming home with me." She had an incredulous look on her exquisite face. He wanted to wipe it off with another earth shattering, soul-sucking kiss.

"Ah, I didn't fall hard enough to knock my common sense loose. I don't even know you. I am certainly not going anywhere with you. For all I know, you could be a serial killer."

That fucking karma bitch. This was payback for his playboy ways. Of course his Moira was as stubborn as the day was long. Kitten was an apt nickname. And his kitten hadn't come declawed.

"You heard the doctor. You need round-the-clock monitoring for twenty-four hours. And you already told us you don't have anyone at home. Since I am responsible for this club in Dev's absence, it is my duty to make sure you are cared for. We look after our own here." *Guilt her?* No shame in that.

"I'm not going home with you. I'll just sleep here tonight then. This couch will be perfectly fine. There are plenty of people who can come in and check on me."

Christ almighty. She was going to test every last ounce of his nonexistent patience. He was going to be forced to use the "P" word again.

"Analise, please. You can't get a good night's rest here. This part of the club stays open well into the night."

"I won't get a good night's rest anyway, no matter where I'm sleeping if I'm being awakened every hour," she countered.

Damn. Point kitten.

He absolutely did not want her sleeping here, but he knew he would never get her back to the estate without using force and he really didn't want to do that. He didn't know much about her yet, but he could tell she was leery of people. He wanted her to trust him and flashing her against her will to an unknown location wouldn't exactly boost him very high on her trust-o-meter scale.

"Fine. I'll accompany you to your place." He'd post Marco and T outside the door for extra security. He was taking no chances with his future mate.

She looked down, hands twisting in her lap. Anxiety and embarrassment pelted him. He gently lifted her chin with his finger. "What's wrong, Analise?"

"I ... I don't really have a place, exactly. I'm staying in a motel. Just temporarily."

"A motel?" There was a definite story here and he aimed to uncover it.

"Yes. And it's a small room with just one bed." His cock went stone hard. *Just one bed, you say?* Nothing wrong with this scenario. Nothing. At. All.

"Okay." He was in.

"No. Not okay. I just told you I'm not spending the night with a stranger." Her defiance demanded punishment. And *Jesus*, how he wanted to punish her.

"Well, that's not exactly what you said, kitten. You said you wouldn't go *home* with me. Not that you wouldn't spend the night with me." He inwardly grinned, fearing repercussions if he let it show. That *was* exactly what she'd said.

"Well, then let me make this perfectly clear, *Damian*. I will not spend the night with you here, there or anywhere. I will not sleep in the same bed or the same room with you. Is that clear enough?" Indignation *and* Dr. Seuss references? Damn that made him hot. His mate was a spitfire. And it was beginning to grow on him quite quickly. Nothing turned him on more than a good verbal sparring.

A light bulb went off. Yes ... it could work. She would be safe and protected, yet still under his roof.

"Okay. Fair enough. I have a neutral place that I think will suit us both. You can get a good night's rest—*in private*—and I will still be able to look in on you to make sure you're okay. It's a win-win, kitten."

If her sigh was any louder, she might blow a lung. "I have asked you *repeatedly* to stop calling me kitten. I hate it." She *soooo* didn't. His kitten wasn't a very good liar.

"Can't make any promises." He could, he would just break them and he didn't want to break a promise to his mate. Ever. "I'm sure you must be exhausted and still sporting a headache." He stood, reaching his hand out to her.

She looked back and forth between his hand and face, indecision written all over her.

"You don't have a choice, ki—Analise. I will not let you spend the evening alone with a concussion. You can trust me."

"I don't trust anyone."

He smiled softly at her, holding her gaze so she would see his truth. "Well, I'll just have to remedy that now, won't I?" He heard her breath catch. His poor kitten was buttoned up tighter than Fort Knox. She was broken and he would fix her. No matter what, or how long it took.

After several more moments, she tentatively put her hand in his. It was a start.

Watching her fine rounded ass, he ushered her up the back staircase leading outside. A hand to the small of her back, they re-entered from the main entrance. For at least the time being, he wanted to avoid the questions seeing the underground portion of Dragonfly would provoke, so he took the long way around.

"I didn't realize there was a basement to this club." *Ohhhh, kitten.* Liars didn't go unpunished and he was quite looking forward to doling it out. If she knew of Dev, she absolutely knew the secrets of Dragonfly.

"It's private. Members only. But I'd be happy to show you another time if you're interested."

He was curious how she'd react to the goings on of club activities. He would love to grind against her sexy body on the dance floor, her pussy getting wet and ready for him as they danced erotically.

She grabbed her purse from the employee lounge, and stood looking at him. "I need some clothes. I didn't bring a change with me."

"Don't worry, kitten. I'm sure we can find something suitable for you to wear." Her birthday suit would do, but if she insisted on clothing, he was sure he could rustle up something from the shelter or from Kate's closet if necessary. Although that was a life-endangering proposition, entering the closet of Dev's mate without permission.

Fury lit up her face.

"Listen, asshole. I'm not going back to your fuck pad and wearing leftovers from the whores who have come before me. I want *my* clothes."

He tried to hold it in. He really did, but he couldn't help it. Before he knew it, he was doubled over with laughter as she stood gaping at him.

"I'm serious!" she screeched. Literally, screeched. It hurt his ears.

"I'm not taking you to my fuck pad, Analise, and I would certainly never put you in whore's clothing. You are much too virtuous for that. If you want your own clothing, we'll stop at your motel and get whatever you need."

"I'm far from virtuous, but thank you. I would like that." *Far from virtuous?* He intended to dig into that a bit more.

He accompanied her to the Economy Lodge—the *Economy Lodge* for fuck's sake—and waited inside her roach-infested room as she silently packed an overnight bag. He didn't see the roaches, but he knew the fuckers were hiding somewhere. There was no way in hell she was returning to this place. Over his dead body. He'd send Marco to retrieve the rest of her things later, paying any outstanding bill. She was feisty and would fight him on it, no doubt. But he would win. He always won.

They rode in companionable silence during the thirty-five minutes to Dev's estate, the soft sounds of *Coldplay* in the background. Analise rested her head on the limousine window, closing her mesmerizing eyes. She surprised him by not making snide comments about the limo, her only give away were crooked eyebrows. She wore her expressions on her sleeve, for which he was grateful. She certainly held everything else close to the vest. Maybe the fight had been bled out of her for the evening. He could only hope.

"Marco, return to that hovel and get the remainder of her things. Bring them to me at Dev's. If she owes anything on the room, take care of it."

"Yes, my lord."

They came to a silent stop outside the shelter portion of Dev's mansion. He thought her asleep when her eyes suddenly popped open, taking in everything. The house was relatively dark, not revealing the expansiveness of either it or the grounds, but she must have gotten the gist as her eyes snapped to his.

"You live here?"

How much to reveal?

"No. This is a home of a friend. There are several empty rooms on this side of the mansion, which is used as a women's shelter of sorts. Long story, better told on a different day when it's not so late and you don't have a head injury."

That earned him a slight smile. Go him! She was incredibly beautiful, but she had one hell of a tough shell to crack. For the hundredth time this evening, he couldn't help but wonder what happened in her short life to harden her so. He suspected she didn't smile often, but if she gifted him with a full-on grin, he didn't know if he'd be able to restrain himself from throwing her down and fucking her senseless on the spot.

"Come on. Let's get you settled." He slipped out of the Lincoln, quickly running around to open her door. He didn't quite make it in time. She stood, bag in hand, gaping at the ostentatious abode. He grabbed the bag and her free hand, pulling her toward the door.

Since it was now nearly midnight, the house was quiet, everyone asleep. He'd only been here once, so he didn't know his way around well, but he knew the girls' rooms were on the third floor. He would avoid that one. No need stirring up more questions he wasn't quite prepared to answer yet. Instead, he led her to the second-floor west wing bedrooms not letting her hand leave his, although she tried several times. They would have privacy here.

The second to the last door on the left opened to reveal a femininely decorated bedroom. Personally, he thought it looked like *My Little Pony* threw up in here, but apparently chicks dug that shit. The fact that he even knew what *My Little Pony* was should shrink his cock at least an inch. Oooh ... he'd have to check that later.

"Wow. This is so ..."

"Nice, huh?" He'd play along.

"I was going to say ... pink. It's very pink." She looked around the room with wide eyes. There was something else in her eyes that he couldn't quite decipher. It looked suspiciously like sorrow.

"Would you like another room?"

"I thought you'd never offer." She laughed along with him.

Tugging her across the hallway, he took her into another empty room. This one was much more serene and neutrally decorated. These particular bedrooms were not all that big, but each did have a comfortable queen-sized bed and its own en-suite bathroom. The comforter had a white abstract pattern running through the light tan color. Slightly darker walls complemented it. There was a simple dresser in the corner, a reading lamp on the nightstand.

"Better?"

"Much. No sunglasses required."

A genuine smile lit her up and he felt himself go hard. She must have noticed, her smile faded, desire clouding her eyes instead. *Christ.* He needed to get out of here before he did something supremely stupid, like take her up against the wall. *Jesus, he wanted her*. He wasn't sure how long he'd be able to hold out; the bonding instinct was almost unbearable to resist. It screamed *Mine, Mine, Mine*. But if he pushed her, she would run.

He cleared his throat. "I'll get some aspirin." In the en-suite, he searched every last cupboard and drawer until he found a small bottle. He returned with two pills, along with a glass of water. She swallowed, setting the empty glass on the nightstand.

"Thank you."

"You're welcome. I'll just be right down the hall in case you need me. I'll check on you in a couple of hours or so."

"Yah, okay."

"Are you sure you'll be okay by yourself, kitten? Because it's truly no hardship for me to stay." He willed her to say yes.

She laughed, shaking her head. He loved the sound.

"Nice try, Casanova."

"Can't blame a guy." He closed the distance between them, running a finger down her bare arm. She shivered watching its path. He used the other to tip her chin toward him.

"Goodnight, Analise," he whispered against her lips before tasting her one last time tonight. "Sweet dreams." Without a look back, he turned and walked out the door. Before he couldn't.

Chapter 12

Analise

She stood unmoving as he closed the door. Lips tingling. Goose bumps a reminder of where he'd touched her. What in the name of all that is holy was going on with her? When he'd asked if she'd wanted him to stay, her heart and body screamed *yes, yes, yes*! But her stupid mouth ran autonomously, like it usually did, telling him to leave.

No, Analise, that's a good thing. He's a vampire. A God-like, sexy, devastatingly handsome, exotic, erotic vampire. Who drank blood ... human blood. Who probably wanted *her* blood. But who clearly knew how to kiss. He'd probably had plenty of practice. That thought made her frown. Funny that. Thinking of him with other women upset her more than the blood sucking. She found that oddly intriguing.

He'd tried to hide it, but he was disgusted with her motel room. No, it wasn't the Ritz, but he didn't have to be a snob about it. Not everyone could afford limousines and chauffeurs. Not everyone could afford a pair of five hundred-dollar jeans. Not everyone could *fill out* a pair of jeans like he could either. She'd felt his arousal earlier, but actually seeing the colossal bulge in the front of his pants ... whew. She needed a fan. *Focus!*

She took a good look around the room. A few knickknacks were scattered about and a flower painting hung over the bed, but it looked sterile, utilitarian. Still, a nice room for a shelter, she supposed. And probably one of the nicest rooms she'd ever stayed in. *Pity party over, Analise.* Damian didn't explain, and she didn't ask, but she wondered what type of women's shelter this was exactly.

She had a sneaking suspicion she knew which "friend's" house this was. This mansion belonged to Devon Fallinsworth. She felt it in her gut. And if Damian was watching Devon's club and staying at Devon's house, then maybe she could still get help, just from Damian instead. Or she could convince Damian to ask Devon if he didn't know how to find Beth.

She didn't think Lord Devon had anything to do with Beth's disappearance, but Smitty had told her that he might know how to find out. And he certainly had the resources and money to help her, if his club and this house were any indication. She didn't have anything to barter in return, but she'd do anything he asked of her. Right now, she just needed help.

And since Devon wasn't around, Damian was her next best bet. Would it be a hardship to offer her body to Damian? *Hell, no.* He'd been more than forthcoming of his desire for her, and just looking at him made her wet. He stirred surprising but enjoyable feelings in her. Would it be a smart idea to sleep with him? *Obviously not.* Would that stop her? She really didn't know.

With a loose plan formulated, she peeled off her black dress, bra and panties. Drawing on her baby blue tank and matching patterned terry shorts, she did her business in the bathroom and plugged in her cell. With tonight's bedtime playlist selected, John Legend's "You & I" played softly from the phone's small speakers. Music was the balm for her tattered soul. Lyrics spoke to her, saving her in dark times, soothing her in sad times, giving her strength to face the future.

As she settled under the soft sheets, she resolved to fortify her walls. She was irrationally attracted to Damian. She wanted him in her bed, in her body. And it terrified her. She'd never really ever been attracted to a man, certainly not like this. *That* night so many years ago had ruined her for the opposite sex. And she didn't bat for the same team, so that left her girl parts pretty much dried up like a prune.

So, yes, being so attracted to Damian was foreign territory and scary shit. And she had no clue how to handle it. She liked him way too much for just having met him. She was not a clingy or needy woman by any means. Why him? Why now?

Your destiny awaits. Could it be true?

No. She wouldn't let anyone in that space ever again. It was—and would remain—completely closed off. Other than Beth, she was incapable of love. Life was just easier that way. Lonelier? Perhaps. But she'd had enough lies, enough hurt, enough subterfuge to last two lifetimes.

Beth was still alive—she felt it—but the clock was ticking. Her focus, her mission had to be solely on finding Beth before it was too late, not sleeping with the sexiest man—*vampire*—she'd ever met. He was not her destiny. Finding Beth was. That must have been what Mara meant.

The lie sat hard, like a heavy boulder in the pit of her stomach. In the background, John Legend crooned in the magical way only he could.

As she drifted off into a restless sleep, she couldn't help herself from wishing that it were Damian singing to her instead. All of her past, her troubles would melt away and it would be just the two of them, and she would be happy. Truly happy. And *she* would be *his* one and only girl.

Sighing, she decided she'd work on fortifying her walls tomorrow. Tonight would be reserved for foolishly daydreaming of things that could never be.

Chapter 13

Damian

He'd made his way back to Dev's office, waiting on Rom. His cock was so hard he could hardly think. He might have to resort to taking care of it himself. He could actually feel his balls turning purple. Strangely, though, as much as he wanted to be inside her body, he wanted to be inside her heart, her soul. He wanted to break through Analise's emotional barriers and be the one person she could trust. *Love*.

He called Frankie. He didn't even know Analise's last name and he needed it for what he had in mind.

"Frankie, I need Analise's last name."

"How is she? Is she with you?" Frankie's whiny voice grated on his last nerve. And he had just a little too much interest in his Moira's welfare.

"Her last name. Now." He didn't have to explain a fucking thing to him.

"Aster."

Her full name was as beautiful as she was. "Did she put a previous address on her job application?"

"I'll have to check."

Silence.

"You'd better be doing it now, human." His firestarter abilities itched to be used; he was ready to turn Frankie into a nice crispy piece of bacon if he didn't hurry up.

"Y-yes, my lord. Please give me a minute."

"You have less than thirty seconds."

"Yes, my lord. Fifty-three, forty-one Wyoming Street, Eau Claire, Wisconsin."

The hairs on the back of his neck stood on end. *Eau Claire?* Lots of women were from Eau Claire, right? It didn't necessarily mean anything.

But his gut screamed differently.

"Don't expect Analise at work tomorrow. I'll let you know when she will return." Which would be never.

He hung up.

"T, I need you to do something for me."

"Yes, my lord."

"Check into an Analise Aster. Fifty-three, forty-one Wyoming Street, Eau Claire, Wisconsin. Find out every single thing you can about her. I want to know her parents' names, if she has siblings, what her favorite food is, her bank account balance, where she went to school, her favorite music, her friends' names. Everything. Also, I want you to physically go to her house and look around. Bring me anything of importance. This is your only priority until I tell you otherwise."

"Of course, my lord."

Analise seemed like a very private person. If she found out what he was doing, she'd have his nuts in a guillotine. They may be medieval death-wielding devices, but he had no doubt his mate would move heaven and earth to track one down, making *Thing one* and *Thing two* her first stop. And he was pretty attached to his *things*, so he would make sure to keep this his little secret.

At that moment, Rom sauntered in. He looked pretty damn sated.

"Did you enjoy Angel?"

"Very much." That's all he'd get from Rom except he surprised him asking about Analise. "And how is your mate, Damian? Did all check out well?"

He nodded. "Bump on the head, but she'll be fine. Although *she* thinks she has a concussion. She's in one of the shelter bedrooms sleeping. After tonight, I'll be moving her over here with me until I return to Boston. Then she'll be coming with me. But she thinks she's only staying here for tonight. I'll figure out the rest tomorrow."

Rom laughed.

"She is a conundrum, though. And a hothead." And magnificent and sexy as hell, he added silently.

Rom silently raised an eyebrow. "Sounds like you two are made for each other."

"Go ahead, yuck it up man. I won't forget this when you find your Moira. Then I'll be the one in the wings laughing my ass off. You're bound to get one that will give you a run for your money."

Rom was thoughtful for a moment. "I'm not sure a mate is part of my destiny."

Rom was one of the oldest vampires Damian knew, but even Rom wouldn't reveal exactly how old he was. Was he imagining it or did

Damian detect wistfulness in Rom's response? No…this was stoic Romaric Dietrich standing in front of him. He'd always been convinced Rom was missing an emotional gene. He'd never seen the guy get worked up or lose his cool. Ever. His emotions were like a flat line, never edging up or down. It was eerily creepy, actually. Rom certainly didn't seem lonely, but maybe he'd been wrong.

"I don't know, Rom. Until tonight I'd actually never thought much about finding mine. Both Devon and I found ours within a short time of each other. I think you're the next to fall, my friend."

Rom chose not to respond to his last comment, changing subjects instead.

"Do we have any further information this evening?"

Damian couldn't help but smile. "No. I need to follow up with Giselle and see if she's connected with the detective yet. I've temporarily reassigned T to another, more pressing matter."

Rom raised a suspicious eyebrow but didn't pry. "I have some business to attend to. We'll catch up later."

"That's fine. I need to check on Analise anyway."

As Rom left, he threw over his shoulder, "You never could have taken me, by the way. You were foolish to even consider it."

"Perhaps not. But I would do anything for her." There was no *perhaps* about it. Damian would have been dead in seconds.

He watched Rom leave without another word, but couldn't shake the air of melancholy he'd felt from his friend.

Huh? Who would have thought?

Chapter 14

Analise

She hid just outside the living room, straining to hear. She could only pick up a word here or there, but Ms. Fuergusen being here wasn't good. She didn't know what Ms. Fuergusen did exactly, but whenever she showed up, Analise was taken away. To another home. To another family that didn't seem to want her. To someone who might hurt her.

This family had wanted her; at least she'd thought they did. This was her sixth foster home in ten years and she'd been here for two. The longest time she'd ever been with a single family. She was finally beginning to relax, to let them in. To love them.

And then Jana, her foster mom, got sick. Analise was still reeling from her death just a few short weeks ago. She'd loved her. Jana was nice. She'd let her watch cartoons and help set the table. She'd taught her how to husk sweet corn and make rhubarb crisp. She didn't like rhubarb crisp, but she liked helping. She had a school backpack for the first time in her life. Disney princesses. And she had a room of her very own. It was painted cotton candy pink. Her bedspread had Disney princesses all over it. She loved pink. Jana read to her every night and helped her practice reading and math. Analise didn't like math, but Jana said it was important to learn it.

Jack, Jana's husband, was nice too, but not as nice as Jana. At least he didn't hurt her like some of the others. He hadn't paid her much attention since Jana died, but that was okay. She was used to taking care of herself. She would take care of him instead.

The click of heels echoed on the linoleum floor, heading in her direction. She scrambled to her bedroom and hid in the closet. She knew something bad was coming, and if she could hide, maybe they'd just go away and forget about her. And she could stay here. They told her they were a family. She'd take care of Jack. He wouldn't have to do anything for her. She would be good, do all the cooking. Be quiet as a church mouse.

"Analise? Honey, where are you?"

She hid further in the corner of the closet, closing her eyes. She was a big girl. Ten years old. She knew closing her eyes wouldn't make her disappear; she just wished it would.

The closet door opened, light spilling in from the bedroom.

"Here you are. Come on, sweetie. Come on out," Ms. Fuergusen cajoled. Analise shook her head, waterfalls cascading down her face.

Ten minutes later, they were pulling away from the only house she'd ever called home. From the only person that ever loved her. Correction. The only person that loved her was buried under the dirt, worms eating her decaying flesh. Anyone who loved her would never send her to what would later become worse than a living hell.

At the tender age of ten, Analise vowed to never let anyone that close to her again. Love led to lies, hurt and betrayal.

For the second time in the last several hours, she awoke to a gentle touch on her cheek. She was completely disoriented and blinked her eyes open, trying to shake off her dream. She hadn't dreamt of her past in a very long time. Staring down at her with affection—*and desire*—was Damian.

"Hello, kitten. How are you feeling?" His voice was silky soft, like feathers gliding over her sensitive skin.

"Is it morning yet?"

"No, it's still the middle of the night. I just wanted to check on you. How does your head feel?"

"Ummm ... I'm not sure." A slight headache lingered, but it was mostly gone. She pulled herself into a sitting position, leaning against the soft leather headboard.

Damian's eyes snapped to her chest. She followed his line of sight, noticing her nipples were as hard as pencil erasers. She could even faintly see the outline of her areola through the thin tank. When her eyes lifted, they connected with his. And just like that, she lit up inside. Her stomach was in a free fall, like every other time she'd looked at him tonight. She was sure the lust on his face was mirrored in hers. Holy guacamole, she wanted him. It was exhilarating and terrifying at the same time.

He swallowed thickly and even his Adam's apple was sexy. Movement caught in her peripheral and, looking down, she watched him grow hard right before her eyes.

"Kitten, you'd better stop looking at me like I'm your favorite saucer of milk or I'm not going to be responsible for what happens next. I'm barely holding it together as it is." His voice was low and hoarse, ratcheting up his sexy status another notch to so-fucking-hot-I-dare-you-not-to-touch-this.

"I want to be inside you so bad, Analise," he groaned.

God, she wanted that too.

How could she be so wildly attracted to a man she'd just met? This wasn't at all like her. Was this some sort of vampire voodoo? She'd heard of this type of thing before. Vampires could make humans do their bidding at will. Was that what was happening here? Was that why she could barely resist the urge to climb into his lap and rub her body all over his ... like a goddamned cat? Like a *kitten*!

She saw red. How *dare* he try to compel her!

"What are you doing to me?" She grabbed the blankets and covered herself completely, putting a ridiculously flimsy barrier between them.

He actually had the audacity to smirk. "You mean besides making you wet?"

She inhaled sharply, her mouth forming an O. He did not! What an asshole. Of course, he'd already admitted as much earlier.

"I want to know what you are doing to me and I want you to stop. Right now," she spat.

"So … I guess you're feeling better then." *Ooohhh*. Fury spiked her blood pressure higher by the millisecond. He pushed every single one of her buttons. Good and bad.

"Do you really get women with that mouth of yours?"

"Ah, kitten, come now. You wound me." He held his hand over his heart in mock hurt. "It's not my *mouth* that gets women."

"You are the most infuriating, cocky person I have ever met." And sexy and handsome and erotic and …

"God, I love hearing the word cock come out of your mouth. I'm so fucking turned on right now, Analise. You have no idea." Lust and desire clouded his eyes.

When had he gotten so close? Unrestrained hunger tightened his stunning face. He had no issues showing or telling her how much he wanted her. It was unsettling … and a huge turn on.

He leaned closer, bringing their mouths within a hairsbreadth of each other. She had only to lean forward an inch and his soft lips would be hers for the taking. He would let her and she wanted nothing more. He scrambled her brains.

God, Analise, stop being such a tramp.

She pushed on his chest, trying to gain some space, some breathing room. He moved only slightly and that was only because he chose to do so. She was under no illusion she'd managed to move someone built like a 747. As she felt the hardness and warmth of his pecs under her hand, she realized touching him was a tremendously bad idea. All she could think of was trailing her fingers down his torso until they reached his greatest treasure.

Whew ... was it hot in here suddenly?

This was not going at *all* according to plan. Granted, she hadn't yet hammered out the details of her elaborate strategy, but letting him have control definitely wasn't in it. And right now, he had it in spades.

"What are you doing to me?" The soft words barely passed her constricted throat. Now, however, she wasn't exactly sure what she meant by them.

His eyes never left hers as he closed the gap, capturing her lips gently between his.

"The same thing you're doing to me, Analise," he whispered reverently before taking them again. How could he make her want to commit murder one minute and melt like chocolate sitting in the hot sun the next?

Damian deepened the kiss, scattering her thoughts to the wind. Next thing she knew, she was on his lap, straddling his hips, his erection prodding between her legs. Had he moved her there or had she done that herself? Strong, muscled arms held her tight against an equally sinewy body. Unable to stop herself, she wrapped her arms around his neck and let her body take over. As Damian ate at her mouth, her hips rolled, the rough fabric of his jeans rubbing perfectly against her terry-covered clit. Their tongues dueled, their breaths quickened.

She ran her hands over his back, down his arms. She couldn't get enough of his toned, sleek body. He caught her wrists, holding them with one hand at the small of her back. Her pulse skyrocketed. She hated being restrained but with Damian she became even more impossibly turned on. She was embarrassingly wet if the dampness on her pajamas was any indication.

Damian scattered hot, open-mouthed kisses on her face, her neck. He'd placed his free hand on her hips, helping them keep time with her pace. She was quickly soaring toward orgasm and he hadn't even touched her ... at least not in the way that counted. This was all kinds of wrong, but she couldn't stop. Her head felt heavy, falling back on her shoulders. She was so close to soaring.

"Come for me, Analise. I need to see you fall apart in my arms." His soft voice sounded raw, husky and was exactly what she needed to push her over the edge into complete paradise. A white light exploded behind her closed lids. Goose bumps blanketed her body as an orgasm ripped through her, setting every nerve ending on fire. She'd never felt pleasure like this. She rode the wave for what seemed like eternity.

When she finally came down from ecstasy, she felt Damian's soft kisses at the corners of her mouth, her eyelids, her cheeks. He'd released her arms at some point and placed one hand at the small of her back and one around her neck. His strong grip felt ... comforting. Right.

As the last vestiges of her orgasm waned, shame flooded her. Her cheeks warmed. How could she have just rubbed herself to climax on Damian's lap, like some wanton hussy? She tried, but couldn't help the tears that formed, spilling over her lids. Great, the last thing she needed was Damian to think she was easy *and* an emotional head case. Christ, let's just multiply her embarrassment a thousandfold.

"Baby, what's wrong?" Too late. *Uhhhh. Shoot me now.* She kept her eyes closed, wishing the whole thing would go away. She'd done that a lot in her life. Hadn't worked so far. Guess she wasn't a quick learner.

"Kitten, talk to me. What's the matter? Did I hurt you?" He sounded slightly panicked.

Did he hurt her? No, not yet. But he would. Just give him time. Everyone did sooner or later.

"I don't want to be another notch on your bedpost," she whispered, inwardly groaning. Where in God's name had that come from? That was not at all what she intended to say. *Get out before I let you fuck me* had been more like it.

"Ahhh, kitten." He pulled her tightly to him, strong arms wrapping completely around her, stroking her back, her hair. Tears fell quietly, wetting his shirt. Pretty soon snot would be running down her face. Great. *Excuse me, Damian, while I wipe my boogers from your two hundred-dollar shirt.*

He held her as he spoke, his voice firm, but full of sincerity. "Listen to me good, Analise. You are *not* another notch on my bedpost. I don't want another woman. Only you." He pulled back cupping her cheeks in his strong hands, forcing her eyes to his. "I won't hurt you, Analise. I will protect you. I will protect your heart. I promise."

The ability to speak vanished. She shook her head. That was all she could do. He sounded so sure, so sincere, so possessive. She ached to believe him. Every word he said resonated deep inside, slowly filling each empty crevice in her very damaged soul. Every word created more chinks in her already fragile armor. For the first time since she was ten years old, she longed to be loved by someone. To *belong* to someone. To Damian.

Stupid, foolish schoolgirl thoughts.

He touched his lips to hers one last time before pulling the sheets back. Sliding in, fully clothed, he pulled her body into his, arranging them comfortably.

"Go back to sleep, Analise. I'll be right here when you wake." He was staying. She was never more grateful … or terrified. Letting him stay was the single dumbest idea ever, but she was simply too exhausted to fight him.

The walls she'd spent so many years building were crumbling quickly and she had no clue how to stop them from disintegrating into nothingness. And that would be so very bad. Because if she allowed Damian into her life, into her heart and he broke her … well, she would never recover. Damian would literally be the straw that broke the camel's back.

Hope. It was a fool's emotion. It was that tiny light at the end of a black tunnel that kept one going in even the darkest of times, but the inevitable crash that followed was all the more devastating because once you reached the end you realize it wasn't a light at all. It had been a sick, twisted illusion all along. She should know. She was Hope's bitch.

Against her better judgment, she drifted off to sleep in the warmth and comfort of his arms, wondering what in the hell she was going to do now. Because in order to find Beth, she needed Damian. And against all that made sense, she couldn't spend much more time with him without falling head over heels in love. But that also meant she could end up eternally broken.

Analise had recovered from heart-crushing devastation and deep betrayal throughout her life, but she knew without a single doubt that she would never recover from loving and losing Damian DiStephano.

He held the power to destroy her permanently.

Chapter 15

Damian

He'd been completely gutted. His Analise was in so much pain. What in the hell had happened to her in only twenty-odd years to create such a fierce distrust of people? He hoped he would find out soon enough from the research T was currently conducting, because he doubted very much he'd get it from Analise.

The sad thing was he could relate to her on so many levels. He'd known almost unendurable pain in his life as well. Time helps heal but it doesn't erase. He was in a far better place now, but even after all this time, that pain was always there. Always a dull ache. Surprisingly, Analise had made that dull ache disappear.

She was the salve to his soul and he knew he was to hers. Even if she wouldn't admit it. The lyrics of Coldplay's "Fix You" ran through his head. They would fix each other. This was why they were fated. They were the healing ointment each other so desperately needed. Together, they would be repaired.

Whole.

Complete.

She was going to completely freak when he sprung the Moira thing on her. She would run away faster than Usain Bolt. So how would he get past her guard? *Could* he get past her guard? He had to. He had no choice. She was already becoming deeply important to him and not only on a sexual level. Make no mistake; he wanted her body with a ferocity that bordered on insanity. His balls ached. His cock would wear the imprint of his zipper before morning. How he was going to lie here with her sweet body wrapped around him for the next several hours and not take her was beyond his comprehension. But he would do it. For her.

He hadn't intended for anything to happen when he checked on her, but sexual tension crackled and sparked in the air. They both felt it. He should have just left her sleeping, but she was fitful. And her skin beckoned to him like a siren's song. He simply couldn't resist touching her.

And when she opened her mouth, feisty words spilled out. It got him rock hard every time she did that. She pushed every one of his buttons when she verbally sparred with him. Before he knew it, she was rocking her pussy on his cock and coming apart in his arms. It was the most erotic sight he'd ever watched. She was simply stunning. And she was his. He'd wanted to throw her on the bed, fuck her hard once before making love to her all night slowly, sweetly. He'd wanted to hear her moan his name as he made her come so many times she lost count.

Then her tears tore him up. She'd needed to be comforted, not fucked.

Utter despair poured from her when she'd said she didn't want to be another notch to him. How she could think that was incomprehensible, but of course, she didn't know what he did—they were meant to be together. What he'd wanted to say, but didn't dare, was not only did he *not* want another woman, but there would never be another woman for him. She'd erased any memory of other women before her. She was it. She would always be *it* for him. But she was *not* ready to hear those words just yet.

Trust was the key to Analise's heart, so he had to approach this carefully. Break her trust once, lose her forever, Moira or not. Guilt beat at his conscience for checking into her background. Unfortunately though, not enough to call it off. He just had to make sure she never found out.

He needed to formulate a plan to keep her with him. Get her to Boston. He had to return day after tomorrow to take care of a few business dealings, one of them being to check on Grina, his new club. There was no way in hell he was leaving her here. He would simply have to turn up his megawatt charm full blast. She fought him—*fought herself*—but wasn't immune to their passion as he'd found out twice this evening.

He aimed to find out what really brought her to town, because it sure as hell wasn't to serve Spotted Cow and fried cheese curds. She had a voice like an angel; singing on the stage of even Dev's posh club was beneath her. And how did she come to know of Dev anyway? All questions he would try to get answered tomorrow. She also hadn't denied knowing he was vampire. Tomorrow he would get her to admit it.

He was too on edge to sleep, so instead he simply enjoyed the feeling of holding his Moira close to him. Hearing her heart beat against his chest, in time with his. Listening to her soft, slow breaths. Breathing in her unique scent. Lavender and slight musk from her earlier orgasm.

He was falling for her hard and fast. And there was no place he would rather be than right here with her tucked next to him.

Chapter 16

Analise

She woke with strong arms wrapped around her, sun streaming around the edges of the closed blinds. Laying completely still, she blinked away the remaining morning fog. Memories of the night before came flooding back. *Damian.*

Fainting.

Concussion.

Kissing.

Limousine.

Orgasm.

She inwardly groaned. Her reaction to Damian bordered on embarrassing. No ... embarrassment was just a speck now in her rear view mirror. It was impulsive, irrational, uncontrolled. She couldn't rationalize her insane attraction to him and it was really screwing with her head.

Why, oh why didn't she tell him to leave when he'd pulled her into his hard, sexy body last night? It would make this morning's fortress rebuilding process that much easier if she didn't have to breathe in his delicious scent with every single pull of oxygen. He smelled of spice, danger and sex. He smelled all male. She should breathe through her mouth. No ... bad idea. Then she would just taste him instead. *Ugh.*

She lay there quietly, mentally rebuilding the stronghold around her heart brick by brick. She envisioned laying the bricks, then the mortar. Bricks, mortar. Bricks, mortar.

"I can hear the wheels spinning, kitten. What's going on in that head of yours so early?"

Sigh. The brick building was not nearly far enough along yet and his husky voice just knocked down a few rows.

"Must you be so annoying first thing in the morning?"

He simply laughed. The sound rolled over her, as soothing as gentle ocean waves crashing on the beach. *Build faster, Analise. Bricks, mortar. Bricks, mortar.*

"How did you know I was awake, anyway?" Subject change. She didn't feel like fighting before she at least had a chance to brush her teeth.

"Well, don't you know us vampires have a very keen sense of perception?"

She stilled. Her heart beat out of its chest. That was the second time he'd referenced being a vampire. She'd ignored it the first time and he let her. Maybe if she did the same thing this time, he'd let it go again.

"I can feel your pulse increase, Analise. I hear the blood rushing through your veins, your arteries, keeping your organs alive. I've had to lie here for hours listening to it pumping through your body. Your intoxicating scent calls my name. It cries to me on a primal level."

Holy fuck. She scrambled to get up, but ended up flat on her back, over two hundred pounds of very sexy, very aroused, very angry vampire pinning her to the mattress, hands held immobile above her head. She couldn't speak. She should be petrified, but instead her core liquefied. She'd lost complete control of her body now, in addition to her mouth. Could things get much worse?

"I can smell your arousal, kitten. It's driving me out of my goddamn mind." He took a deep breath, closing his eyes for a moment. When he opened them, he pinned her with a hard glare, eyes alight with desire. And anger. "Why did you come to Dragonfly?"

She swallowed, hard. *Yes*. Yes, things could get worse. She opened her mouth to speak when he spoke over her.

"And don't even think of lying to me Analise. I can smell subterfuge a mile away and you, my kitten, are full of it. The truth." He ran his nose along the side of her neck, nipping along the way. Her breath hitched. Her eyes closed. Pleasure ricocheted throughout her body.

"I'm waiting," he groaned while continuing his assault, this time moving to the other side of her neck. Was she arching to give him better access? *Oh my God Analise! Have you no shame?*

"I—I can't think when you're doing that?"

He chuckled. "Was that a question or a statement, kitten?"

'"Stop." She couldn't take any more of his seduction. She'd be naked in less than sixty seconds if she didn't get him to stop. He pulled back, a smug look on his face. He was so stunning it almost hurt to look at him.

"Get off me."

"Answer the question." He turned deadly serious. She still wasn't frightened, even though she could sense his darkness. Turned out she believed him when he said he'd protect her. Maybe not the heart part, but she knew he wouldn't physically harm her.

"I want to know why you were at Dragonfly and why you were looking for Devon," he demanded. She was not getting out of it this time.

What the hell, why not? She didn't trust him; well ... maybe she did a little. Right now, he was her only shot at finding Beth.

"My friend is missing and I heard that the owner of Dragonfly may have the resources to help find her."

He regarded her for a moment. "And how did you hear about the owner of Dragonfly?"

Now this she was *not* revealing. He would start digging too deep and she wasn't prepared to answer questions about her past. Not now. Not ever. Least of all to someone she found so attractive. If he ever found out the things that she had done ... well, she just wasn't going there.

"I plead the fifth."

"Jesus, Analise. This isn't a court of law. You can't plead the fifth."

"I think I can and I think I did. Next question." Bastard.

His head fell back on his shoulders and he took a deep breath. "You are the most infuriating woman I've ever met."

"Pot, meet kettle."

He laughed. A full belly laugh that echoed through her body, on account of the fact he was still sitting on top of her. Her confined arms were starting to tingle.

"Fine, I'll let it go. For now." He leaned down until their noses were almost touching, not even trying to hide his now glowing eyes. "So you know Devon is vampire?"

She nodded slightly, never breaking eye contact. The fact that she wanted him to stop talking and kiss her senseless wasn't lost on her when a minute ago she wanted to throttle him. Her emotions were as jumbled as a Sudoku puzzle around him.

"And you know that I'm vampire as well?" Desire emanated from him, his eyes glowing more brightly than ever before. They were spectacular, mesmerizing. Golden light bathed her face.

She nodded. His gaze shifted to her lips and she licked them unconsciously.

"And you're not afraid of me?" For the first time since she'd met Damian DiStephano she sensed his cocksure bravado falter, though he tried to hide it. The answer to his question was more important than he would let on.

She softened her voice and let her body relax, answering honestly. "No."

The word had no sooner left her lips than his mouth crashed to hers. She didn't hold back one ounce of desire for him. She couldn't fight this insane attraction to him anymore. He'd woken up something inside her and she craved the warmth it provided. He made her feel alive.

His kisses were bruising, punishing. She relished it. She craved his dominance. It was refreshing to turn herself completely over to someone. Gentle fingers stroked up and down her arm, her torso. A complete dichotomy to the way he pillaged her mouth. Her legs had eased open and once again, his denim-covered cock rocked against her most sensitive parts. His free hand cupped her breast, his thumb rubbing circles around her areola, not quite touching her hardened nub. She ached for his mouth on her.

As if sensing her need, he pulled her pajama top up and took the rigid peak into his hot mouth. It was pure rhapsody. He sucked and nibbled. A long moan escaped her. His hips never stopped their assault and she could feel her wetness seeping through her thin terry shorts. Her head was spinning; sensation overwhelmed her. He was everywhere, but not close enough.

His hand snaked down between their writhing bodies, over the outside of her soaked bottoms. The long, deep groan that left his throat lit her up inside. She was so drenched now she should be embarrassed, but she wasn't. Instead, she felt empowered because he loved it. He slipped a finger underneath her tiny bottoms and dragged it through her saturated slit.

"Christ, Analise," he whispered before roughly taking her mouth again. His kiss was ripe with lust, longing, and an unspoken promise.

Her sex ached with emptiness and she moved her hips in an attempt to coax him into working her sex faster, moving his fingers inside her. But he took his time exploring, starting at the top of her lightly curled mound, down one side of her outer lips and back up the other, like he was mentally mapping every dip, every curve, every nuance. Her arousal now coated the entire hot space between her thighs.

"Damian, please," she unashamedly begged.

Careful to avoid her clit, he finally pushed one, then quickly two fingers inside her craving body and she could have wept with unadulterated joy. She'd never experienced pleasure like this at the hands of any man.

He broke the kiss, murmuring, "Your pussy feels like silk, kitten. Hot. Smooth. Mine."

Oh. My. Sweet. Lord.

His wicked tongue forged a wet path back toward her engorged breast while his talented fingers never stopped their sensual assault to take her over the edge. He cleverly curled his fingertips inside her just right, as his thumb finally circled her sweet spot. She rode his hand now with complete abandon, never needing to reach a climax more in her life, while at the same time trying to stave it off as long as possible to draw out this unimaginable pleasure.

"Come. Now, kitten."

His hot mouth closed tightly over her hard nipple, taking the nub between his sharp teeth. When he bit down, pain and pleasure collided, setting off an unexpected orgasm. Ecstasy coursed through every single cell as she bucked and thrashed beneath him. She heard herself moan his name as waves of bliss overtook her, scattering all thought into the stratosphere.

When she came back into herself, her eyes slowly opened to see Damian gazing both hungrily and worshipfully at her. He made her feel so beautiful, so special. Almost loved. *Stop Analise ... it was just an orgasm, not a marriage proposal.*

"You're fucking amazing, Analise." His voice was low and raspy, his desire for her evident. She felt bereft when he removed his hand and, while she shouldn't have been shocked when he brought his fingers to his mouth and sucked them clean, she couldn't help but gasp. His hips were now once again moving against her cloth-covered sex and she felt the tingling sensation of a second orgasm looming.

"I can't wait to have you tied to my bed, at my mercy. I'm going to spend all night gorging on my new favorite meal."

She took a sharp breath. No one had ever talked so blatantly sexually to her. His face became taut with lust, sharpening his beautiful features.

"That turns you on doesn't it, kitten? You crave my dominance." He nuzzled the delicious little place where her neck met her shoulder, nipping slightly. A thrill shot through her. "You crave my bite. You want to know what it feels like when I pull your sweet essence into me. You need to know what it feels like to have my mouth all over you. To have my cock inside your sweet, tight pussy as I'm taking your blood. Your desire to know what it's like for me to own every delicious inch of your body is written all over your face."

She wanted to lie and tell him no. But every word he'd said was spot-on and she knew he could see the truth reflected in her eyes.

"Christ, Analise, I want you so goddamned bad. I'm in absolute agony with the need to be buried balls deep inside you, making you mine." He groaned as he touched his forehead to hers. "But you're not ready yet. And when I fuck you, make no mistake about it, you will give me all of you. Body, heart, mind and soul. All of you will be irrevocably mine. Forever."

Whoa.

What?

His?

Forever?

Could she only think in one-word sentences?

Her heart raced. That bitch, Hope, reared her foolish head. Made her dream of things that could never be.

Love.

Trust.

Belonging.

His words were like music to her ears. He wanted her. For more than just a quick lay? And while she may want it to happen, it never could. Never would. Things like this just didn't happen to her. Other than Beth and Jana, she hadn't been truly wanted by anyone in her whole life. Or loved. She was unworthy.

Damian had the power to irreversibly break what was left of her damaged heart into a million pieces. She liked him way too much already for her own sanity. She was getting in far too deep here, on a speeding train that had lost its brakes. And the only thing that could happen in that scenario was a huge fiery crash when it eventually jumped the tracks.

"You're thinking too much, kitten. Get out of your own head. This"—he motioned between the two of them—"us. It's going to happen. It's only a matter of time and you'd best accept it. Sooner rather than later, because I honestly don't know how long I can hold back from taking you."

He placed another searing kiss on her lips before getting up from the large bed. She lay there, unable to move, her mind swirling.

"If you feel rested enough, why don't you take a shower and I'll be back to get you in an hour. We'll eat some breakfast and talk. I want to hear more about your missing friend. Okay?"

She could only dumbly nod. He walked toward the door and she couldn't help how her eyes traveled to his very fine ass. He turned back just before he reached the door. *Whoops ... busted.*

He gave her such a gentle smile it almost made her cry. What he said next did.

"Oh, and, Analise ... you are worthy, my love."

Tears slid down her face as he turned and silently walked out. If he noticed, he didn't say a word, and for that, she was grateful.

Chapter 17

Damian

Damian entered Dev's office, barely acknowledging T.

Forty-five minutes before he could return to Analise. Being separated from her made his heart ache. Being with her made his body ache. He hadn't lost his erection once in the twelve hours since he'd met her, so he'd had to take a quick shower and empty his pipes before he burst. It was hollow, not gratifying, but served its purpose and the pressure had been slightly eased. At least maybe he could stand to be around her a little longer before he threw her against the closest object and fucked her into next week.

He could already hear her thoughts. Even if he couldn't, she broadcast them loudly. It was like standing next to speakers at a rock concert. It took every ounce of strength to walk out of that bedroom when he saw her crying. He'd essentially already staked his claim on her, making his intentions known, and he knew she needed time to process his words.

The fact that she thought herself unworthy of love absolutely gutted him to his very soul. He had a ferocious need to know her, inside and out. How did his precious Analise come to know such pain and agony?

"I have some information on the girl."

He glared daggers at T. "She's not a fucking girl, she's my Moira. And you'd do well to treat her with the respect she deserves."

Surprise briefly flashed across T's sharp features. If Analise was a conundrum, T was a complete enigma. No one knew much about the guy and Damian had never really given his story too much thought. He was a great asset, a great warrior. That was all he'd needed to know. He'd never asked. T never offered. Now that he'd met Analise, however, he couldn't help but wonder what his story was.

"Forgive me, my lord. I had no idea."

"Well, now you do." Damian was acting like a bastard, but he was on the razor's edge, the sharp blade threatening to cut deep.

"Analise Lisbeth Aster is her full name. She was a ward of the State of Wisconsin from birth."

"Fuck," he whispered. *Could it possibly be?*

T regarded him briefly before continuing. "She was in and out of no less than a dozen foster homes before she ran away at the age of fifteen. She was off the grid until the age of twenty, when she got her GED. She's taking classes at the U of WI. Sociology major. She lives alone in a run-down duplex in a shitty part of town and has less than fifty bucks to her name. She's behind a month on rent. She worked at some trucker diner until just a few days ago, right before she showed up at Dragonfly. She also occasionally has singing gigs at coffee shops and bars to earn extra cash."

"What have you uncovered for the time she was off the grid?" Because in addition to being in and out of foster care, which he was sure was hard enough, the time she spent on the street no doubt molded her into the woman she was today. His gut churned at what she would have gone through to survive.

"Nothing yet, my lord. I'll need more time. I will hit the streets myself this evening and see if I can find someone that knows her."

"Yes, do that. Did you find anything out about a friend of hers named Beth?"

"No, my lord. But I'll check into that as well. Do you have a last name?"

"No ... not yet." He wasn't sure he wanted to know the answer to his next question, but he had to ask. "Any boyfriend?"

T tried holding back a smirk, quite unsuccessfully, he might add. His death stare shut that shit down. "No, my lord. No boyfriend, no friends really to speak of that I could find. She's quite the loner."

It wasn't much information, but it certainly gave a small glimpse into her psyche. Shuffled from home to home, living on the streets, no real friends, no real relationships, no acceptance, no love. She'd only known abandonment, hurt and distrust. So much made sense now. But he still had so many questions. How much would his kitten tell him about herself? Little, he was certain. She was fiercely prideful and would never want him to know of her past. Could he tell her about his? As much as it would hurt, the answer was a resounding yes. Give a little to get a little.

"Keep digging. I want you to uncover every nugget of information available."

"Yes, my lord."

T had just left when Damian's cell phone rang. Unknown number. He almost let it go to voicemail, but his gut screamed this was important.

"Damian."

"My lord, it's Frankie Durillo, the manager of Dragonfly."

"I know who you are, Frankie. You don't need to give me your fucking title." Fucker.

"Yes, of course. I'm sorry. I just got a call from my head bartender and thought it strange, so I decided to call you."

"Human, you are making no fucking sense. Either spit it out or I'm hanging up." Jesus, was this guy always ready to piss his pants? He really needed to talk to Dev about this asshole. Maybe he should fire him and replace him with someone actually competent. Dev would likely thank him. Yes, he'd add that to his to-do list. Besides, he didn't like the possessive way Frankie acted about his mate.

"My apologies, my lord. Someone came looking for Analise last evening, shortly after you left."

Ice froze his veins. She'd been here for just a few short days. Who would be looking for her? "Who?"

"I don't know, my lord. He refused to leave a name. Said he was an old friend. He asked when she was working again."

"Pull up the security footage and send it to my phone. I want it within the next thirty minutes, max. I want to see this asshole."

"Yes, of course."

Damian hung up and dialed Giselle. It was highly inconvenient sometimes to not be able to speak telepathically with all vampires, but such was the ways of their kind. They could only speak in that manner with their mates and those in their own Regent. They didn't even have that ability between the three lords themselves and they didn't even have that ability with those in their Regent if they were too far away.

"Giselle, I need to see you now." Her response was a heavy sigh.

Fucking woman. He prayed for patience.

Several minutes later she came sauntering into the office. He held back a retort about what took her so damn long. If his suspicions were correct, they may not need the detective's work, but it would certainly help verify what he felt in his bones to be true.

"Have you reached out to the detective yet about the Eau Claire baby?"

"No."

He breathed. In and out. In and out. *Hold your tongue, Damian.*

"That needs to be done today. Please." Christ that hurt. Physically painful.

"Fine. I'll see him this morning." He nodded and she left. She was getting one nicety from him today. That was it.

He knew what the detective would find about the Eau Claire baby delivered so many years ago. T's comments from yesterday came racing back.

"He did say that the Eau Claire female was left with the family in the winter months, December or January timeframe. That one was kind of a debacle and the adoptive parents called the cops on him, so he left the baby and ran. We don't know whether the parents kept that baby or not."

His money was on not. That female became a ward of the state. Bounced around from foster home to foster home until she'd had enough and ran away, living on the streets. His gut was wailing loudly now. His Moira was in danger. He felt it with every fiber of his being. He knew the man he'd see on the video wouldn't be human. He would be vampire.

Which meant that they'd just found Xavier's second daughter. His Moira, Analise Lisbeth Aster.

Chapter 18

Mike

He watched her from his bay window. His heart raced. She was like a feast for a starving man's eyes. She'd been pacing on the front porch for damn near twenty minutes now. Hadn't rung the doorbell. Hadn't just *poofed* herself into his living room like she owned the goddamned place, her usual M.O. She looked nervous, unsure. She was different. Not at all like the self-confident, guarded, cocky seductress she generally portrayed herself to be.

Now he knew better. Underneath her self-imposed frosty persona, Giselle was just as fragile as everybody else. She wanted acceptance, validation ... possibly even love. Giselle put on a good front, but he could see beneath her complex layers into the real woman ... *er, vampire* ... she tried so desperately to cover up.

He recognized a kindred spirit when he saw one. She'd suffered greatly, as had he. Perhaps that was why he was so drawn to her, against his better judgment. Against his will even. Their sadness, their pain, their darkness called to each other. He despised this unwanted attraction to her. Despised himself and to some extent, her. She was everything he'd loathed for nearly a dozen years. Not her, per se, but her kind. What the vampire species had done to Jamie, the woman he'd planned on making his wife someday, was unforgettable. Unforgiveable.

His heart and body were fucking traitors. Perhaps physical desire didn't play by the species rules, but his emotional desire? He actually *cared* about Giselle ... her feelings, her well-being. Her hopes and dreams. *Pussy alert.* The very bloodsuckers he was now attracted to had ripped away from him the last female whose hopes and dreams he had cared about.

Logically, he knew it wasn't Giselle. She had nothing to do with Jamie's kidnapping and subsequent torture. She'd wanted to stop the rogue vampires just as much, if not more, than he. Yes, logically he knew that, but his heart had a tough time separating the two.

However, standing here with the biggest hard-on he'd had since the last time he'd almost fucked Giselle in Dev's office, he knew he could put those feelings aside. There were no ifs, ands or buts. He was unnaturally attracted to Giselle. And she was here standing on his doorstep.

She was breathtakingly, painfully beautiful. He leaned toward brunettes, but loved Giselle's angelic golden blonde locks that hung like silk to the middle of her back. He'd fantasized countless times about holding a fistful of it while he pumped into her tight sheath from behind. Her vibrant eyes were mesmerizing, the most unnatural color of cerulean blue he'd ever seen, dotted with tiny violet-like flecks. They were the doors to her untainted, pure soul.

She now stood still staring toward the street, her back to him. He'd already decided he'd wait for her to make the first move. Maybe she would be more amenable that way? No ... this was still Giselle they were talking about here. As if sensing him, she turned around. Their eyes locked through the thin fabric shrouding the window. The mask she wore to perfection snapped in place once again, but too late, for he caught a glimpse of her vulnerability. She strode to the door and rang the doorbell. Interesting ... why didn't she just flash her way in?

He took his time answering. If she could act, so could he. They'd both play the parts they'd been given. Her, the self-righteous bitch, him, the hostile fucking asshole. Both disinterested, hateful even. Never mind he'd spent the last several weeks wishing he could see her exquisite face again, taste her lips, shove his cock to the hilt in her sweet body and make her forget any man who came before him.

"Giselle," he said politely as he stood in the open doorway trying not to openly gawk at her. She wore a cream-colored see-through blouse, her black bra standing out starkly against her fair skin. She'd paired it with a short leather mini-skirt and knee-high black leather boots. *Fucking A*, how on earth was he going to be able to hide his erection?

"Detective," she purred, lacking her usual conviction. She was bruised and bleeding inside though she tried hiding it well. He stood silent waiting for her to make the next move. God, she really was exquisite. The mold had been obliterated after she was created.

"Aren't you going to invite me in?"

"I wasn't aware you needed an invitation. I thought vampires could flash anywhere at will."

"We can, asshole. Just trying to be polite." She breezed past him, walking into his small living room.

He held his snide reply back. It was so easy to fall into this trap with her and before they did, he really wanted to see how she was.

"By all means, make yourself at home, Giselle." Suddenly, he was assailed with anger. He'd been calling her for three long months and she didn't have the courtesy to even send him a damned text or email back, yet here she stood in all her glory, wanting something from him. Because let's face it, she wasn't a coffee girl and it was a little too fucking early for happy hour. Attraction or not, she was going to get an earful.

"Why are you here?" He was barely holding his fury in check now. He wanted to throttle and fuck her simultaneously.

"Aren't you going to even offer me a cup of coffee or a soda? Tsk, tsk ... where are your manners, Detective?"

In an instant, he had her backed up against the wall separating his kitchen and living room. He was under no illusion he could hold her there against her will, for her strength was far superior to his, but right now he didn't give a flying fuck. Her flippant attitude was going to be excised. By his cock.

"Why didn't you return my calls?" He held her arms tightly at her sides and ran his nose up and down her cheek, her neck, inhaling her unique citrus scent. *Jesus*, he'd missed that. He'd been eating oranges and nectarines by the bushelful in an attempt to remember how she smelled. Yes, he was beyond pathetic.

"I'm not at your beck and call, Detective," her breathy voice replied. They still had the same effect on each other. Good to know.

He pulled back, cupping her cheeks, pinning her to the wall with his hips instead. Her spellbinding eyes grew wider. He was hard as a rock and now he wanted her to know it.

"I don't want a fucking beck and call girl, Giselle." Then he kissed her with all the pent up desire and frustration that had been building inside him for months. He plundered her mouth, taking everything he wanted. His hips pumped into her, hitting her sweet spot and he swallowed her moan. His tongue demanded entry into her hot mouth and he savored her taste like a death row inmate eating his last meal.

He left her mouth, tasting her neck, nibbling her ear harshly before soothing the pain with his tongue. His hands now ran wildly over her body, cupping her breasts, her ass. There wasn't room for a sheet of paper between them, but she still wasn't close enough. He was so caught up in her, in the fact she was finally here in the flesh that he didn't register her tears until he caught a salty taste on his tongue. He immediately halted everything, looking into her red-rimmed eyes.

"Baby, what's wrong?" He was in a near panic as tears streamed in rivers down her splotchy face. She wasn't even trying to hide the fact she was crying. He cupped her cheeks in his hands, trying to wipe away the waterfall, but it was like a dam had burst and he couldn't keep up. He pulled her into his arms, but she was stiff as a board. Silent sobs wracked her body.

"Giselle, baby, I'm sorry. Please tell me what's wrong." He had a feeling Giselle had been buttoned up tighter than a hazardous containment unit, her emotions now in a free fall through the leak he'd created.

He bent slightly and with one arm beneath her knees, the other behind her back, picked her up and carried her to the soft, brown leather couch. She now clung to his neck like a child, openly sobbing into his shoulder as he made her comfortable in his lap. He held her tightly, gently stroking her hair, her back, and whispering over and over again that she would be okay that he was here for her as long as she needed him.

After an hour, she quieted, and only an occasional heave shook her exhausted body. Other than his consoling words, they never spoke. He knew she was sleeping when finally all tension in her body was gone, and her breathing slowed and evened out. Careful not to wake her, he gently laid them down, the wide sofa comfortable enough for their long frames. Tucking her into his side, he wrapped two protective arms around her.

No doubt when she awoke she'd be embarrassed, throwing up her walls so fast it would make his head spin. He was constantly dizzy around her, either from her barbs or his desire.

The question when she roused was ... where would they go from here?

Chapter 19

Analise

She lay on the made bed, buds in her ears, waiting for Damian to return like some lovesick puppy. Or kitten. *Christ, she was pathetic.* She should go in search of him, not wait around here for him to fetch her like some kenneled animal. But she vaguely remembered that they took many twists and turns to get to this room and she wasn't sure she trusted herself not to get lost. She'd never been in any place like this before. Plus she was a little afraid of running into anyone else. Other vampires, for example. *So ... stay put it is.*

The last twelve hours played through her mind on a continuous loop. She hadn't let a man touch her for nearly ten years. In fact, over the last twelve hours, she'd let Damian touch her more than any other human being since she was ten years old. And that didn't really count, because this was far different than motherly or fatherly affection.

She was wildly, absurdly attracted to him. To let him hold her while she slept took an incredible amount of trust and she hadn't placed that kind of trust in any man. He was the first. What did that mean exactly? She was so very confused. She wanted to stay; she wanted to go. She hadn't stopped fantasizing about him since she first set eyes on him. And she *never* fantasized about men.

Ever.

She'd had sex, unfortunately, yes, but she'd never had an orgasm. At least not given to her by another. Her right hand had become her sexual BFF, sad as that was. Orgasms by her own hand were always empty, unfulfilling and most definitely lonely. But she'd adjusted. Now, though ... now that she'd had a taste of true rapture, she didn't know if she could go back. And they hadn't even had sex yet. She wanted more. She wanted the whole enchilada now, with a side of supreme nachos. And fried ice cream for dessert.

When he mentioned tying her to his bed, she wanted to scream, yes, yes, please yes. She had been ready to give herself completely—*well, her body anyway*—to him at that moment, consequences be damned. Never in her life had she imagined that such a thing would turn her on, but it did. Oh boy, did it ever. Then he had to go endear himself to her even more by not taking advantage of her. He could have, she would have let him. But he didn't. And she had so much more respect—and daresay trust?—for him because of that. She had a feeling he knew exactly what he was doing in that regard.

She'd never met anyone who knew exactly the right thing to say at exactly the right time. "*You are worthy.*" How he knew to say that floored her. It was like he'd read her mind. *He's a vampire; of course he could probably read minds, Analise.*

The part that scared her, however, was how adamant he was that he was going to make her *his*. *"This ... us. It's going to happen. It's only a matter of time and you'd best accept it. Sooner rather than later, because I honestly don't know how long I can hold back from taking you."* That thought both terrified and thrilled her.

As she listened to Justin Timberlake's "Not A Bad Thing", Damian walked in like he owned the place. What if she'd been naked? The thought made a burst of heat rush through her. Along with the familiar anger that always simmered below her surface.

"Don't you knock? What if I'd have been naked?" she asked, pushing herself into a seated position. She wasn't about to just jump up and act all giddy that he'd finally come for her a half hour late. Even if she was.

"I wouldn't have minded one bit, kitten. In fact, if you want to strip right now, I certainly won't protest."

She threw a pillow at him, which missed by a mile. He had showered and was now wearing a fresh pair of dark blue jeans, this pair with small rips all over. His gray T-shirt stretched tautly across his chest, showing off his sinewy, sinful upper body. The short sleeves allowed her to see more of his tattoos. He had several on each arm, his biceps covered. She cursed that shirt, no matter how good it looked on him. She wanted nothing more than to see his naked chest. His naked everything.

Holy hotness. She reached up to see if drool was running out of her mouth.

He sauntered over to the bed and scooped her iPhone off the mattress. "What are you listening to?"

She tried grabbing it and he held it high out of her reach, laughing. "Give it back."

Instead, he unplugged her ear buds, and JT's buttery voice resonated through the small bedroom.

She expected him to laugh, to make fun of her. Instead, he looked deeply into her eyes before he spoke the most beautiful words she'd ever heard leave someone's lips.

"JT can go fuck himself. *I* am that man, Analise. Me. I see your brokenness, your darkness, but I also see your light and I'm drawn to it. I crave it like my next breath. I can see the shattered pieces of your soul and I will put them back together. *I* am the man to heal you, Analise. Let me heal you. Trust me to hold your heart in my hands like it's the most precious gem in the entire universe. To protect it with my life, because I will. I will never hurt you. Piss you off, yes. But hurt you ... never."

Analise had never been much of a crier, but for the second time this morning, he'd managed to bring her to tears. She couldn't speak past the thick lump in her throat, so she launched herself into his lap instead, hanging on for dear life. She was barely holding it together, but being in his arms was by far the safest place she'd ever felt in her life.

What is he doing to me?

"Thank you," she managed to choke out. He held her tightly in his warm embrace.

"Kitten, you don't have to thank me. It's how I feel. I know this may all seem sudden to you, but you don't understand how things work in my world. I'll explain it all when you're ready to hear, but know that I mean each and every word I've spoken to you."

He gently drew her back, cupping her cheeks. He wiped away her tears, kissing her softly. A feeling of rightness swept over her. Like she was meant to be here, with him.

"Now, let's go eat some breakfast before I eat you instead." Heat crept up her neck. He certainly didn't mince words. "Then we can discuss your friend."

Beth. She couldn't forget why she was here. It wasn't to fall into bed or in love; it was to find Beth.

She let him lead her through the large estate into an entirely different section. She refrained from asking questions, even though they were rapidly firing through her head. The house was obscenely large, ostentatious even. Who needed this much space? It was sinful really.

He led her to a large dining room, which he said was the smaller of the two. Really? This one could probably seat over twenty people. Could the other one hold an army? Ridiculous. She tried not to gawk or look like trailer trash. She didn't want to let someone as sophisticated as Damian know how utterly *un*sophisticated she was.

There was a giant spread of breakfast options on the large, dark table. Maple was it? She wasn't good at this stuff, having lived in abandoned warehouses, under bridges, or in cardboard boxes. Occasionally on a really cold night she'd go to the women's shelter. She might not be any safer, but at least she'd be warm.

"Wow, is someone else joining us? This looks like a lot of food."

"Just you and me, babe. Eat up. You look like you could use a few extra pounds." She may be a tiny bit on the thin side, but she certainly did not need to gain any weight. She always ate as healthy as her meager salary allowed, which was sometimes challenging. But she had to admit it all looked amazing. She filled her plate with scrambled eggs, fresh fruit medley and splurged on a powdered sugar donut. She also poured herself a nice big cup of coffee. That was a must in the morning and she was usually at least three cups in by this time.

Damian's plate overflowed with eggs, bacon, a bagel, fruit and three different types of pastries. How on earth did he look so fine if he ate so much? He had a large glass of orange juice instead of coffee. They ate in silence. It was nice. Comfortable. After they'd finished, he took their plates away, returning after a few short minutes.

"Come. Let's talk somewhere more comfortable than the dining room." She took his hand and they walked into a small, cozy sitting room. A fireplace took up the wall opposite the door. An oriental rug adorned the hardwood floor.

A loveseat sat to her left and two wingback chairs to her right, facing each other in a configuration meant for conversation. Built-in bookshelves lined the walls, and while they held some books, there were many knickknacks as well. Definitely a woman's touch. For the hundredth time, she wondered where exactly Damian had taken her.

He led her to the loveseat, sitting next to her, legs touching. His bulky arms flung over the furniture, he guided himself comfortably into a corner. She put one leg underneath her butt, turning toward him.

"Tell me about your friend, Beth."

She'd started to talk, stopping when he leaned toward her ever so slowly, eyes never leaving her lips. He was going to kiss her now? Her body reacted the same way every time he did this. It was like she was stuck in neutral and someone held down the gas pedal at full throttle, flooding her body with fuel essential to her existence. Her eyes involuntarily closed when his lips touched hers. His tongue explored the outside of her mouth before leisurely dipping inside, stroking hers. Every nerve ending was on fire.

All too quickly he was pulling away; undisguised lust shone in his brilliant eyes as he settled back on his side.

"You had powdered sugar on your lip. I couldn't resist."

He'd completely thrown her off-kilter once again. Shaking her head, she had no comeback, unable to help the small smile curving her lips. She sat quietly for a few moments to regain her composure. The slight smirk on Damian's face meant he knew what he was doing to her. Bastard.

"Anyway, like I was saying ... my friend Beth disappeared about three weeks ago while walking home from work. She lived in a pretty rough part of Chicago, so we kept in daily contact when she was coming and going. She always called or texted me on either end so I knew she was safe. So when she didn't call me, I immediately knew something was terribly wrong. I filed a police report and the Chicago PD have been less than helpful, even suggesting that she was just getting banged by some guy and she would show up any time now." She paused, needing a minute.

"I even went to Chicago myself to see if I could find any clues and got the super to open her apartment, but I didn't find anything out of the ordinary. Her purse, her phone, it was all gone. Beth would never stay out of contact with me for this long. We're all the other has." Her voice cracked on the last part. She would not cry, she would not cry ...

"Okay, and what makes you think Devon would be able to help you find her?"

She knew this question was coming and she'd been wracking her brain for a plausible explanation. Nothing. She had to tell the truth and hope she didn't sound too crazy. She took a deep breath and began.

"I just feel things. I've always had some type of sixth sense when it comes to being able to sense danger." For the longest time she'd thought it was because she'd grown up in dangerous situations all the time, but she knew that wasn't it.

And her premonitions of life-altering changes still bombarded her. She'd thought maybe meeting Damian was the change she'd been expecting, and that was part of it, but it wasn't it entirely. Something else big lay around the corner for her. She knew it.

"That doesn't explain why you thought a vampire would be able to help, kitten." Damian's eyes bored into hers, daring her to lie. In for a penny, in for a pound.

"I don't know how to explain it exactly. I know a vampire is responsible. Do I know that to be an *absolute* fact? No. But I'm not often wrong when I get this feeling, so I've learned to trust it. And ... I know people. I've heard there are other missing girls and I know for a fact vampires are responsible in those cases. I was given Devon's name as the Midwest Vampire Lord and was told he may be able to help find her. So here I am." She might have sounded brave, but inside she was trembling.

"What sort of people do you know?"

She began to shake her head. "I'd rather not say." If she started down this path, she'd be forced to reveal far more about herself than she could stomach. Her back met the loveseat and dark, penetrating eyes stared into hers.

"I don't particularly care whether you'd rather not say, kitten. I want to know how *exactly* you ended up finding out about Devon and I want to know now." *Would he hurt her if she didn't answer?* No, she didn't think so.

"No," she answered, voice steady. Bravo to her.

"Analise ..." he growled. She'd come to learn something about Damian in this short period of time. When he was serious about something, he called her by her given name. It was *kitten* when he was more playful. "Spill it. Now."

"Bully for you. I'm not talking and there isn't anything you can do to make me." Well, there probably was. Like torture, brain sifting, or sex. God, she would so spill in the heat of passion. She was so very weak.

"Well, that can be arranged, kitten. I have every confidence I can break you." She could feel his erection growing swiftly against her lower belly. Her stomach dropped. She was equal parts scared and turned on. They stared at each other, neither willing to give an inch.

A throat clearing interrupted them and Damian looked up. Yah ... she won. Anger twisted Damian's beautiful features into something truly terrifying. Since she was still lying on her back, faced away from the door, she couldn't see who had made him so irate, but she instantly knew she wouldn't want to be on the receiving end of that. He was utterly terrifying.

"What the fuck do you want, witch?" he barked.

Witch? There were witches too? Of course there were. There were all sorts of things that went bump in the night. There were many monsters out there, human and not. She ought to know.

"I sensed a change in the energy and came to check that the shields were still effectively in place, my lord."

My lord?

What. The. Hell?

Damian was a *lord*?

She tried pushing him off and he reluctantly moved, standing to face the interloper. When she sat and turned toward the door, she gasped. The noise caught the witch's attention and now she was staring at Analise with wide eyes. Damian's head was now moving back and forth between the two women, clearly confused.

Analise was sure she'd never met this woman in her entire life, yet she seemed *familiar* in the strangest way. She sensed a kinship with this woman, this witch.

"You'd better tell me what the fuck is going on here and fast." Damian spoke, anger vibrating in his voice. What was he so upset about? She stood and went to his side, placing an arm around his waist. He grabbed her, holding onto her for dear life. She was totally confused. Why was he acting so strange?

"I don't really know, Damian. I feel like maybe I know her, but I can't. We've never met before." The woman standing before was a bit older with a large growth on the end of her nose. When one thought of a witch, she would be the image they would conjure.

"You are the spitting image of her. It's uncanny," the witch whispered.

"Of who, Maeve?" Damian growled. Finally, she had a name. She didn't feel comfortable calling the woman *witch*, even though that's what she was. It seemed derogatory, but Damian obviously didn't care.

"Of my niece, Mara. She went missing close to twenty-eight years ago now. Was never found."

Analise became dizzy, broke out in a cold sweat, and had Damian not been holding her up, she would be on the ground. They were both talking to her now but sounded so far away. She felt herself being lifted and settled into a lap, strong arms surrounding her. *Damian.* Her protector. She felt so safe with him.

She didn't pass out, but it took her several minutes to completely recover.

"Kitten, are you okay?" Damian's voice was laced with concern. And fear.

"Yes, I'm fine. I'm sorry, I don't know what happened." But she most certainly did know. She just wasn't sure she could voice it.

"Sometimes when fate stares you in the face, the mind has a hard time accepting it," Maeve quipped. Wow ... Maeve was far more right than she knew. Analise knew that the instant her eyes met Damian's.

"You think I'm her daughter. Mara's." Not really a question, for in her heart she already knew the answer. Her mother had never really left; she just wasn't able to be with her in person, visiting her dreams instead.

"I know you are. I would recognize her aura anywhere. And Mara was a very powerful elemental witch." *Elemental witch?* Of course, it all made sense now. Mara, her mother, had been teaching Analise in her dreams all these years. The dizziness returned and she swayed slightly.

Damian's arms tightened almost painfully at Maeve's last statement. She could feel the hate emanating from him. Was it just Maeve he didn't like or all witches? And she apparently was one or the daughter of one anyway. Before they even had a chance to begin, she'd probably lose her chance with the one man who had awoken feelings in her she'd thought long dead. And for some reason, the thought made her incredibly sad.

Analise had truly stepped into Wonderland. She'd met the man of her dreams—a vampire—*and* she was a witch's daughter.

What else did fate have in store for her? Because she was quite sure that hateful bitch wasn't done yet.

Chapter 20

Xavier

"My lord, she was already gone for the evening when I arrived. I will try again this evening. The bartender thought she was scheduled at six p.m.," Geoffrey explained.

"Did you find out where she's living?" Xavier demanded.

"Yes, my lord. She was living in an Economy Lodge, renting a room week to week. I went there, but the front desk clerk said she'd checked out. A man paid her bill just last evening and said she wasn't returning."

"Fuck!" Xavier roared. Could nothing go his fucking way? The lords were behind this somehow. They were all following the same trail, after all. Damn Marcus to hell!

Those motherfucking lords found his daughter before he did and now they had two of them. They were HIS! He wanted them back, goddammit!

"You are to camp out at that goddamned bar until she returns. Do you understand me? And dig around the city for any information on the lords. I know one or all of them are still in Milwaukee and are responsible for this. When you return tonight, don't talk to anyone but the manager. I don't care how you get information from him or her, just fucking get it."

"Of course, sire." Geoffrey was the epitome of Zen, nothing ruffled the vamp's feathers and sometimes that just plain pissed him the fuck off.

"If you don't return with her, I'm going to rip your motherfucking heart out with my bare hands." He hung up and dialed the lab. "Tell Philip to get his ass in my room thirty minutes ago."

A couple minutes later, Philip stood before him out of breath and sweating.

"What have you found out about any other living daughters, human?"

Philip's pasty skin paled even more. Jesus, the guy looked like Casper. He swallowed thickly, looking ready to vomit. "I'm afraid I haven't had any success yet, my lord. I'm working as fast as I can."

Philip found himself pinned against the wall by nearly two hundred forty pounds of incensed vampire.

"You'd better fucking work faster, human. The lords always appear to be one step ahead of me and if they find another one of my daughters before I do, you're dead. I don't care how fucking brilliant you are." For good measure, he sunk his fangs deeply into the human's neck and drank, pulling his bitter essence into his mouth. He detested male blood. Female blood was so much sweeter, more satisfying. The human screamed, nearly breaking his eardrum.

He pulled away, not bothering to close the puncture wounds. "Consider this a warning. Next time I won't stop until I've drained every single drop of putrid blood from your worthless fucking body."

With that, he shoved the human toward the door. He went crashing to the floor, scrambling for purchase. "Now get the fuck out of my sight before I change my mind and gut you right now instead."

As hard as it was to believe, Xavier didn't kill indiscriminately very often anymore, except the females he fucked, but his anger raged like a dormant volcano, demanding to explode or else it would cause more damage to the earth underneath. If he exploded here, he'd destroy this compound and everyone with it. As immediately satisfying as that might be, it would do more damage in the long term.

He had to get out of here and kill some goddamned humans. Now. Tomorrow, in some small town in Canada, there would be a media frenzy about a mass murder. Which would forever be unsolved.

Chapter 21

Damian

Damian felt like the biggest bastard ever. Hell, he *was* the biggest fucking bastard ever. Hands down. After the witch dropped her Hiroshima bomb and Analise recovered from nearly passing out—again—he'd ushered Maeve out and told Analise he had some business to take care of. Leaving her in the sitting room. By herself. He didn't even let her talk to her supposed family. He was A. Fucking. Asshole.

His head was spinning like a merry-go-round and he'd sat in the office for the last three hours trying to process everything that'd happened this morning. He'd ditched his Moira after her life-altering news. Like a pussy. He should be comforting her, but here he sat instead. All by his lonesome, trying to come to grips with all that he'd learned. But he couldn't make himself go to her. Not yet anyway. He was starting his bonding off with a big ass bang. He swore he'd never hurt her and he'd already broken that promise.

There was no doubt in his mind Analise was Xavier's daughter, for earlier he'd seen Geoffrey, Xavier's second in command, on Dragonfly's video footage, confirming those fears. Why would Geoffrey be after Analise otherwise? So in addition to being half vampire, his Moira was half witch. *A goddamned witch.* He could hear the Fates laughing at him right this very minute.

He abhorred witches. They'd ruined his fucking life. Took away everything that'd mattered. His mind involuntarily drifted to a time long ago. A time that he wished could be scrubbed from his steel trap of a memory ...

How long had he been here? Months? Years? Time had lost all meaning—days and nights blending together endlessly one after the other. He was in constant agony, often wishing for death but dreaming of revenge. Why hadn't his family rescued him yet? Why had they forsaken him?

He heard his cell door creak but was too weak to open his eyes. They starved him, keeping him anemic, near death. Preventing him from using his powers to escape. A lyrical voice spoke to him, demanding he look upon her. He wanted to tell her to fuck off, but that took too much energy. His eyes cracked open with great effort. She was beautiful, but a wolf in sheep's clothing. A devil disguised as an angel.

"My lover, I brought you a treat." His monthly pint of blood. The bare minimum he needed to simply survive, but far from what was necessary to thrive. What he would be required to do to earn it made him want to deny her. But his body wouldn't let him. Already his incisors had dropped at the smell of the sweet nectar. His gut clenched in anticipation of the life-giving substance. His head flew off the concrete floor toward the bowl she held, but was vehemently jerked back by the bindings. He

was naked, all extremities bound, in addition to his neck and torso. Magical bindings he had no way to expel.

"Ah, ah, ah, lover. First things first." She began to disrobe, baring her perfectly formed body. His traitorous cock became hard at the sight of her. As always, he willed it down, but the fucker wouldn't heed his command. He'd sooner cut it off then stick it in her. She eyed him up and down like a candied treat and he could smell her arousal. It made him physically sick and he turned his head to dry heave.

She sauntered over, lowering herself onto him. He closed his eyes in both agony and ecstasy. She knew better than to get too close to his mouth, for given the chance, he would surely find enough energy in reserve to rip her fucking throat out. He'd done it before.

Instead, she sat back and rocked her hips back and forth, up and down moaning in pleasure. She was an expert. Not all could make him come, but she could. She always did. When they first sent her, he fought orgasm sometimes for hours, but in the end she always won. The outcome was always the same. Now he raced to climax so it would end sooner. She hated it, as she liked to draw out her pleasure. As soon as he'd uncovered that little fact, he'd changed tactics.

As he peaked, she reluctantly eased off him, using the glass vial to catch his semen. He roared in sheer misery as she rammed her sharp fingernail into his scrotum, taking a thimble full of blood as always.

She quickly poured the bowl of blood down his throat, making him choke, spilling the precious liquid down the sides of his dirty face.

She dressed quickly and got the hell out of his cell. The blood would renew his cells, providing a short burst of strength. While he'd never completely escaped, he'd come close a couple of times, killing the witches unlucky enough to stand before him. She apparently valued her pathetic life too much to gloat.

And so it went. This same pattern unceasingly repeating itself. What they did with his bodily fluids he didn't know, but it couldn't be good. They were witches after all.

He awoke in confusion. Had he heard a scream? No ... the only sound he ever heard was the opening and closing of his prison door. How long had it been since a witch had visited him? It had to be close to a month now. He felt himself slipping away. If he wasn't rescued soon, he would die at the hands of these vile creatures.

A shrill cry broke the silence. Then another. Followed by yet another. His ears filled with the agonizing, pained cries of the witches that held him hostage. It was bliss. After all this time, had his family finally arrived? He was close to death, but even if he perished, it would be with the knowledge that these vicious witches suffered the same fate. That was his last thought before he blacked out.

His next thought was that he wasn't dead. He slowly opened his eyes, fully expecting the attack on the witches' coven to be a dream, but as he focused on the thatched roof, he knew it to be true. He had been rescued. But by whom? He was weak. Could barely turn his head. His body was in anguish.

"You're awake," said a deep voice. A large imposing male vampire stood in his peripheral vision; he turned his head to get a better look. The male was not familiar to him. He scanned the room for his family. Where were his papi and his brother, Thaddeus? His mimi?

"They are dead, I'm afraid. In their quest to find you, they all perished at the hands of the sorceresses. I am sorry."

Grief smashed into him like a falling boulder. So his family had *been looking for him. All this time. The witches had taken more than his life; they had also taken his family's. Wrath quickly replaced grief. He would get his revenge. Once he regained his strength, he would kill each and every last witch walking the face of this earth as painfully as possible, starting with the coven that had kidnapped him. He would set them ablaze with his fire, burning them alive. His anger and grief would be fuel for vengeance.*

"Who are you?" he croaked. He needed some water. And blood.

"I am Romaric Dietrich. Your mimi asked for my help after your papi and brother disappeared. I am a hunter of sorts."

"How did you find me?"

"It wasn't easy. The sorceresses were very powerful, but I am more so."

"I need blood." He needed to regain his strength. He needed to get the hell out of here and plot his reprisal.

Romaric was quiet as he handed him a goblet filled to the brim with blood, which he downed in only three gulps. He handed him three more, dealing with them in a similar manner.

"They are all dead, Damian." At his confused look Romaric added, "The sorceresses. The entire coven is wiped out." While he was grateful, he was equally angered. He wanted revenge by his *hand, not another's.*

It had taken Damian a month to fully recover from his seven-year ordeal. At least physically. It took several centuries to recover mentally. To this day the urge to murder every fucking witch alive still lingered.

Rom had stayed with him for the entire month of his physical recovery. They'd struck up quite a friendship and, as his whole family had been slayed at the witches' hands, he'd followed Rom, learning at the hands of the most powerful vampire he knew.

As the United States was discovered and became more inhabited, and therefore more unruly within their world, they'd divided up the U.S. into three Regents, with Rom becoming lord of the West, Devon Lord of the Midwest, and Stefan Moor, Lord of the East until he was beheaded more than one hundred years ago. Damian worked under Rom until he was able to take over the East Regent after Stefan's demise. Damian was also responsible for Stefan's death when he'd challenged the tyrant for control. Stefan was a vicious bastard who ruled the East with fear and deceitful intent, often breaking their only two covenants.

"You know, my friend, you have a mate that's been waiting for you."

Meddling Rom. You couldn't get anything past him.

"She's a witch." He hadn't meant to say anything; it just slipped out. He could solve his own damn problems now.

"I know," Rom replied flatly. That caught his attention, his eyes snapping to Rom's.

"What do you mean you know? How do you *fucking* know?" If Rom knew and hadn't said anything to him, he was going to cut off his head. Friend or not.

Rom smiled. Actually fucking smiled. Mark the calendar.

"I knew the moment I laid eyes on her. Her aura shines bright, like a star. She is a perfect mate for you, my friend." Rom was very matter of fact, like he was reading the goddamned *New York Times* instead of telling him he knew she was of a species he detested.

Damian was speechless for a full minute. "How could you not tell me?" he finally uttered.

"Damian, you cannot define someone by *what* they are, but rather *who* they are. You have never learned that lesson over all of these centuries, no matter how many times I tell you. Not all witches are evil, just as not all vampires are evil and not all humans are evil. There is evil in every species, but there is also innate goodness. Your mate has goodness in spades, and if you shun her simply because of *what* she is, you will lose the best thing that ever walked into your lonely life. Think about that. And then get your fucking ass back to her. She needs you, you asshole."

After the tirade, Rom walked out, leaving him gaping. In addition to his unusual swearing, that was the longest number of words he'd heard Rom string together ... ever. And they were pretty fucking powerful words.

And he was right. Rom was always right, even if Damian fought against him. It was not a surprise—he was the oldest, most powerful vampire he knew.

With that, Damian went in search of Analise in an effort to make up for his larger-than-life failure today.

Chapter 22

Analise

She couldn't process the images in front of her. This could not be real ... yet she knew it was. How could she be here? Where *was* here? Why hadn't she dreamt of her before now? She felt evil all around her, seeping into her pores. It was so thick it oozed from the walls, ceiling and floors. Malevolence hung in the air like black, sticky tar.

And Beth was in the middle of it. Lying on a thin mattress resting on the concrete floor, staring vacantly at the water-stained stucco ceiling. Her glassy eyes didn't blink. She lay unmoving even though she wasn't restrained.

It had only been three weeks, but she'd lost significant weight. Weight she couldn't afford to lose on her already slight frame. Her beautiful blond hair was matted, gnarly and dirty. She wore a filthy white bra and panties. Her wrists and ankles were bruised and bloodied. She had visible bruising in the shape of fingerprints on both biceps as well.

It was then she noticed the blood that soaked the mattress where Beth lay. Oh God, was she even alive? Analise whispered her name. Ridiculous. It was a dream. Beth obviously couldn't hear her.

Except ... was it her imagination or had Beth moved her unfocused eyes slightly? She tried again.

"Beth. Can you hear me?"

This time, Beth's eyes began roaming around the ceiling, her brows drawing together in confusion. Holy shit. Had she really heard her?

"Beth, it's Analise. Can you hear me?"

Tears brimmed in her eyes, spilling down the side of Beth's face.

"Analise," she whispered on a broken sob.

Analise started sobbing, making Beth cry harder. She didn't understand what was happening at all, but she needed to pull herself together and help her friend.

"Beth, where are you?"

"Analise ..."

"Beth, concentrate. I need you to tell me where you are."

"I ... I don't know. Oh God, I'm losing it."

She ignored that comment. She thought maybe they were both losing it, so she couldn't really reassure her.

"Beth, honey ... think. Tell me anything you can that seems useful. Anything. Hurry."

"Where are you?" Beth was now looking all around the room in confusion. Analise felt she was running out of time and this was going in circles.

"Beth, focus, please! Any details you can share will help me find you."

"I don't know where I am, Analise. Someone jumped me on my way home from work. They drugged me and I woke up here. They are vampires, Analise. Vampires."

Analise felt sick. She had been right all along. She'd been right to seek out Devon Fallinsworth.

"What else, Beth? What else?"

"They do things to me. Horrible things."

"How many are there?"

"I don't really know. I've seen at least a dozen different ones. There are also humans here too. Doctors or something. And other girls like me." Beth started crying hysterically. "Please help me, Analise. Please help me."

The turning of Beth's doorknob stopped their conversation short. Beth's sobs turned to screams as a ginormous vampire walked into the room, a malicious grin on his otherwise handsome face. "It's time, female."

Beth started to scream in earnest now ... *"Nonononono ..."* Then ... silence. Beth simply went limp. Stopped screaming, stopped flailing. Analise could only watch in horror as the giant vampire picked her up like a feather and carried her from the bare room, closing the door behind him.

Analise awoke screaming, and Damian burst through her bedroom door, smashing it to smithereens. He sat on the bed, rocking her in his strong arms until she stopped crying and babbling nonsense. He repeatedly asked her what was wrong, but she simply couldn't respond. She could do nothing but shake her head for several minutes.

"Kitten, you're scaring me. What's wrong? Please tell me, baby." He was stroking her softly, her head tucked underneath his chin. She'd missed him, not understanding why he'd suddenly taken off when she'd needed him most. The other vampire she'd seen in the club, Romaric, had escorted her back to her bedroom when she got lost. He was scarier than hell.

"I saw Beth. I fell asleep waiting for you and I saw Beth in my dream. I talked to her. And she talked back."

He froze. "Have you ever dreamt of her before?"

"No. I don't understand what's going on. We carried on a fucking conversation *in a dream*. How is that possible?" Her pitch increased with every word.

"What did she say?"

She pulled away from the comfort of his chest. "I just told you I talked to my missing friend—in a dream—and you ask what the conversation is about? Don't you find that line of questioning a little odd?" She'd never stopped to think that was exactly what she'd done with Mara all these years, talking and interacting, but surely it was different, right?

He smiled. "Oh, kitten. I have much to tell you. I think I may know what's happening. But first, tell me what happened."

"Vampires have her." She relayed the specifics of her dream, best as she remembered. Some of the details were a bit fuzzier now.

"So you don't know where she's being held?"

"No. We didn't get that far before a barbaric vampire hauled her off to do God knows what." She added, "We need to find her."

"We will. I promise you, Analise. We will." He pressed a lingering kiss to her temple.

Analise was quiet for several minutes, trying desperately to understand everything that was happening to her. "You know what's happening to me?"

He nodded. "Come with me to Boston."

"What?" That came completely out of left field. She pulled back, looking to see if he was serious. He was.

"Boston. I live in Boston and I need to return for some business that can't wait. I want to take you to *my* home, talk to you on *my* couch, show you *my* club." He nuzzled her ear, whispering, "Fuck you while you're bound in *my* bed."

She was stunned, speechless and so very horny. He wanted her to go to his home? Show her his club? He had a club? There were so many things she didn't know about him. Would it be smart to just run off to another city with him, getting in deeper and deeper until a dump truck couldn't dig her out? *Not.* Was she considering it? *Yes.* A sudden memory surfaced from earlier today.

"You're a lord? Like Devon?" His lips had drawn into a thin white line before he nodded sharply. In fact, every time she mentioned Devon, they did. He was jealous. That almost made her giddy. "I don't want Devon, you know. I just wanted his help to find Beth." His lips loosened enough they regained their luscious dark pink color.

"I have to work tonight," she said.

"You're not going back there, Analise. You only came here to find someone who can help find your friend. *I* am that someone. I can help you find her." She should be mad that he was telling her what to do again, but he was right. She only came her for a resource to find Beth.

"Do you know who took her?" There *Hope* went again ... building her up only to callously push her off the mountain when she reached its peak, laughing evilly as she fell back to the hard, unforgiving earth.

"I have a pretty fucking good idea," he growled.

Against her better judgment, she made an impulsive decision. "Okay. I'll go with you." She had no sooner acquiesced than she felt a strange tingly, dizzying sensation overcome her. One minute she was in the bedroom at Devon's mansion and the next she was in a strange high-rise apartment.

As soon as she got her bearings, she was screaming at Damian. "What the fuck did you just do?"

"Sorry, kitten. I got a little overexcited. I should have warned you."

"What. Did. You. Just. Do?" She got in his face ... well as close as possible. With an almost foot differential in height, it was challenging.

Standing on her tiptoes gave her another couple of inches at least. Okay, so she came up to his neck, but she was still damn intimidating.

"Pretty neat, right? It's a vampire skill I possess. Flashing. It's better than spending all day on a germ-infested, defy the laws of gravity plane." Asshole was grinning ear to ear. He was actually proud of himself.

"Are you for real?" She started punching his chest. *Ouch*. "Next time you decide to go all *I Dream of Jeannie* on me, will you at least give me a damn heads up? Say bippity-boppity-boo! Something!"

He started laughing ... *really* laughing. While the sound was glorious, she continued to hit him, only managing to hurt herself in the process. His body was harder than a rock. At that thought, she suddenly desperately wanted to see what lay beneath his tight T-shirt. She wanted to explore each and every tattoo in detail. Wanted to trace each one with her fingers, her tongue.

Damian stopped laughing. His face taut, acute hunger replaced the laugh lines which only moments ago adorned his stunning face.

"Don't tempt me, kitten. I'd love nothing more than to feel your hot tongue all over my body."

She was flabbergasted, mouth hanging open. How the hell did he know what she was thinking? That was the second time. He surprised her when he gently picked her up in his arms, cradling her like a child. He carried her over to a soft-looking ivory leather couch and settled them on it, keeping her on his lap.

"We need to talk." Damian was such a fun-loving guy that his serious side scared her. She wasn't sure she would like what he had to say, and the feeling that her world would once again turn on its axis intensified. Suddenly, she didn't want to know anything else. Burying her head in the sand wasn't her style, but in this case it was warranted.

"Denial doesn't suit you, Analise. You're the strongest woman I have ever met. You can handle what I'm about to tell you. I wouldn't discuss it if I didn't think you were ready."

Knowing Damian would do what he wanted anyway regardless of what she said, she nodded.

"I can't believe how clear your thoughts are, kitten. It's incredible. It's so fucking arousing." She felt him grow hard underneath her bottom. "Maybe having you on my lap isn't such a good idea, but I just can't seem to let you go."

"It's fine. I like being here." Something about Damian made her filter vanish. Most comments that she would generally keep to herself came spewing forth instead.

"First of all, I'd like to apologize for leaving you earlier this afternoon. Quite frankly I was stunned at the news and I have a ... less than desirable past with witches."

"So you don't like witches. I knew it." Her heart sunk. She knew this was all too good to be true. She'd never deserved someone like him.

"Oh, Analise ..." He cupped a cheek with one hand, stroking it softly with his thumb. "It is I who don't deserve you, my darling. If you only knew how unworthy I am, you'd be running for the hills. But I would follow and drag you back because that's the kind of selfish bastard I am. I want you, regardless of what you are. You're mine and I will never let you go."

His eyes were so soft and warm that her insides turned to mush. She could not only see the truth in his words, she *felt* them. They wrapped around her like a warm, fluffy blanket, providing the comfort and security she so desperately craved. He kissed her lightly before continuing.

"Let's start at the beginning. I am Damian DiStephano, Lord of the East Regent. Devon Fallinsworth is Lord of the Midwest Regent, and Romaric Dietrich is Lord of the West Regent. Being a lord means we are responsible for all vampires in our Regents. We maintain order, we enforce our laws, we lead our people. Lords are the strongest of all vampires. I am four hundred ninety-nine years young."

At the last piece of news she gasped. "Are you kidding me? You're half a millennia old?"

"Now, now ... don't be insulting me," he smirked.

"I'm sorry. Just trying to wrap my mind around what you've seen in your lifetime." She was in awe. She had no idea vampires lived to be that age, but what surprised her was her intense jealousy at the women that came before her. Had he ever been married? Had he ever been in love? Of course, the answer to these questions had to be yes. He was almost five hundred years old after all.

"Too much, I'm afraid." Did she detect an undertone of wistfulness in his voice?

"Will you tell me sometime?" She couldn't help but press. She wanted to know everything about this man that she'd come to care for so much in such a short period of time. Yes, she realized that was in complete contradiction to her earlier thoughts of not getting too close to him.

"Yes, kitten, but not today. We already have a long talk ahead of us. And the sooner we get that over with, the sooner I can get you underneath me in my bed." She was in a constant state of arousal around Damian, but his sensual one-liners made her pussy weep. If he didn't actually take her soon instead of just talk about it, she was going to die.

He groaned before continuing. Did he know he was rocking his pelvis gently, his very erect cock rubbing against her? "Fuck, Analise. You have to stop these thoughts or we'll never get this conversation over with."

"Well, then stop making it so easy for me to think them. For the next hour, you make no sexual innuendos and I'll think no sexual thoughts. Deal?" One last not so gentle thrust of his hips and he was hauling her off his lap, settling her to his side instead.

"This is the only way I'll be able to honor our deal," he said sternly.

"Why can you hear my thoughts anyway?" She'd been dying to know the answer. "Is it because you're a vampire?"

"Yes and no. I want to tell you a few other things before we get to this, though, okay?"

She nodded. He was contemplative for a minute before he started again.

Her stomach rolled. *Here it comes.* The news that would forever change her life.

Chapter 23

Damian

Damian couldn't believe she was here with him, in *his* penthouse, in *his* city. He wanted to introduce her to his world, on his turf, on his terms. She would soon find out he meant to keep her forever. She was his.

But he had to get some things out in the open first before they could move on together. He had to reveal her parentage. She needed to know the danger she was in, but that he would die to keep her safe. She needed to know about her dreamwalker skills and most importantly he needed to tell her she was made specifically for him and him alone.

And her thoughts about other women and marriage? He just hadn't been able to address it at the moment without throwing her down on his Italian leather couch and screwing her brains out first, so he chose not to even acknowledge it. He'd get around to that soon enough and ensure she knew that anyone that came before her was completely irrelevant. They always were.

"So, in addition to having some sorceress genes, I believe you also have vampire genes."

"What? No ... no that's not possible," she vehemently shook her head.

"And why is that so impossible, Analise? Do you know your parents' history?" That stopped her short. Of course she didn't know because she'd been a ward of the state for the first fifteen years of her life until she'd run away to live on the streets. But would she fess up was the question.

They stared at each other; he waited patiently for her response. *Please tell me, kitten,* he thought silently. *You can trust me.* Her eyes widened slightly before she finally answered. Good, she was starting to hear his thoughts as well. He couldn't wait to push every single dirty thing clouding his mind into hers. Everything he wanted to do to her. All too late he remembered their deal and discreetly adjusted himself.

"No. I don't know my parents. I've never known my parents. Neither of them wanted me and I spent my life in the foster system." She wouldn't meet his eyes, her face downturned. He gently placed his finger under her chin, raising her face until their eyes locked.

"Analise, you have nothing to be ashamed of. Those were circumstances beyond your control." For the first time, he actually listened to the words he was speaking to his mate. The same ones Rom had repeated to him almost verbatim all of these years. The ones he'd refused to believe ... until now. He finally got it and now he'd do everything in his power to help Analise believe them too.

Tears formed in her golden eyes and she fought hard to not let them fall. Fuck it. He was holding her on his lap again. Deal or no deal.

"Why do you think I'm part vampire? I don't have any unusual abilities. Not really anyway." She leaned her head against his chest and he inhaled her always-enticing scent. Now he knew what heaven was like.

"Ah, but you do. Maybe not vampirism, but the dream you had about Beth solidified my suspicions. You're a dreamwalker, Analise. Except I've never heard of a dreamwalker being able to interact with their subject during a dream. That is unusual and I'll have to ask Big D about it. But in any case, I believe you were sired by a vampire named Xavier.

"Xavier is, unfortunately, a psychotic rogue who's been kidnapping young women for years, trying to build his own army with world domination in mind, blah, blah, blah. The stuff Hollywood movies are made of, except in this case it happens to be true. It's highly probable he has Beth and he kidnapped your mother. So you see, your mother most certainly didn't abandon you willingly."

She started to talk, but he cut her off. "Let me just get this out, kitten; then I'll answer your questions." He felt her nod against him.

"A vampire is born from a male vampire and a female human. We are born full-fledged vampires, but vampirism has to be activated by drinking blood several times throughout childhood, a small amount at birth and then twice again. Once at age fifteen and once again at age twenty. With each blooding, you get stronger and more of your vampire abilities are formed, with full vampiric skills by age one hundred. If the appropriate blooding doesn't occur, you're just an exceptional human being, not a full-fledged vampire. You may have some underlying skills or senses but are never able to fully tap into them, like a full-fledged, blooded vampire could."

While it was a sad truth, some families did just what he'd described with their female offspring. They didn't blood them, leaving them weak and unable to fend for themselves. It was a harsh reality of their kind. She sat up straight now, keenly interested in his story.

"Unfortunately in our world, only male vampires can reproduce. Female vampires are not rare, but are fewer in number and they are unable to carry young. Makes no sense, but *c'est la vie* as the French would say.

"So back to Xavier. It's a long, complicated story, which I promise to tell you later, but the short of it is Xavier didn't know you previously existed, as you were supposed to be eliminated. For what Xavier has in mind, he had no use for female vampires who could not bear young. Now we believe he knows that you're alive and he's on the hunt for you. I'm quite sure his intentions aren't so honorable." He chose to leave out the part about Kate and possibly a third daughter for now, as this was surely going to be overwhelming enough without throwing the fact she had sisters into the mix. He'd tell her later once they verified through DNA she was Xavier's daughter. He heard her jumbled thoughts racing, making no sense.

Her tears were now all dry. "So I'm a vampire, but not a vampire?"

He chuckled. "You carry vampire genes, but, no, you're not a full-fledged vampire. And you never will or can be." Quite frankly that made him very happy because if she was vampire, she couldn't be his Moira.

"And I'm in danger?"

He nodded once. "Yes, I believe so. Last night after we left the club, a vampire came looking specifically for you. Asking for you by name. It's highly likely he was able to find out where you live. You're not safe to return to either that motel or your original home, I'm afraid."

Her now dry eyes became wet again, this time not even attempting to hold in her sobs. Her hands flew to her mouth as she mumbled, "Oh God."

Grabbing her by the shoulders, he repositioned her so she straddled him. "Analise, listen to me. You are safe with me. I promise that I won't let anything happen to you. He will *never* touch you, do you understand? The other lords and I are doing everything in our power to find and destroy this sick son-of-a-bitch." He left out the fact they'd been trying to do that for centuries. Not exactly a confidence inspirer.

"Nod if you believe me." She instantly complied. He pulled her into his arms, pouring every ounce of comfort and love into her. *Love?* Yes, he loved her already. And it felt so fucking good. It was a high he'd never gotten from the strongest alcohol, the immense pleasure of killing an enemy or his most intense orgasm. He held her quietly until she was ready to continue. Content to simply have her in his arms.

"How will we find her? Beth?"

"We're already doing everything we can to find Xavier, Analise. Beth's not his only victim, I'm afraid." He couldn't bring himself to tell her all of the depraved things he thought Xavier was doing. It would unnecessarily scare her. He just had to hope they found her friend before the same fate befell her that had so many others.

"Devon already rescued several victims a few months ago and his mate set up the shelter where you stayed last night to re-acclimate them to society and provide counseling before they returned home, if they wished. Several are still there," he added.

She thought on that for a few minutes, but her next question surprised him. "Why can we hear each other's thoughts? I gotta tell you, it's damn unnerving."

She still lay with her head on his shoulder, arms tightly wound around his neck. She was hanging on for dear life and he couldn't blame her. He'd sprung a hell of a lot on her and it was about to get deeper. He prayed she was ready for what he was about to tell her.

"Because, my sweet Analise, you're my Moira and I am yours. In simpler terms, it means we are fated mates. You were made especially for me and me alone. I've told you before that you are mine and I'll never let you go." He wanted to tell her that he loved her, but that would be the stupidest thing to do at this point. She was about to find out she would spend the rest of her days with him and only him.

She drew slowly back and regarded him, her brows drawn together in confusion. "What does that mean exactly?"

"You know what it means, kitten," he said softly. "We are destined to be together. I know you feel the magnetic pull between us just as much as I do. Our bodies, hearts and souls are drawn to each other. They recognize their kindred spirit, their soul mate, even if your mind refuses to accept it."

Her face in his hands, he continued. "I knew it the moment I laid eyes on you, Analise. I knew you were mine. Vampires have only one Moira, one Destiny, and they recognize them immediately, and if you were honest with yourself, you would admit I am meant for you, as you are for me. You're trying so hard to protect your heart even though it's crying out for me, for my love. I'd know what you're doing even if I couldn't hear your thoughts. You're trying to keep me at arm's length so you don't get hurt. But, baby, what you don't even realize is that I've held your heart close to mine, protecting it as violently as I would my own, since I laid eyes on you." Holding back those three little words stung. He wanted to pour his entire heart out to her.

Water cascaded down her gorgeous face. "I've done more crying around you than I have in years, you know that? You must think I'm an absolute basket case." He wiped them away, but they continued to flow.

"No, I don't. Tell me what you're thinking, kitten. I'm in emotional agony here." His heart was on the table, hers for the crushing.

"I ... I don't know what to say." His face must have dropped because she quickly continued, bringing her hands up to cup his face. "Damian, you're right. I am scared. The feelings I have for you are so powerful, so overwhelming, I don't know how to deal with them. I've never had them before for another living soul."

She dropped her hands, leaving him bereft. She breathed deeply before continuing. "I have been through unimaginable pain in my life, Damian. Yes, I was in the foster system, but what you don't know is that I was in and out of more than a dozen homes by the time I was fifteen. The one woman who loved me, the only real mother figure I ever had, died when I was ten and her husband, whom I called father for two years, couldn't handle the grief and returned me to the system. To hell. I haven't trusted anyone in a very long time, Damian, and it scares the shit out of me that I trust you. And I do ... trust you. You're also right that I don't want to get my heart broken. I'm damaged goods and I'm not sure even you can glue me back together. You don't even like witches and I obviously can't help what I am. I don't know if I can take a chance on love, to love you, only to be rejected again. I just wouldn't survive it this time."

His heart ached for her. If he could take away every ounce of pain she'd had in her life, he would. In a fucking heartbeat. He made a snap decision he hoped he wouldn't regret.

He'd not talked about this with another living soul besides Rom. But Analise needed to know. Together their broken pieces snapped together perfectly. She needed to know he was just as broken as she, shards invisible to the naked eye long buried in the dirt so there was no way he could ever be whole again.

Or so he'd thought. Now he knew Analise was the key. He heard the click in his soul the minute he saw her and in retrospect he realized he'd felt profound relief. They only needed each other to be whole. Like a transplant, their hearts and souls would be new and the dying tissue surrounding the rotting organ would refresh and regenerate making the whole body even stronger than before.

"When I was a young vampire, I was tricked by a witch. I thought she was ... well ... turns out they were looking for a pet. Someone their coven could torture and experiment on. I hadn't come fully into my powers yet, so with their sorcery, they were able to overpower me. I was held captive for seven long years, starved within an inch of my life, restrained on a cement floor, and repeatedly violated. Rom rescued me. Barely saved me in time. Those same witches killed my entire family as they searched for me. My parents and my brother wiped from existence for nothing other than trying to rescue me."

She had gone ghost white, quietly sobbing. While the story was gut wrenching to tell, it was cathartic in a strange way too. Now there was nothing he held back from her. She knew all of him. He hoped she'd accept him, blackness and all.

"It changed me, Analise. I'm not gonna lie. I was emotionally vacant for more than a hundred years. It took me almost three hundred to truly recover, but it still lurks inside me. The darkness. The pain. The rage. But then I met you. And your light penetrates even the blackest recesses of my heart. It's so bright, it's blinding. I almost wept with joy when I saw you. I haven't felt truly alive since I was rescued and you've changed that. While our pasts are not exactly the same, we're both familiar with betrayal, anger and pain. So you see, kitten, we are both broken. But together, we can be whole. Only together can we be complete. Let me in, Analise. Let me love you."

He had to pause a moment to regain his composure, clearing his throat. Then he murmured softly, "Love me back."

Chapter 24

Analise

Her lips crashed to his. Screw her fucked up past. Screw her fucked up view of people, of relationships, of love. If this beautiful creature before her could be brave enough to strip away every single protective layer and bear his soul to her, she could do the same. She felt his sincerity, his passion and his love swirling in the air around them like a living, breathing thing. She hadn't known him long, but she knew she was falling hard. She should have asked more questions about the Moira thing, but she couldn't think beyond this present moment. He made her feel worthy of his love and she was tired of fighting this pull between them. It was exhausting.

He stood, her legs automatically wrapping around his waist, their mouths working feverishly against each other's. Her lips would be bruised, but she didn't care. He moved with the speed of light to the bedroom across the massive penthouse, depositing her on an enormous king-sized bed. She was so damned horny right now she didn't look at her surroundings, not caring if the room was pink, purple or rainbow striped. She just needed to get him inside of her.

After giving her one last heated kiss, he stood and gazed down at her, his glowing eyes alight with lust. He took a few steps back and grabbed a soft plush cream covered chair, taking a seat. What the hell was he doing?

"Strip," he commanded thickly.

"Strip?" She swallowed hard. Was he for real? She wanted *him* to rip *her* clothes off and ravage her aching body.

"Kitten ..." he growled. "Stand and strip. Now."

"A little bossy, aren't you?" He looked like he was ready to snap, so pushing him this way wasn't very smart, but this banter had quickly become their thing.

He stood and stalked toward her, pulling her by the heels until her butt was on the end of the bed. She felt like prey. He looked so fucking sexy, all she could think of was him using his powerful thighs to thrust into her from this position. His eyes looked like sunbeams, they were so bright.

"I told you I had darkness in me, kitten. And it extends to the bedroom. In here, yes, I am the boss. And if you're a good little kitten I will reward you with unimaginable pleasures, I promise you. But I don't like to ask for things twice, let alone three times. This is the third and final time I will tell you to strip. I will then dole out punishment if you do anything other than follow my command. Are we clear?"

Oh my. Everything he said should've had her cowering in fear, but instead she felt her pussy ooze, liquid literally running between her butt cheeks. She had never been so aroused in her life. She could only nod her agreement.

"Good." He turned and walked the short distance back to the chair and sat back down. She stood and was reaching for the hem of her blouse when he barked, "Stop. Just one moment." He reached into his pocket, pulling out his iPhone. A few moments later, sultry music echoed from ceiling speakers throughout the colossal bedroom. She instantly recognized the sensual music of Enigma, but couldn't place the specific song. No matter. It set the mood for her first striptease. Damian's thoughtfulness would never cease to amaze her.

"Continue. Slowly," he rasped.

She focused on the erotic man in front of her instead of the nerves threatening to turn her legs to jelly. The soft, sexual music flowed through her, relaxing her just a bit. The desire etched into his face, coiling his every muscle fueled her confidence. He wanted her and she reveled in her power to bring such a powerful man to his knees.

Swaying to the music, she again reached for her blouse, pulling it ever so slowly over her head. Oh, how she wished she'd worn a button-down shirt for she didn't want to miss even a second of his eyes raking over her.

Next she unbuttoned and unzipped her denim jeans deciding to turn around so her back faced him. She shimmied out of the confining fabric, taking care to bend forward seductively as she completely stripped them off. Since she was barefoot before, she didn't have socks or shoes to contend with. She slowly turned back around, now standing in front of Damian clad in only her black lacy bra and panties. Thank God she'd had the foresight to put on the best lingerie she owned this morning.

There was never a more nerve-wracking moment than when you stood before a man for the first time in your skivvies, bearing every single one of your flaws. Analise had curves, ample breasts, and a very flat stomach. But she thought her hips were a little too wide and her body was marred with several scars that Damian would question. However, watching how Damian eyed her with fascination and longing blasted every one of her negative thoughts to dust.

"All of it, Analise." His hoarse voice was firm and laced with lust.

Her heart raced double time as she reached back to undo her bra, letting it fall to the ground once she straightened her arms. His eyes traveled to her breasts. Her nipples had become hard and they ached for his mouth, for his bite. Every nerve ending was on fire and only he could provide sweet relief.

She hooked her thumbs into her panties. His eyes snapped back to hers as she began slowly dragging them down her legs, the wetness from her desire smeared along her inner thighs. She watched him watching her as she dropped her panties to the floor, stepping out of them one foot at a time. His eyes burned with desire as his gaze scoured her nakedness.

"Turn around," he croaked. Her only desire right now was to please him. If he told her to bend over and touch her toes, she would ... shamelessly.

"Get on the bed. Lie in the middle with your hands above your head, wrists crossed." Oh boy. Was he really going to tie her to his bed? She wanted to touch him. She wanted to map every inch of his honed body with her tongue.

When she was in position, only then did he move from the chair to the bed. And only then did she notice the black silk he held between his fingers. Her heart was now in her throat and breathing became more difficult. He was quiet as he crawled beside her, gently taking her wrists and tying them expertly to the headboard. She tested the bindings. Not too tight, but she wouldn't be able to escape. How many other women had he brought here and done the same thing with? That thought made her frown.

He growled at her. *Growled* ... animal-like. "I don't bring women here, Analise. This is my private space reserved only for me. And now you, my mate. Only you." He moved back, sitting on his haunches, eyes raking over every exposed inch of her now vulnerable body. She tensed.

"Analise," he whispered reverently, "you're so fucking beautiful it almost hurts to look at you. I can't believe you belong to me." Once again his words melted her. How could someone she just met know her so intimately?

"Jesus, the things I want to do to you, kitten. I'm going to take your blood into my body tonight, but I'm not going to make you completely mine yet. Bonding in the vampire world is irreversible and you need some time to digest what we talked about tonight. I need you to want this as desperately as I do. But make no mistake about it; I will make your soul mine very soon. Tonight, though ... I will make your body mine."

Her eyes closed on a moan. She couldn't help it. He was right, she needed to think about what he'd told her, ask questions. The thought of being bonded for life sent a rush of excitement through her veins, but at the same time terrified her enough to want to flee. This was all happening so fast her head was swimming. But there was no denying she wanted Damian DiStephano to own her body. Her heart, however? That was another question.

"Open your eyes. I want you to watch everything that I'm doing to your delectable body." She complied, but her heavy lids made it difficult to hold them open. The way he looked at her caused every thought to fade, bringing her back to the moment at hand.

Starting at her face, he gently ran a finger across her brow and down her cheek. He continued working his way downward, over her neck, her collarbone, between her breasts. He softly circled her areolas, not touching her aching nipples.

"Please," she moaned, as he moved down her stomach.

"Patience, kitten. I've waited for you for almost five hundred years. I'm not rushing this now."

"You're torturing me," she whined.

"Au contraire ... I'm *savoring* you. You'll know when I'm torturing you." His fingers had moved down her long legs and were now tracing every toe delicately. Both hands wrapped around her ankles and he now ran them up her shins, pushing her legs apart when he reached her knees. Her pussy was now fully open to him and he could see the evidence of her desire.

"Jesus Christ, Analise, you are so wet for me." He leaned down, inhaling deeply before running his nose along the outside of her labia. She should be mortified, but she didn't care. Her body was on fire. She was strung so tight, she thought she might orgasm the second he touched her.

She felt his hot breath right before his tongue descended, licking her from back to front, avoiding her clit. She cried out, her hips bucked and he used his free arm to hold her in place.

How was she going to survive sex with Damian DiStephano when she was ready to die from simple foreplay?

Chapter 25

Damian

She smelled so fucking good. He wanted nothing more than to sink his fangs into her clit and draw her essence into him, driving her to an endless orgasm. He was holding on to his sanity by a thin thread. In equal parts, he wanted to ravage her—as she wished—and he wanted to savor her, as he was currently doing. His kitten was right, the savoring was torture, but it was sweet, fulfilling torture. Besides, he didn't think she had been with a man for a very long time, and he was very large. He needed to prepare her properly, not rip her to shreds with his cock on their first night together.

When his tongue touched her pussy, he swore he saw stars. She tasted musky and spicy and her lavender scent was stronger here. He'd never tasted anything finer or sweeter in his long life. He could eat her for days on end. The hunger to drive her to orgasm so he could lick every single drop of her come fueled him to devour her in earnest now.

He plunged his tongue into her pussy, mimicking what he would do to her shortly with his cock. He licked his way up to her clit, circling it for the first time since he'd gone down on her. She cried out and he looked up, their eyes locking. He circled her clit slowly with his tongue as he eased two fingers into her weeping passage.

"Jesus, kitten, you're so fucking tight."

He had a lot of work to do before she could take him. She'd closed her eyes and he commanded her to open them again, which she did. His kitten was very obedient, which made his cock throb with the need to be inside her. He eased out, now thrusting in three fingers, pumping in and out, all the while softly circling her clit with his tongue. He applied more pressure, flicking his tip back and forth. Her hips tried moving in time with his tongue, but he held them firm. She would learn he was in control in the bedroom.

Her breaths indicated she was close to exploding. "Come for me, kitten," he commanded right before he sucked her clit hard. His name never sounded so sweet as it did falling from her lips while she shattered on his lips, in his mouth. He licked and sucked, savoring the taste of his efforts. Her head thrashed against the pillows he had her piled on.

He couldn't wait any longer. He had to be inside her. He climbed off the bed, divesting himself quickly of his clothes. Analise had opened her eyes and was now watching him disrobe with fascination, eyes wide.

Not many vampires had as many tats as he did. It was an obsession for a while after his torment. Relieve pain with pain. But then he turned his depravity to the bedroom instead and it was a more cathartic release anyway. While he found he definitely wanted to do kinky things with Analise, the drive to release his demons in debauched ways was strangely absent with her.

"I want to touch you," she murmured. "Please untie me."

"Not a chance. I'm barely hanging on here, Analise, and if you start touching me, I *will* lose control. And neither of us wants that. I'll let you touch me, I promise. Just ... not right now." He wouldn't let her touch him. He couldn't. How long could he come up with excuses to avoid that? Her disappointment gutted him, but he just couldn't do it, even with her.

"Let me love you, kitten. I want to so fucking bad." He didn't give her a chance to respond before he was back between her legs, driving her up again. The need to sink his fangs into her fleshy mound was too overpowering to resist this time and he struck fast. She screamed, her orgasm riding her hard while she bucked and thrashed beneath him. She called his name over and over again, the sound music to his ears. This right here ... between her legs, her blood pooling in his mouth, was pure nirvana. He took three quick pulls before closing the wounds, only barely sating his insatiable desire to have her lifeblood running through his veins.

Rising to his knees, he grabbed under her thighs. "Wrap your legs around me." She obeyed, eyes glazed with lust and satisfaction. His chest puffed that he was able to bring her to that state, though they were far from done. "Look at me. Don't look away."

He guided the tip of his cock into her sheath, groaning at the tightness he already felt. Their eyes held as he slipped in slowly, inch by agonizing inch, tension coiling every muscle in his body from holding back the urge to simply slam home. After several minutes, he was finally buried balls deep in the tightest pussy he'd ever felt. She was like a second skin. He was wrong before. This … this was pure nirvana.

"Fuuuuuuck, you feel so good," he gritted through clenched teeth.

Gazing down at their joined bodies laid out on *his* bed, her hands tied to *his* headboard, pure satisfaction on her face, he'd never felt more fulfilled, never more content. Never more right.

He started pumping into her furiously, leaning down to swallow her moans of ecstasy with his mouth. She broke the kiss; trailing wet kisses down his neck, over his broad shoulder, baring her creamy neck to him. He latched on, sucking and nibbling, murmuring, "I'm not hurting you, am I?"

"God no. It feels too good. Please don't stop. Never stop," she panted.

Her skin was flushed and her blood sang to him, calling his name, begging to be taken by its mate. For the second time, he struck, relishing in her sweet, honeyed, life-giving taste. He was fucking in love with this woman who was perfect for him in every single way.

Her taste.

Her touch.

Her smell

Her light.

Her heart.

He thrust in earnest, chasing his own pleasure. Feeling her tight pussy clench around his shaft, he knew she was on the verge of another orgasm. But he wanted to go over the edge of bliss together.

"Damian, please don't stop. I'm going to come," she wailed.

"Yes, Analise. Come apart for me, baby." Her pussy tightened like a fist around his cock and two furious thrusts later he fell over the cliff with her, ejaculating harder than he ever had before. Divine pleasure infused every cell in his body and they cried each other's names in unison. Several long moments later, his hips slowed. He showered her face with kisses, as she lay limp beneath him, a goofy smile on her face.

"You okay, kitten?" he asked. If her screams and moans of ecstasy were any indication, yes, but he still wanted to her hear her say it. Males like validation...*all* males.

She nodded. "More than," she choked out. He drew back to look at her, sensing something was wrong. Her watery eyes scared him.

"Analise, what is it? Did I hurt you?" Oh Christ, he'd never forgive himself if he went too fast. He knew he should have taken more time to get her ready.

She shook her head, a few tears leaking out in the process. "No. You didn't hurt me. It was incredible. I never knew it could be like that. I've just never been so ... happy." She paused. "Or felt so cared for." Her voice broke on a sob.

He held her face between his hands. "Oh, Analise. This is how it will always be between us, except it will only get better and better, especially once we bond." He withdrew his still stiff cock, quickly freed her and rolled onto his back, pulling her tightly into his side. They fit together like a puzzle that was missing its pieces.

He wanted to hold her in his arms all night, making love to her between bouts of sleep she would need, but he needed to get to Grina. He was actually looking forward to taking Analise to see his pet project.

Since she had none here, earlier he had asked Katrina to purchase some clothes for Analise and bring them to the penthouse.

"Why don't you sleep a bit, kitten, before we shower. I need to go to one of my clubs tonight and you're coming with me." She rose on an elbow, looking down at him. Her tears had dried and now she just looked like a very sated woman.

"I don't have anything to wear. You flashed me here without anything but the clothes on my back, remember?" Did he sense a little hostility?

"I'm taking care of that. You'll have fresh clothes here within the hour and something very appropriate to wear to Grina, I assure you." Katrina was Devlin's mate, a member of his security team. She had very good taste and he was confident she'd deliver something worthy of his mate.

"I don't want some guy picking out my panties, thank you very much."

"Neither do I, kitten. That's why I'm having a woman do it." A flash of jealousy scrunched her pixie nose. She was as easy to read as a book. "She's bonded, Analise. She's not a former lover."

He sat against the headboard, pulling her to straddle his lap. "I don't know how many times I have to tell you this before you believe it, but you are the only woman for me, kitten. Because of my longevity, I can't change the fact that other women came before you, but I can promise you ... *none* of them meant a fucking thing to me." He grabbed her neck, pulling them nose-to-nose. "You are the only woman to ever have my heart, my soul and my every breath. Do you understand?"

She closed her eyes and he felt her relief. His Analise would need regular reassurance of her worth, of his love. Fuck it, he was going to tell her.

"I do love you, Analise. I know you may think it's too early, but it's not. Nothing has ever felt so right or perfect. You are my life now. And I am completely and irreversibly in love with you and I want you to know it. That has everything to do with the woman you are and nothing to do with the fact that we are fated. "

She nodded but didn't reply. Although it stung more than he would admit, he felt her love. She was just too scared to admit it out loud. Saying it made it real. He'd waited such a very long time for her that he was more than ready to jump into this headfirst. His main objective now was to make her feel safe and loved. He wanted to throw her down and bond with her right this minute, but he would wait until she was ready.

"So, I've been thinking about some questions."

Good, that was a good sign. "Shoot."

"Okay. What's entailed with this bonding thing, exactly?" He wasn't sure what she was going to ask, but that wasn't it. His still hard dick swelled even more and she was sitting squarely on it. Her eyes widened as she looked down between them.

"Sorry, kitten, involuntary reaction to your question. Thinking of bonding with you gets me hard. Can't be helped." A shy smile lit up her face like a thousand suns. "So … this bonding thing. As I said before, a vampire bonding is far more serious than a human marriage. There is no divorce between vampire mates. Most vampires are male and there is only one human female mate for us. Once we complete the bonding ritual, we will be bound together forever. You will wear my family crest mark on your left thumb, as will I. Then all vampires will know you are permanently bonded and because I'm a lord, they will all know to whom."

"Okay, but what is the bonding ritual, exactly? I mean, what do we do?"

"Ummmm…" He grabbed her hips, pulling her more firmly against his stiff erection. One thrust and he'd be buried inside her again, but he used every ounce of restraint to hold back. His eyes glowed with fierce desire. "The bonding ritual is pretty simple, kitten. We make mad, passionate love until we see fucking fireworks and then we exchange blood. I take yours and you take mine." He remembered Dev saying something about bloodlust with Kate, so he was cognizant he'd need to be careful. He didn't have a place to restrain a blood-crazed vampire in his penthouse.

"Oh," she breathlessly replied. He rocked his hips, the head of his cock slipping in between her wet folds, still dripping with his come. Her head fell back, a moan escaping her parted lips. She was fucking perfection in every way.

One thrust and he'd hit the end of her womb, able to penetrate deeply in this position. He was getting ready to do just that when a knock echoed in the main room.

"Sire, Katrina and I are here with the clothes you requested." Devlin.

Christ.

In her lust-filled haze, Analise hadn't noticed the knock and she was now rocking to get him further inside her. He groaned, pulling out. "Someone's here, kitten. Go jump in the shower and I'll be right back. It's your clothes. We'll finish this later." He kissed her passionately, hinting at where they would pick up later.

Easily lifting her from his lap, he set her on her feet and swatting her butt, pointed toward the bathroom. "Shower."

He could tell she held back a smart-ass retort, instead sauntering slowly into the expansive bathroom. She was definitely exaggerating the swing of her very fine ass. He was so tempted to punish her cheekiness, but they needed to get going.

Instead, he called, "You're going to pay for that, kitten."

Her laugh followed him all the way out of the bedroom.

Chapter 26

Mike

He sat on his couch, nursing a beer in his hand. He should just throw it out, warm as it was by now. The TV was off and he was simply staring out the bay window into the darkness, alone.

Giselle had reacted exactly as he'd predicted she would. And when she awoke, her steely resolve slammed firmly back into place. She'd slept for a couple of hours and during that time he couldn't help but savor simply holding her in his arms, acting as her protector. Which was ridiculous, because her strength exceeded his tenfold. But this was far beyond physical protection; he was her emotional guardian. She needed one, whether she would admit it or not. She held everything so tightly to the vest she was going to fucking explode.

Whether she knew or would admit it, she trusted him. No one would let himself or herself be that vulnerable if they didn't trust the person they were with. And he was deeply grateful he was her person. She wasn't too happy about that fact when she woke up, however.

"What the fuck are you doing, Thatcher?"

Ah ... his foul-mouthed sleeping beauty was finally awake.

"Giselle, can we just lie here in sweet silence a bit longer?" She jumped from the couch so

goddamned fast he thought she might have broken a spring or two.

"Are you out of your damned mind? Why are you holding me like we're lovers anyway? We are not *lovers, Detective." Defensive much?*

He slowly stood, stalking toward her until he was just inches away. "Not yet, we aren't, Giselle. But it would be my pleasure to remedy that if you'd like."

She blushed. Actually full-on blushed, redness rising from her neck into her exquisite pixie face. She was seriously off her game and what was he doing goading her into a fuck anyway? Complete role reversal.

"You fell asleep in my arms and I thought you'd be more comfortable lying down." He didn't know why he felt the need to explain himself to her. After all, she should be the one explaining why she had a nuclear meltdown on him, but he didn't want her to think he'd taken advantage of her. The way she was acting, he had no fucking clue why he cared. But he did.

"Oh." Oh. That was it. And that's all he would get as she started in on what the bloodsuckers needed from him this time. Other daughters. Eau Claire. Adoption agencies. Police reports. Yada fucking yada.

So they'd spent the next several hours working side by side, neither one discussing or acknowledging the energy that hummed around them like an electric storm. They'd confirmed that a baby was dropped off with Child Social Services after a call from parents on a potential adoption scam. Analise Aster was the child's name. She'd been in and out of foster homes until fifteen, when she ran away. She had no police record, not even a jaywalking ticket. Pretty impressive for a kid on the streets. They'd tracked down her last known address, still in Eau Claire, and then Giselle took off, not saying whether she'd be back or not.

Her reaction to their intimacy only solidified her vulnerability. Giselle did not let anyone into her inner circle, sarcasm her most powerful defensive weapon. Such dirty things should not fall out of the mouth of such a beautiful woman.

His head fell back, resting against the couch. Huh, his ceilings needed painted. There were old yellowed water stains everywhere from when the roof leaked last summer. His hand found the cell phone in his pocket and a sly smile crossed his face. While Giselle had been sleeping, he'd looked at her cell phone. The foolish vamp hadn't bothered to lock the screen.

He was now the proud owner of her phone number. So maybe she wouldn't answer his calls, but she also wouldn't be able to escape him completely like she had the last three months. Texting was a *brilliant* invention. Kudos to that guy.

The question rolling around in his brain was—did *he* want more? He couldn't stop thinking about her. Her taste, the feel of her body next to his, her perky breasts squished against his chest. Her tight ass filling his palms. He'd had a massive hard-on the entire time she was in his arms, one that he had to take care of the second she'd left. It had taken about five pumps before he was spurting all over the tiled shower wall, fantasizing it was her pussy milking him instead.

The answer was yes, he wanted more. *But how much more?* Would one hard fuck get her out of his head? He'd like to say yes but, truth be told, he was scared shitless the answer was a resounding *fucking no.*

Chapter 27

Xavier

"My lord, the female is not at work again this evening; however, I now have a detailed description of Analise Aster. Of interest, I did speak with Dragonfly's manager, a human named Frankie. I have reason to believe she is with Damian DiStephano. According to Frankie, she left with him last evening and Damian called her in sick this evening. She hasn't returned to the motel either. I have checked other hotels and she is not registered at any of them."

"What the fuck is the East Regent Lord doing in Milwaukee?"

"Well, I was able to get some very interesting information from Frankie before his untimely demise. It seems as if Dragonfly is owned by none other than Devon Fallinsworth. And while the main part of the bar is for humans, there is a lower level that's reserved for vamps only. Oh ... and the females they feed on. Hired help. Seems like Devon is running a safe feeding club and this likely isn't his only one."

Brilliant. Xavier should have suspected they would do something like this, noble as the lords thought they were. Provide a safe haven for vamps to feed and fuck, without killing their prey. Stupid fucks.

"Were you able to get into the lower level?"

"Of course, my lord. I simply looked around, gathering information until I could get further direction from you. It appears Devon is out of the country on his honeymoon and won't return for several weeks. The club is under the watch of Damian DiStephano and it appears that Romaric Dietrich has also been frequenting the place the last day or two."

My, my, my. Could this be easier? Or was it too easy? He smelled a trap and wasn't about to rush into a battle without a detailed plan of attack.

"For now I want you simply to keep watch. Frequent the lower level, sample the goods, but play by their rules so as to not draw attention to yourself. If you see Damian or Romaric, you are to let me know, but take no action and for fuck's sake. Make yourself invisible. They both know who you are and won't hesitate to try severing your head from your body." And as powerful as Geoffrey was, he wouldn't be able to hold his own against two lords without backup. Especially if Romaric was in town.

"Of course, my lord. I will report nightly."

This could be the break that he'd been waiting for. Devon may be out of the country, and it looked like the lords got to his daughter before he could, but he still had the upper hand. They didn't know he knew about Dragonfly.

He was already plotting his next move and it would be brilliant. Devon would return from his sweet honeymoon to complete and utter devastation. Once again.

Chapter 28

Analise

They walked into Grina, the heavy bass reverberating throughout her body from Iggy Azalea's "Fancy." She was sexually frustrated from not only their last little bedroom session, but the limo ride. He kindly offered to take the limo versus flashing and she'd readily agreed.

During the forty-minute drive, they'd made small talk, learning little facts about each other. She loved her car; he'd never driven. They shared a passion for music. Damian raved about her angelic voice and told her she could sing in Grina if she wanted to. Of course, she said yes. She hated soup, loved pizza and brussel sprouts, but not together. He hated brussel sprouts. He'd read tens of thousands of books, so many he'd lost count. He had more than a hundred different tattoos, some inked over multiple times. She'd always wanted a tattoo, but could never afford it and couldn't decide what she'd want permanently inked on her body anyway. Damian said he wouldn't allow her to mar her perfect skin with any mark other than the bonding one.

When she'd asked about the unusual name of his club, Damian's eyes turned glassy with hunger seconds before she was flat on her back against the seat, his mouth plundering hers. His hands clawed at the top of her beautiful Persian blue dress, so low her ample cleavage practically poured out. Her nipple easily popped free and pleasure coursed through her as Damian took the rigid peak into his mouth, sucking hard. Then he bit down, hard enough to draw blood and she cried out in euphoria as he lapped it up with his tongue.

His driver interrupted, announcing their arrival at the club. After straightening themselves, he leaned over and softly kissed her lips, murmuring, “It means passion, kitten. In Basque.”

“Wow ... okay. That’s original.” Her chest still heaved as he helped her from the car.

They made their way through the main section of the club and Damian proudly showed off his new renovations, which had only recently been completed. Grina’s doors opened a few short weeks ago, but it was already a hot spot, located on the east side of downtown Boston, just south of Cambridge.

The interior walls were rough dark limestone and the ceiling pipes were left exposed, but painted black. Grina had a large, open area with a center stage taking up a fair amount of space, along with the dance floor. The outskirts of the floor were lined with tall glass tables and chairs and there were comfortable leather couches and chair configurations on the outside perimeter. Sexual energy hummed in the room and the soft lighting added to the ambiance. A massive bar, lit with soft blue and red colors, was the first thing you saw when you walked through the doors.

Damian took her through several separate, smaller rooms offshooting from the main one. Each had a different type of music: rock, pop, jazz and rap. Each replicated the main area but on a smaller scale.

"Come, kitten. Let's go downstairs and I can show you my lair." He laughed evilly, eyebrows wagging. She chuckled along with him, loving that he was so carefree and fun. It'd been a long time since she'd let herself have any.

She'd been heartbroken listening to Damian's story earlier, and for the first time she thought about sharing a bit of her past with someone else. Someone who understood some of the pain and suffering she had gone through. But she didn't want to bring down the vibe of the night. She was having fun and for once in her life, was going to just go with the flow.

Damian moved them through the crowded bar with finesse. Of course, when one looked as intimidating as he did, people moved out of the way, their protective instincts kicking in as if innately sensing danger. Pretty soon they were in the back of the club, Damian punching a series of numbers into an alien-looking keypad. Downstairs, the more sophisticated system required a retinal scan. Wow ... they took security seriously here.

"Welcome to Grina Bi, Kitten," he purred.

"Grina Bi? What does that mean?"

"It means Passion Too, in Basque of course." He grinned from ear to ear, bobbing his eyebrows up and down for proper effect.

Once the steel door opened, sultry music flowed through her. It was so dark, she could barely see, her eyes taking nearly a minute to adjust. Once they did, she was stunned. Bodies, many nearly naked, writhed on the dance floor, almost like snakes. The smell of blood and sex assailed her nostrils, and while it should repulse her, it had the opposite effect instead. Damian's head snapped toward hers and she felt his hand tighten around her fingers.

"Oh, kitten, we're gonna have fun tonight," he said devilishly.

She couldn't help the smile that broke out. Yes, they were going to have fun. She was horny and felt uninhibited. It was probably the pheromones in the air, and she may regret it tomorrow, but tonight she didn't care. She was going to live in the moment. Whatever Damian was game for, so was she.

Someone called his name and soon they were surrounded by a group of very large, very male vampires. Damian tucked her tightly into his side, sensing her uneasiness and introduced her as his Moira. Even though they weren't bonded yet, every time she thought about it, butterflies took flight in her stomach and comfortable warmth spread throughout her body. The more she thought about it, the more she wanted to just say yes, but she needed to be one hundred percent sure. Forever was a very long time. Plus with her human and him vampire, how long would their forever really be?

A familiar song began playing and he begged his leave, dragging her away from the throng … directly to the dance floor. People cleared, making way for the almighty Vampire Lord. As Massive Attack starting singing the lyrics to "Angel," Damian stopped, grabbed her hips and slammed them into his. With her four-inch heels, she was still several inches shorter, and his erection was now low on her belly, hard as granite. He watched her with an intensity she hadn't seen before, like he was going to devour her any second, his eyes bright with love and unquenched craving.

He was so goddamned sexy in his custom-tailored black suit. He'd paired it with a shirt whose shade matched her dress perfectly. With the top two buttons undone, his erotic tattoos peeked through.

His eyes pierced her with incredible passion as he softly sang the sultry lyrics that nearly made her barely-there panties melt. *Fan, please.*

Everyone else faded away and there was nothing but him and the erotic music echoing in the background. Moving his hips in a slow and grinding motion, she threw her arms around his shoulders, hanging on for dear life. He moved their bodies in time to the slow beat and bent down taking her lips with his, whispering the dirty things he wanted to do to her between kisses. Her breasts pressed against his hard chest, nipples poking through the thin fabric of her bra and dress. Every rub against him set them on fire anew.

Hot kisses blazed a fiery trail to her ear. "You look fucking amazing in that dress, Analise. I can hardly wait to be inside that hot, tight pussy of yours again. I'd take you right here, but I'm not sharing my Moira with anyone else."

Her legs nearly buckled, only his strong arms holding her up. The hand on her back snaked down to her ass, his finger tracing between her butt cheeks. "I want you everywhere, kitten. Soon," he taunted.

Her core flooded, her thong absolutely drenched now. He filled her pussy to the brim, how would he ever fit there without doing permanent damage? She felt him smile against her cheek.

With one hand on her hip keeping them in rhythm, the other cupped her cheek before his lips crashed into hers. Every ounce of desire he felt for her was put into that one kiss. His tongue invaded her mouth, sweeping against hers, dominating. Tugging her bottom lip between his, he bit hard enough to draw blood, then groaned when it hit his lips. She couldn't help the moan that escaped her. Her body was ablaze. She ached to have him fill her, make love to her, make her his.

Turning, she ground her backside against his erection, swaying against his perfectly honed body. His hands firmly grasped her hips and she drew her arms overhead, wrapping them around his neck. Her hands ran through his dark locks as one of his trailed up her torso, cupping her breast.

He thumbed her nipple through the imprisoning fabric, the sensation going directly to her clit as if they were wired together. She was so damned turned on she might have an orgasm right here.

Lips caressed her neck, teeth lightly nipping, but not hard enough to break the skin. Angling her head for easier access, Damian took full advantage. He alternated between aggressive sucking and erotically scraping his teeth along her neckline. She wouldn't be surprised if she had a hickey come morning. Both hands now cupped her breasts, his thumbs lightly teasing the top of her dress, trying to dip inside.

"I can smell your wetness, Analise. It's driving me out of my fucking mind." His voice was gravelly, thick with desire.

"I want you," she moaned. "Please." She sounded desperate. She was.

He turned her around, pillaging her mouth once again as he lifted her in his arms. She wound her arms around his neck and her legs around his waist and he never let up the pressure as he quickly walked them off the dance floor. Wherever they were going, it had better be close; she was about to explode. One touch from him and she would detonate.

Moments later she heard the door open and close, not bothering to open her eyes until Damian deposited her on a soft couch and released her from his grip. She was literally ready to open her legs and rip off her own thong to get him inside of her.

"Now you have the right idea, kitten," he purred. *Another game?*

Still breathing hard, she slid back on the soft leather and watched him get a chair from behind a large wooden desk. She briefly looked around now, noticing they were in an office. It wasn't anything fancy, filing cabinets filling one side and bookshelves the other. Since they were underground, there were no windows to the outside and the walls were cement. The leather couch was the only real luxury in the room.

Damian set the chair down about ten feet away and sat facing her. Her stomach clenched. She could hear the music pounding outside the closed door, albeit muted.

"Lose the panties." Dominant Damian had returned. Jesus, he made her so horny when he was like this. Every smart retort drowned in a sea of desire.

She stood and obeyed, setting them next to her on the couch. "Ah, ah ... hand them over." She did, reluctantly. When he brought them to his nose and took a big inhale she just about lost it. She wanted to strip him naked and suck his cock.

He smiled brightly. "We'll get to that." Damn him. Was nothing a girl thought private anymore?

"Stop broadcasting your thoughts so loudly, and I won't hear them as often. They're like a bullhorn in my head." She opened her mouth to speak, but he continued. "Now, the dress. Off."

The scrap of fabric he'd had someone named Katrina get her could hardly be called a dress. It was held up by two thin straps, hugged every curve and barely covered her ass. The front dipped so low, the bra she wore nearly showed and her cleavage bounced with every step she took. She'd almost told Damian she couldn't be seen in public in such a getup, but when he saw her wearing it his eyes practically bugged out of his head like a cartoon character. So the dress stayed, of course.

She began to kick her heels off when he stopped her. "Those stay on."

She tilted her head, raising her eyebrows. He simply smiled seductively, his eyes ablaze. Two can play at that game. She slowly, slowly unzipped and dropped the dress, kicking it out of the way. She was now standing in only her new baby blue lacy bra and black fuck-me heels.

His eyes scoured over every inch of her exposed flesh. "Fucking perfection," he murmured. "On the couch, legs up with your heels hooked on the edging. Spread your knees so I can see how wet you are for me." She opened her mouth to ask if he was kidding, but thought better of it at his intense glare.

She backed up, eyes locked with his, until her knees hit the leather. She slowly sank down and scooted toward the back so she could comfortably comply with his command. Comfortable was relative, she'd never felt so exposed in her life. When she was in the desired position, she watched him—watching her. Heat prickled her cheeks, but desire sat low in her belly, swirling like a tornado. She waited with anticipation for the next command.

"Pull down the cups of your bra so your beautiful nipples are fully exposed, kitten." His voice was low and rough. She delighted in the fact she could affect him so much. She could only imagine the vision she made with her legs spread open and glistening, boobs now perky due to the bra's support, desire etched across her entire face.

He stood, removed his suit coat and rolled up the sleeves of his shirt. Sitting back down, he crossed his arms and legs and leaned back in the chair. He looked casual, like he might be having a business lunch, except for the rock hard erection straining his zipper and his lust-filled, hooded eyes.

"Touch yourself, kitten. I want to watch you make yourself come."

"What?" She couldn't have stopped the question if she'd tried.

"Analise." His voice was hard, unyielding. They held each other's gazes, each waiting for the other to break. She started to pull her knees together and he was immediately in front of her, holding them back. Damn, he moved fast. He leaned forward until they were nose-to-nose. And he didn't look happy.

"Are you itching for a punishment, Analise? Because I'm itching to give you one." She shook her head slowly. He closed the gap, giving her a heated kiss. Pulling back, he whispered, "I want this. You want this too, if you can get past your unfounded embarrassment. You're a vision sitting here like this, all spread for me and obedient, even though I know it goes against your grain."

He was right again. "Okay."

She wanted to please him; she did want this. She was just embarrassed about doing something so private, so intimate with an audience, especially him. He nodded and returned to his seat, assuming the same position.

"Touch yourself, Analise."

She let the longing reflected in his eyes intoxicate her as she slowly reached down to caress her wet folds. Hearing a sharp intake of breath, she knew it came from Damian. Slowly she moved her middle finger up her wet slit, from back to front. On her next pass, she dipped inside to gather her wetness so she could spread around her natural lubrication.

Damian's ravenous eyes followed her every move and she suddenly felt very emboldened. She wanted to be his fantasy come to life. She wanted him to watch her fall apart. She wanted to drive him mad with desire.

She dipped two fingers inside, never able to hit the sweet spot that a man could, but it still felt amazing under the watchful eye of her lover. Slowly she slipped her wet digits in and out, but the only way she could orgasm by herself was to pay attention to the special hard bundle of nerves at the top of her mound, so she dragged her damp fingers back up to her clit, circling lightly. With her free hand, she teased her exposed tight nipples, heightening her own arousal.

She could practically feel the heat radiating from Damian, even ten feet away. He was an inferno that chilled her cold skin. She was so excited she wouldn't last long. She increased the pressure, circling quicker until she felt the telltale tingling in her groin signaling the warm rush was right around the corner.

Damian's eyes flicked up to hers, knowing she was close. "Watch me, Analise. Don't look away." Her breathing increased at a rapid pace and it was difficult to keep her eyes locked on his.

"Jesus Christ, kitten, you're so fucking hot. I can't wait to lap up every drop of your climax."

Once again, his wicked verbal skills pushed her over the edge. Intense heat and pleasure radiated outward from her core as her orgasm washed over her like a tidal wave. She could no longer keep eye contact with Damian as she threw her head back and cried her pleasure, fingers slowing as the nerves became more sensitive.

After several moments, minutes maybe, she rolled her head, cracking open her eyes only to see Damian stripping with intent. Then he was upon her, carrying her in his arms until her back hit the wall. Wrapping her legs around his waist, he lined up his rock hard shaft with her moist center and thrust hard, impaling her on his manhood. She cried out in both pleasure and pain, her head falling back against the wall. His mouth was everywhere. Her lips, her neck, her nipples. Everywhere, but it still wasn't enough.

"Harder," she begged. She didn't want him to hold anything back. She was desperate for all of him.

And he didn't. His raw thrusts were almost brutal, but she reveled in it. *She* had brought out this passion in Damian. He wanted *her* with unbridled ferocity. It was a heady feeling. The bite of his fangs stung briefly before the deepest pleasure she'd ever felt soared through her, his name falling on a breathy moan. He soon followed, muscles taut as hot spurts warmed her insides … making her whole. Damian may have darkness inside him, but his rays of sun shone brightly into her soul and she craved their warmth.

Suddenly she panicked. They had used no protection either time they'd had sex. She wasn't all that worried about pregnancy, but Damian had likely been with a lot of women.

Damian drew apart their sweaty bodies, his arms still holding her tightly. "Vampires don't carry disease and there's no chance of pregnancy until we bond, Analise. Once we bond, I'd love nothing more than to watch your belly grow round with our child."

She nodded slightly as guilt stabbed at her. Her heart sunk at not being able to give Damian something as precious as his own child someday. She should tell him, but she just wasn't ready and she needed to keep those thoughts hidden until she was.

They cleaned and redressed, Damian ever attentive to her. He'd told her he needed to talk to his manager before they left. She hoped it was soon because she was starting to fade, even though her body was still on central time.

Damian kissed her sweetly, drawing her into his side. "We'll get you home shortly, kitten."

They left the privacy and relative quiet of his office. Now that she wasn't in a desire-filled haze, she had a chance to look around. The walls were painted blood red and there were several doors on either side of the long, unusually wide hallway. She noticed each room had a window, and several had a congregation of people outside, peering in. As they made their way through the crowd, she glanced through an open window and the sight before her made her freeze. It was like a train wreck. She shouldn't watch, but she couldn't turn away either.

Save for thigh-high black boots, a completely nude, blindfolded woman was strapped to a piece of wood that looked similar to an X. She had clearly been whipped, as her fair skin was a deep pink all over, her breasts and torso the darkest in color. Analise absurdly wondered what her back looked like.

The woman struggled against her bindings, not because she was trying to get free, but because a fully clothed man was on his knees in front of her, head buried between her legs. She thrashed and wailed, but the man held her pelvis firm with his arm. Finally, the woman screamed her pleasure, her previously tense body now relaxed. She assumed the man was a vampire, but couldn't tell as his back was to her.

After gently bringing the woman down from her bliss and removing the blindfold, the man drew away and she noticed blood smeared on his lips. The woman had puncture marks at the very top of her inner thigh. Vampire confirmed. A movement in her peripheral caught her attention. She'd been so enthralled with the scene she didn't notice another man sitting in the corner of the room, watching. The seated vampire stood and began disrobing. *Oh my. Was every vampire hung like an ox?*

It was clear the woman was sated, but also equally clear the scene was not over. He stalked slowly toward the restrained woman, who had slightly recovered from her orgasm and was now watching him with pure lust reflected in her hooded eyes. Leaving her hands bound, vamp number two untied the woman's leg restraints, wrapped her legs around his waist and thrust hard, causing her to scream, likely in both pleasure and pain.

The sensation of being watched crept over her. Remembering where they were and who she was with she looked over at Damian, who wasn't looking at the scene in front of them, watching her with outright interest instead.

"Does that excite you, Analise?" She'd heard that in her head, for Damian's lips hadn't moved. The thought that she could hear him made her giddy. Their eyes locked, the ever-present electricity thrumming between them. She contemplated how she would answer. Did it excite her?

"Yes," she answered honestly.

"Would you like to try it sometime?" Holy shit. The very thought had every neuron in her brain rapidly firing.

"Maybe." She added quickly, *"But not in front of a crowd."*

He grunted. *"Absolutely fucking not. I already told you no one gets to see that sweet body of yours but me, kitten."* He added, *"Our connection is deepening. You carried on this whole conversation silently. That pleases me a great deal."*

She smiled and he grabbed her hand, hauling her down the hallway, but not before she heard the woman howl her delight yet again, followed closely by an almost deafening male roar. *Yowza.* This time she kept her eyes forward as they wound their way through the crowd into the main club.

Analise met Damian's club manager, a very nice, very handsome vampire named Frederick. She was beginning to think all vampires were gorgeous, but she hadn't met a one yet who made her heart flutter like Damian did.

While Damian and Frederick carried on their quiet conversation, Analise took in the enormity of the lower level. In addition to this area, there was a small open balcony above the main dance floor. The walls here too were painted blood red, with very dark wood accents. Scattered soft lighting shone above the bar. Black candles sprinkled about the rest of the club flickered softly. The mass of bodies continued to writhe on the dance floor, but the music had changed in genre to

Ted Nugent's "Stranglehold". There were several couples copulating in plain sight, no care to who was watching. This place was sex personified and she found herself getting impossibly excited again.

Damian was true to his word, getting them out of there in record time, and though she fought against it, she was out cold two minutes into the drive home.

Home? She'd thought of Damian's place as home. How odd and comforting at the same time. She'd known Damian for little more than a day, but it already felt like a lifetime. He felt comfortable, like toasted marshmallows on a fall day or lying in front of a roaring fire naked with your lover.

It felt good. More than good. Maybe all the trials and tribulations in her life had led her here, straight to Damian. Straight to the one person she was meant to belong with, belong to.

Belonging to someone ... was it too good to be true? That was the last thought she had before sleep took her under.

Chapter 29

Damian

While Analise slept in their bedroom upstairs, he sat in his oversized leather chair, behind a sleek contemporary black desk with Marco, Devlin and Sebastian. They were beefing up security plans for both himself and Analise. Now that he had an Achilles' heel by the lovely name of Analise, he would be even more of a target than usual. And Analise, well, the fact that she was likely Xavier's daughter *and* his mate ... that made her especially vulnerable.

He'd underplayed this whole Xavier thing to her, not wanting to worry her, but he was absolutely petrified. Now he knew exactly what Dev had gone through a few short months ago. Was still going through, really. With Xavier on the loose, their mates were not safe. He'd just found her. The thought of losing her now made his body shake with unbridled rage.

"Devlin, Sebastian, I want you both on Analise when I can't be with her."

"Yes, my lord," they replied in unison.

"Also, beef up the security stationed outside the penthouse. I want double the men we have today and one of you is to be with them at all times. I don't want anyone allowed in unless it's personally approved by me, do you understand?"

They both nodded.

Besides Marco and T, they were his two strongest vamps and he knew she would be safe in their care. He didn't intend on letting her roam the goddamned city by herself, that was for sure, but he couldn't keep her prisoner here either. This was now her home, whether she knew it or not, and he wanted her to feel safe coming and going. He would try to be with her at all times, but the reality was he wouldn't be able to. As the lord of this Regent, he had responsibilities, some of which were not appropriate to bring his mate into.

"Did you check the security feeds?"

"Yes," Sebastian replied. "The camera in the parking garage was out and has now been replaced. We installed several other cameras in questionable areas as well as three additional cameras on the outside perimeter."

"Good. Very good." He owned the entire block his building was housed on and his penthouse spanned the four top floors of the skyscraper. All windows were bulletproof glass and only one elevator went up to his place. And only his top four security people could access it. Marco, T, Devlin and Sebastian.

Infrared retinal scans and blood analyzing technology used in his security arsenal were deterrents to most vamps who tried getting to him in the past. And other than him, no one had the ability to flash into his penthouse, so no surprise attacks could take place. The only thing he'd used a witch for. While Dev had preferred to use the mystical powers of witches to shroud his estate, Damian preferred the power of technology. Now, however, he had to wonder about the benefits of using shrouding. The only problem was that it was much more challenging to make an entire skyscraper in the middle of a metropolis disappear than it was a country estate. Humans would surely notice a giant gaping hole in the middle of a city block where a sixty-five-story building used to be. If he wasn't confident in their safety, he may just have to consider moving somewhere where shrouding would be a possibility. Two days ago someone could have stuck a hot poker in his heart before he'd even consider working with a witch. Funny how a woman—the *right* woman—could change a man's entire perspective, making him consider things he never would have imagined in his wildest dreams.

"Devlin, did Katrina get more clothes for Analise?"

"Yes, my lord. She's also offered to take her shopping to pick out more things to her liking."

"That was very kind of her. I'll talk to Analise, but I'm sure she would like that. It would be good for her to make a female friend as well."

Devlin nodded.

"Sebastian, did you check into what I asked you to do earlier?"

Sebastian looked wary. He knew the way Damian felt about witches, not the specifics, so, of course, his request seemed highly unusual, even absurd, to the vampire. "I did, my lord."

"And?" Jesus, guy ... spit it out.

"She would be delighted to see Analise when you return to Milwaukee."

"Well, she'd better be delighted to see me because Analise isn't leaving my side."

His stomach churned violently at the thought of having to spend any time with a witch—other than Analise—but this woman was apparently family and Analise desperately needed family. No matter her species, he certainly was not going to be a wedge between them or she would eventually come to resent him. She hadn't asked to see Maeve, hadn't even spoken of her newfound information, but he hadn't really given her a chance either. He'd whisked her off and fucked her senseless for the last eight hours, the thought making him hard all over again.

Analise hadn't been able to rely on anyone in her short life, and as much as it pained him to admit it, she needed more than him. She deserved a whole sea of people around her, loving her, protecting her. She had a frantic need to belong and he would make that dream come true. Guilt stabbed at him for not telling her about Kate, who was most likely her half-sister. He would tell her, soon. One overwhelming thing at a time.

She also needed to learn about her latent sorceress abilities, as another avenue of protection against Xavier. If she tried to use it on him, though, she was going to find out the meaning of punishment and right quick. He'd withhold her orgasm for a month.

"Okay, then. I think we're set. I have a few business meetings before dawn, but I'm going to take them as calls instead. I don't want Analise waking up in a strange place without me here. As of now, I plan to return to Milwaukee day after tomorrow for a few days, unless something urgent comes up before then. Devlin and Sebastian, you will accompany me this time as well."

They all departed except for Marco, who hung back, looking like a cat had his tongue.

"What is it, Marco?"

Marco had been with him since he'd earned this position. He'd been a loyal friend and confidant and Damian was grateful to have his advice. His business savvy was like no other and, while Damian was highly skilled at playing the stock market, even Marco had taught him a few new tricks, which had more than doubled his already impressive net worth. Marco usually didn't mince words, his natural born filter somehow absent. While it had pissed Damian off more than once, it was refreshing someone would bust his balls when he needed it.

Marco cleared his throat. "I just wanted to congratulate you, my lord." Damian must have looked confused as he added, "On finding your Moira. I can already see how much she means to you and you to her. I'm happy for you."

Damian was stunned silent. Out of anything he thought the guy could say that was certainly not it. This felt a lot like a chick moment. So he did what he did best.

"Jesus, Marco, you're such a pussy."

Marco laughed as he walked toward the door. "Fuck off, my lord."

Over the next several hours, Damian finished his business calls for the day and adjusted his calendar for the next two so he'd have uninterrupted time to spend with Analise. He turned his attention to his favorite job ... day trader. As he determined the best adjustments to make to his portfolio, what should have taken him a half hour took almost two. His mind kept drifting to the sexy, naked woman sprawled in his bed just one flight above him and the incredible emotional and physical connection they'd shared so far.

Only two short days ago Damian thought he had it all, but since Analise breezed into his life, he realized how very empty and shallow an existence he'd truly had. She was a breath of fresh air in his stale life. She challenged him. While infuriating, it was also exhilarating. Except for Marco, no one challenged him for fear of their lives, of course. But Analise simply didn't give a shit. She was not afraid to back down from him and it made his blood burn for her. Made his dick hard for her. She was intelligent, witty, independent and a survivor. A survivor just like him.

Fate. Destiny. Predestination. They were a theory, a belief, a feeling ... whatever you wanted to call them. He'd thought them to be a bunch of bullshit. Until her. Fate, in her infinite and fucking twisted wisdom, had chosen to give to him the one thing that had shattered him beyond repair so very many years ago. A witch.

But with her he felt lighter.

Comfortable.

Whole.

Happy. Truly and profoundly happy. It was like he could take a full, deep, life-giving breath for the first time in his nearly five hundred years. She was warmth, light, joy. She was home. And she was *his*. He wanted to be a better man for her. He wanted to be a better man *because* of her. That was probably what struck him as most insightful. His selfishness had simply melted away from the moment he saw her.

Even in the bedroom. While he was a generous lover, in the bedroom it had been about his wishes, his desires, his ultimate pleasure. With Analise, his need to dominate her was even more overpowering, but now all he wanted was *her* pleasure. To fulfill her desires, her fantasies. He would never make her do anything where she truly felt uncomfortable or unsafe, but he would push her boundaries because she needed that. And in no way could she hide how much his dominance excited her.

When she'd watched the scene on the St. Andrew's cross in fascination, he could see the cogs spinning in her pretty little head. He'd caught a brief glimpse but was so fascinated with her reaction he couldn't tear his eyes away from her. And when he saw the lust in her eyes, when he smelled her excitement, his cock was straining in his pants desperate to get out and back inside its rightful place.

Since he never brought women to his penthouse, he didn't have a playroom installed here. However, that was already well on its way to being remedied. By the time they returned from their next trip to Milwaukee, the largest two bedrooms on the third floor would be converted. It would require knocking out a wall, but it would be quick work. Money talked.

He'd pretty much done it all in the BDSM world, except a few things he considered too taboo, even for him. No asphyxiation. No electricity play. Humiliation didn't do a damned thing for him. He'd had more threesomes, foursomes and orgies than he could remember. He'd used every single piece of equipment, every toy, every flogger ever created. Sometimes the best toys weren't even those specifically made for that purpose. A good household item like a hairbrush, a clothespin and even something as innocuous as an electric toothbrush could be used very creatively.

He'd custom ordered all of the equipment, including a very beautiful cherry wood St. Andrew's cross, which he couldn't wait to try out. The room would be stocked with various toys, restraints, paddles, floggers, nipple clamps, Shibari ropes and the like.

Kink was part of him, it was in his blood, and he could see it captivated Analise. Another reason fate had chosen correctly. He couldn't wait to show her a whole new sexual world existed. But it would only be the two of them. He would not share her.

His cell rang, bringing him out of his fantasies. Caller ID indicated it was Ronson. He'd had a bad feeling since he'd left Milwaukee that something significant was going down.

"Ronson," he said as he answered the call.

"My lord, my apologies for bothering you, but I thought you should know that Frankie is missing. When I questioned Bart, the head bartender, he indicated he was at the club earlier this evening and then was seen talking to a man. A very large man. Then he was just gone. While nothing is visible, Frankie's office smells of fresh blood. I also reviewed the security footage and saw a very large vampire enter the club shortly before Frankie was last seen. All of our customers know to use the back entrance versus the main one, so I have reason to believe this vamp was the one responsible."

"Fuck. Send me the footage. Like an hour ago." He was certain it was Geoffrey. And if Geoffrey was back *talking* to Frankie, then they were made. There was no way Frankie could have kept the owners identity secret. Which meant they also knew about Damian and Rom as well, and Frankie would have most certainly revealed that Analise left with Damian. Double fuck.

"What would you like me to do from here, my lord?" Ronson wasn't stupid. This put every human and vampire alike in that club in danger, but Damian needed to be more strategic than Geoffrey and Xavier.

"Do nothing for now. If the footage confirms my suspicions, I believe it's the same vamp that came in the other night looking for Analise. He'll be back and he'll be looking to get into the lower level, if he hasn't already made it in. Let him. But keep a very close eye on him. Geoffrey is an indiscriminate killer, so if he breaks the rules restrain him and call me immediately. He's a very strong vamp, Ronson, so if you need help, you'll need to let me know. In the meantime, I'll get someone to look for Frankie's body, although I'm not sure we'll find much left of him. Geoffrey is known for dicing up his victims like Humpty Dumpty. No fucking way someone could put them back together again."

"Yes, my lord. What about Lord Devon?"

Yes, what about Dev? Would this news make him cut his honeymoon short? It didn't matter; he needed to be made aware. He'd try to convince him to stay away. After all, with Xavier sniffing around, it was probably still the safest place for his mate to be.

"I'll take care of it, Ronson. Send me that footage and call me if anything else comes up."

"Yes, my lord."

Damian dialed Rom. Damian had a love for technology, but Rom was on the opposite end of the spectrum. Rom hated it. Damian had to break down and buy the guy a new cell phone a few months ago. Rom still carried a flip phone. A *flip phone* for fuck's sake! He'd bought Rom the newest iPhone and spent two hours teaching the guy how to use it. He wasn't sure he'd learned anything other than how to use the phone keypad and his favorites menu. And Rom sending or responding to a text? Good fucking luck. He'd said his fingers were too big, to which Damian had replied, "Use the talk to text feature." That was the end of that conversation.

"D, shouldn't you be with your mate instead of calling me?"

"She's sleeping. Listen. I need to bring you up to speed on a few items. Xavier has a bead on Analise. Geoffrey showed up at Dragonfly night before last asking for her by name." He probably should have updated Rom before now, but he'd been kind of distracted with a certain leggy brunette.

"Fuck."

"Yep, that about sums it up. I took Analise with me to Boston last night, but I plan on coming back to Milwaukee in a day or two. I'll be bringing additional security with me for her protection."

"Okay."

"And I just got a call from Ronson that Frankie, Dragonfly's main bar manager, is missing. Well, likely dead, and Geoffrey is the primary suspect. I'm waiting for the security feed to come through, but I suspect it's him. There is no way Geoffrey didn't find out what really goes on in that bar and who owns it. And at minimum they know that Analise is with me."

"Are you sure it's wise to bring her back to Milwaukee?" He'd been wondering the same thing, but he'd made a promise to Dev and even though he was convinced his place was air tight, with Dev's estate protected by shrouding, he thought perhaps it was a safer place for Analise instead.

"Yes, I'm sure."

They spent a few minutes discussing his strategy and how to lure Geoffrey in. Rom agreed with his approach. He'd learned from the best. Although he didn't think Geoffrey would talk, it would be a blow to Xavier to lose his second in command. And they'd take great pleasure in torturing the fucker to see if they could get a lead on the other missing girls or the children before they put an end to his pathetic existence.

"I'm also going to have Giselle get with the detective to track down Frankie. Or his body."

"Parts, you mean." Rom was also well aware of Geoffrey's predilection.

"I know, but we need to try." He may not have liked the guy, but he didn't wish his body to be spread out all over Wisconsin farm fields either.

"We need to call Devon," Rom said.

"I know."

They disconnected and Damian gathered his thoughts, deciding to put off a call that would ruin his friend's honeymoon for day or two. He couldn't help thinking that they still had the upper hand.

Xavier didn't know how many of his daughters were alive. They did. And the last one couldn't be found fast enough. Neither Kate nor Damian's own mate was safe, but at least they were both under the protection of men who fiercely loved them and would give their lives for them. What Xavier had so callously discarded many years ago he now suddenly wanted back.

Well, fuck that. This little family reunion would happen over his dead body.

Chapter 30

Analise

She woke to an empty, cold bed. In Damian's penthouse. In Boston. She sat, called out to him and was greeted with silence. Flopping back down, she wondered what to do next.

Looking down at her naked form, memories of last night wove their way into the forefront of her brain. She blushed remembering how she'd readily complied with Damian's wicked demands. She'd performed her first strip tease and publicly masturbated. Well ... maybe not *publicly*, but close enough. Masturbating beneath the covers in the privacy of your bedroom was far different than being completely exposed, someone watching your every move.

If she moved her hands down right now, she knew she'd find herself wet. His dominance over her body was overwhelming but oddly gave her relief at the same time. She'd spent her entire life taking care of herself and it was almost cathartic to let someone else call the shots and take care of her for once.

The thought that Damian's touch lit her body on fire instead of making her cringe made her heart soar. Before Damian, when someone touched her, she felt like bugs were crawling all over her skin, boring themselves into her pores.

She reflected on their conversations over the last day. She had been too overwhelmed with information yesterday, needing time to digest it.

First and foremost, after twenty-six long years she'd discovered her parentage. Her mother was a witch and her father probably a psychotic vampire. Yah her. How did they find out for sure if she was this guy's daughter? She'd have to ask Damian.

You couldn't choose your DNA, but you could choose what to do with it. Good or bad, she wanted to learn more about both sides of her family and, whether Damian liked it or not, she would. After hearing his heartbreaking past, she had empathy to his aversion of witches, but like it or not, she was one and that was something she would dig into further. How her vampire half factored in she wasn't sure. Did she have latent vampire powers as well? It was both exhilarating and terrifying at the same time.

She also was a dreamwalker. She still wasn't sure exactly what that meant. Could she make herself dream about things? Were there others like her? Why hadn't this ever happened to her before? Why now? Could it have anything to do with meeting Damian and the fact they were fated to be together? It was confusing and she needed to find out more.

Determined to get answers to the questions racing through her mind like a thundering pack of wild horses, she left the bed in search of clothes. This was the first time she'd had a chance to really look around the bedroom and what she saw didn't disappoint. The master bedroom was oversized with a sitting area to the left, which led to a massive covered balcony. The oversized four-post king bed sat in the middle of the room on a raised platform. There were slats in the headboard that were perfect for binding her. Her blush returned full force.

Hanging on the wall opposite the bed was the biggest damn flat screen TV she'd ever seen. She wasn't sure how it stayed on the wall without falling down. It had to be seventy or eighty inches across. To her right were French doors, which she assumed led to the closet, so she headed there thoroughly enjoying the feel of the plush carpet on her toes. She hoped to at least find an oversized T-shirt of Damian's she could wear. Her clothes from yesterday were dirty and she wasn't donning that sexy dress again unless she had no other choice.

When she entered the walk-in closet, she froze. On the left side hung row after row of high-end dress shirts, suits, dress pants and jeans. Open shelves held dozens of neatly folded T-shirts, mostly dark colors like blacks, charcoals and grays. There were several built-in shoe shelves, all lined with various dress and casual men's shoes.

But that wasn't what surprised her, for hanging on the right side of the closet were brand new women's clothes. She knew they were new as they all had the tags still attached. There were stacks of jeans and several dozen shirts, blouses, dress pants and even a few dresses. She checked the sizes of several pieces and they were her size. She checked the various shoes stacked in the shoe rack, all size eight. Opening a few drawers, the most beautiful lingerie peeked out at her. Rows and rows of lacy bras and panties, spanning every shade of the rainbow and then some.

Damian got these? *For me?* When? Tears pricked her eyes as she tried to gain her composure. No one had ever done anything remotely like this for her before. These were high-end clothes; the person who'd left them hadn't bothered to remove the prices. One of the dresses alone was over two thousand dollars. Where would she ever wear a two thousand-dollar dress? A pair of shoes was eight hundred dollars. For something that would just get dirty when you walked in the dirt? And two hundred-dollar underwear? On what planet did people pay two hundred dollars for one pair of panties? That was simply asinine. While she appreciated the thought, she could not accept these gifts.

She found the cheapest pair of underwear she could and ripped off the tags. They were still one hundred fifty-two effing dollars. Jesus that made her stomach churn. She could shop for practically a year at the thrift shop on one hundred fifty dollars. How she would pay Damian back, she had no idea, but she would. Maybe she could sell them on Craig's list. People bought all kinds of weird shit on that site.

She grabbed a neatly folded gray short-sleeve tee and, while she wasn't pencil thin, the XXL fabric engulfed her frame. The hem hung to mid-thigh, arms falling several inches below her elbow. Even her ample breasts were hidden by the excess fabric. Well, at least she was covered in case she ran into anyone besides Damian.

She left the comfort of the bedroom and began winding her way through the spacious apartment. She found a set of stairs going up, but was drawn downstairs instead. She could simply *feel* Damian's presence down there but didn't understand why. As she entered the main level, she drank in the unbelievable sight. The modern room was open, with ultra-high ceilings, a built-in bar on the far back left and a black marble fireplace clearly the centerpiece of the expansive room. To her right she noticed the edge of the black marble kitchen countertop, but from her vantage point she couldn't see much of anything else.

But to her the most impressive thing in this room was not the expensive leather furniture, priceless wall hangings, or the cream-colored carpet that felt like silk under her feet. No. The most impressive thing was the view of the city from the floor-to-ceiling windows lining the entire left wall. These windows must have been at least twenty feet high and the entire lengthy room was lined with them. At night this must be breathtaking.

She noticed a hallway straight ahead, just from the front door. That was where she would find Damian, no doubt. He said he had business to take care of while here, so she suspected she would find him in an office of some sort. She followed her intuition and quickly located him several doors down. She was just about to knock but pulled up short when she heard her name.

Yes, she shamelessly put her ear to the closed door like the little eavesdropper she was.

"The missing friend is Beth Murphy," said an unknown voice. "She worked as a sous chef at a new restaurant named *Prime* in downtown Chicago. Went missing on June twenty-sixth. I checked out her apartment and there was nothing of use there, so the snatch must have happened between work and her apartment. I talked to her boss and he's clean. Analise and Beth met on the streets and were thick as thieves.

"Tracked down a street rat named Smitty who knows her. He admitted to being the one to provide Analise Lord Devon's name and where to find him. He didn't remember where he'd heard his name, but I talked to a few others and it's a pretty common rumor actually. He didn't really even believe the information he'd given to Analise, but he said she sounded desperate and he was just trying to help."

"How does he know Analise?" Damian growled. She couldn't believe her ears. Damian had someone check into her background? How could he do that to her? He'd told her to trust him. And like a goddamned lovesick fool, she had.

"He said they'd spent time on the streets together. Nothing between them other than friendship, not that *he* didn't wish for more I could tell. He saved her life when he caught a group of guys trying to rape her. She'd been beaten up pretty good and stabbed in the stomach by the time he came across her. He took her to the hospital, saved her life. Apparently the doctors said a couple minutes later and she would have bled out."

"Fuuuuck."

Shame washed over her like a tidal wave. Of all people, she did not want Damian to know this. She'd made a horribly bad decision and trusted the wrong people. She was eighteen and drugged out of her mind when that incident happened. And Smitty didn't catch them quite in time as she'd led him to later believe.

At first, she honestly couldn't remember what'd happened that night, but a couple months later, she thought she was dying with the worst abdominal pain of her life and ended up at the same emergency room again. Ectopic pregnancy. She lost the baby along with a fallopian tube. The doctors told her the remaining one had been severely damaged from the previous stabbing and her chances of getting pregnant would be pretty much nil.

For the second time in two months, she'd almost died. After that incident, she didn't touch even as much as a cigarette and vowed to drag herself out of the sinkhole she was trapped in. And she'd succeeded. She'd had three jobs at one point early on, but had gotten her GED and enrolled in college. Life was still hard, but it was on her terms. *She* owned her life, not the other way around.

The next thing she heard brought her out of her musing.

"... sister," Damian said.

"You haven't told her about Kate? No offense, my lord, but when do you plan on doing that? She deserves to know she has other family out there."

"I know," she heard him reply in a resigned voice.

She had a sister? And Damian knew but didn't tell her? What the hell else was he keeping from her?

Crushing devastation almost brought her to her knees. This man called himself her mate, told her repeatedly to trust him ... that he'd never hurt her. He couldn't have hurt her more if he'd reached into her chest cavity and crushed her heart in his hand while she watched.

She was destroyed. He said he loved her, for Christ's sake. Yet he went behind her back snooping into her life and lied to her about family. Did he know about her witch blood, but kept that from her too? Given his background, quite possibly yes.

Bitter tears sprang against her wishes, which she viciously wiped away. He did not deserve her tears, or anything else from her for that matter. She was so fucking out of here.

She fled back up to the bedroom, quickly dressed in her dirty clothes from the day before and quietly headed for the front door. She didn't know where she would go in Boston without any cash or how she'd get back to Milwaukee, but she'd figure it out. She'd always been resourceful. Damian was the worst liar of all and she was the worst kind of fool. He was the first man she'd actually allowed herself to envision a future with and she'd bought his lies like a foolish, lovesick girl.

She felt her heart physically shattering into a million pieces as she walked through the front door and pushed the button, calling the elevator to their floor. Her hands were empty, as they'd left Milwaukee with nothing but the clothes on her back.

A sudden voice behind her made her jump five feet in the air and she spun around, ready to fight. Her heart raced as two massive vampires, almost as large as Damian, stood on either side of the penthouse door.

"Where can we accompany you, ma'am?" Lefty said. Her eyes flitted back and forth between them, confused. Thank God they weren't there to harm her. But it would be a cold day in hell before they accompanied her anywhere either.

"I'm fine, thank you. Just going out for some fresh air."

"I don't mind keeping you company then. I'm Sebastian, ma'am," he said as he held out his hand. So lefty now had a name. She tentatively shook it, unsure how she should handle this.

"I'm sure you don't, Sebastian. But I don't need company. Thanks for the offer. I'll be right back up." Liar, liar pants on fire, Analise. If he knew she was untruthful he didn't say anything, only smiled kindly.

"In any case, I'm afraid you are to be accompanied at all times, ma'am. We're your new security team."

What. The. Hell? Security team?

"What are you talking about?" She was utterly confused now. Just then the front door opened and Damian stood there, taking up the entire doorframe with his massive body. Her breath caught as she drank him in. He was devastatingly beautiful in his faded blue jeans and tight gray T-shirt, which looked far better on him that it had her. *He may be a sex God, but he's a liar, Analise. Stop letting your lady parts short out your common sense.*

"Going somewhere, Analise?" His face told two different stories. His eyes had you believing he was confused, while his lips showed his smugness.

Mother. Fucker.

"Yes. Away from you. Asshole." She turned to stab the elevator button once again. *Why wasn't the damn thing here yet?* She squealed as tight arms surrounded her, carrying her back into the apartment.

"Put. Me. Down. Now," she huffed. Her legs were flailing and she tried to connect with any body part of his she could. He made an *oomph* noise when the heels she wore caught his shin. Well, that was one use for a pair of eight hundred-dollar shoes. Self-defense. Since she had been flashed here barefoot, and her only shoe choices were various forms of high heels, she'd had no choice but to don a pair in her escape. Correction ... *attempted* escape.

"Analise. Calm the fuck down. What is going on here? Why are you trying to leave?"

By this time, he'd turned her in his arms and effectively stopped her flailing by pressing her back into the closest wall. His legs held hers immobile. Fighting against him was a losing battle, so she let her body go limp. She'd fight this battle with words instead.

"Oh, I don't know, Damian. Why don't you hire your little private detective to find out for you? He seems pretty good at uncovering ghosts people have buried deep in their closets."

A look of surprise crossed his face so fast she would have missed it if she hadn't been paying attention. But she was. She was paying attention to every little nuance as Damian tried to lie his way out of this too.

"Christ," he uttered under his breath as his eyes darted away from hers.

"That's what I thought. Now let me go," she demanded.

"How much did you hear?" Was this guy serious? How much *didn't* she hear was the real question?

"Enough to know that you're a liar, just like everyone else that's been in my life. Except you're the worst kind of liar, Damian. You made me believe I could trust you. You made me believe you wouldn't hurt me. You made me believe you actually *loved* me. I may not know a lot about relationships, but I do know you don't go behind someone's back and snoop into their past if you claim to fucking love them." Her voice broke.

Don't you cry, Analise. He's not worth it. The problem was she didn't believe the lies her own mind tried to tell her this time. Damian *was* worth every tear in her body.

"You're right," he whispered

She was stunned silent. "What?" He wasn't trying to build more lies on top of lies to justify his actions?

"You're right, Analise. I went behind your back and it was wrong of me." He paused, blowing out a deep breath. "Can we do this somewhere other than pressed up against the kitchen wall? Please give me a chance to explain." She could see remorse, regret and guilt swimming in his onyx eyes and that was the only reason the next clipped word came out of her mouth.

"Fine." She had to be out of her ever-loving mind. Once a liar, always a liar.

He tentatively let her go, ready to catch her again if she tried to bolt. She considered it, but now that she'd been caught, getting out of Damian's apartment wouldn't be so easy. So she might as well listen to him while plotting her next move. Damian snuck her a knowing glance as he firmly grabbed her hand, leading her to the couch. At least he had enough sense to keep his trap shut.

Once they sat, she tried to pull her hand away, but Damian simply held on tighter. "Not letting you go, kitten."

Kitten? He didn't know how close to the truth he was. She smiled, feeling its bitterness. "You're about to get your eyes scratched out with my claws." She may look under control on the surface, but beneath her anger churned as hot as a sleeping volcano. One wrong word and she would spew fire and ash all over the place. It wouldn't be pretty. In fact, it would be downright fugly.

They sat in momentary silence, eyes locked in a battle of wills. The question was ... could anyone really come out victorious?

Chapter 31

Mike

As suspected, his calls all went unanswered. Because she hadn't set up a voice mailbox, he couldn't even leave a damn message, so he'd resorted to texting. That was an hour ago and although she'd read every one of them, he didn't get one reply. He'd text her every ten minutes for the next three fucking months if he had to.

6:15 a.m.: How r u today, Giselle?

6:22 a.m.: When r u coming to see me again?

6:31 a.m.: I dreamt of u last night.

6:45 a.m.: U looked edible yesterday, btw. Nice boots.

6:52 a.m.: I can't get the taste of u out of my mouth.

7:02 a.m.: Giselle, pls.

7:19 a.m.: Ur driving me out of my effing mind woman.

His doorbell rang. Who the hell was here? The only people that visited him these days were Jake and the bloodsuckers. And he doubted either was at the door at this time of the morning.

He was so concentrated on his phone, the lack of response bubbles mocking him, he threw open the door without checking the peephole first and was stunned silent at the beauty in front of him.

Today Giselle was dressed in tight black leather pants that left nothing to the imagination. She wore high-heeled patent red leather pumps and you could barely see her first two toes. He didn't know the name for those particular type of shoes, but who fucking cared. He would bow at the feet of the man or woman who'd invented them. She wore an off the shoulder sheer red blouse, with the sexiest red push-up bra he'd ever seen. It molded her boobs perfectly.

The sun hit her at the perfect angle, looking as if it was radiating out of her body instead of a bright ball of gas in the sky. Anger emanated from her in waves and she looked like either the angel of death or the devil incarnate.

His erection strained in his jeans. It took every ounce of willpower he possessed not to haul her inside, throw her up against the wall and ravage her. That hadn't worked out so well yesterday and would probably go over like a lead balloon today, given how pissed she looked. He tried to discretely adjust himself, but Giselle's eyes flicked toward his hands as he shimmied. Busted.

He cleared his throat. "Good morning, Giselle."

"How the fuck did you get my phone number?" She hadn't bothered moving from the spot to which she now seemed rooted.

"Would you like to come in or do you want to do this in plain view of the neighborhood? I'm cool either way, but Mrs. Hansen, my neighbor across the street is the neighborhood busy body. She regularly sits in her front window with binoculars to spy on everyone. You wouldn't believe some of the shit she's seen, especially with my neighbor to the left. Mark. He's twenty-two and apparently likes to host orgies and doesn't bother closing his blinds. Not that I care, mind you. What one does in the privacy of their own home should remain in the privacy of their own home. As long as I don't see naked people stumbling out of his house, I could care less. I've since had to tell Mark to close his damn blinds. I—"

She shoved her way past him into the house. Guess she decided to take this inside. He smiled inwardly. Steps one and two successful. She was here and inside.

"Jesus, do you ever shut up?"

"I just didn't want anything between us to be fodder for neighborhood gossip." True. Partially.

"Let me make one thing clear, Detective. There *is* nothing between us." She tried to sound convincing but fell as flat as a pancake. He decided now was not the time to goad her, pointing out she needed to brush up on her acting skills. That would likely earn him a swift kick to the family jewels.

"To what do I owe today's honor, Giselle?" He didn't really care how or why she was here, just that she was.

"We need to find a missing person. Frankie Durillo. You know Dev opened up a new club downtown a few weeks ago. Dragonfly." Yes, he knew and he also knew what happened below Dragonfly as well. And as much as he disliked

Devon and the other bloodsuckers, he had to reluctantly admit that providing a safe place for vampires to feed with willing participants was a good fucking idea. Apparently the lords owned quite a few of these feeding places all over the country. It was another one of the many reasons that he was starting to doubt his whole hatred of vampires and open himself up to the possibility of at least considering something more with Giselle. Something that didn't require a facemask and boxing gloves like their usual verbal spars.

"...could be dead." He'd just caught the tail end of what she's said.

"I'm sorry, could you repeat that?"

She sighed heavily, rolling her eyes for the full effect. "What were you dreaming of, Detective? Spanking the wank?"

He smirked and let his eyes shine with undisguised lust. "No, doll, I was imagining you wearing nothing but your thigh-high black boots on your knees in front of me, sucking my cock dry." He hadn't been thinking of that at all, but now that the image was in his head, fuck if he was going to be able to get it out. Guess that barb backfired.

Giselle was visibly flustered and it took her several moments to recover. Her beautiful blush was back too. "As I was saying before you so rudely drifted off, Damian got a call early this morning that Frankie was missing and was last seen talking to Geoffrey, Xavier's second in command. Blood wasn't found but could be smelled in Frankie's office. We've been asked by Damian to try to find Frankie's body or his parts before anyone else discovers it, especially humans." *Humans*. Right.

He shook his head. Why, oh why, had he agreed to work for Devon? He knew exactly why. And she was standing in front of him in all her exquisite glory. "You think this guy is in pieces? Why?"

"That's Geoffrey's M.O." She shrugged.

"Christ." Sick fuckers, the lot of 'em. "And why is Geoffrey here in town anyway? Or should I ask?"

"He's doing the same thing we are. Looking for Xavier's long-lost daughters of course." *Fucking great*. The most powerful vampires on earth were converging upon his city and he couldn't do anything but sit back and watch the show unfold before his very eyes. And pray he survived.

Giselle had moved their little conversation into his meager living room and was now sitting on a deep red club chair closest to the gas fireplace. The fabric was pilled and had seen better days, but he'd be lying if he said she looked anything other than a queen sitting on it, especially given her attire today.

He also knew why she sat there. Every other time she'd been here, she'd sat on the couch, but that also allowed him to sit beside her. Today her walls were reinforced with five-inch thick steel doors and he'd have to find another way around.

"How did you get my number?" Back to that, were we?

"Your phone fell out of your pocket while you were sleeping." Not true, since he saw it tucked in her bra instead. There were no pockets to be found in that tiny skirt she wore yesterday.

"I didn't have pockets," she snapped. Her ire was back in full force.

"Oh."

"Oh? That's all you have to say?" Cue the steam.

"Yes. Oh." Fuck if he would give her more than that.

"I could make you tell me, you know," she purred, back to the seductress. Looked like her bipolar had kicked in.

He sat back on the couch and crossed his arms, purposely letting his legs fall farther apart. Giselle took the bait, glancing a little too long at his stiff cock before their eyes locked again. Which way would she play this? Seduce or attack?

Attack, it was.

"Yes. I can compel you to tell me the truth." She was lying. She couldn't compel him. No vampire had ever been able to compel him and, quite frankly, he wasn't sure why. He understood it was a very rare human who couldn't be compelled. But he'd play along.

"Okay. You can give it a shot. If how I found your phone number is *really* that important to you, I'm game."

Anger caused her brows to crease and her lips to thin. "Fuck you," she spewed.

"I thought you'd never ask, Giselle." He held her furious glare with a straight face. For several moments he felt pressure like a headache coming on, and then ... nothing. It wasn't a new sensation. He'd felt it many times before.

"Is that all you got?" he goaded. He couldn't help himself. She was the matador provoking him with a red flag and he was the bull. She just brought out the bastard in him.

Next thing he knew his back was digging into the broken couch spring and a sexy, volatile, furious female straddled him. "How did you do that?"

"Are we still talking about the phone number?" Her sweet spot was perfectly straddling his still erect dick and her breath caught when he slightly ground into her.

"No. I want to know how you resisted my compulsion." Her little act of aggression was quickly going to shit. He was affecting her and she failed miserably in trying to hide it.

"You're changing subjects so fast I'm getting whiplash, baby." Was it stupid to needle a pissed off female? *Yes.* Was it even more reckless to prod a pissed off female *vampire*? *Fuck yes.* Did he care? *Not one iota.*

She leaned down, running her nose along his jaw. She none too gently scraped her teeth down his neck, along his collarbone. It was his turn to catch his breath.

She murmured, "I could end your sad, pathetic life in just a few short minutes, Detective. I would even make it pleasurable for you, although you're an asshole and don't deserve such kindness."

He wrapped one strong arm around her waist and another around her head, holding it tightly to his neck. He thrust his hips hard into her as if she was riding him naked and he was trying to bury himself balls deep. *If only that were true.*

"Go ahead." When she didn't move, he added, "Do it, Giselle. End me." He wasn't aware how much he truly meant it until the words were out and for the first time since he'd resolved to devote his life to retribution, he just wanted it to be over.

His life was sad.

It was pathetic.

It was lonely.

He was full of self-loathing, anger and hate. He had nothing inside of him to give Jamie, Giselle or any other woman. Hell, how could he when he was an empty shell of a man?

He half expected to feel the sting of her bite, but instead felt the softness of her lips as they skated along his neck. Her tongue darted out, and he actually shivered. A slight moan escaped her as the hand gripping her head tightened and his hips drove into her leather-covered pussy.

How many times over the last few months had he imagined her mouth willingly on him? *Countless.* The reality of it, however, was so much better. His fantasies had been blown to bits, scattering like shards of glass. If he was going to die, he wanted to do it while inside her sweet body. Yes, he was a selfish bastard.

It was his turn to moan as she got more aggressive, now lightly nipping his skin, kissing her way up toward the shell of his ear. He wanted to grab her head and plunder her mouth. He wanted her underneath him, legs wrapped around his waist as he pumped ruthlessly into her. Hell, he might not even make it inside her, he was ready to blow his load right this fucking second.

Then she stopped. Her ragged breath echoed in his ear. Shit, was she going to break down again? Christ, a minute ago he'd accepted death. Now he wanted nothing more than to hold Giselle in his arms. He held her tightly to him, waiting for her to speak, move, do *something*. Several minutes slowly ticked by and she remained quiet. At least his raging hard-on wasn't begging to be set free any longer. But Jesus, did his balls hurt.

"Giselle?"

"We can't do this," she whispered.

Ummm ... what? She was a vampire. Didn't they love fucking? Now he just felt slighted. He wasn't good enough to be used for even the most basic of human or vampire needs?

Rage and embarrassment welled. His mental middle finger shot up at her rebuff.

"You're right." His hold was so tight his knuckles were cramped and it took several seconds to loosen them up enough to let her go. Even with his arms completely removed, she lay still, head buried in his neck, chest heaving. He was so irrationally pissed, he grabbed her shoulders and none too gently shoved her away. He was never rough with a woman, well, unless it was mutual, but this was Giselle they were talking about. Her multiple personalities were harder to keep up with than a *Scandal* episode and he was done with it.

He stood as she scrambled out of the way. "Why don't we split up on this one? We can cover more ground faster. We've already established I have your cell phone number and you have mine, so I'll call you if I find anything." And he wouldn't have to be around the psycho bitch.

After splitting up the areas deemed most likely to dump a body, half an hour later he went his way and she hers. Giselle had mentioned Dev and Kate were on their honeymoon. Don't ask don't tell was the vibe he'd gotten, so he didn't ask. When Dev returned, however, Mike was going to speak with him about working with Giselle. As in *not*.

This was the last time he would do this with her. Not only was this torture for his cock, his mind was constantly tormented. He might be a masochist bastard, but these unpredictable interactions with Giselle were even more than he could handle.

After this task if he saw her again, it would be too soon. And most definitely not good for his own fucking sanity.

Chapter 32

Damian

He was screwed. How could he be so careless as to let T update him with Analise in the house? The better question was why did he check her background in the first place? He knew the answer to that, but Analise wouldn't accept it. Nor would she accept anything less than the truth. Which was no less than she deserved.

Fucking hell.

He'd completely blown it. She was damn pissed and deservedly so. She may be his fated mate, his Moira, but that didn't mean she had to agree to *bond* herself to him forever. He had to lay it all out on the line and hope that she could forgive the biggest mistake he'd ever made in nearly five hundred years. Not letting go of her hands, he began his confession. At the end of it, he'd either earn her forgiveness or her rebuff. He honestly didn't know if he would accept any decision other than for her to stay. He couldn't. He *wouldn't.*

"The night I met you I asked T to dig into your background because I knew you were mine and I wanted to know every piece of information about you I could get my hands on. You were buttoned tighter than a straightjacket and I was impatient."

Insults ... maybe not exactly the best way to start off an apology. He paused, waiting for any reaction. She regarded him stonily, but emotion swirled beneath the surface, so he continued.

"After I found out your full name and that you were a ward of the state, that's when I suspected that you were Xavier's daughter. Well, I had a gut feeling was more like it. And I always trust my gut.

"What I didn't tell you was we believe Xavier sired several female vampires. Apparently Xavier can only produce female offspring, which is unheard of. At the time, Xavier didn't see the value of these female offspring and at his command his minions were to eliminate all of the females he'd sired. However, they managed to save three by trying to place them with families on the adoption registry. We think perhaps your placement went awry as we knew one baby ended up being turned over to social services."

"And you're positive I'm his daughter?" Her voice was small, childlike.

"We haven't verified it with DNA yet, but, yes, I do believe you are his daughter. I was going to have blood samples taken when we return to Milwaukee so it can be verified." He continued. "So we believe Xavier likely still has three daughters alive. Devon's mate, Kate. You. And a third we haven't found yet."

"I have two half-sisters?" Her voice was laced with disbelief ... and hope.

"One for sure. Kate. As I said, we haven't found the other child yet, so perhaps she's not even living anymore." While it might make it easier if she wasn't, he truly hoped that wasn't the case. If for nothing else than Analise's sake.

Her body was tense, eyes alight with fury once again. "You kept the fact that I have sisters from me. How could you do that?"

"Analise, we haven't even confirmed that you're Xavier's daughter. Even though I think that's the case, maybe I'm wrong. And if I'm wrong, you'd be far more devastated to think you had sisters and have them ripped away than to just wait a few more days and know for sure. I was only being cautious." It was the truth. He just hoped she'd see the prudence of his decision.

Her eyes flicked to the floor. Bingo. She knew he was right. One bullet dodged. They snapped back to his quickly, anger still very much present.

"Okay, fine. I can agree that you were right to not say anything just yet. But you were wrong to look into my past, Damian. If you wanted to know something, you should have just asked me."

He held her eyes, challenging her. "Would you have answered *anything* I asked?" He saw her waver and again knew he had her. No, she wouldn't have and she couldn't sit here and deny it. At least not honestly.

"Maybe. Maybe not. But you didn't give me that opportunity, did you?"

He stood and walked to the windows. It was a cloudy day in the Boston area and he could see a summer storm rolling in off in the distance. He'd turned his back on her and while she may be tempted to bolt, she wouldn't. She wanted an explanation. And he would give it to her.

"Analise." He spoke toward the window but watched her in its reflection. "I can't even begin to describe to you what it's like for a vampire to find his Moira, his fated one. Every protective instinct I had kicked in when I met you. Hell, before I met you just two short days ago, I had no fucking clue what I was even waiting for. Not only was my imagination of you an enigma, but the real you is as well. You're a mystery, a puzzle, a conundrum that I desperately wanted—*no, needed*—to solve. I want to know the good, the bad, the ugly. The black, the white and the endless shades of gray in between. You have no idea how deliriously happy I am now that you are in my life. You are a soothing balm to my dark soul and if I lose you, it will be irrevocably lost in the burning pits of hell."

He turned around to face Analise, her face rapt with attention, her eyes shone brightly with unshed tears.

"Yes, what I did was wrong. And you're right. I should have given you the benefit of the doubt to tell me your story in your own way in your own time. Life dealt you a shit hand and I was frantic to fix it. I didn't need to have T look into your background to know that. I sensed it from the moment I saw you. One look and I knew that you, my sweet kitten, were broken."

He walked over, sitting on the coffee table across from her, their knees touching. Speaking softly, he hoped she would know the truth of his words. "And how can I know how to put you back together again if I don't know what broke you in the first place?" He felt something wet on his face and, reaching up, discovered it was his own tear.

Analise was full-on sobbing now. He reached for her, but she put her hand up to ward him off. He was gutted. He wanted nothing more at that moment than to comfort the woman he loved. The woman whom *he'd* caused immense pain.

"I am truly sorry. Please forgive me, Analise." Her head hung low, fingers twisting nervously together.

"I can't have children," she whispered. *What?*

She looked up, her watery gaze meeting his. "I can't have children. I thought you should know."

He felt her pain as his own knifing sharply through his heart. He was sure he didn't want to know, but had to ask nonetheless. As long as he had her, he didn't give a damn that she couldn't have kids, but this was a pivotal conversation to the future of their relationship.

"What happened?"

Taking a deep breath she was silent for so long, he didn't think she'd continue. She refused to look at him, so he knew this would be bad. Really bad. *Fuck.* He thought back to what T told him about her being attacked. He forced himself to not react no matter what she told him.

"I was raped when I was eighteen. I was blitzed out of my mind on coke at the time of the attack and thought I had only been stabbed." She laughed bitterly. "*Only* stabbed, right? A guy named Smitty happened upon me and saved me. I would have died if not for him. The doctors wanted to do a rape kit and I refused. Two months later I ended up back in the same ER with an ectopic pregnancy and a lost fallopian tube. They told me the other was severely damaged in the attack and that I wouldn't likely have children."

Savage rage and brutal agony boiled within him. All he saw was a haze of red cloud his vision. He would find those responsible for this senseless attack and he would slowly flay the flesh from their bones before he worked his way from the outside in removing fingers, toes and limbs, taking care to painfully castrate them before pulling a Lorena Bobbit. Then he'd slit them open and gut them like the animals they were, leaving their entrails behind as a warning to all others who would cross his path.

He was so distracted planning every detail of his retribution for what they'd done to his mate that he almost missed what she said next.

"It was my fault."

He could sit still no longer and flew off the table. He was shaking with such fury he didn't trust himself to touch her until he calmed down.

"Analise. Listen to me. Rape is *never* a woman's fault. I don't care the circumstances under which it happened. It. Was. Not. Your. Fault." Then he had a thought.

"Have you ever received counseling for this? Ever talked to anyone?"

She shook her head. So many things came together in that moment. She'd been abandoned by family after family, she'd lived a tough life alone on the streets, only to become a statistic. And she'd almost died. And because of all that, she didn't think she was good enough for him. She still thought herself unworthy. He needed to get her to the shelter for some immediate counseling. As much as he wanted to think he could fix her, he couldn't do it alone. He knew that now.

"Oh, baby." He pulled her into his arms, stiff as a board. She cried into his tee, arms tightly at her sides. "I don't care if you can't have children, Analise. I don't care. All I need is you. And I still love you, no matter what happened in the past." Sobs poured from her, his shirt now soaked with her grief and misplaced guilt. She finally softened and while she didn't wrap her arms around him, she did lean her body into his for support.

Minutes later she stiffened again and he let her go.

"I need some time to think." His heart sunk, his dreams crushing under the heavy weight of it. After all he'd said it didn't matter. She was going to leave him anyway.

Because they were fated, their bodies may crave each other, but that didn't mean she had to love him. She had to give that gift freely. Raw possessiveness roared through him. He would *not* let her go. No matter her decision. He would spend eternity earning her forgiveness and getting her to admit her love for him. No, he would not let her go, but he would give her time to think.

"Fair enough. But you'll stay here. I'll leave for a couple hours. I have some things to take care of anyway." He didn't, as he'd worked his ass off earlier getting his business done so he could spend the day making love to her. When he leaned in to kiss her lips she turned her head away. *Fuck me.* He made his way to the front door, talking to Sebastian before turning back to Analise.

"Please don't leave the penthouse, kitten. You're not a prisoner here, but you are still very much in danger and I'd prefer you here where you are safe." She nodded slightly. He pinned her eyes with his. "We are meant for each other and you know it. Don't throw it away because I made a foolish mistake with honorable intentions. I meant it when I told you I would always protect you and your heart. You may not always agree with my methods, but anything I do is out of my intense love for you and absolute need to make you happy."

Without another look back, he walked out, leaving her to her thoughts. He only hoped he wasn't making the biggest mistake of his life by giving her space. Analise was her own worst enemy and right now she could talk herself out of the Hope Diamond if she tried hard enough.

Chapter 33

Analise

The second Damian closed the door she knew she'd made a mistake. She sagged into the couch in despair. She was hard wired to vet the bad in people. It'd been engrained day after day, year after year until it was now second nature. Can't teach an old dog new tricks? That phrase was coined after her. Her mind wandered to a time long ago.

Why are you taking me back there? "Because I can't afford the food you shovel in your mouth." She would eat less next time.

Why can't I stay? "Sorry, kiddo. My kids don't like you." She'd be quieter next time.

I don't understand why you won't keep me. "Because you're an unlovable, ungrateful brat." She'd heard it enough, so it must be true.

"Sorry kiddo. You'll be fine. I'm sure you'll find a great family." I'm sorry. I'll do better. I promise. She wasn't fine and she never found a great family.

Reject, reject, reject. So she did the only thing she could to emotionally survive. *Protect, protect, protect.* Brick after brick she built her castle, complete with reinforced steel doors, armored guards and a moat. And she hid in the corner of the deep, dark dungeon so no one would find her. Where she was safe.

Then she met Damian. And in a matter of minutes, the guards disappeared, the moat evaporated and the mortar began to crumble under the burdensome weight of her loneliness. She was left unprotected, vulnerable and scared shitless. Damian had woven a sensual spell around her that she couldn't escape. If she were honest with herself, she'd been looking for a way out since the very first second they'd met and at the first inkling of duplicity, she dove head first out the door. Literally.

But his challenge held true and that stung. If he'd asked, she wouldn't have told him the truth about her past. Hell to the no. As far as she was concerned, that door was locked, the key long lost. The harder he pushed to know her, the harder she leaned against the door, afraid the rusty lock would shatter under his pressure.

His explanation about her sisters made logical sense. Of course, he wouldn't tell her anything until her DNA was verified. No need to pile crushing disappointment on top of crushing disappointment. She should have confronted him instead of assuming the worst and trying to run. She ran so hard and fast from people one would think she was an ultra-marathoner. Sadly, her butt and thighs didn't reflect her efforts.

She was a fool's fool. She'd felt Damian's love in every command, every question, every action. She didn't know this man at all, yet she did to the bottom of her soul. She trusted him, as was evident by the fact she'd spilled her deepest, most shameful secret. She'd never told another living soul the entire truth of that horrible night and subsequent weeks, not even Beth.

Randomly, one of her favorite songs, "Mirrors", popped into her head. Who translated feelings and emotions into a song better than Justin Timberlake? Damian was her mirror. Her soul reflected back when she looked into his eyes. Two damaged souls that, by themselves, were full of cracks and crevices, but when overlaid on the other, all cracks vanished like they'd never existed and all crevices now overflowed with bursting love.

She thought back to the words Damian spoke which simultaneously destroyed and repaired her heart. *"And how can I know how to put you back together again if I don't know what broke you in the first place?"* No one had ever spoken sweeter words. And then she sent him away. Bitter tears bit at her eyes at the horrible mistake she'd just made.

Suddenly, she felt exhausted, even at this early hour. She was so very tired of the heavy burden she'd been carrying around by herself. She was a snowball rolling downhill, fresh snow hitching a ride until it became unwieldy and out of control, unstoppable. Everyone jumped out of the way or risked being crushed. But not Damian. Damian stepped directly in front of the raging snowball and under his command it'd melted.

She lay on the couch and let sleep pull her under, praying when she woke that Damian would be there, holding her in his arms and able to forgive her incessant need to push people away.

It was time to stop running in the wrong direction.

ഌ൫ൄ

She was there again. In the same room Beth occupied last time. Only it was empty. Blood stained the thin, flat, pale yellow mattress. There was a bucket in the corner she hadn't seen before. Feces floated on top of yellow liquid. *Oh God.* She felt like vomiting, adding to the putrid mixture. Could she vomit in her dreams too? She didn't want to find out.

She wondered what to do next. Would she be able to leave this room? What went on in this horrid place? How many others were here?

Frustrated, she closed her eyes and visualized herself outside this room, but it didn't work. What good was being half vampire, half witch if she didn't have any goddamn powers! She'd have to talk to Damian about that.

Suddenly she remembered her dreams of her mother.

"Concentrate Analise," demanded Mara. "Everything here is simply energy and you are the conduit. You control it. It bends to your will and only your will. You want a fire? Start a damn fire. You want that candle lit? Make it so. If that oak tree is in your way, don't go around it, move it instead. You are powerful. You are commanding."

She had moved objects with her mind in her dreams with Mara. Countless times. At first it was the smallest of things. A pencil, a feather, a piece of paper. Over the years, they gradually increased the complexity of her tasks until she was moving houses, starting raging fires and digging holes thousands of feet deep.

Could she do it here too? There were only two objects with which she could try. The bucket in the corner, doubling as a toilet, and the thin mattress that lay on the hard floor. The mattress was the safer play. Listening to her mother's words, she closed her eyes, visualizing the mattress lifting just an inch or two off the cold cement floor. When she opened them, she nearly laughed out loud with joy.

Hovering in front of her was the mattress, but nearly a foot off the ground. The doorknob turning caused her to lose control and the mattress flopped back to the ground with a soft thud. Oh God, she hoped the person on the other side hadn't heard.

In walked an undeniably gorgeous, but monstrous vampire, an unconscious Beth in his arms. Oddly, he laid her carefully on the mattress and pressed a reverent, lingering kiss on her forehead before turning to leave, whispering that she'd be okay. After he was gone, she called Beth's name but there was no response. She concentrated, hearing Beth's soft breathing and the blood pumping through her veins. The last part freaked her the hell out, which was her last thought before she was ripped from her dream.

She lay there for several minutes reflecting on what had just happened. In her dreams, she was powerful. In her dreams, she had control. In her dreams maybe, just maybe, she could help Beth herself. But *how*?

Sitting up she looked around the living room, disappointment made her heart sink. No sign of Damian. The clock showed that it was only ten thirty. Damian had been gone only an hour, but it felt like days. If she knew his number, she'd call begging him to return. She supposed she could ask Sebastian, who was probably dutifully stationed outside the door.

Opening the door, two large vampires stood there, blankly gazing down at her. Neither of them was Sebastian. "How can I help you, ma'am?" Biggie one asked.

"I ... I was just looking for Sebastian," she mumbled.

"He'll be back shortly, ma'am."

"Oh. Okay. Thanks." She quickly shut the door. And then locked it for good measure. *Like a locked door would keep a vampire out, Analise.*

To kill time, she decided to shower. She needed one anyway after two rounds of deliciously hot sex. Making her way back up to the master bathroom, she stripped out of her dirty clothes, and eventually stepped under the hot spray of the largest shower she'd ever been in. There were eight showerheads hitting her in all directions. It had taken her five minutes to figure out how to use them and adjust the water temperature. She'd managed to practically scald her skin off at one point. Who knew she'd need a damn owner's manual to work a shower, for God's sake?

She lingered for nearly half an hour, enjoying the feel of the massaging jets on her shoulders and back. After toweling off, she decided she had no choice but to dig into some of the clothes that Damian had somehow procured for her. She felt uncomfortable wearing such expensive things, but it was either that or run around naked, and while the thought of sitting in her birthday suit on the buttery couch waiting patiently for Damian to return sounded somewhat appealing, she didn't dare in case someone else walked through the door instead. Like Sebastian.

She picked a beautiful lavender billowy sundress and a strappy pair of nude wedges. Underneath she wore a deep purple push-up bra and matching thong. Seemed like whoever had purchased her lingerie had a thing for thongs since that was all she had to choose from. How one small scrap of fabric could cost so much damn money, she couldn't fathom. It looked like Damian had enough of it to waste, though, given the size and splendor of his place.

She made the bed and tidied the room before heading downstairs. So sue her, she liked to get into a nice tight bed every night. Since Damian was still a no-show, she rummaged through the kitchen and found some bread and peanut butter. Having had so many PB and J sandwiches as a kid, peanut butter wasn't her favorite, but it would have to do since his selection was limited. She couldn't even find coffee. *Ugh.* Who didn't own coffee? That was sacrilege.

All the while she'd been performing these mundane tasks, she'd thought about everything that'd happened since she'd met Damian. She knew some of it had to be verified yet, but Damian seemed so sure, she believed it to be true.

One. She now knew her parents' identities. Her father was a self-absorbed psychotic vampire who kidnapped young women and was apparently on the hunt for her. And her mother slash guardian angel was a very powerful, but very dead, witch who'd been teaching her magic in her dreams. And here she'd thought *she* was the fucked up one. *Was that a white rabbit that just ran by?*

Two. She also had other family. She had at least an aunt, Maeve, and possibly two half-sisters. She smiled. She'd never had a *real* family before. Her smile quickly turned into a frown when she remembered that she and her sisters were all in danger from daddy dearest. *Lovely.*

Three. She was half vampire, half witch and something rare called a dreamwalker. And even more rare apparently, a dreamwalker who could interact with those people she dreamt about. As soon as she stepped out of the twilight zone, maybe she could wrap her head around this one.

Four. Your destiny awaits. She'd met a Vampire Lord, not the one she'd been looking for, mind you, but the one she was destined to find. Who claimed to be her fated one. It was more than a claim ... her mind, body and soul knew it was true. Instead of revulsion, his touch sent comfort, pleasure, joy and ecstasy through her entire being. As unrealistic as it sounded, she was already in love with him. He was it for her. *Sigh*.

When Analise was nine, Jana and Frank had taken her to the Eau Claire County fair. She'd never been to a fair before and she'd never forget the smell of fried food or cow manure. Not a pleasant combination when you're nine. If she thought hard enough, the smell still lingered in her nostrils today. Jana spoiled her rotten, buying her cotton candy, caramel apples and funnel cakes.

When she spied a ride called the Zipper, she begged Jana to go on it with her. Jana tried telling her she'd had too much to eat, but Analise was unrelenting. Finally, Jana gave in and took her on the ride, much to her regret. The Zipper was an egg-shaped cage that spun relentlessly for the entire ninety seconds they were trapped in it. Even though Jana held her hand the entire time whispering words of comfort, those were the longest ninety seconds of her life and of course, she was sicker than a dog after they'd been released from their steel prison. Someone would have to hold her at gunpoint before she'd ever get on another ride.

But that was kind of how she felt now. She felt like she'd been forced onto an out of control carnival ride from which she couldn't escape and the only person grounding her in all of this mayhem was Damian. So here she stood, hoping her anchor would come back to her after she'd so foolishly asked him to leave.

She finished her crumbly toast, now like paste on her tongue, cleaned up her mess and settled back on the couch to wait. Wait for the man who had turned her world upside down in such a small amount of time. Her mate, her anchor. Her destiny.

Chapter 34

Xavier

"There is no sign of the girl or the other lords, my lord. I scouted the place last evening, but everyone is pretty buttoned up. They are all very loyal to Devon."

Mother. Fucker.

"Did you at least hear specifically when Devon would return?" He had to ruin all that Devon had built before he returned. But more importantly Xavier wanted to get his hands on his daughters.

"Only that it would be a few weeks yet, my lord."

"Okay, you know the plan. Keep frequenting the place until a lord shows up. Then you know what to do."

Silence greeted him and he knew the problem. "You've taken quite a shine to one of our girls, I've noticed." Xavier turned and poured himself a tumbler of his favorite scotch.

"I want her." Geoffrey shrugged, trying, but failing, to play it cool. His fighting stance and coiled muscles belying his cool demeanor.

"And there's nothing more to it than that? You just ... *want* her." Xavier took a sip of Dalmore and sighed. Bliss.

"Yes," Geoffrey replied stonily. Lies. He should cut off his fucking head right now.

Xavier watched him quietly. This really was an unfortunate turn of events, but one he would work to his advantage. Geoffrey's skills were invaluable and he really did not want to lose him. Not at this stage of the war. Fine, he'd let him have his plaything. That was the least he could do to reward such a loyal servant.

"The female will not be touched again." If one hadn't been as observant as Xavier, one would have missed the subtle way Geoffrey's muscles relaxed. Geoffrey was ready for a fight and that could only mean one thing.

"Return to Milwaukee to complete the mission. I don't think I need to tell you not to disappoint me, Geoffrey. I certainly can't guarantee this female's *safety* otherwise."

Geoffrey's lips thinned in fury. "Of course, my lord."

Xavier relaxed. Sated from last night's events, he savored his drink. There was a slight chance this plan of his would backfire and he'd lose the best lieutenant he'd had in many decades anyway. However, there was a better chance this plan *would* work ... at least for one of his objectives. Geoffrey was strong and possessed a skill that he didn't think the lords were aware of.

Xavier hadn't a clue where Devon had moved his operation and he'd been looking for a replacement witch since he'd worked the last one into the ground. Literally. Six feet under. Yes, for now this was the best, and only, course of action.

Besides, what better way to undermine the enemy than from the inside?

Chapter 35

Damian

He hadn't expected to be away from Analise this long, but the moment he'd walked out the door he knew exactly where he was headed. To Eau Claire, Wisconsin in search of one human male named Smitty, resident of Gibson and Main. He would track down the fuckers that had so horrifically violated his Analise and make them pay.

It took him over an hour to locate this Smitty person. And he was surprised to find he was one of the biggest, blackest humans he'd ever come across. He could see how this man had saved Analise's life. He'd scare the fuck out of any human.

Smitty was quite cooperative, only too happy to help him track down the vermin that were responsible. Only two of the five still breathed the same oxygen as his precious mate. One died of pneumonia, one was shot in a drive by, gang related, and the last was recently found beaten to death in an alley. That was a far kinder death than any of them deserved. He wanted to resurrect the animals so he could torture and kill them again. Painfully and repeatedly.

Instead, he now stood in an abandoned warehouse—as luck would have it the same one where they'd held Analise—with fuckheads one and two tied tightly to stainless steel chairs. Marco and T had happily agreed to accompany him on his quest to put every one of these scum in the ground.

While one of their basic laws was not to kill humans, these two animals in front of him could hardly be considered human. Damian was one of the few vampires that had the ability to sift memories and the depraved things these vermin had done deserved an eternity of endlessly burning in the fiery pits of hell. And even that was more than they deserved. But before they sent them to an eternity of fire, he was making their last few hours hell on earth.

As vampires, although most appreciated the female taste, they weren't too terribly picky on human blood, however his lips would never touch such foulness. Instead, it pooled on the floor in dark puddles around their feet; its coppery tang repulsed him. While this had been cathartic, he was ready to finish and get home to Analise. And make it clear to her that she was not leaving him. *Ever.*

Making one final deep slit from ear to ear, the three of them flashed out of there, leaving the humans to painfully bleed out. They'd flashed to Devon's so he could clean and change into fresh clothes before returning to Analise.

Once cleaned, he flashed back to his Boston penthouse. He was the only one who could flash in and out, but instead of going inside, he wanted to check in with Sebastian first. When he appeared, his men had already assumed a fighting stance. He knew he was right to put them on Analise's protection team. They would guard her life as their own.

"My lord." Sebastian nodded, relaxing slightly.

"How is she? Has she tried to leave?" Damian knew Sebastian wouldn't let her leave, but he'd been gone so long he wouldn't put an attempt past her.

"No, my lord. She came out shortly after you'd left asking for me, but I was checking a potential security breach downstairs and Raymond was in my stead. She never returned so I don't know what she wanted."

Huh? He opened the front door to an empty room, but it took him all of two seconds to pinpoint where she was.

Standing in the doorway to his office, he watched his love with fascination. Of everything she could be doing in there, she was reading yesterday's *Wall Street Journal*. She looked intrigued by an article and hadn't noticed him standing there, drinking her in.

Living up to his asshole reputation, he'd planned to storm in there and forbid her from leaving. She'd given herself to him already and he'd made it clear that once she did that, there was no turning back. She was his. Forever.

But first he wanted to memorize every feature of her face. Her perfectly shaped brows were pinched together, causing several wrinkles in her forehead. Long, dark lashes framed her hazel eyes as they quickly scanned the paper. Her pert nose crinkled slightly as teeth chewed on her full bottom lip, which was glazed in a light pink gloss. She had absolutely no idea how incredibly beautiful she was. Inside and out.

"How long do you plan on staring at me?" she asked, eyes never leaving the paper. He couldn't help the laugh that escaped him. She was spectacular.

"Until I get my fill. I've been away from you about five hours too long." True that. If it were up to him, he'd never have left in the first place. They'd be naked and probably trying out their fourth room by now. He wanted her in every room, on every surface of his home. *Their* home.

She finally looked at him, her irritation clear. "Where have you been? You said you'd be gone only a couple hours." He was enjoying her perusal of him from head to toe, until the next words came out of her mouth. "And why are you wearing different clothes?"

"I'm not letting you leave, kitten." When in doubt, divert.

She sat back in his oversized leather office chair, crossing her arms, letting a smirk turn up her gorgeous lips. "Is that so?"

What he heard instead was *I'm staying*. He'd already known that the moment he saw her sitting in his office reading the paper, like she was simply waiting for him to return home from a hard day at the office.

"Come here, kitten." She sat stock still holding his gaze, clearly trying to decide how she was going to play this little game she'd started.

"We need to talk, Damian." Disobedience it was then.

"Analise, I asked you to come here." He'd been away from her too goddamned long and he wasn't going to waste any more time talking. At least not with his mouth. Well, not with *words*, anyway.

"One, you didn't ask, you demanded. And two, we're not fucking until we talk. End of."

In an instant, he was nose-to-nose, leaning over the chair that dwarfed her small frame. "Let's get one thing straight, kitten. I am not going to *fuck* you. Not this time anyway. I'm going to *make love.* To. My. Moira. End of." He closed the small distance between them and, never breaking eye contact, gently took her lower lip in between his, biting down softly until she moaned, closing her eyes. He repeated the same process with her upper, tasting the fruitiness of her gloss. The muskiness of her arousal filled his nostrils and his dick throbbed with the frantic need to be inside her.

He pulled away and she groaned her protest. The thought of taking her in his office rolled like a movie reel in his head. He imagined her over his desk with her ass high in the air. The thought of her naked on his couch or riding him in his chair almost made him abandon his original plans. But not today. Today he had other plans. For making her *his*. Permanently.

Without a word he held out his hand and she hesitated only momentarily before taking it. He ushered her into the living room and started the fireplace with only a thought. Yes, it was June and yes, it was blasting hot in Boston in summer, but for what he had in mind, he wanted the ambiance of a roaring fire, even in the middle of the day. Because he was not going to wait one fucking minute longer for this.

"Sit." He gestured toward the couch. Once again, she hesitated but did as he'd requested, demanded. Whatever. He flashed to the bedroom and returned quickly, arms filled to the brim with pillows and the plush comforter. He situated them all in front of, but not too close to, the fire.

"Damian, what are you doing?" Her voice shook slightly as she spoke. Once again, she was an open book, her emotions clearly written all over her face.

She was shy.

She was nervous.

She was hesitant.

But she was also excited and confident this was their destiny. Her eyes were alight with desire and, dare he hope ... *love?*

He momentarily ignored her question as he set about his last preparatory task. Love of music was one of the many things they shared and he knew how to pick the perfect song to display his feelings. Maybe it was a pussy thing, but he didn't give a shit. It made her happy and that was all that mattered. When he'd picked the perfect song, he walked slowly toward her, holding out his hand for hers. This time there was no hesitation as he gently helped her to her feet and walked to the center of the room.

"I'm making you mine, Analise," he whispered as he took her in his arms.

Chapter 36

Analise

She fought to hold it together when Damian wrapped his arms around her just as John Legend's "All of Me" began playing. All thoughts of talking had completely vanished. *I'm making you mine, Analise* played on a continuous loop through her head, the words comforting yet frightening. Her heart beat double time and her stomach was in knots.

She knew Damian well enough already to know that he didn't pick this song without intention. John Legend may be singing, but it was Damian speaking. He accepted her the way she was, imperfections and all. He knew placing her heart in his hands was the hardest thing she could imagine doing, yet here she was doing it anyway. She was ready to skydive out of a plane five thousand feet above the earth and he would be there to catch her wherever she landed. And did she mention she was terrified of heights?

His gaze was supernova intense and she couldn't have looked away if the whole damn place burned down around them. They swayed slowly, bodies moving as one, completely in tune with each other.

"You want to be mine, Analise." It wasn't a question. It was a statement. And it was true. Damian had known from the moment he'd come back she'd decided to stay, even though he was arrogant enough not to bother asking. That should piss her off, but for some reason all she felt was relief. Relief that he still wanted her, even though she was hesitant only a few short hours ago. For even though he'd done nothing to the contrary, she was worried he'd change his mind and think she wasn't worth the effort.

Damian had bared his soul every time he spoke to her. He'd not held back one speck of emotion, unlike her. And it was time for that to end.

"Yes," she replied softly, but confidently. "I give you all of me, Damian." His face, already taut with lust, now looked razor sharp. His eyes, already bright with desire, bathed her in his light, his warmth, his love. His arms, already tightly wound around her, crushed her so tightly she could barely breathe. And his mouth, hovering just millimeters above hers finally crashed down, taking ownership of hers.

She wound her hands in his inky hair, holding him fast to her lips as they ate at each other. His hands were all over her now, cupping her ass, her breasts. His mouth broke from hers, kissing and suckling down her neck. His teeth scraped her collarbone, causing her to inhale sharply. She turned her head to allow him better access, causing him to hiss.

"Fuck, Analise, I want you so much," he growled.

"Yes. I'm yours." She wanted to be his more than her next breath. She ran her hands over his biceps, his back and down to cup his buns of steel. This was the first time she'd been allowed to touch them and damn if she didn't want to spend an entire day just worshipping his fine ass.

He pulled away, taking a few steps back. Disappointed, she'd come to expect this from Damian. As much as she didn't like to be touched, he must abhor it for she hadn't been allowed yet to touch him. Every time she'd tried, he'd secure her hands somehow or distract her in other ways.

But that was going to end today. If they were going to be each other's forever, she would be allowed to touch him. She'd been dying to map his body with her mouth, her lips, her tongue. She wanted to explore and trace every tattoo and he hadn't allowed her proper access to his very fine physique yet. She wanted his cock in her mouth, his pleasure under her complete control.

"Take off your clothes," she demanded.

"No, kitten. That's not how this will work," Damian chuckled. "And as fan-fucking-tastic as that dress looks on you, right now it will look better on the floor."

"Damian, I want to touch you. You haven't let me touch you yet." Her whiney five-year-old alter ego had returned, stomping her feet and flailing her small body.

"Oh, I know what you want to do to me, Analise. You want to map my body with your mouth, your lips and your tongue. You want to suck my cock and just thinking about that makes me want to blow." Was he mocking her?

"No, I'm not mocking you, Analise, but I can't give up control in the bedroom. It's not in my nature." He was serious.

"I'm not asking you to give up control, Damian. I can accept that part of you." She wouldn't verbally admit to liking it, although she very much did and he knew it. "But I can't accept never touching my mate. That's not in *my* nature."

They regarded each other silently, the sexually charged moment now morphing into something else entirely. She felt like she was in a cowboy showdown, dusky, dry dirt swirling around them as they stood in the middle of a run-down town, guns drawn, neither one backing down. They were on the precipice of something more profound than just vampire bonding. The future of their entire relationship stood precariously in the balance because of this one simple request.

Damian sighed and dropped his head, hands now on his hips. He looked so damned beautiful in his black denim jeans and white T-shirt, stretched taut across his beefy chest. Her mouth watered at the thought of doing all the things she wanted. All the things Damian had been denying her.

"Why won't you let me touch you, Damian?" She had a pretty damn good idea, but she wanted him to tell her. She hoped that would the first step to moving past it.

"Analise," he growled.

She closed the physical gap he'd created between them. She could only pray he'd close the emotional one. She knew that she wanted to bond with him more than anything she'd ever wanted, but couldn't do it with this one last black cloud forever hanging over them.

"Damian, please. I'm not asking to tie you up. I simply want to touch what's mine. You can't deny me that."

His face turned hard, all desire now replaced with anger. "I sure as fuck can."

For the second time today, devastation nearly crushed her. Whoever said that words couldn't hurt you was full of complete bullshit. Words were the sharpest, most hurtful weapons man possessed. Her heart physically ached. She was a pretty fucked up person. She admitted it. Human touch sent her cowering in fear. Trust was simply a pretty word steeped in lies. Love was a fool's paradise. But she was here, willing to try putting all her fucked-upedness aside. For him. And he wasn't willing to do the same. And she simply couldn't live with that.

She turned and walked toward the bay of windows that lined the east side of Damian's penthouse. The view of the harbor was clear today and she marveled at its beauty. She'd been landlocked her entire life, never really understanding the allure of the ocean. She loved it already. And this was the last time she'd look at it before she returned to her lonely, solitary life in Eau Claire. Hopefully, Damian would honor his word and still help find Beth.

"I can't be with you, Damian. I have to go," she whispered. The words tasted bitter and foreign on her tongue, the truth of them as painful as being flayed with a butter knife. Girlish fantasies of how this day would end were now weighted down with sadness and emptiness. She was right when she'd thought loving and losing Damian DiStephano would destroy her. She felt obliterated. Completely annihilated. Worthless.

She remained with her back to him, unable to look at him for fear she'd crumble, pushing aside something that meant so much to her. No. She wouldn't be able to look upon his face ever again.

"I hope you honor your word to help me find—" She didn't get to finish her sentence before she was whipped around and pressed against the cold glass by one angry vampire. She didn't have to look at his face to know he was pissed. She felt the anger emanating from him. *Don't look at him, don't look at him* she chanted to herself repeatedly. And that might have worked, had he not grabbed her chin firmly between his finger and thumb and lifted it so her gaze was forced to meet his.

"I thought I'd already made it clear that you were mine, Analise." Anguish, anger and determination caused several rows of deep wrinkles to crease his forehead.

"This isn't a dictatorship," she quipped. *Oh, Analise, you stupid, stupid girl.* You don't goad the shark with fresh chum in the water and expect to swim away in one piece.

Damian smirked, but it was laced with piquant, and for the first time in his presence, she felt a tiny twinge of fear. He was a dominating, formidable male who was also a Vampire Lord. Which meant people didn't tell him no. Or if they did, they regretted it pretty damn fast. And that was about the place where she was.

"Oh, kitten. You're so very wrong there. This may be America, but we vampires don't live by the old U. S. of A. democratic rules. We very much live in a fucking dictatorship and here ... *I'm* the motherfucking king."

Anger, her very best friend, returned with a raging vengeance. No way was she backing down now.

Bring.

It.

On.

Fang.

Boy.

"You're a fucking asshole."

"Unoriginal." He ran his nose along the underside of her jaw, inhaling deeply. As usual, her hands were held immobile above her head in one of his. His other hand palmed her bare ass, courtesy of the skimpy thong she'd worn. Déjà vu hit and she remembered a similar position just a few days ago in Dragonfly's office.

"Damian, stop." Perhaps it would have worked better if she'd put more conviction behind her hollow words. She had to get out of there before her resolve completely crumbled like a rotted out piece of wood.

"Analise, I know you don't want to go." When he nipped her earlobe her core flooded with desire. Damn him and his irresistible allure.

"I can't think when you're doing that," she breathed.

"That's the point, kitten," he groaned as he ground his steely shaft into her stomach while continuing his sensual assault on the other side of her neck now. He knew exactly the right spot that drove her insane. His free hand now reached behind her and began pulling down the zipper on her dress.

She decided to take a different tactic. If she continued down this path, she'd end up bonding with Damian without resolving this wedge he'd unconsciously put between them. Then she'd have no way out.

"I know it's because of the witches." It worked. His hands and mouth froze and his body, seconds ago strained with lust was now vibrating with restrained fury.

"We are not having this conversation, Analise." He released her, turned and walked toward the fireplace, muscles rigid. She felt cold and bereft. Abandoned.

As hard as it was for Damian to talk about his past, he'd done it. *For her.* Now it was her turn. If she couldn't return the trust in kind, she had no business standing before this man asking him to peel back his last layer of protection. She'd never felt more vulnerable than she did right now and she'd felt plenty vulnerable over the last few days.

"My earliest memory of a foster home was when I was five, but that was already my fourth home." She had to force herself not to turn back toward the window. Nothing would be gained if they both had their backs to each other. "The Farbers. That family had eleven foster children ranging from seventeen to me. I was the youngest. I'd heard that the babies of the family usually have it easier, but that's not quite how it worked out for me. I became the older children's plaything instead."

At that, Damian turned around to face her and she fought to hold his penetrating gaze. This was so much harder than she'd thought it would be. She could get through it, though. She could. Those experiences made her strong, invincible.

She'd often wondered how the foster system could be so vile, so broken. Sure, she'd known kids who were placed with loving parents, who were later adopted, who grew up in really great homes. She'd just never been that lucky and now she had to wonder if it was for a reason. As if she was meant to live that life in part for Damian. For this very second.

"My bed was a blanket on the floor in one of the bedroom closets, which they locked at night so I wouldn't wander around. I couldn't go to the bathroom. I was a bed wetter and would often wake up lying in my own urine. When that happened, my punishment was spending the day locked in the same closet with no food. They wouldn't let me change my clothes or my bedding."

Damian looked horrified. Her stomach churned with the need to purge the vileness of her memories.

"They didn't keep me more than a few months. The next foster home wasn't much better. They had two foster kids in addition to their three. Food was scarce and I'd already lost quite a bit of weight from the last place and was very unhealthy. I became pretty sick and they dropped me off at the emergency room, never to return. It took a few months to place me again. I think CPS decided they'd better get me well before farming me out again."

Damian began walking toward, but she held up her hand, stopping him short. She couldn't do this if he was touching her. His face had completely morphed to one of sympathy, pain and agony.

"I went through a couple more homes before being placed with Jana and Frank. I loved them and they loved me. At least Jana did. I had a room all my own, decorated in pink." Damian's eyes shined with the understanding of why she'd freaked out about the pink room at the shelter. "Jana treated me like a real daughter. She let me help her cook and grocery shop. She bought me toys, clothes and books. I was placed with them when I was eight and Jana died of cancer when I was ten. Frank couldn't handle her death and sent me back to the system." To hell on earth.

"Let's just say my next few homes were not quite so loving. The last foster home I was in before I decided to stick my middle finger up to the system was the worst. Eric and Lillian Greenbreier. Eric had everyone fooled. By then I had a pretty healthy set of girls and a lean, but curvy, body. And Eric noticed."

Damian now radiated with nearly uncontrollable rage, but she knew it wasn't directed at her. She could barely get the words out, but she'd come this far.

"His wife worked nights at the hospital. She was an emergency room nurse. Eric took the opportunity when she was gone to visit my bed. I tried to fight him off, but he was a cop. He was strong, he was armed and he was a sadistic bastard. I knew the second CPS pulled up to their house that I would be in trouble there. I begged them to take me back that it wasn't the right home for me, but they wouldn't listen. I was in hell for three months before I had a chance to escape. Eric kept pretty close tabs on me so it was hard. He took me to and from school. Wouldn't let me spend time with friends. Finally at Christmastime there was a party at the hospital that his wife made them attend. Adults only. So I grabbed the extra cash I could find in the house and a few extra sets of clothes and took off. I didn't return to CPS or they would have just shipped me back there, so I had no choice but to live on the streets.

"Since he was a cop and I was now living on the streets, I had to take care to avoid him. He saw me one time, but I hid in an alley dumpster until he left. I fought to survive, falling into a life of drugs and well ... you know the rest."

The fight to hold back the waterworks failed miserably. They now stood only a foot apart, but it felt like the Grand Canyon. Damian was clearly struggling to control his emotions as well.

"So you see, Damian, I was a prisoner myself. Only I was a prisoner of the foster system versus a coven of witches. I know all about pain and suffering. I know all about dark and hate. And I know all about how abhorrent another's touch can be."

She finally closed the distance between them and laid her hand on his chest, which was heaving up and down with the effort to stay back and respect her space. She gazed lovingly into his molten eyes before continuing.

"You are the only being alive whose touch I can bear. You are the only person I trust with my heart, with my life. You were right when you said we are the light to each other's darkness. I am nothing without you. I am dead inside without your warmth. You were also right when you said I didn't want to go. I don't. The thought of never seeing you again is far worse than anything I have been through. I love you and I want to be your mate, but will you return the same trust I've placed in you? Will you let me heal you, just as you have done for me?" What she really meant was *please, will you let me touch you?*

"Jesus, Analise," he mumbled, wrapping his arms around her waist and putting his forehead to hers. He closed his eyes, breathing deeply. "I'll try," he breathed, barely above a whisper. "For you, I'll try."

Chapter 37

Mike

They'd searched all day for the body of Frankie Durillo. He'd checked in with Giselle several times, directing her to other remote spots she should scout, but both of them came up short. They'd decided to check out the club first and Giselle confirmed there was indeed a faint scent of blood in Frankie's office. They'd been to Frankie's house, which was a smelly pigsty, and no sign of him.

The guy had the biggest stash of porn he'd ever seen though. At least it was adult ... that he could tell. He wouldn't have been a bit surprised to log onto his computer and find some kiddy shit stashed in a folder or bookmarked on Bing. Magazines and videos lined his living and bedroom floors. He'd found several male sex toys in the pervert's nightstand drawer and even a fucking blow up doll in his closet. Who looked like she was real, for fuck's sake. It was creepy. If he did happen to find Frankie alive, he might beat the shit out him on principle alone. Jesus, just buy a hooker for the night, dude.

When he'd talked to Giselle throughout the day, it was strained. They'd decided to call it quits and she said she'd update Damian, so he headed home where he now sat in the back on the slab of concrete he called a patio, a cold bottle of Miller in hand.

He stared at his lawn, almost so long it was seeding. His bushes were out of control, not having been trimmed since last spring. His neighbor would probably call in a complaint on him pretty soon. He should just hire the shit done. It's not like Devon wasn't paying him enough for his gopher services. Yeah, he'd get on that. Tomorrow. He finished his beer and grabbed another cold one from the cooler he'd brought out with him.

As hard as he tried, he couldn't get Giselle out of his head. The feel of her lips on his skin. The electricity zinging through his blood at the first scrape of her teeth. He could still feel her on his lap, his body pressed close to hers. He'd never been so close to ejaculating outside of a woman's body before, even in his prepubescent years. He'd given up trying to fight this mysterious attraction to her and decided to just accept it and see where it ended up.

As he'd had time to reflect today, he realized he'd overreacted at her vacillation earlier. Giselle had been through something traumatic. Something she hadn't yet come to terms with so she could begin the healing process. Yes, he was a fucking a hypocrite. He'd been in a self-induced living hell for eleven years, ever since Jamie went missing. Maybe it was time to pull himself out of the quicksand he'd been willingly stuck in and turn his sorry life around. God knows if he wanted to be any good for *any* woman, he needed to get his own shit together. His bitterness and anger and vengeance were a burning, heavy weight on his soul.

Yes, Mike Thatcher was going to make a change. Be a better man. Be a better citizen. Be a better neighbor. He downed his beer and went into the garage, gassed up the mower and started on the front lawn.

It wasn't lost on him that the very species that turned his life to shit so very many years ago had also been the inspiration he needed to pull it back together.

Chapter 38

Damian

He was sweating fucking bullets. His gut felt like it was on fire. If he didn't know better, he'd think he was getting sick, but vampires didn't get sick. Ever. He'd had plenty of gashes, cuts and burns and those hurt like a mother, but he'd healed quickly. He had never known what it was like to have a cold or a sore throat. Or what it felt like to be diagnosed with something as horrific as cancer, which killed you slowly from the inside out. And he'd had no damn idea what heart palpitations felt like ... until this very moment. Even in captivity he hadn't felt like this.

But he'd told Analise he would try and he would. For her. For *them*. He wanted nothing more than to throw her on the makeshift bed he'd made for them in front of the roaring fire and make her his. But he had to get through this first.

So as he lay down naked on the bed he'd made for Analise, he watched her slowly strip out of her clothes. She was getting quite good at that. She looked fucking amazing in that purple dress, but the lingerie underneath ... wow, come to daddy. He would have to remember to thank Katrina personally.

"Leave the lingerie." He looked down at the wedges that framed her ruby red painted toes. "And the shoes." It would be easier for him if she had at least some clothing on. Then he could look forward to removing it when she was done with her exploration.

She slowly sauntered toward him and, with trim legs on either side of his hips, lowered herself on his lap over his rock hard erection. The thin barrier of her panties was the only thing keeping his cock from entering her, which it wanted to do of its own accord. Fucker was twitching like mad. Maybe she should be naked. Maybe he'd be better able to handle her touch if he was setting a punishing rhythm with his dick inside her, taking his mind off of what her hands would be doing.

Jesus. *This was a supremely bad idea, Damian.* He hadn't let a woman touch him in hundreds of years. He hadn't been on his back at a woman's mercy since he'd lain on a cold dirt floor, shackled to a wall. His heart raced, feeling it reverberate in his fingers and toes. His stomach clenched and he thought he might actually vomit.

"I'll go slow," she whispered softly. Sade played through the ceiling speakers and her syrupy voice serenaded them in the background. He thought he might actually be on the verge of a panic attack. He needed to get his breathing under control. *Concentrate on the music, Damian.* Closing his eyes at her first tentative touch, he couldn't help but flinch. She immediately pulled back.

"Damian, are you okay?" He nodded, not opening his eyes. "Damian, look at me, please." He cracked one eye, deeply ashamed at his reaction to his Moira's touch.

"We can do this another time, it's okay." She moved to get up and he grabbed her hips, firmly pulling her back to his lap.

"No. Stay. I *need* to do this, kitten." As much as he didn't *want* to do this, he did *need* to. But he needed her lips on his first. "Kiss me."

She tentatively, but greedily, obeyed. At the first touch of her lips to his, his body raged with fire but in an entirely different way from before. His arms wound around her nearly naked perfect form and held on for dear life as he claimed her. His tongue swept inside her hot mouth and he mimicked with his tongue what he wanted to do with his cock.

As he ravaged her lips, her hands tentatively cupped his face. He tensed only briefly, focusing on her lips, her mouth, her tongue instead. She broke away and hesitantly kissed the side of his mouth, placing hot, open-mouthed kisses on his cheek, moving slowly toward his ear. She nipped his ear sharply before sucking the lobe into her wet mouth. All the while she lightly stroked her hands down his neck, over his collarbone and his broad shoulders, running them down his arms.

She was doing a fantastic job distracting him with her mouth, but if he concentrated on only her hands, he found that the feeling of them on his skin wasn't so bad at all. In fact, her light, gentle touch was soothing, warm and comforting. Healing.

Suddenly he craved more. He wanted her hands everywhere. Tracing the tats on his chest, nails digging into his back, fingers kneading his ass. Stroking his cock. He grabbed her shoulders and gently pushed her back, so she was now sitting once again over his straining shaft.

"I'm sor—"

"Touch me," he rasped. "Touch me all over, Analise. Heal me," he begged. Her hazel eyes were a pool of muddled emotions.

Relief.

Happiness.

Excitement.

Lust.

Love.

She held his burning gaze, slowly reaching her hands toward him. Light fingertips grazed over his jutting collarbone before gently tracing down his sternum to his pecs. He closed his eyes in pleasure as her index fingers gently scraped his flat masculine nipples, bringing them to hard points. His cock was now painfully hard, regret eating at him for the silk that kept her hot sheath from him.

Her sultry voice penetrated his thoughts. "What's this one?"

He knew exactly what she was tracing. The tat over his heart he'd gotten in tribute to his dead family. Mixed among the black tribal tattoo were three red script letters ... CBE.

"They are a memoriam to my family. My papi Cedric, my mimi Beulah and my brother Elias." Because the color faded, he had to have them frequently redone.

Her smile was sad. "That's lovely, Damian." He was hanging on by a very thin thread now. The need to be buried inside her was so great he had to fist his hands in the blankets beneath him.

"I need you naked, kitten. Now," he growled as he thrust his cock into her drenched panties, her desire evident.

She gasped. "Not a chance, vampire. I'm not nearly done exploring your smoking hot body yet."

"Analise, I'm close to losing it here." In about ten seconds she was going to be beneath him and filled to the brim with his unyielding manhood.

"Please, Damian," she whispered softly. "We have all evening to make love. Please let me do this." *Christ.* He couldn't deny her. He would never be able to deny her anything.

"Since you asked so sweetly, kitten, how can I say no?" Taking a deep breath he willed his disco stick down. Gotta love Lady Gaga.

The next thirty minutes were both heaven and hell. Analise ran her hands all over his body, tracing each and every tattoo with her fingers and tongue. She especially loved the ring of fire, which covered his entire back. He'd demanded several more times that she remove her bra and panties, but she'd refused, saying it would distract him from her task. Little did she know, but she was going to receive some punishment for her disobedience when he took back the reins, which was right fucking now.

He was reaching for her hands, when she stroked them straight down to his aching cock. She was tentative at first, getting bolder with each pass.

"Analise, that feels so good," he croaked, his voice gravely and thick with lust. He wanted to watch her, but his heavy lids couldn't stay open.

If he'd thought her hands felt good, her mouth was pure paradise. At the first touch of her tongue on his cock, his hand flew to her head, grabbing a fistful of her silky hair. When she took the tip into her hot, wet mouth, he was sure he'd died and gone to heaven. No woman's mouth had ever felt as good as this.

When she took him in as far as she could, he couldn't help the groan that escaped his lips as he involuntarily pumped his hips. "Christ." His voice was raw, primal. And when she started sucking and licking, he nearly blew. He was embarrassingly close to the edge and she'd only just begun. When she started gently fondling his balls that was it. He couldn't stop himself from fucking her mouth in earnest, using the handful of hair he held as leverage.

He looked down to ensure he wasn't too rough and her beautiful hazel eyes caught his, alight with desire. Their gaze never broke as she took everything he gave, giving back equally.

"That feels too fucking good, kitten. I can't hold back." He couldn't remember ever coming so fast, but she'd had him so wound up with her hands and mouth all over his body. Her touch was pleasure he knew only Analise could deliver. He was seconds away, the base of his spine tingling, and he wanted to give her the chance to pull back, but instead her suction increased and she bobbed her head up and down faster.

"Come," she demanded silently, eyes blazing into his.

Her command was like a siren's song, pulling his seed roughly from low in his balls until it hit the back of her throat. She swallowed quickly, never missing a beat. Never breaking eye contact. Never letting up until he was completely spent.

Every muscle in his body felt weak. He was boneless as he sagged back against the plush pillows.

He felt cleansed.

He felt healed.

He felt reborn.

Analise had crawled up his body to snuggle and with great effort he wrapped his arm around her, holding her tightly to him. They were comfortably quiet for several minutes.

"Thank you," he rasped.

"Ditto," she softly replied. She was an incredibly amazing creature that he did not deserve. But fuck if he was going to give her back either. She was his.

He couldn't fight the pull of sleep that beckoned him, his last thought of how he was going to protect the precious thing he now held in his arms from the evils that lurked in the night, waiting to snatch her away.

Chapter 39

Analise

Damian surprised her with another evening out to *Grina*, but this time she was the main attraction. She was five minutes from stepping on stage to sing in the underground, or *Grina Bi*, as Damian referred to it. Nerves ate at her stomach like termites devouring a pile of decaying wood. He'd sprung this on her as they lay in front of the fire so she hadn't had much time to prepare, albeit she was singing a short set. She was always nervous before she sang, but it was doubly so tonight as Damian's attention would be one hundred percent on her.

After a brief nap earlier, they'd spent a couple of hours simply lying in each other's arms talking. She'd told him about her guardian angel, which turned out to be her mother. His only comment was, "Stranger shit has happened." In his world, she guessed it did.

While lying in each other's arms was heavenly, she was also anxious to complete the bonding process with him, but he was insistent they wait until after she sang so he could spend the rest of the night worshipping her. They'd driven here again, but he'd already prepared her that after her set was over, they were flashing back to his place because he "wasn't going to wait forty-five more fucking minutes to ravage her body and make her his." She was so happy, it would take a stick of dynamite to wipe the sappy smile from her face.

Damian was far more damaged than she'd realized. She didn't know if he'd ever tell her the full story, and quite frankly she wasn't sure she wanted to know. She took a risk by pushing him, but in the end he'd had a breakthrough, even enjoying her touch. As damaged as she was, she felt giddy at the thought that *she* could help begin Damian's healing process. She could physically see brightness around him that hadn't been there before.

She'd picked only four songs to sing this evening, two of them she'd not performed before, but selected just for Damian. Against his protests, he'd brought her early so she could practice a couple of times with the house band before she actually performed live. One was a duet and she'd absolutely needed to practice so she didn't make a fool of herself.

It was time. She took a deep breath and took the stage. Her first two songs went quickly. Damian stood in the back of the club, his heated eyes never wavering from hers. When she began her third song, Evanescence's "Bring Me To Life", she saw his body tense, holding back the effort to come throw her down on the stage and take her right there. She'd chosen that song because the words called to her, just like Damian had. He'd brought her back to life, saving her from the nothing she'd become. Her final song, "Nights in White Satin", was her love anthem to Damian. She began singing, pouring every ounce of emotion she felt into the words.

She'd only gotten through the first verse when he pushed his large frame from the wall and started stalking slowly toward the stage. He moved with such grace, such ease, it was hypnotic. He was an animal on the prowl and she was most definitely the prey. The fire in his eyes burned with such intensity she could feel the heat they threw all the way from across the room. A shiver of anticipation ran through her as he closed the distance between them.

She was on the last chorus by the time he'd reached her and once again, the world narrowed to the two of them. Everyone else faded away and she poured her whole being into the sultry song she sang only for him. Passion emanated from his every pore, weaving a sensual haze around them that shimmered and glowed so bright, it was blinding. Her body was nothing but white-hot energy, feeding off the life source standing in front of her.

When she finished her last note, he gently reached out his hand, the gesture in complete contrast to the raging need she felt rolling off him in drowning waves. He helped her off the stage and surprised her with a soft, gentle kiss right there on the dance floor.

He tenderly cupped her cheeks in his rough hands, looking deeply into her soul. "You own me, Analise. Every breath, every thought, every beat of my heart." His voice was strained, rough, raw. "I need to make you mine. Right. Now."

Hot tears sprang up, threatening to spill. No moment had ever been so perfect. All she could do was nod before the dizzying effects of flashing consumed her. Seconds later her back was pressed up against the cold bay window in Damian's living room and he was plundering her mouth with such ferocity she was sure she'd be bruised. Like she gave a shit ... she planned to give a few bruises of her own.

As his mouth worked her over, his hands were everywhere ... unzipping, tugging and pulling her dress off, revealing deep red lingerie underneath. She'd chosen her undergarments with care and purpose. Tonight they would complete their bonding with the exchange of blood and the silky red bra and panties set called to her the moment she'd opened her drawer.

"You are so perfect, kitten. So perfect," he muttered between kisses. Her breathing was shallow and erratic as he unhooked her bra, letting it fall down her arms to the floor. Her sex was dripping from her desire as he hooked his fingers in her panties, slowly drawing them down her legs. She was now standing completely naked against the glass window and while they were high in the air, so were several other buildings. Could anyone see in?

"Privacy windows. No one can see your delectable body pressed against the glass, I can assure you of that. I don't share what's mine." From his squatting position, he spread her legs and took a single finger, running it through her slick folds. He groaned, "Fuuuck, you are drenched." He slowly brought the wet digit to his mouth and sucked it clean. *Oh my God, that was so hot.* Damian was sex incarnate, his lack of inhibitions liberating.

She sucked in a sharp breath when his talented mouth replaced his finger, nibbling and licking with fervor. Pleasure coursed through her as he speared his tongue in and out of her slick channel. He spread her nether lips with his hands, while applying light pressure to her clit with his thumb. It wasn't enough.

Her head fell back against the glass and she moaned in pleasure. "More, more," she begged. The anticipation of tonight had her on the precipice of an orgasm since she'd dressed for the evening. So when Damian thrust two fingers into her while suckling her clit, she immediately detonated. An explosion of lights ignited behind her eyelids as pure bliss radiated outward from her core. His name fell like a mantra from her lips while she convulsed with pleasure. He brought her down slowly, never taking his mouth from her until every last shudder stopped.

He rose and started to disrobe, the moonlight that shone through the windows casting an ethereal glow around him. His bright eyes locked with her heavy-lidded ones, the promise of insanely intense pleasure hung heavy in the air. Damian had produced a long, black ribbon from his back pocket before he dropped his pants. He radiated hot, sinful masculinity and if she didn't get him inside her this instant, she was going to spontaneously combust.

"Damian, please. Make me yours." She felt empty, aching with need, her body vibrating with passionate lust. She automatically offered her hands, palms up, waiting for him to bind her with the silk. She loved to touch him, but tonight ... tonight she *wanted* to be bound for his pleasure. He gifted her with such a bright smile it lit up her insides like the Fourth of July.

"Behind your back, kitten. It's safer that way in case blood lust takes you." She nodded her acquiescence and he bound her quickly. "Let me know if you're in any discomfort."

"Okay," she murmured. The only discomfort she was in right now was the aching need for his cock and the sting of his bite.

"Legs around my waist," he rasped as he lifted her hips. She'd do anything he asked. If he'd told her to squat on the floor and quack like a duck, she would do it.

"I'm sorry, kitten, I can't be gentle. I've waited too long for this. For you." With that, he seated himself inside her with one hard thrust and instantly set a punishing pace, bringing her close to the edge again almost immediately. She marveled at the sense of belonging and wholeness she felt when he was inside of her. Their mouths were fused so tightly together, it would take a welding torch to part them.

"I love you, Damian."

"And I you, Analise."

"I want to be your mate. I want to worship you for all of eternity."

The noise torn from his throat could only be called animalistic as he left her mouth, latching onto her neck instead. He sucked hard, his teeth grazing and teasing. A trail of fire followed his lips as he kissed his way to her breast. A sharp bite of pain caused her to cry out before her body exploded in utter bliss. Shooting stars pierced the blackness of her eyelids and she felt herself floating between space and time.

Her orgasm was unceasing and a warm, coppery taste unexpectedly met her lips. At the first drop, she felt hunger so powerful the pain was nearly crippling. The only thing that could satisfy the famine was her mate's lifeblood. Latching onto Damian's wrist, she held it tightly to her mouth like he might take it away any second. She drank in earnest; the spicy flavor filled her mouth and cooled the hot flames burning deep in her belly. It was sheer ecstasy. Unimaginable hedonism. And with each pull she felt stronger, consummate, invincible.

Everything around her became sharp and clear. It was like she'd been living in a thick, dense fog her entire life and it had finally lifted. Like she'd been eating tofu and had now been introduced to prime rib. Colors were brighter, sounds were louder, her senses sharper and unfettered.

Damian's blood was an aphrodisiac. She'd never get enough in a dozen lifetimes. She could vaguely hear Damian shouting as his thrusts became almost brutal. The pleasure of his climax coursed through her veins like a freight train as she felt the hot spurts of his release bathing her insides. Her body and soul felt scattered to the wind as she broke into a million pieces.

She was born anew.

Repaired.

Resurrected.

Truly alive for the first time. She became aware of softness on her skin and realized they were now in Damian's bedroom. *Their* bedroom. He was gently rubbing her now freed wrists. When she managed to crack her eyes open, the vision staring back at her was surreal. Damian had a bright hue of red surrounding his dark, magnificently sexy nude body. *His aura*. He was utterly splendid.

"You're staring," he quipped.

"You're beautiful," she replied, smiling dumbly at him. He gifted her with a glorious smile in return that she would never tire of.

"How do you feel, kitten?" He'd moved his ministrations up to her shoulders now and between the amazing sex, blood and the massage, she felt sleepy.

"Deliriously happy," she settled for. Everything else she felt paled in comparison to how unequivocally content she was at this moment.

"You're mine now," he crooned in her ear. "Mine to command, mine to cherish, mine to love."

"I will concur with the last two, but only to the first in the bedroom, vampire." She turned her head slightly, meeting his mouth for a gentle kiss. "I love you, Damian."

He gathered her into his arms and settled them under the silky soft sheets. "And I you, kitten. Now get some sleep because I'll be ready to make love to my new mate again in very short order."

He kissed her softly and with a goofy grin plastered on her face, she let the healing sleep take her under, never feeling safer or more loved.

Chapter 40

Damian

They'd returned to Milwaukee two days ago, Analise's meeting with the witch, Maeve, had been postponed until this evening. She was nervous about it but excited at the same time. He would be with her the entire time, not trusting Maeve as far as he could spit. He may trust and love Analise, but that was as far as his tolerance for witches would ever go.

Blood tests taken by Big D yesterday confirmed his suspicions. Analise was, in fact, the daughter of Xavier. And Kate's sister. Damian really needed to call Dev. He couldn't put it off any longer. Not only did he need to update him on what had gone down the past few days, Kate also deserved to know she had a sister. He was sure they would insist on coming back immediately, cutting their honeymoon short, and for that he felt bad, but it was the right thing to do. He was sorely remiss in not calling him already and he made a vow to do it. Tomorrow.

Giselle and the detective had yet to find Frankie's body, and he wasn't sure they ever would. He'd keep them on it for another couple of days, but after that he had another project for Detective Thatcher. He would track down the pedophile that had assaulted Analise as a teenager. The man who was supposed to be her protector, her mentor, her caregiver, but had resorted to violating a young, vulnerable girl instead.

And then *he* was going to pay Mr. Eric Greenbreier a personal visit. He could easily be the vile monster that so many humans thought vampires were. Just give him a good enough fucking reason … and hurting his mate ranked at the top of the list.

There seemed to be no more sightings of Geoffrey, which both concerned and confused him. He had to have known about the underground of Dragonfly and Damian knew Xavier wouldn't give up that easily if he were sniffing after Analise. That traitor was lurking around somewhere and he was going to find him. Tomorrow night he and Rom would head back to Dragonfly to see what they could find, leaving Analise in the protection of Devon's home. Of course, Sebastian and Devlin would stay back to guard her with their lives.

"Hi, babe," she sang sweetly, walking into the office. She was freshly showered and her intoxicating lavender scent hit his nostrils the second she was right outside the door. Swiveling in his chair so she could step between his legs, he placed his hands possessively on her curvy hips.

"Hello, kitten. You smell unbelievably delicious." Pulling her down so she straddled his lap, he nuzzled her neck, drinking in her inebriating smell. Vampires couldn't get drunk or high, but he swore he'd been constantly buzzed since they'd bonded. Everything about her was dizzying. Now he understood why Devon wanted to get away with Kate for a month. He wanted to do nothing but stay locked in a bedroom with Analise day and night, eating, drinking and making love. Screw his responsibilities. She was perpetually on his mind and he was constantly voracious for her.

Already he sensed the changes within her. She was stronger, faster, her tiny teeth sharper. And unbelievably he could visibly see the violet aura that Rom had spoken about. It radiated from her like a bright beacon in the night, protecting fisherman from the rocky shores.

They held each other quietly for several minutes. "I missed you," he whispered against her neck.

"I was gone all of thirty minutes," she jibed. He could feel her smile against his cheek. Happiness radiated from her like a moonbeam, bright and strong. His male ego puffed that *he* was the one who had done that ... who'd brought her back to life.

"Well, it was thirty minutes too long." He couldn't stand to be away from her for thirty seconds, let alone thirty minutes. He was one whipped mofo.

"My lord, the witch has arrived."

"Give us five minutes."

He was loath to leave the warmth and comfort of her body only to share her with the witch. "Our guest has arrived, kitten." He kissed her passionately before reluctantly letting her up.

They'd settled on the couch just as a soft knock sounded at the door. "Come in," he said. The door slowly opened and Maeve tentatively walked in. If he'd thought Analise was anxious, Maeve radiated nervous energy. If he said *boo*, he was sure she'd either drop dead on the spot or jump and latch onto the ceiling like a big ugly hairy spider. Huh, he ought to just ... try ... it ... out ...

"Ouch," he grunted, rubbing his arm. He looked over at his mate and the daggers coming out of her eyes looked sharp enough to cut off his balls.

"I wasn't really going to do it." He so was.

She sighed heavily, shaking her head in disappointment. Standing, she warmly greeted Maeve, but kept her hands to herself. "Thank you so much for coming, Maeve."

"My pleasure, dear. I'm happy to be here." Maeve shifted nervously.

"Would you like to have a seat?" Analise asked.

"Yes, dear."

They turned back toward the couch, where *he* sat, and the look she gave him was a *move-your-ass-now* look if he'd ever seen one.

"Oh, kitten. You'll pay for that later. And I look forward to every minute of your punishment."

"Damian, be nice. Please."

"I'm doing this only for you, Analise."

She walked over and surprised him with a sweet kiss. "Thank you," she whispered.

When he stood, he noticed Maeve watching them with shocked fascination. "I'll be right outside, kitten." He placed a soft kiss on her forehead and against his better judgment, left his precious mate alone with her aunt.

See ... he *was* growing.

Chapter 41

Analise

"So, you and Lord Damian ..." Maeve hedged after Damian had shut the door. Analise noticed her glancing down at the black bonding mark, which spanned the width of her left thumb. It was so beautiful, so surreal; she could hardly take her eyes off it herself.

Her defensive claws immediately emerged. Family or not, she wouldn't let anyone look down on her new mate. "Yes," she retorted. "What of it?"

"Oh, I didn't mean any offense, Analise, I promise. I'm just surprised. That's all." Maeve was clearly lying. Analise was very good at spotting a fake.

"You may be a great witch, Maeve, but you're a terrible liar," she snipped. She stood to pace the room, this meeting was going to shit and suddenly she wished she hadn't agreed to it. She was about to call Damian back when Maeve spoke so softly she almost didn't hear her.

"Mara, your mother, dated a lord shortly before she disappeared." Shock almost stopped her heart.

"What?" she choked. *Damian dated her mother?* No, that couldn't be right.

"It's true, Analise. We thought he might have something to do with her disappearance as she went to meet him one night and never returned."

The sound of the door being thrown open startled her, as did the sight of her furious mate. She'd never seen him so livid. His aura was fiery red and the heat emanating from him was uncomfortably hot. She wouldn't be at all surprised if fireballs started shooting from his eyes.

"What kind of bullshit are you filling Analise's head with, witch?" If looks could kill, Maeve would be twenty kinds of dead.

Maeve stood up and finally grew some balls. "It's *not* bullshit. She told me that they were in love, but because of his position he'd wanted to keep their relationship a secret so she wouldn't be placed in harm's way. But she described you, Lord Damian. To a 'T'." And now was probably not the smartest time for her to grow them.

Damian got right in her face and Analise thought he was going to strangle her. For real. He made fists so tight his hands were nearly white. Holy shit, this was bad.

"You listen up, witch, because I'm only going to say this once. Before Analise, my mantra was the only good witch was a dead witch. I have never dated a witch. I have never been in love with a witch until I met my mate. And I sure as hell never *fucked* my mate's mother. Now ... you pack up your little spell book, your dead spiders, and your broomstick and you get the hell out of here before I rip your goddamned head from your shoulders."

Maeve's lips drew into a thin line; she squared her shoulders and walked silently out the door.

Damian turned to Analise, grabbing her forcefully by the shoulders, shaking her slightly. "Analise, you have to believe me. I have never even met your mother."

She did believe him, but something was off. There was something more going on here than met the eye and a feeling that her life was in danger washed over her. Of course, it was in danger ... her deranged father was hunting her like an unsuspecting deer. She nodded her head. "I believe you, Damian. I do."

He hugged her tightly and they stood there clinging to each other in the aftermath of the weirdest encounter she'd ever had. Little did she know that circumstances set in motion years ago had set her on a path from which she could not veer. There were no forks; there was no turning back. There was only the slow, methodical movement ahead into the wide black abyss of the unknown, from which she'd need to use every skill she'd been taught and tap into every ounce of grit she had to survive.

ꟃꟃꟃ

"Why didn't you tell me?" Angry tears filled her eyes and Analise furiously wiped them away.

"You weren't ready, my dear," she replied softly. "I was always with you, my child. I gave you the tools you will need to survive the fight ahead of you. That was always my objective."

"But I needed a mother, not a teacher." Betrayal cut so deep, she wasn't sure she would be able to forgive her.

"What is a mother but a teacher with a different title?" she countered. Analise wasn't a mother, would never be a mother, so she couldn't argue with her mother's logic.

"Is it true?" Please say no, please say no. Her mother knew what she was asking.

"Not everything is what it seems, Analise," she replied sadly.

"What does that mean? Stop talking in circles!" She was frustrated. She needed answers dammit, not more riddles to solve.

Mara held her hands now, rubbing her marked thumb until it felt so warm it was almost uncomfortable. "Be careful, my darling girl. Not everyone is what they seem."

Analise woke with a start, bolting upright. Her thumb still burned slightly from her mother's touch. She sat there for a moment contemplating their conversation. While Analise felt betrayed that her mother never revealed her true self during her dreams all these years, she thought Mara might be right. Until she met Damian and was sucked into this bizarre world, she's not sure she *would* have believed her or accepted the fact she was her mother. And knowing herself, she probably would have pushed Mara away, even in her dreams. She was pretty stubborn like that.

Damian still lay sleeping next to her and she stared, drinking in the sight of his beauty. How did she get so lucky that Fate blessed her with not only the finest male specimen she'd ever laid eyes on, but also someone with the biggest heart she'd ever known? Damian's love and concern for her was boundless. She remembered her mother's words during the last dream ... *your destiny awaits*. She now knew Mara had been speaking of Damian and Analise had almost foolishly let him slip through her fingers.

After the Maeve debacle, they ate a quick dinner and retired to their room, making love for hours. She was deliciously sore in all the right places. Looking at the clock, she'd only been asleep a couple of hours but already felt refreshed. She lay down quietly so as not to disturb her mate, the conversation with her mother and the events of the past several days playing in mind.

Her mother's words replayed in her head ... *not everyone is what they seem*. Like she didn't know that already. She was, unfortunately, very intimately familiar with wolves in sheep's clothing and all that ... but she knew her mother meant more than that. It was a warning. Once again, dread washed over her. Something bad was coming. She felt it. She was in grave danger and she knew it had everything to do with her evil father.

After the blood tests had confirmed she was his daughter, Damian finally told her all about him.

His history with Lord Devon, the kidnappings, the baby factory ... all of it. He'd told her about Xavier kidnapping Kate and that he was now sure Xavier knew Kate was his daughter, as well as Analise.

He'd told her about the rescue of some of the kidnapped women and how her sister—God she would never get used to that—started the women's shelter that she'd stayed in a few nights ago. He'd even offered to take her there tomorrow and show her around. With her background and education in social work, he'd said maybe she could help out while they were in Milwaukee. If she wanted. She wasn't sure she was ready for that yet, but she did want to look around and meet some of the girls.

Kate seemed like an amazing woman, and how much of a coincidence was it that her sister was also married to a lord? Analise didn't believe in coincidences.

While she was excited to have a sister, she was sickened by the fact she shared the same blood and DNA with such a toxic creature. She was a combination of Damian's two most hated enemies, yet he'd assured her it made no difference to him. She believed him, but it was hard to understand how he didn't just kick her ass to the curb. There was bound to be more grief and drama in their lives than necessary because of her heritage. Guess what they said about love was true ... it really was blind.

"Kitten, stop it," Damian firmly demanded, sleep causing his gravelly voice to catch. He was so damn sexy. He pulled her closely, tucking her into his side. She threw her legs over his, entwining their bodies closely.

"Your cogs are working so hard, I could hear them in my sleep," he joked.

"I'm sorry," she murmured against his sinewy chest. She lightly began tracing his tats, concentrating on the precious ones over his heart.

"If you don't stop that you're going to end up tied to this bed, being ravaged by your very hungry mate." His voice had lowered an octave and she became impossibly wet and horny.

"That doesn't sound so bad," she breathed. Her fingers traced a path down to his navel. They didn't reach their final destination before Damian's strong grip encircled her wrist. "Hey," she whined. "Let go." His hard shaft beckoned to her. She could practically hear it whispering her name.

Instead of releasing her, he brought her hand to his lips, brushing kisses along her knuckles. "Tell me about your dream," he said between grazes.

"Don't you want to make love to me?" His rejection stung a little. Damian was game for sex all the time.

He tilted her face toward his and she clearly saw the mutual desire mirrored in his dark eyes. "Analise, I want to make love to you every second of every day, but I also want us to talk with our mouths, not just our bodies." Soft lips grazed her forehead and she shut her eyes in bliss.

"Open your eyes, kitten," he said softly. She obeyed, unable to deny him anything. His gaze was full of so much warmth it set her insides ablaze. "Our bodies may be together because that's what the Fates chose for us, but our hearts ... they are our own. Our hearts are one, Analise, because we not only see the intrinsic goodness in each other, but we also accept the bad and the flawed. I love you no matter *where* you come from, understand?" She nodded slightly before he placed a chaste kiss on her lips. "I heard a song the other day that reminded me of us. I think it should be our official song. Chicks like that stuff, right?" He winked with a broad grin.

She couldn't help but laugh as he reached for his phone. A few clicks later and a new song from one of her favorite bands started playing. She had no idea Damian even listened to Adelita's Way. The gravelly voice of Rick DeJesus began singing one of her favorite tracks, "Undivided". They were lost in each other and she listened to the words with all new meaning. She felt like she might burst at the seams when Damian began singing softly to her, his deep voice cradling her tenderly in his love.

By the time the song ended, happy tears flowed freely down her face. He leaned in and lightly took her lips between his, their eyes never leaving each other. All too soon he pulled back.

"We're undivided, kitten. I will never run. I will remain by your side, always. It's you and me through thick and thin, no matter what." After several beats, he crooked his eyebrows slightly, waiting for her response. It was not that she didn't want to respond, she couldn't.

"No matter what," she finally managed to choke through the golf ball-sized lump in her throat. They lay in silence, bodies wound tightly around each other.

"Go to sleep, my mate. You can tell me about your dream with your mother in the morning." Damian knew. Of course, he knew. Sudden lethargy overtook her and her eyes fell shut of their own accord.

As she drifted off, as happy as she was, the premonition of peril had latched on like a leech in the pit of her stomach. Thick and slimy, she felt it ever so slowly draining the happiness from her body, much like a real leech would suck your lifeblood in order to sustain itself. Except unlike a leech, which detached itself when full, her metaphorical leech wouldn't stop until she was decimated. Until every drop of contentment and joy and serenity was dried up and gone.

And since she had a psychotic vampire after her, the parallel of her analogy was a pretty freaking apt one.

Chapter 42

Mike

He'd just hung up the phone with Lord Damian, who'd given him a task that, for once, he was all too happy to fulfill. A dirty cop was the worst cop. Plus he was thrilled for the distraction since it meant he wouldn't see Giselle today. He'd spent the last few days having to interact with her on this missing person's case and his nerves were starting to fray, and like exposed wires, someone was bound to get electrocuted any second. He needed to unplug himself. Call it self-fucking-preservation, because the one bound to get hurt here was sure to be him.

Their face-to-face interactions had been brief, but during each one Giselle said they'd needed to talk and he'd told her to piss off. Nicely, of course, but piss off nonetheless. He just couldn't bear her excuses, not because he didn't want to hear them, but because he *did*. Desperately. He wanted her to tell him she wanted him as much as he wanted her. That he actually meant something more to her than just a chew toy you'd throw to your dog. He wanted ... hell, he didn't even *know* what he wanted and that right there was part of the problem.

Every day she clouded his mind a little more, crowding out any female before her. Including Jamie. *Especially* Jamie. And it pissed him the fuck off. How he'd let her get under his skin in such a short period of time when no other woman had come close, he just couldn't comprehend.

Some may call it Fate. He called it Misfortune. Giselle was the epitome of everything he detested, especially in a woman. She was cocky and bullheaded and a femme fatale. But most importantly, she was a bloodsucker. So the fact that he was inexplicably drawn to each and every one of the characteristics he so despised in her was a conundrum indeed. If he could solve that puzzle, perhaps he could eliminate this near fatal attraction he had for her. And he had no doubt it would end up fatal ... for him. Either physically or emotionally. Maybe both.

Christ, she made his heart beat a little faster, his blood pump a little quicker, and his dick harder than fucking titanium. Oh, his dick worked just fine and he'd been with plenty of women since Jamie, but they were all empty, faceless shells. He'd used them to fulfill a physical need, plain and simple. He was the quintessential wham, bam, thank you ma'am kind of asshole that no respectable girl would take home to meet her parents.

He'd tried to make himself believe that's what he'd wanted from Giselle too. In the infamous words of his favorite eighties hair band, Poison, 'don't need nothing but a good time'. For the last eleven years, that had been his mission statement with women. Hell, he'd even thought about having cards printed with his motto so he could hand them out before he fucked a girl, but that seemed too crass, even for him.

But his mission statement rang hollow in Giselle's case. For the first time in a very long time, he wanted more. And that scared the living crap out of him.

Mike had spent the last few days trying to get his shit together. He'd cleaned his house and garage, top to bottom, purging old items he didn't need or use anymore. He'd hauled two truckloads of shit to Goodwill. He'd connected with a couple of old buddies, meeting them for beers one night. During his search for Frankie's parts, he worked his body relentlessly, his muscles more sore than he could ever remember.

He'd even called his mom, not remembering the last time he'd talked to her. She was so thrilled she spent the first five minutes of their conversation crying. He was the worst kind of son, and now that he had a little more time on his hands, he vowed to make it up to her by coming to visit her in Illinois some weekend soon. Hell, he could use a break from the hamster wheel he was running on. Stupid hamsters. He used to laugh at them in the pet shop when he was a kid, wondering why they would spend hours running, going nowhere. Who had the last laugh now? he wondered. The fucking hamsters, clearly.

Yep, off one wheel and onto another. Just a bigger, more dangerous wheel, with man-eating sharks swimming in the dark, choppy, unforgiving waters below, waiting ever so patiently until you tire and can't stay on the wheel any longer. Then you're shark bait ... or in his case, vampire bait. Same end result. You're not getting out of the murky waters alive.

He needed a distraction, at least for the next few hours. Had someone told him a year ago that he'd be one vampire's bitch and half in love with another, he'd have had them committed. Hell ... maybe he should voluntarily commit himself. Thirty days in a psych ward might do him some good.

"Enough introspection for the day, Thatcher," he mumbled to himself. "Time to earn your keep."

He picked up the phone and started to dial, trying to banish from his brain this goat-fucked situation he'd landed himself in. He didn't know the cop Damian had asked him to find, but he did have an academy buddy in the Eau Claire PD. If this Greenbreier character had stayed in the area, Jimmy would know where to find him.

Chapter 43

Damian

Analise was anxiously pacing the small space as he and Rom spoke to Dev on speakerphone. He'd wanted her to lounge by the pool while he had this conversation with Dev, but she'd insisted on being here. She wanted to hear every single word that was said, because as she'd so bluntly told him just minutes ago, "I am your mate now and what concerns you, concerns me. The only way you'll keep me out of that room when you talk to him is to tie me up. But be warned, Damian, if you do that you'd better sleep with one eye open for a very long time." Christ, by the time she'd gotten through her tirade, all he wanted to do was throw her up against the wall and fuck her senseless. But he didn't have time since Rom was on his way down. Damn the luck.

"So you're telling me that Xavier can only sire females and there are two more female offspring alive and your *mate,* who is also a dreamwalker, is one of them?" Dev asked unbelievingly. Yes, even he couldn't believe this quick and bizarre turn of events. When they'd first started their conversation, relaxation oozed through the phone. Now he could feel tension building with every word.

"Yes, that's what I'm telling you," Damian replied. He hated having to repeat himself, but it was almost too surreal to believe himself.

"And you haven't found the third female?" Dev asked.

"No."

Dev sighed heavily on the other end of the line.

"And there's more, I'm afraid," Damian continued. He spent the next five minutes getting both Dev and Rom up to speed about Frankie, the potential compromise of Dragonfly from Geoffrey, who was now after Analise, and revealed the fact that Maeve was Analise's aunt. He left out the parts about Analise originally looking for Devon and the fact that her mother had been teaching her witchcraft in her dreams ever since she could remember.

"This is like *Days of Our Fucked Up Lives,*" Dev retorted. Damian heard Analise stifle a laugh and, had she been anyone else, he'd have shot her a shut-up-before-I-make-you look, but since she was his bonded mate, instead he shot her a *please*-shut-up-before-I-make-you look. She smirked, eyebrows high in the air, daring back an I'd-like-to-see-you-make-me-do-anything look. Jesus, she was simply glorious.

"...next?" He heard only the tail end of Dev's question.

"What was that again?" he asked.

Rom piped up, his usually stony face now barely able to contain his smirk. "If you'd stop making googly eyes at your woman, you'd have heard the question the first time, D."

This time Analise full-on laughed and he couldn't help but smile. Her laugh was angelic, like her singing, and when she made that glorious noise, he felt beams of light from heaven shining down upon him. Who knew he could be so goddamned poetic? If only Rom could hear him now ... he'd never live that shit down for the rest of eternity.

"Fuck off, Rom," he replied. "Come again, Dev."

"Jesus, I leave for a few short days and Damian gets bonded to a female vampire slash witch slash dreamwalker sired by Xavier, who also happens to be my new witch's niece and Kate's sister, and is also is being hunted by daddy dearest; while my new club is compromised by Xavier's sick fuck of a lieutenant who's also likely chopped my club manager into fish food. Is that about right?"

This time Damian had to stifle a laugh. This did sound like *Days of Our Fucked Up Lives.* "Yup, that about covers it."

"Jesus H. Christ. What's next?"

Damian chuckled. "What's next? What's next is we find Xavier's third daughter and kill Geoffrey before he gets his hands on Analise. Then we find Xavier and wipe his sorry ass off the face of the earth after we rescue the remaining missing girls and children. That's what's next, my friend."

That effectively cut the tension that had built to volcanic proportions.

Dev sighed. "We'll be home in a couple of days."

"There's no need for you to cut your honeymoon short, Dev." If it were Damian, he'd be torn. Stay away and keep his mate safe, or safer as it were, or jump back into the fray. It was a tough call. It certainly wasn't in a lord's nature to stay away from the battle, but both he and Dev had other more important things to think about now. They each had an Achilles heel and that was a very bad thing to have in their positions.

"The second Kate heard the word 'sister', she started packing. Since I haven't had nearly enough time alone with her, I'm going to try convincing her twenty-four more hours won't mean the end of the world. We'll see you in a couple days and I'll let you know if we have a change of plans." Dev disconnected the call.

"Well, I'd say that went well," Rom flatly stated. "We headed to Dragonfly tonight?"

"Yes. Analise will stay here with Sebastian and Devlin. I don't want her anywhere near that sick bastard because I'm quite sure he's hanging around waiting for my mate." Damian held his hand out to Analise and she quickly came, throwing her arms around his waist, burying her head in his chest.

"You okay, kitten?" he whispered. She nodded. The movement caused her face to rub against his pecs and his cock immediately swelled. He would never get enough of this woman.

Rom regarded their little exchange with amusement. "We need him alive, D."

Damian agreed. "Unfortunate. I'll meet you here at eleven p.m." Rom nodded sharply and departed, leaving them alone once again.

"He's very scary," Analise said the moment Rom had closed the door. She'd disengaged herself from him and he didn't like it. At all.

"I suppose, but that's part of his undeniable charm," he retorted. To a human and hell, to most vampires, Rom was incredibly intimidating. His physical appearance—bald head, goatee and crystal clear blue eyes—only added to his dangerous façade. Damian reached for her again, but she evaded. He frowned.

"I thought we were going to the shelter this morning?" she countered. "If I let you get your hands on me, we'll never make it there." There was no denying that, but so what?

"Damian," she cooed, "let's get the shelter out of the way and then we can spend the rest of the day in bed. Deal?"

"Are you trying to get back at me for last night? Because I wanted to talk instead of fuck?"

She considered him for a few moments, her playful mood replaced instead with annoyance.

"Crass is not a good look on you, Damian." She walked toward the door, throwing over her shoulder, "Are you coming with me or are you going to stay here and pout like a toddler whose sucker just fell in the dirt?"

Well ... shit. Point: kitten. He'd met his match with her.

"Coming," he mumbled under his breath. He'd finally met the one person in the world who could make him come running with the simple crick of her finger. He used to laugh at guys like that, who were led around by their women like they had an invisible leash tied around their little necks.

And now he was one of them. He shook his head and followed his mate, thinking of ways he could punish her when they finally made it to the bedroom. For fuck's sake, he had to maintain the upper hand somewhere ... *right*?

Chapter 44

Analise

They walked into the kitchen of the shelter just as the staff was preparing lunch. Her spidey senses tingled and she couldn't get over the unease she felt. Damian gave her a reassuring squeeze of the hand and she felt mildly better.

There were several people flitting about, one cutting vegetables for salad, one at the stove, stirring food in several pots. The undeniable scent of pasta filled the air, her very favorite food, except that wasn't Ragu bubbling over the hot flame. It was definitely homemade. Her stomach growled, loudly.

"Wow, that smells amazing," she gushed, approaching the lovely old woman who juggled several hot pots.

"Thank you, dear. My great, great grandmother's recipe. She hailed from a small town in northern Tuscany north of Agliana."

"Yum." Analise breathed deep, inhaling a lungful of the aromatic, spicy sauce. "Would you mind if I tried a small taste?"

"Of course not, child. Be careful, it's very hot." She grabbed a spoon and scooped up some of the savory sauce, handing it carefully to Analise. She blew on it for several seconds and, unable to resist any longer, took a bite too soon, burning her tongue and the roof of her mouth in the process.

"Yikes," she yelped, dropping the spoon and the remaining sauce on the kitchen floor. Her tongue throbbed only briefly before it started to soothe. Within seconds, the burning was completely gone, as if she hadn't scorched the tender flesh away at all. She could actually feel her skin repairing itself, which was a little unnerving.

Huh?

"One of the many benefits of being bonded to a vampire, kitten," Damian whispered softly from behind her. She turned with a puzzled look on her face when Damian answered, "She knows."

Well, thank goodness for that. She didn't really know all of the rules yet and who knew or didn't know about their kind and certainly didn't want to be responsible for a very kind old lady's untimely demise. Yes, she was now including herself in 'their', because she was also part vampire.

Damian told her she'd gain all of his very impressive powers since she was now his mate, but it happened over time. Every mating process was different, so there was no general rule of thumb for how long it would take her to come into her full capacity. She'd gotten used to the sound of blood pumping through everyone's veins, so that was a good thing. For the first day, it was deafening. Every day she felt more power coursing through her veins, humming underneath her skin like an electrical current. But she just didn't quite know how to harness the energy it would provide. Damian said he'd know when she was ready, so she had to rely on his expertise.

She looked down at the mess she'd created. "I'm sorry," she started, only to be interrupted by the kind old woman.

"No worries, dear. Easy enough to clean."

Just then two young women walked into the kitchen, talking and laughing. They stopped short, all chatter cut off when they saw Damian and Analise standing there. Their gazes flicked nervously back and forth between them.

"Sarah, Meagan, this is Analise, my mate," Damian announced gently. So gently, it reminded her of how one might speak to a cornered animal or a tortured victim. *Victim*. Because that was how Damian saw them. But they weren't. Not anymore. They were survivors now and she was sure they'd want to be treated as such. She did.

"Hi, I'm Meagan. Nice to meet you, Analise," she said meekly. Meagan wasn't classically pretty with too round of a face and stringy dark brown hair, but her soft brown eyes were piercing, haunting. And they couldn't hide the pain and suffering she'd been through. Analise didn't know her exact story, but she could relate on too many levels.

"Hi, Meagan. Pleased to meet you." She held out her hand and Meagan looked at it like it was a cobra, coiled and ready to strike venomous poison into her bloodstream. Finally, Meagan reached out, tentatively shaking it. At her touch, Analise pushed every ounce of comfort and healing she could into the frightened girl. She didn't know if it would work, but it certainly couldn't hurt. She physically felt something pass between them and saw

Meagan's eyes widen slightly before pulling away quickly.

She turned to Sarah and was struck dumb by the immediate sense of kinship she felt. They were kindred spirits, Sarah and her. Again, she didn't know Sarah's story, but knew she'd had been to hell and back and survived, just like Analise. And she was the stronger for it.

Sarah had reddish blond hair that was pulled sleekly back into a low ponytail. Her soft brown eyes were framed by fashionable thick black glasses. On most other women, they'd look ridiculous, but on her they looked striking. She was very beautiful.

"Hi, Sarah. I'm Analise." Once again she held out her hand and unlike Meagan, Sarah shook it quickly and firmly. Sarah had a strong mind and an even stronger will. Analise felt a powerful connection with her and hoped they could become friends.

"Nice to meet you, Analise," Sarah said genuinely. "Hi, Marta. Whatever you're cooking today smells divine." Sarah walked over and gave Marta a quick hug before grabbing a spoon and taking a taste of the heavenly sauce. "Yum. Tastes fantastic!"

Sarah turned back toward Analise, who could do nothing but marvel at how *normal* Sarah acted, despite the circumstances. "Are you staying for lunch, Analise? Marta makes a mean spaghetti sauce. Noodles are homemade too."

"Ummm, yes sure. Is that okay?" She didn't want to intrude and could tell Meagan felt uncomfortable with her and probably more likely Damian's presence. She didn't want to make them feel unwelcome in their own home.

"More than okay, right, Meagan?" Sarah had sensed Meagan's discomfort as well. In just the few short minutes she'd met her, Analise had Sarah pegged. She was the mother hen. She was the caretaker of the other girls here. She exuded strength and resilience and people were drawn to her like moths to an open flame.

"Y-yes, sure," Meagan stuttered. Analise smiled warmly at Meagan, trying to put her at ease.

"Lunch is ready!" Marta exclaimed. "Everyone to the dining room. Tut tut."

Through lunch, Meagan barely uttered a word, unless prompted by Sarah. And Analise could tell something wasn't quite right with Sarah either. She looked a little peaked and Analise had asked a couple of times if she was okay. She'd reply with a tight, pained smile and politely answer yes, but Analise knew it was a lie. She'd barely touched her food, pushing it around on her plate instead to make it appear she'd been eating.

Through their brief conversations, she'd learned about Olivia who was also a dreamwalker, as were Sarah and Kate. For this dreamwalker thing being so rare, she now knew of four people who shared this unique gift. How could that be a coincidence? It wasn't, that was how.

Just as that thought entered her mind, Sarah gasped and doubled over, clearly in agony. "Sarah, what's wrong?" Analise rushed to the other side of the table where Sarah was bent in half, struggling to breathe, her skin ghostly white.

"I ... I don't know," she choked. Sarah grabbed her arm, her grip so punishing it would leave bruises. She was very strong for such a tiny woman. "Get ... get the ... doctor. Now," she panted.

Not saying a word, Damian swiftly drew Analise out of the way, picked up a now crying Sarah, and quickly left the dining room. Analise, Meagan and Marta quietly followed Damian through a maze of hallways and downstairs into a medical clinic waiting room. Except for the fact that it was empty, it resembled any other normal physician's waiting room, with several chairs lined up against the wall and a rack filled to the brim with magazines.

As they walked through the empty waiting area toward the back, Duchess Kate, holding a sweet baby Prince George, stared back at her from the latest issue of *People*. She couldn't help but think about how happy the Duchess looked and how cruel it was to showcase a woman living a fairy tale life while these women lived in the aftermath of unspeakable horrors.

They'd made their way to an exam room and Damian gently deposited an agonizing Sarah gently on the exam table. Sarah curled into the fetal position, wet tears of pain streaming down her face. Analise recognized the doctor waiting for them inside as the one who'd taken her blood just a few days ago.

"What happened?" Big D asked, snapping on a pair of rubber gloves. Analise looked to

Damian, neither of them quite sure what was happening.

"She was fine one minute and doubled over in excruciating pain the next," Damian replied, confused as everyone else.

The doctor softly lay a hand on Sarah's shoulder. "Sarah, can you tell me where the pain is?"

"It's ... it's all over." She breathed heavily, indicating her abdominal area. Big D asked several more questions about nausea, appetite and pain elsewhere as he gently poked and prodded Sarah and cursed under his breath as several more people streamed into the confined space. They were also medical professionals if their scrubs and white coats were any indication.

Sarah cried out in agony as Big D barked orders to the rest of his team, something about an ultrasound and blood typing and ordered all non-medical personnel back to the waiting room. Analise was glad to get out of the fray, but she was loath to leave Sarah alone. Someone should be with her.

After Damian told the doctor to keep them updated, they all walked silently back the way they'd come. Damian softly kissed her temple. "I'll be back in just a few minutes, kitten. I need to change my clothes."

For the first time, she noticed red sauce splattered down the front of his shirt. It must have spilled in the chaos. "Okay," she replied quietly.

Sarah didn't deserve this. She'd already suffered so much. Meagan was trembling beside her now, clearly trying to contain her sobs. Analise could see that Sarah was Meagan's rock and without her Meagan was lost in a vast sea of nothingness. The sea would soon open up and swallow her whole and Meagan would be lost to its blackness forever. None of these victims, including Beth, deserved what had been done to them by the cruel, malevolent hands of her father.

Her eyes flicked again to the mocking *People* magazine. The wrongness and unfairness of this entire fucked up situation caused anger to well inside her so intense it was like someone had struck a single match to a truckload of brittle kindling.

Suddenly Duchess Kate was in flames, ashes from the burning magazine falling silently to the ground. Analise looked on in complete and utter horror. She felt Meagan and Marta's eyes upon her, but she couldn't look away from the red, orange and yellow colors dancing before her. Nothing else was ablaze, only the God-awful magazine that had caused her raging fury. The flames slowed and died and all that remained of the offending article was a pile of black ashes on the carpet below.

She had done that ... but how?

"What the hell?" Damian's deep voice rumbled causing a shiver of desire to run the length of her spine and ending right between her thighs. *Jesus, Analise, what a completely inappropriate reaction.* She'd officially turned into a sex addict, but one could hardly blame her with a mate as sinfully handsome and sexually skilled as hers.

"How did you do that?" Damian asked, confusion lacing his deep voice. When she finally tore her eyes away from the mess she'd created to look at her mate, she saw the sincere bewilderment on his face. "You shouldn't be able to access your powers yet, let alone control them with such precision."

"I ... I don't know. The magazine made me angry and all of a sudden it just combusted." Jesus, she could have burned the entire place to the ground killing everyone inside. She was completely mortified.

Damian smirked, the corner of his stunning full lips turning upward. "Wow. I can't imagine what kind of offense a stapled, glossy piece of paper did to earn such retribution, but remind me never to piss you off."

She tried to laugh, but it came out choked, sounding more like a pigs snort instead. Great, now she was making farm animal noises. "I'm sorry," she replied sheepishly.

His strong arms wrapped around her. She breathed deep and took in the scents of crisp ocean, fabric softener and sin. She loved this man so much it almost hurt.

"No harm, no foul. But now that you're able to tap into your powers, we need to refine them."

As the wait dragged interminably on for word about Sarah, Analise couldn't help but worry. Over an hour later, Big D came rushing into the waiting room calling her name.

"Analise, we need you," he said frantically as he grabbed her arm, dragging her toward the back. Damian immediately put a stop to anyone manhandling his mate when he stepped in front of the doctor, his hard gaze as sharp as a surgeon's scalpel. She felt the telltale warmth when Damian got angry and Big D's hand let go of her immediately.

"Explain," he growled, pulling Analise into his side.

"My apologies, my lord, but Sarah's appendix burst and we took her immediately into surgery. During the operation, a vein was nicked, but it shouldn't have caused this much bleeding. We finally got it under control, but she needs a blood transfusion to replace the significant amount she's lost. The truth is, we just don't know the full extent of everything that Xavier was pumping into her, but right now it's irrelevant. Sarah needs blood and she has a rare blood type. When we cross matched her to the database, only three people came up as a match. Analise is one of them."

They both gaped at him. How could she possibly be a match for Sarah's blood type? Unless …

"Please, my lord. We have no time to waste."

Damian looked at her questioningly and she knew what he was asking. Was *she* okay with it? "Yes. Yes, of course. Let's go." If she had the ability to save Sarah by giving a little of her own blood, that was a no brainer.

"I'm not leaving her side," Damian demanded, challenging the doctor to deny him.

"Of course, my lord. This way." He turned and led them in the back, down a series of hallways, every step taking them closer to Sarah. Analise and Damian exchanged knowing glances, neither of them voicing what they knew to be true. Analise was the only option, for the only other two people that matched would be her other sister, Kate, and their sick, twisted father.

As impossible as it seemed, Xavier's other living daughter—*her sister*—had been right beneath their noses this entire time. And while she may be safe from Xavier, her life was still in danger, nonetheless.

Chapter 45

Damian

"How are you feeling?" he asked as they cuddled on the couch in the living room. They'd been listening to the soft sounds of good ol' blue eyes while discussing the day's events. Sarah was out of immediate danger, but still in the infirmary for the next couple of days. Analise had donated a couple pints of blood, but he'd replenished her with his. He still couldn't believe that all this time, Xavier's other daughter had been right here.

His blood was strong, but Damian could tell Analise was still tired and lethargic. "I'm fine, Damian. For the hundredth time," she replied in annoyance. "I swear if you ask me that one more time it's you that will get punished."

He laughed but without humor. "Don't make idle threats you can't make good on. I assure you, the only one getting punished later will be you, kitten."

"Me?" She pulled back from the warmth and comfort of his arms, scooting toward the corner of the worn leather sofa. He didn't like it. "And what, pray tell, have I done to earn said punishment?"

That little devil on his shoulder, the one he should most definitely ignore in this situation, overrode the angel on his other who was whispering for him to just tell her. "I didn't realize I owed you an explanation," he stated flatly. Their eyes locked in a battle of wills, neither looking away, neither backing down.

"Okay, what's really going on here, Damian?" she asked.

Damian was like Oz. Almighty and powerful, yet with Analise he felt powerless. Control was slipping through his fingers like grains of sand to which he couldn't quite grasp onto and the only place left for complete and utter domination was the bedroom. No goddamned way would she take that away from him. Once again, that fucking annoying angel gave him very sound advice. *Talk to her, she'll understand.*

"Nothing is *going on* here, Analise. I thought I made it very clear that I, and I alone, dominate the bedroom. Period. The only one doling out any punishment will be me. What I want, when I want and how I want." Guess he gave that cherub bitch a one-way ticket south. Way south.

After several tense minutes, she rose from the couch and started walking out of the room. He called after her, "Where are you going?" Jesus, he was a bastard. He had no idea why he was acting like someone had stuck a hand up his ass, working his mouth like a ventriloquist. Every time he opened it, he had no control over what came out.

"I'm tired. I'm going to lie down for a while. I'll see you when you get back from Dragonfly." She took a few more steps before turning around to face him. The look of disappointment in her eyes made him feel about two inches tall, which was, quite frankly, more than he deserved. "However, if you're still going to be a fucking prick when you get back, maybe I'll just see you in the morning instead. If it's all the same to you, I don't really think I'm up for *punishment* tonight at the hands of a selfish asshole." And with that dressing down, she left.

Fuck him! He *was* a selfish asshole! There was no excuse for the way he'd just treated the love of his life. He should go after her, he should have stopped her, he should have apologized. He should have done a lot of things ... but he didn't. He sat there instead and watched the empty space she'd just occupied, wishing he could go back in time and undo the last five minutes. His angel tutted her disappointment while his devil tried to high five him.

He flicked that motherfucking pitchforker off his shoulder, vowing to never let him return. At least not in the presence of Analise. He'd better prepare himself for days of endless groveling to make up for his latest round of insolence, which was the very least that he owed the woman who'd turned his life upside down in the most magical of ways. And yes, that irony wasn't lost on him.

ꕤ

Damian walked into Dragonfly, senses on full alert. Since they'd learned that Sarah was the third daughter they'd been looking for, it was decided that Rom would stay back at the estate to provide additional security and Damian would scout Dragonfly alone this evening. He could handle anything Geoffrey threw his way. He scanned the upper level, and finding nothing out of the ordinary, headed downstairs.

Ronson met him upon entry. "My lord, so good to see you again."

"Ronson." He inclined his head in greeting. "Any unusual sightings?"

"No, my lord. No sign. I have every eye peeled and I've watched the security tapes myself from every evening. Nothing."

"Stay diligent. Geoffrey's slimy."

Damian ordered a Patrón neat and leaned against the bar watching the action for many long minutes. Dragonfly was packed wall-to-wall tonight, pheromones dancing provocatively in the air. His mind drifted to the dance he'd shared with Analise back at Grina before he'd ravaged her in his office, his cock hardening painfully at the erotic memory.

He noticed several women blatantly checking him out, running their eyes over every inch of his honed body, including the two he'd spent the evening with just several short nights ago. The night before he'd met his mate. He remembered thinking that night that they were beautiful women who took very good care of themselves, but all he saw when he looked at them now was blandness. Analise had effectively rendered every other woman a dull matte gray, while she shone with such color, such brightness, it was blinding.

And like the goddamned idiot he was, he'd come here without apologizing, without making things right between them. He was wrong and he wanted nothing more than to return home, crawl into bed and worship her all night long. Turning to do just that, something in the corner of the room caught his eye, stopping him short. Not something ... *someone.* Fucking Geoffrey. How the hell was he here when Ronson had everyone looking for him, guarding the entrance with an iron fist? His gut burned. Something was way off about this situation, but not looking a gift horse in the mouth, he flashed directly in front of Geoffrey, grabbed him by the neck and slammed him back into the wall, cracking the stone.

Damian shoved a knife to the hilt in Geoffrey's chest, just millimeters away from piercing his black heart and he held his windpipe so tightly Geoffrey gasped for air. The smell of Geoffrey's coppery, revolting blood only fueled the demon clamoring inside to be set free so he could decimate the vampire who dared to come after his love.

"Give me one good reason why I shouldn't end your pathetic, sorry existence right now, vampire," Damian spat. He knew they needed Geoffrey alive, but the inferno blazing inside him was like a backdraft, waiting for that little bit of air to turn it into a living, breathing ball of fire so it could engulf the vampire in front of him. Geoffrey's eyes widened, knowing Damian held his life precariously in his hands.

"Because we both want the same thing. To end Xavier."

"Forgive me if I don't believe a fucking word that comes out of your filthy mouth. You're a disgrace to your species." Damian needed a mirror to make sure he didn't have the words *stupid fucker* tattooed across his forehead as that was the only way someone would fall for Geoffrey's bullshit.

"Believe me or not, but it's true. Xavier has my Moira. I want to rip the motherfucker limb from limb, but I'm not strong enough to do it alone. I need help from you. From the lords."

Damian sensed the truth in Geoffrey's words. Why he gave a rat's ass, he didn't know, but having just found his own Moira, he knew the certain agony Geoffrey would be going through knowing that she was suffering and he could do nothing but sit by and watch or risk her being slaughtered right in front of him. Because that was what Xavier would do. Guess he really needed that mirror after all, for he was actually *considering* this asshole's request.

Damian would never forgive himself if this were the break they'd waited for and he killed the rogue instead. This was possibly an inside lead to wipe Xavier from the face of this universe once and for all and if he chose instead to gut the traitor, spilling his entrails all over the dance floor, he'd never forgive himself if it put Analise in more danger. *Shit!* What a catch twenty-two.

"I swear to you by all that is holy, if you are lying to me you will have something much greater to fear than Xavier Illenciam. My wrath will know no bounds. And that includes *all* you hold dear." Geoffrey's face hardened at Damian's subtle threat against his Moira and before Damian could change his mind and against his better judgment, he flashed them to Devon's estate.

Once he had the rogue secured in the dungeon, he went in search of Rom, hoping he hadn't made the biggest mistake of his life in bringing the enemy so close to the only thing he loved.

Chapter 46

Analise

She lay in bed still fuming mad at the way Damian had treated her earlier this evening. She got him, more than he thought. She knew he felt a little helpless. She'd turned his perfectly organized, perfectly commanded world upside down and he was grappling to adjust. She felt the same way. But that didn't give him the right to treat her like some submissive wife who was expected to follow every wish, every command, not allowed to think for herself. If that was what he expected, forever took on a whole new meaning ... in a very bad way.

She felt the energy in the room change and, anticipating her mate, pretended to be asleep, turning her back to the door. Unless the first words out of his mouth were *I'm sorry*, he could just get the hell back out. If she could flash out of here so that he'd find an empty bed, she would.

Sadly, they hadn't practiced that and she didn't want to end up scattered to the wind, not able to retake a solid form. Damian told her they'd start practicing all those *vampire* things tomorrow. He'd told her of Xavier's particular skill of stasis and while she'd tried hard, she couldn't immobilize anyone.

She was beginning to wonder if she was really his daughter, as she couldn't seem to do a damn thing. It was frustrating. He also promised to find her another witch besides Maeve so she could learn sorcery in a real state, instead of just a dream one. She'd only had that one odd incident with the gossip magazine and she wasn't sure if that was Damian's firestarter ability or her own sorcery ability. She felt woefully inadequate as a vampire mate. And a witch.

She smelled blood seconds before Damian flashed in and immediately knew something was wrong. Her angry thoughts vanished in a puff of smoke and she jumped out of bed, moving quickly toward the door. Toward her injured mate. The second he appeared she knew something was wrong. *He* was wrong. It was Damian, yet it wasn't. The man in front her had a bright orange aura, unlike her Damian, whose aura was deep, vibrant red. But too late she'd realized her mistake, for before she could warn Sebastian or Devlin, his beefy arms wrapped around her and the telltale dizziness that accompanied flashing washed through her.

The next thing she knew, she was locked alone in a small, nondescript room, the Damian doppelganger nowhere in sight.

What the hell just happened?

She yelled and screamed until her throat was raw, pounding on the door that was sans a handle. She tried starting the door on fire, she tried unlocking the door with her mind, she tried everything she could possibly think of and nothing worked. She was sweaty from her exertion and her hands hurt from pounding relentlessly on thick wood. Finally, she decided to preserve her energy instead.

A slow look around the room revealed it was very similar to the one Beth was held in, except this room didn't even have a mattress. There were four cement walls, a concrete floor and a door that led to freedom, which she couldn't access.

She'd been kidnapped, from what was supposed to be the safety of Devon's estate, taken to an unknown place by an unknown captor for an unknown reason. A sharp, bitter pang of fear ran through her like ice water in her veins, chilling her from the inside out. Fear for herself, fear for her mate, fear for their future.

It didn't take a genius to know who was behind the abduction, but who was the doppelganger that kidnapped her? It was a vampire, that much was clear, but while he could take on Damian's physical appearance, he hadn't been able to fool *her* one bit.

Fear churned her stomach, but not for her. For Damian. *Was Damian hurt?* Would she feel it if he actually *got* injured? How long would it take him to discover that she was missing? And the biggest question of all was how the hell was he going to find her?

As she paced the small, suffocating space, pieces of the puzzle rapidly fell into place. The sinking premonition, the riddled words of warning from her mother, the strange conversation she'd had with Maeve. This was what she'd felt.

Her mind raced back to her mother's words. *"Not everyone is what they seem."* Maeve's words tumbled in the muddled mix. *"Mara, your mother, dated a lord shortly before she disappeared." "...she described you, Lord Damian. To a 'T'."* Holy shit. This vampire had been impersonating Damian for years? But to what end? It didn't make a lick of sense to her. And could he only impersonate Damian or was it anyone? So many questions, yet no damn answers.

After what seemed like an eternity, she sat on the cold floor in the corner of the room where she had the best vantage point to the door and waited. What Fate laid before her on the other side, however, was the million-dollar question.

She would soon find out, because the door finally began to open ...

Chapter 47

Damian

He was crazed with worry and sheer terror. Overcome with guilt, functioning was nearly impossible. He hadn't slept at all in three days. He'd barely eaten, hadn't showered, hadn't changed his clothes. *He* was responsible for the fact that his Analise was missing, kidnapped ... vanished. And he was no closer to finding her three days later than he was the second he'd found Geoffrey gone, along with Analise. He'd torn up this whole goddamned country, using every single resource he had available to him, running into brick wall after brick wall. It was like they'd vanished off the face of the earth. He'd fucked up royally and deservedly tormented himself every single second of every single day because of it. And to make matters worse, he'd spoken unforgiveable words the last time he'd seen her.

They'd at least been able to piece together what happened that fateful night. Geoffrey had the skill of mimicry. He could take on the form of another person and obviously quite successfully, for he must have convinced Analise to go willingly with him. Sebastian and Devlin were right outside her bedroom door. No one entered from the outside and they hadn't heard a thing. There was no sign of a fight, no struggle. No blood, nothing. Not one thing to indicate that Analise didn't willingly leave with him. The thought that Geoffrey could still be impersonating him and doing God knows what with Analise made him fucking homicidal, as the guard he'd sent to watch over Geoffrey had, unfortunately, discovered.

He'd been gone all of two minutes tracking down Rom and by the time he'd returned, Geoffrey was gone. He had been *let go* by the guard. Geoffrey had convinced him that *he* was Damian, that there was an intruder in the house and he'd been shackled to the wall like a dog while the intruder roamed free and his mate was in danger. Like Damian would ever let that fucking happen. Two minutes, one hundred twenty seconds that changed the course of his life, ripping his only love away from him. He might as well have handed her over to Xavier on a freshly polished silver platter himself, complete with all the trimmings and an apple shoved in her mouth.

"Maeve is here," Dev said, walking into the living room where Damian now sat, Patrón in hand, staring into a roaring fire. Fire calmed him and right now he was a raging volcano, spewing fire without control, so to be any good to Analise, he needed to find his center again. Clear his head; get a new game plan. The only ones who'd dared approach him the last twenty-four hours were Devon and Rom. Even his own men gave him a wide berth, fearing he'd involuntarily burn them to a crisp where they stood. It wasn't unfounded, he supposed. *Was that only yesterday an unsuspecting source had spontaneously combusted?*

"If I even get a whiff of that witch, I promise you, Dev, she's dead." Damian didn't bother even looking at Dev, the mesmerizing colors of the blaze entrancing him. Already he was starting to feel a little more grounded, but he certainly wasn't feeling forgiving toward that ... *thing*. Especially given the lies she'd spewed the last time she was here.

"Well, that's a shame given she knows where Analise is."

Damian's head whipped around so fast, he felt his brain rattle. "What do you mean she knows where Analise is?" He started toward the door, but Dev held him back.

"Damian, stop. Look, I *personally* know what you're going through, but if you don't remain calm and rational, you'll do your mate no good and could even put her in more danger. You are a lord for a reason." What he left unsaid was—*act like it.*

Dev and Kate had returned the day before yesterday to complete and utter chaos. Analise was missing, Sarah was still recovering from her brush with death and Damian was on the warpath, mowing down everything and everyone in his path on his quest to rescue the only person that had ever really mattered to him.

But Dev was right and he was ashamed to admit it. He needed to take a step back, strategize and stop acting like a goddamned lunatic. "Bring her in, but I'm warning you, it's in her best interest to be as far away from me as possible. And you may want to get a bucket of water handy."

Dev smirked and left to get Maeve. Dev thought he was kidding, but he wasn't. In the least. Several minutes later, in walked Maeve, Dev, Kate and Rom. A sharp pang of jealousy stabbed his heart when he saw Dev's mate. While it was clear Kate was worried about a sister she hadn't met yet, she was also glowing from her pregnancy. The soft swell of her belly was already more prominent since he'd last seen her.

While Damian and Kate weren't particularly close, she came to him, laying a comforting hand on his arm. "We'll find her unharmed, Damian. I feel it." He forced a smile, hoping she was right, because hope was about all he had left to grasp onto and she was a wily bitch, taunting and teasing him, as he'd found out over the last several days.

Maeve took a place over by the bookshelves on the far side of the room and out of his peripheral he noticed that Ren, Circo and Marco had taken up position right inside of the door. Jesus, he really was off-kilter if everyone thought he'd go all pyro on his own family. And along with Analise, that was what these people were to him. His family. And they'd been doing nothing but trying to help him over the last several days. And as usual, he'd acted like a bastard. He straightened his spine, took a deep breath, and pulled his shit together. For Analise.

"Maeve, thanks for coming. What do you know?" he asked as politely as he would have in a general conversation with Dev or Rom. In glancing around the room, he almost burst out laughing.

Everyone's eyebrows were cocked high on their foreheads in disbelief. Christ ... he *could* be nice if he *chose* to be.

His genuine sincerity particularly threw Maeve off her game and she stumbled over her first few words, having to restart. "I ... Mara visited me in a dream last night. She told me in her last dream with Analise, she'd warned her of danger and put a locating spell into her bonding mark."

Analise's mother had put a locating spell in her bonding mark during a dream and didn't tell Analise? Or perhaps she did and Analise hadn't had a chance to tell Damian. With all that had happened with Sarah and then their argument, they'd never gotten around to talking about Analise's dream with her mother.

"Who the hell is Mara?" Ren interjected.

Damian had been so focused on finding Analise that no one was fully up to speed on all that had happened in Dev and Kate's absence.

"She's Analise's dead mother," Damian clipped, eyes never leaving Maeve. There would be plenty of time for explanation later. Right now, he needed to find his mate. "Where is she?"

"I did a locating spell when I woke and she's in a remote location east of Olcott, New York. I have specific coordinates."

Damian looked at Rom and Dev. "We need a plan." And while it gutted him to wait another damn second to flash to Analise, they needed to formulate a solid strategy not only for Analise's rescue, but Xavier's future. To capture or to kill became a heated topic of conversation. For every ounce of pain he may have caused Analise, his vote was instant but painful death and Dev was one hundred ten percent on his side, but Rom had made some very good points for capturing him instead.

While trying to help him locate Analise, over the last couple of days Rom had apparently spent quite a bit of time talking to Big D about the coincidence that Xavier not only sired three female vampires, but that all three were dreamwalkers. The chances of that were billions to one, which meant that for all his abhorrent fucked-upedness, Xavier had an unheard of ability. But in the end, they decided on death. Xavier simply couldn't be kept alive.

After several hours they had a plan, plus several contingencies. Dev, Marco and Giselle would stay back, protecting Kate and Sarah, while Rom, Ren, Thane, Circo, T, Manny and two-dozen others would accompany Damian to the small town right off the banks of Lake Ontario. They were going in blind. No idea how many enemies would be present and whether Analise was being held with other missing girls or if she was alone with Xavier.

Either thought made the ever-present acid in his stomach churn like a blender on full speed. The bitter taste burned a slow path up his throat, threatening to choke him with its causticity.

They flashed to the designated location, two miles from where Maeve indicated they should be and began scouting the area. Against her wishes, Maeve was glued to Damian's side until they invaded Xavier's compound. Then he'd leave her with one of his men, far enough from the melee, but close enough to assist, if necessary. Much to his dismay, Xavier wasn't an idiot. He'd be expecting them, likely setting some fun little traps, but the bigger risk was that he would flash away with Analise to another, unknown location. His only hope, if that happened, was that Maeve could find her again.

"She's still in the same location," Maeve whispered.

Vampires had a keen sense of hearing, but not two fucking miles away. "There's no need to whisper, witch. The enemy can't hear you this far out."

Embarrassment tinged her cheeks. He really needed to work on his spiteful comebacks. He could do *far* better than that.

Since Ren had the ability to sense vampire and human presence and Manny could see through shrouding, they'd been sent to scan the area, only just returning. There was no shrouding and Damian wasn't sure what to make of that. Either Xavier was getting sloppy or he *wanted* to be in plain sight. He voted for the latter, which meant they had to be extra cautious.

Ren reported, "There are roughly twenty rogues posted outside the compound and I sense only twenty or so inside as well. There are also thirty-two humans, some in clusters, some in individual rooms just as with the last raid we conducted." Ren filled them in on the layout and the specifics of where the vampires and humans were as of now. With three floors, it would be more challenging getting everyone rescued without casualties.

Damian recalled Dev's words of warning. *"Xavier works closely with witches. When I was in his last lair, there was a spell of sorts that prevented me from flashing outside the compound once I had Kate. I had to wait until I was clear to get her to safety. He'll likely have the place spelled in a similar manner again, so be prepared and get out of Dodge as fast as you can."*

Duties split, it was time. Rom was assigned to Xavier, while Damian, Ren, Thane and T would rescue Analise. The rest would rescue the other humans. When he got closer, Damian hoped he could reestablish his connection with her, but if he couldn't, the bonding mark would allow him to at least sense where she was.

Damian had always been confident in his abilities as a lord, as a vampire and as a warrior. He'd not once worried about the outcome of the battle, ever assured he would be victorious. But the outcome had also never mattered as much as it did right now. For the first time in almost five hundred years, doubt, like the fingers of deadly toxic smoke, crept its way into his head and he hoped he didn't fail. He quickly pushed those poisonous thoughts aside. Doubt got one killed on the battlefield and he wasn't about to die today. After three long, agonizing days, he was getting his Analise back.

Hold on, kitten. I'm coming.

Chapter 48

Analise

She opened her eyes, all too aware of her surroundings. Her eyelids felt like sandpaper scratching her corneas raw. She was hungry, dehydrated and every muscle in her body ached.

She was still here—stuck in hell—with Lucifer playing the role of doting father and the Four Horsemen as his minions. Well, it was more like forty horsemen, but that didn't quite fit with the horror story. If Xavier had his way, the Apocalypse would rain down on the world and he'd sit high on his throne, watching as the earth burned and chaos erupted. And he expected *her* help with that.

"Ummm ... that's the offer of a lifetime DAD, *but I think I'll have to pass. Thanks anyway."* Needless to say, that response hadn't been too well received. She'd received a nice heave against the wall and lost consciousness for several minutes for that particular retort.

She knew she should keep her smart mouth in check, as it had gotten her *punishment* more than once over the past several days, but right now that was the only thing also keeping her alive. Xavier *liked* that about her and while she was disgusted being anything he enjoyed, she had to keep her wits about her until the cavalry arrived. And she knew they were coming. Damian was coming. Her bonding mark had heated up twice now ... once in front of Xavier, almost revealing the magic her mother had unknowingly weaved. And that would most certainly be the death of her. She'd gritted her teeth so hard against the white-hot pain, she'd truly felt a tooth crack.

Her mother came to her in more than dreams now. She would see visions of her while awake, she heard her voice whispering instructions in her ear and whenever she succumbed to the drugs they'd given her to keep her pliable, she was there. Teaching and helping and *mothering*. Analise thought back to just a few short days ago and the first time she heard her voice while awake.

After hours of being alone with these stone walls, the door finally opened and she was frozen in fear.

"Fire, Analise," her mother whispered urgently.

"Mother?" she murmured back.

"Now. Hurry!" Mara replied. "There is no time!"

What. The. Hell?

Instead of overanalyzing, the second she'd set eyes on the enormous, menacing vampire walking through the now open door, she'd focused all her anger and all her fear and all her thoughts on one thing. F I R E.

And with one foot inside the door, the sick bastard erupted into fiery flames, screaming and moaning and thrashing in agony until he dropped to the floor in a dead heap. He was pulled quickly out and the door shut, leaving Analise alone once again. She abhorred violence, but couldn't even make herself feel sorry for doing it. He'd intended her harm and it was time to do or die. And she didn't intend on dying. Not when she finally had life beating within her.

Several minutes later, still stuck to the corner wall, she heard a slow, mocking clap but couldn't locate its source. Turned out ... it was Lucifer calling.

"Well done, Analise Aster. You're more powerful than I'd hoped. And while I would love to see what other tricks you may have up your sleeve, I can't have you harming any more of my men. I need each and every one for what you and I will accomplish, together with your sister when she joins us. We'll be a family, at last. As it should be. As it always should have been."

Xavier's voice slithered over her like a hundred centipedes, the creepiest, nastiest insects on earth. The noxious feeling it left in its wake was beyond repulsive and a dozen showers wouldn't scrub it away. This was it ... Xavier was her happiness sucker.

"I think you may be a bit delusional, Pops." That *was her brilliant reply? How about* not in your fucking lifetime, *or* whatever you just took a hit of must have come from a bad batch.

He cackled, and if his speaking voice was akin to centipedes, his laughter was akin to a thousand knitting needles being repeatedly stabbed into her skull. It was agony. "I am most definitely delusional, Analise. You'll come to love that most about me, I guarantee it. Now, I'm truly sorry that it's come to this, but I'm afraid it's time for you to sleep. I'll see your pretty face when you wake and are more ... secured. It's time for a long overdue father-daughter reunion."

A toxic fog began seeping from the ceiling. She lay on the floor holding her breath, trying in vain to escape. Finally, she had to take a breath and couldn't help the fingers of sleep that came to take her directly to the devil himself.

"Play along, Analise. Appear malleable, but a little recalcitrant. Be reluctantly agreeable. Appear confident, but be scared. He needs you, but he will not think twice about killing you. If you're too accommodating, he'll see right through you, and you're dead. Most importantly and probably the most difficult will be convincing him you do not love Damian, but in order to survive until he arrives, that you must."

Mara vanished as Analise was yanked from her guidance with freezing cold water to the face. How cliché.

Her hands and feet were bound and she was sitting in an oddly comfortable leather chair that didn't seem to mesh with the meager surroundings. And standing in front of her was the most monstrous, hideous creature she'd ever had the displeasure to lay eyes on. This was her father, no doubt.

She was reminded of the first time she saw a picture of Ted Bundy, one of the most infamous serial killers in the United States. Ted didn't exactly get her womanly juices flowing, but he wasn't repulsive either. The point was, he didn't look *like a serial murderer. Her father, however? Next to the words sinister, vile and malevolent was a picture of his hideously scarred mug. His aura was the blackest of blacks, oozing poisonous toxins. He stood statue still, regarding her with an eerie silence. Her stomach rolled. It made her physically sick to be in the same vicinity.*

Her mother's words reverberated around like a steel ball hitting the flippers in a pinball machine. '...the most difficult will be convincing him you do not love Damian, but in order to survive until he arrives, that you must." *You must. Why couldn't she just set him on fire and be done with it? She began to do just that when her mother appeared as solid as a live human being directly in front of Xavier. Analise gasped.*

"You mustn't, Analise."

Well, why the hell not?

"What are you mumbling about, girl?" said Xavier stonily.

Did he not see Mara?

"No. He can't see me. If you want to make it out of this alive, you must follow my instructions exactly, Analise. Exactly." Then she vanished again.

'Hey. Mom, I know what would have really helped. A damn heads up that I was going to be kidnapped, that's what!' she screamed in her head. Except she did do that, didn't she? Just with a brainteaser she hadn't been quick enough to solve.

"Were you enjoying your stay with the lords, Analise?" Xavier asked, still nonchalantly leaning against the wall like she was here for tea and

crumpets. But his cool façade wasn't fooling her, anger wafted from him in dark, crashing waves that rolled over her like sticky tar.

"About as much as I'm enjoying our little visit," she retorted. Analise needed to draw on every single acting skill she'd developed over her short twenty-three years.

His grotesque smile didn't reach his eyes. "Well, you must have enjoyed it a little," he quipped, glancing at her bonding mark.

Oh shit.

"Sex is sex." She would have to be more convincing than this if she wanted to live past the next five minutes. Movement to her right caused her heart to sink into her stomach. It was the vampire she'd seen worshipfully touching Beth ... like Damian would touch her. And although he didn't resemble Damian now, she would recognize his aura anywhere.

Double shit.

She was screwed. How could she feign indifference when he'd clearly seen how concerned she was about Damian?

"Is that so?" Xavier pushed himself away from the wall, stopping directly in front of her. Her own betrayal cut through her like a piece of dull jagged glass as she uttered her next words, taking something Damian had said with such love and caring and twisting it into something mean and cruel. She was Judas and the pain that stabbed her heart when she uttered the words cut deep.

"My heart is my own. I may have given my body, but that's it." Don't cry, don't cry, don't cry.

You're dead if you cry, Analise. *She also couldn't look at the vampire standing in the corner while she used all of her skill trying to convince her father she wasn't in love with Damian.*

He leaned down, his putrid breath feathering across her face, his hard stare delving into her soul. "I think you're lying."

"You don't know me well enough make that determination," she replied flatly.

Xavier smirked, now taking a seat in the chair across from her. "She's got fire, doesn't she, Geoffrey?" Another piece of the puzzle fell soundly into place.

Geoffrey, the vampire sent to Dragonfly to kidnap her, answered, "I think she demonstrated that earlier, my lord." Their gazes connected and she knew he knew. Geoffrey knew she was lying, yet he remained silent. Why?

"Well, it's a shame you made such a hasty decision, Analise. We'll have to work that much harder to undo the effects of the bonding. But never fear, I'm sure my researchers can figure that out in short order. In the meantime ..." Xavier held a hand out to Geoffrey, who placed a very large, very scary-looking syringe filled with a clear liquid in it. Was she mistaken or had she seen a twinge of regret in Geoffrey's eyes?

Okay, Mom. Now would be the time for some direction, some instruction, anything. *But her mother remained silent as Analise was stuck with the painfully large needle right in the thigh, the thick fluid burning as it was pushed in.*

Analise began to panic. What if they were giving her something to reverse her bonding to Damian? She would never forgive herself. Why was she listening to her mother anyway? She should have ashed Xavier's ass the second she opened her eyes.

"Why don't I get her something to eat, my lord? We'll need her in proper shape." Geoffrey briefly glanced at her again and she read his intentions as clearly as if he'd spoken them aloud. Get your shit together or you're dead. *Why was he helping her when he brought her into this hellhole to begin with? She felt like she'd entered an alternate universe and she had no clue where the damn door was to get back home.*

For the last several days, they'd fallen into a similar pattern. She'd be gassed, wake up tied to a chair and Xavier would grill her about the lords, about where they lived, could she find their homes, did they know where Xavier was? He asked her about Kate, about her pregnancy, which was a shocker. Damian most certainly did not tell her she had a niece or nephew on the way. Oddly enough, Xavier didn't mention anything about a third child; he only ever discussed her and Kate, so she assumed he didn't know. She gave him half-truths, generalities. Enough to appear cooperative, but not enough to put her family in danger. At least she hoped not. The fact of the matter was, she didn't know the answers to most of his questions and that simply angered him more.

She'd been stabbed with the terrifying needle each day, but Xavier wouldn't reveal its contents, no matter how much she'd begged. Which was often. Strangely enough when her mother was absent, Geoffrey grounded her, keeping her from a complete meltdown and out-and-out despair. He even protected her from Xavier's wrath, convincing Xavier not to hurt her—*much. Remember the plan, my lord*, he'd say. But it was clear Geoffrey was treading a thin line with Xavier as well. Xavier was like a rabid animal, unpredictable. You never knew when he was going to attack.

"It's time," her mother whispered.

"I know," replied Analise quietly, unable to keep Hope from bubbling over. If there was ever a time she needed to believe in the ever-elusive *Hope*, it was now. She concentrated all her hope and light and love into one swirling blast of protective energy. A battle was brewing and she needed to not only protect herself, but to be a beacon for her mate to easily find her.

Today, the gassing would end. Today, the needles would end. Today, the endless inquiry and threats would end. Today, her hell would end. Because today, Damian was coming for her. And he was close.

Chapter 49

Damian

During this battle with Xavier, they'd have a couple of very powerful secret weapons. Circo had the ability to sense what skills another vampire possessed. That came in very handy during an operation such as this. With that knowledge, they were able to quietly and efficiently eliminate the twenty rogues outside the compound with few injuries sustained, except for Manny, who was bleeding profusely from a gaping hole in his shoulder. Damian thought if he held a flashlight to it, he'd be able to see clean through to the back.

"Stay back with Maeve," Damian ordered.

"With all due respect, my lord, I'm fine. And I'm not babysitting a witch again while everyone else gets in on the fun." Manny's insolent tone set his teeth on edge, even though he understood. Manny had been stuck back with the traitorous Esmeralda during the last raid on Xavier's lair when Kate had been kidnapped.

"If I let you get killed, Dev will have my head. Or Kate, which is probably far worse come to think of it." Manny was still Kate's personal bodyguard and she had quite a fondness for the vamp. It was already bad enough he would return him injured, although it would only take a few days to fully recover.

"Fuck!" Manny snapped.

Damian slapped his good shoulder in understanding. Shifting his attention. "Ren, how's it looking on the inside?"

"Recon showed twenty-two rogues spread out over three floors. Fifteen are on the first floor, which is also where most of the humans appear to be, so this time it appears they are very heavily guarded, which wasn't the case last time. At the bottom of the first set of stairs, there are twenty rooms that line the hallway straight ahead. Each room contains one human, which we have to assume are the missing girls." Ren looked pointedly at Damian. "I sense something different about a human in the second to the last room on the left."

Ren wasn't able to confirm that particular human was Analise, but Damian's gut was wailing it was. He nodded sharply. That would be the first room Damian checked out.

"A dozen humans occupy the lowest level, mostly concentrated in a room at the north end of the building. If this is anything like the last time, those will be Xavier's human minions and we need them alive if at all possible. Two rogues are on the middle floor and the remaining five are on the lowest level. Remember the last time, we couldn't flash while inside the building, so expect that to be the case this time as well."

"Can you talk to your mate?" Rom asked.

No. And it scared the living shit out of him. He didn't respond, and an uncomfortable silence hung thickly in the air.

"Xavier and Geoffrey?" Damian asked. Because Circo could sense a vampire's unique skill, they should be able to pinpoint Xavier and Geoffrey's exact whereabouts, *if* they were here. He personally wanted to remove Geoffrey's head from his shoulders and, given the chance, he would gladly do so.

Circo was quiet for several beats, almost trancelike. "Geoffrey is in the lowest level. I'm not sensing Xavier. I'm sorry, my lord."

Shit! "That doesn't mean anything. Xavier masked his presence last time, so he could be doing it again with the help of a witch."

Damian and Rom exchanged knowing glances. Looked like Rom would get the honor of killing Geoffrey since his one and only mission was on level one and Xavier might escape their clutches yet again. So be it. All that mattered right now was Analise.

"Let's go."

ꟿ

After breaking the flimsy lock on the outside that any human thief worth his salt could conquer, they entered an abandoned building, which looked like an empty, dilapidated storage unit on the inside. It didn't take but seconds for Ren to locate the hidden door that led downstairs.

The battle started before they'd breached the heavy steel secured door at the end of the stairway as two mammoth rogues flashed directly in front of them. A white-hot pain knifed through his skull, the sonic scream let loose by one of the rogues deafening, nearly bringing him to his knees. He let loose a string of expletives under his breath. A lesser vampire would have succumbed, losing his own head in the process. But with one swipe of his razor sharp blade instead, the rogue's head rolled at his feet. It was blessed fucking relief. And with simply a thought, his remains were nothing but ash.

Rom had easily taken care of the other rogue, doing what he did best, but for good measure Damian ashed him as well. With the power of negation and absorption, Rom could not only resist whatever power another vamp used against him, but he could then take it as his own. Rom said the vampire would retain some of their power, albeit weakened, but he'd only tested that once early on. Rom was pretty unforgiving when another vampire was trying to kill him. Rom's skills were kind of like a human campfire story. Were the stories real or lore? Damian was convinced that was one of the reasons Xavier had avoided Rom all these long years. Even with Xavier's impressive skills, he was no match for the formidable Romaric Dietrich. Damian was only glad Rom was on their side and not the enemy's.

They'd decided during their strategy session that even if they could flash inside they wouldn't. It was too dangerous and those were the tactical errors that got less experienced vampires killed. So they went in the old-fashioned way instead...through the door. Now flashing out ... that was a different matter altogether, if they could.

Upon entry, they were attacked from all directions. Damian could hear war shouts and screams of agony all around him within seconds as he tried to make his way down the hallway to Analise. The vampires they'd brought on this mission were seasoned and extremely skilled. The best of the best and he worried little for their safety, so with a singular focus on getting to Analise, he easily ashed two rogues who were blocking his path as he quickly made his way toward her.

He was halfway down the narrow space when the first real attack occurred from a rogue with vortex breath, which was the ability to freeze a person in a solid block of ice within seconds. He was mid-stride when his muscles began to quickly solidify. Luckily for Damian, his fire elemental ability could easily negate the ice, but they were matched in their vampiric power, and every time Damian tried to ash him, the rouge would simply put out the fire with a thought. The rogue actually smirked at him ... taunting *him*. Damian fucking DiStephano, Regent Vampire Lord.

Damian had felt Analise's energy calling to him the moment he'd stepped foot into this hallway and he was getting tired of this cat and mouse game with an insignificant, far less experienced vampire than himself. Damian unleashed his animal instinct with a roar of fury. This fucker was going down.

He tried flashing and was surprised when it worked. The smirk was now permanently wiped off iceman as his body lay in a pool of his own blood, head rolling like a lumpy bowling ball somewhere down the long hallway. *Buh-bye Mother. Fucker.* He silently passed the flashing tidbit off to T, who would make sure the other men on their team had it.

He turned back toward Analise and flashed to the door behind which she was a prisoner. For the first time, he wished he had the superpower of x-ray vision. He didn't want to flash inside as his enemy would anticipate, and be ambushed, so this was the better way. In retrospect, he'd look back on the next several seconds and swore they took a lifetime. But had they been more than several seconds, he would be dead and his mate lost to him forever.

He was mid-kick when he felt a sudden calmness blanket him and his foot dropped down with a thud to the floor. All of his emotions went numb, like he'd taken an entire bottle of Xanax and was floating in the air watching the scene unfold as if it were happening to someone else. There was no anger, no fear, no hate, no love.

Why was he here again?

An angelic voice cut through the dense fog that had permeated deep into his brain, wrapping it in cellophane. A voice he vaguely recognized but stirred a strange feeling deep in the pit of his stomach.

"Damian, help me. I need you."

She needs me. Who needs me? Her lyrical voice sounded once again and the words she spoke shattered the haze that had fallen over him into a million pieces.

"We're undivided, Damian. It's you and me."

Analise. He turned, shoving his knife to the hilt in the chest of the empathy rogue, but not before he felt the bite of the blade through his own torso, barely missing a lung. *Jesus, that hurt.* He stumbled back against the door and unleashed his wrath with a vengeance. The white-hot fireball took two more rogues out, along with the empathy rogue. With a swift kick, the door standing between him and his mate was in pieces and there she was, huddling in the corner, eyes wide with fear.

"Damian," she cried, launching herself off the floor and into his arms. Even though his midsection was on fire from his wound, he wasted no time getting them out of the melee, flashing them to Dev's estate. He wanted nothing more than to take her to his penthouse, but she might need medical care and the best person for the job was Big D, who was waiting at the shelter. He'd lost a lot of blood with his injury and the flashing made him dizzy, but nothing, not even his own injuries, concerned him more than her well-being.

She was alive and finally back in his arms and he would never, ever let her go again.

Chapter 50

Geoffrey

They were here. *Took them fucking long enough.* The loose plan he'd formulated over the last week was finally in motion and he once again questioned the prudence of it. But this was the only way out. The only way to throw Xavier off track. The only way to get his Moira to safety.

Geoffrey had served Xavier for close to five long, torturous centuries. As his lieutenant, the last one hundred had been by far the longest, and since he'd discovered the truth about his existence, about his *family*, he'd been strategizing for this exact moment.

Xavier was a mean, sadistic, black-hearted, egotistical motherfucker and it made him ill to think of the things he'd done under his command. He was fucking done. He only hoped he had enough information to bring the monster down once and for all and didn't die in the next five minutes before he could put the second part of his long plan into motion. If he did, he'd at least die with the knowledge that *she* would be rescued and in part, it was because of the actions he took to get her the hell out of here.

For countless decades, he'd watched, he'd learned, he'd tucked information away in his brain for later use. He'd been plotting, strategizing. But the minute he'd laid eyes on subject number four hundred eighty-two, it was all over. Poof ... up in a plume of smoke. *She* was now his number one priority and it was only a matter of time before Xavier figured it out and just for the sport of it, tortured and killed her while forcing him to watch. Hell, he'd probably make him do it just to prove his loyalty. And he couldn't—*wouldn't*—let that happen. Not ever. All that mattered now was *her*. And this plan was his only shot to get her away from these vile monsters and to safety.

He'd been waiting for the lords to show up and rescue Damian's mate, so he'd personally been scouting the area, telling Xavier he was extra cautious. The minute he'd sensed them, he'd told Xavier there was a problem at the Kentucky lab that needed his immediate attention. Only Xavier could handle it. Of course, it was a very timely *problem* that may or may not have been created by him.

Taking a deep, fortifying breath, he stepped into the hallway. His first objective was to personally kill every single vampire and human down here that had laid a fucking fingernail on his Moira. He'd protected her from being brutally raped by these savages this long, but Xavier was onto him and he needed to get her the hell out of here. Yesterday. *He* wanted the honor of painfully gutting each and every one of them. Unfortunately, there were several vampires upstairs guarding the girls that he wouldn't get the chance to slice open, but in the end they'd be dead and he'd have to live with that. All that mattered was that they were wiped off the face of the planet for the wrongs they'd done.

Striding down the hallway, he adopted his new persona. Mimicry was something he could only hold for a reasonably short period of time. A few hours at best. And if he was severely injured, he reverted back to just plain old Geoffrey. He'd found that out the hard way once and nearly lost his head. When he mimicked someone, he sounded like them, acted like them, his mannerisms were like them. But the one downfall of his skill was that while in mimicry, he still retained *his* powers, not able to take on the special skill of the vampire he mimicked. Humans were easy to mimic, vampires were much more challenging.

Only minutes later, having killed each and every vile creature on the lower level—plus Xavier's favorite pet researcher who'd orchestrated his mate's torture— and covered from head to toe in his enemies blood, he stepped back into the hallway only to face the most intimidating vampire he'd ever come across. Looked like they'd sent the big guns. This might not turn out so well for him after all.

He was shitting bricks. The Reaper, in the flesh. He'd heard rumors about Romaric Dietrich, but couldn't believe the tales that a single vampire possessed such mind-blowingly powerful skills. And he didn't really want to find out firsthand either. Geoffrey was a very powerful vampire in his own right, but Romaric Dietrich was not a vampire he'd ever hoped to cross paths with. It would be like jumping into a lake full of flesh eating piranhas. Foolish, painful and life ending.

He couldn't keep Xavier's persona for the next part of his plan to work. He had no choice but to morph back into Geoffrey, hoping Romaric didn't take this opportunity to capitalize on his vulnerability and behead him on the spot.

Back to his six-foot-six bulky stature and hands held in the universal surrender position, he spoke, "I, and I alone, have information that can bring down Xavier once and for all, so it's in the Lords' best interest to capture versus kill me."

Romaric regarded him with cool interest.

Before another thought formed or he could utter another syllable, Geoffrey felt red-hot, blistering pain leak into every single pore of his body. Hc looked down, fully expecting to see himself ablaze or his skin falling away, but outwardly he was fine. It felt like acid was eating his flesh, burrowing its way greedily into his veins like thousands of African driver ants. He couldn't even drop to his knees or scream in agony because every one of his muscles was held immobile, including his voice box.

His last thought as he succumbed to the beckoning, blessed darkness was that he hoped his Moira made it out alive and that he'd see her again in the afterlife.

Chapter 51

Analise

"How are you feeling today, Analise?" Big D quietly asked her as he patted the exam table, indicating she should sit. No doubt he didn't talk louder because he couldn't.

She felt good, more than good. She'd honestly never felt better. "I'm feeling great actually. Have you been able to find anything yet?"

This was the third blood draw in the last five days ... since Damian had rescued her. Trying to respect her privacy, Big D had asked Damian to wait outside, but quickly changed his mind when he found himself pinned up against the wall, depleted of oxygen on account of the hand tightly wrapped around his neck. Damian now stood stoically at her side, a possessive arm around her shoulders.

He hadn't left her side for one second since they'd returned. He even followed her to the bathroom for the first three days, which she finally had to put an end to. He would only agree if she left the door open. She couldn't even fart in private! *Gah!* Stubborn vampire.

While he hadn't left her side, he hadn't touched her either. Not in the way she wanted, in the way she needed. She was ready to throw a temper tantrum like a five-year-old in a grocery store whose mother denies her that pretty rainbow-colored sucker in the checkout lane. Damian would never know what hit him.

The foolish vampire was unable to forgive himself, blaming himself for her abduction, but she knew this path had been predetermined long before either of them could influence it. She just wasn't sure to what end. She'd told him all about her mother's help during the abduction—her mother had remained strangely absent since her rescue—but for some reason she had left out the part about Geoffrey. She was afraid if she told him, she'd have to confess her act of betrayal in the worst way, for which she hadn't yet forgiven herself.

"I believe I finally know what was injected into your bloodstream, but I would like one final test to confirm it," Big D said, getting the phlebotomy kit ready. *Ugh. Another goddamned needle.*

"What is it, Doc?" Damian demanded, his sinewy body coiled with tension.

Big D flicked his gaze nervously between Analise and Damian. Analise reached out, laying a soothing hand on his arm. "It's okay, Dirk. I'd just rather know." Damian grabbed her hand back, tucking it into her side. She promptly elbowed him in the stomach with the other, hoping that the daggers she fired with her eyes landed on their mark. He was being absolutely ridiculous.

"You were injected with the pregnancy enhancing hormone that Xavier's minions developed." *Well, yikes.* She hadn't really seen that one coming. Damian stiffened beside her, his grip becoming painfully tight.

Her mind spun with possibilities. Clearly Xavier had planned to farm her body out, hoping to make grandbabies. He'd referenced a *family business* several times during their conversations. She'd just foolishly thought he was referring to herself and Kate—and Kate's baby—and that was why he was so upset she'd bonded with Damian. Damian had told her how difficult it was to procreate with a mate, let alone without one, which was supposed to be impossible.

More puzzle pieces knitted their way together, but more questions plagued her as well. *Her mother knew.* Her mother knew all along what Xavier's intent was. But *how* had she known? Could she somehow have been responsible for orchestrating this entire thing? It didn't seem feasible, but since she was officially living in Narnia—a world where anything was possible—she couldn't definitively say she hadn't.

But the one question that kept rising to the top above others was ... could she now *possibly* get pregnant? Could she have Damian's baby? Would *he* even want to?

By the time she'd come out of her reverie, Big D walked out of the exam room, mumbling something under his breath she didn't catch.

"Kitten ..." Damian's voice broke with pained emotion. He was on the verge of breaking down and her own tears pricked at his agony. They held each other for an indeterminable amount of time. This news wasn't the end of the world. In fact, the more she tested it, the happier she was about it. If the three days she had to spend with that monster resulted in her ability to bear a child with Damian, the love of her life, she'd do it all over again. No hesitation, no questions, no doubt.

She needed to help him get over his guilt so they could move on from here, but how? She recalled what Sebastian had unknowingly revealed yesterday during a hushed, clearly private conversation with Damian. Hey, could she help it if she now had super-sized hearing? When she'd cornered Sebastian in a rare few minutes that Damian had left her alone to speak with Dev, he'd revealed some very enlightening facts about Damian's little home improvement project.

"Damian, let's go home," she mumbled into his chest. She'd spent a fair amount of time with Kate and a little with Sarah since she was still recovering from her near death experience, and while she didn't want to leave her sisters, she needed time alone with Damian. They could come back at any time on a whim.

"I think we should stay here until we get the final results back from the doctor, Analise," he replied, his voice firm and unyielding. *Uh oh.* Domineering Damian had returned, and there was only one place she wanted that persona to make an appearance. And if she had her way ...

Pulling back, it was time to put her foot down. "No. We already know. And there is a thing in the twenty-first century called a goddamned phone. If anything comes up that we don't already know, the doctor will call and we'll even come back if necessary. But there won't be, because for the umpteenth time, I. Am. Fine. Now, I want to go to *my* home with *my* mate and make love in *my* bed. You can't deny me that, Damian."

She knew the moment she had him. For not knowing anything about relationships, she was getting pretty darn good at this pretty darn fast.

"Okay, kitten." He gently brushed her lips with his. "Anything for you. Do you want to say goodbye to your sisters first?"

"Yes. Thank you, Damian."

He smiled, but it didn't reach his sad eyes. Hopefully, by tomorrow morning, she'd have her cheeky, fun-loving Damian back.

Since they were already in the shelter, they made their way to see Sarah first. She'd been released from the infirmary but was on strict bed rest, and Damian graciously waited outside so they could have a private conversation.

"Come in," Sarah replied to her knock, her voice sounding even stronger than yesterday.

"Hi, Sarah. How are you doing today?" Analise asked as she closed her door and sat on the edge of the bed.

"Better. Every day I feel a bit stronger. The incision is still a bit sore, but otherwise I'm good."

"Good, I'm glad to hear it." Analise considered her words before asking her next question. "How are you *really* doing, outside of the appendicitis, I mean?"

Sarah looked her square in the eye and Analise knew that her sister would not only recover, she'd use this experience to make her stronger. Much like Analise had.

"I'm getting there, Analise. I'm much better." While her voice was soft, there was confidence and strength lying underneath, trying to crawl their way to the top of the complex and ever-shifting emotional mountain.

Analise had taken a deep breath before she told the only person outside of Damian her survivor story. "When I was eighteen, I was raped, got pregnant and ended up losing the baby. Ectopic pregnancy." Analise looked down at the pale ivory Damask bedspread. "Even though I went through the worst thing a woman could possibly endure—on many fronts—I was devastated at the loss of that baby. I didn't realize how much I wanted him until I didn't have him anymore." The last part she'd not mentioned to a single soul, not even Damian.

She looked back at Sarah who now had tears brimming in her golden brown eyes.

"My point is that, to some degree, I do know what you're going through. I know you weren't raped, but you were traumatized and you're still going through the same emotional rollercoaster, Sarah. I spent years locking myself away in my own little castle, or more accurately locking everyone else out. Never trusting anyone enough to tell them my story so I could heal and move on. Not everyone in this world is evil. Not everyone is out to harm you. Meeting Damian has helped me realize that I'd done myself a complete disservice by not talking about it, not letting it out.

"You're strong, Sarah. I can see the fire, the grit, the determination in your eyes. There are people here who love you and want to take care of you. I'm proud to call you my sister."

Sarah launched herself into Analise's arms and they both cried. "Thank you, Analise," Sarah rasped. "I'm so glad I have you."

"Ditto," she choked through the lump in her throat.

"I'm going back to Boston for a few days, but I'll call you every day, okay?" Sarah just nodded, her grip tightening. Analise was torn, but her mate had to be her first priority. She pulled back, gently holding her by the shoulders so Sarah could see she meant it. "Call me anytime, Sarah. Okay?"

"I'll be just fine, Analise. See you when you get back. And thanks for trusting me with your story."

Analise kissed her on the cheek, saying goodbye.

She had one more stop to make before she searched for Kate. Analise and Damian exchanged knowing glances and he stayed put in the hallway while Analise walked down a few doors.

She knocked and opened the door at the same time. Beth had been pretty emotionally unresponsive since Damian's men rescued her. Kate said that most of the time she just lay on her bed, unfocused eyes staring at the ceiling. While her physical scars were healing, it was obvious her emotional ones weren't. Once again, guilt battered Analise. Her sister, her friend … they needed her and all she could think of was getting Damian's body inside hers. *Ugh ... she was a terrible person.*

"Beth, how are you today, sweetie?" No response. She sat for a few minutes like she did every day for the past five days, talking to her about inane things, like current events, Beth's favorite TV show and finally told her she'd be returning to Boston for a few days. Squeezing Beth's hand as she rose, Analise made her way to the door, but Beth's voice stopped her cold.

"Where is he?" she whispered so softly Analise didn't know if she'd heard right.

"Where is who, Beth?" Her skin prickled in anticipation of Beth's answer. As she'd seen the attentive vampire in her dream of Beth, she knew exactly to whom Beth was referring. Analise didn't have an answer, except that he was presumed dead. Xavier's team was massacred in the battle. Not one of his rogues survived.

"My savior," she said simply. Beth's head turned toward Analise, looking at her for the first time. Beth's soul was haunted and it cut her to the quick to see her best friend in such emotional pain. She wasn't about to cause her any more by telling Beth that the vampire she'd come to care for, even if he might be associated with a psychopath and one himself, was likely dead.

"I don't know, Beth. I don't know." Beth closed her eyes on an exhale and turned back toward the wall. Analise slipped out quietly and Damian was right there, arms around her, knowing exactly what she needed. He *always* knew what she needed sometimes even before she did.

"We have to go. I'll call Kate when we get there. Right now I just need to go home, Damian. Please," she begged. This place was full of pain and sadness and selfishly she needed an escape, if only for a little while.

Within seconds, they were blessedly at the penthouse and Damian had them settled on the couch. He held her in his lap, her head on his shoulder and not for the first time in the last few days, she relished in the feel of his strong arms around her, comforting her and protecting her and loving her.

And now it was time to bring the domineering, confident, sometimes infuriating man she fell in love with back to her.

Chapter 52

Mike

He stood at the window in the plush, ostentatious room with a nice amber scotch swirling in his glass, watching a flock of birds in the distance. He'd prefer a nice bottle of beer to the scotch he now held, but alcohol was alcohol and he needed its mind-numbing effects. *It's five o'clock somewhere, right?* And apparently Dev was clean out of beer. Who the hell runs out of beer? That's just criminal.

He'd been *dispatched* to Dev's for some unknown reason and he should have been getting used to that by now, but fuck if he was. Ren, who'd 'retrieved' him, sat silently on the couch, more interested in his phone than conversation and that suited him fine.

It had been almost two weeks since he'd heard from the bloodsuckers. He'd found the dirty cop Damian had requested, passing that information along, but he'd never heard a word back. Every day he searched a few more places for the body of Frankie Durillo, but that proved to be a bust.

He hadn't seen, talked or texted with Giselle in almost two weeks either. Actually, it was twelve days, fifteen hours and forty-two minutes, but who the hell was counting. *He sure wasn't.* And that was precisely the reason he needed the liquid courage.

Because if he saw her today, he wasn't sure how he would react. Would he be indifferent, which was how he *wanted* to act, or would he let his desperate need for her bleed through his eyes until it was spelled out clearly at her feet? If he were a betting man, it would be the latter.

"She's not here, man," Ren finally quipped. "But she should be back. Any. Minute. Now." Mike stood stock still with his back to Ren, pretending he didn't hear him. Apparently that didn't deter the meddling asshole as he continued blabbing his trap. "The text I sent should get her back here right quick."

Mike whipped around wishing he had a goddamned knife so he could shove it deep into Ren's chest. "What are you playing at vampire?" he spat.

Ren didn't miss a beat. "Well, I'm playing matchmaker, you stupid fuck. You both need to pull your heads out of your asses and just screw already. You could light up an entire city for a goddamned year with the amount of energy you've wasted trying to pretend you don't want in each other's pants. Jesus Christ, man, it's *exhausting.*"

He sat there just staring at Ren in ... confusion? Amazement? All he'd really heard in his tirade was *she wants me*. And damn if that didn't make his heart swell just a little teeny, tiny bit.

Obviously he wasn't as good at hiding his attraction to Giselle as he'd thought. And neither was she. He was speechless. For once in his sorry life, he had no witty or hateful comeback. Luckily Dev saved him from the shame of silence, which in

Ren's eyes would be akin to agreement and that was the last thing he needed.

"Detective, thanks for coming. Someone has requested to see you." Mike shot his glance back toward Ren, who just shrugged like he had no idea what was going on. If this were some type of group intervention, he would go absolutely ballistic. Goddamned vampires thinking they could tell him who to fu—

"It's Jamie."

Now his eyes snapped to Dev's and he could feel the confusion clouding his own face. "Jamie asked to see me?" he muttered.

Dev nodded once. "Kate is bringing her down now, but I wanted to talk to you first." Dev gestured for him to sit, which he did gladly. His legs were feeling rather like a newborn calf's.

"While she's recovered physically, she's in bad shape emotionally, Mike." *Mike* ... that was the first time the vamp even acknowledged he had a first name. This was getting more bizarre by the second. "She's hardly left her room for three months. Kate has finally convinced her to attend some counseling sessions and interact a bit with the other girls, and she's making some progress, but she's not revealed much about what happened. I don't know who she was before, but I can guarantee you she's not the same girl you knew and you need to understand that before you agree to see her."

Agree to see her? Like he would turn her away? And he already knew she would be different. Who the hell could survive what she'd been through and be the same? Not one living soul. Mike nodded in understanding.

"And if you say or do anything to upset her, you'll have me to answer to, human. Understand?" Now there was the Devon he was all too familiar with. Again, he simply nodded. Devon didn't know him very well if he thought Mike would upset the only woman he'd ever loved.

Ren took off, leaving Mike and Dev alone. They sat in pensive silence for several minutes until Kate walked into the room, holding Jamie's hand and Jamie was holding onto it for dear life. Head down, she stared hard at the carpet underneath her feet like she was walking into a pit of snakes and they would attack at any minute. *Jesus. Jamie.* His heart was bleeding.

Kate led Jamie to a chair opposite the couch where he sat and Jamie sat down, still not making eye contact with him. Kate whispered something in Jamie's ear before standing up. Dev held a hand out to Kate and she walked into his arms like that was the only place she was ever meant to be. She looked happy. *They* looked happy.

A seed of envy planted itself deep within his gut and he felt the roots starting to grab hold. Time for some *Weed-B-Gone* on that shit when he got home. Mike Thatcher did *not* do envy.

Everyone left the room, giving them privacy. He had no illusions that they'd gone too far, though. They were probably eavesdropping just around the corner. He didn't give a rat's ass. He would never hurt this fragile woman sitting in front of him. Her eyes remaining on the floor, they sat in uncomfortable silence for what seemed like a lifetime. Well, uncomfortable for her maybe, but it gave him an opportunity to really drink her in. And Dev was right ... she had changed.

Physically, she'd filled out, her face less gaunt, which was good because Kate told him when she was recovered she was nothing but skin and bones. But she looked far from the young woman he'd known. At least he didn't *see* any bones visibly protruding. It was hard to say under the long sleeve Henley and dark jeans she wore. Her long brown curly locks looked healthy and just as he'd remembered. Or maybe he was projecting his images of old Jamie onto the new Jamie. At this point he had no fucking idea because his head felt like a jumbled, unwound ball of yarn.

Physically she looked fine, healthy even. But even though he'd yet to look into her eyes as she'd refused eye contact, there was no doubt she was haunted. Sadness surrounded her like a protective shroud and his heart bled for all that she had been through. All that he couldn't protect her from.

"I wanted you to know that I don't blame you, Mike," she said softly. *Absolution?* He didn't deserve it. He should have done more to protect his woman from those vermin.

But all thought vanished and his breath stopped the moment their eyes connected. No, Dev was wrong. *His* Jamie wasn't gone; she was simply drowning so far beneath dark, murky waters she might never find her way to the surface again. He wanted to help her. She deserved to take full fresh lungful's of life-giving oxygen again. She deserved to live the rest of her life happily and carefree. And for this woman who was once his entire world, he'd move heaven and earth to make that happen.

She continued as he'd apparently lost his ability to speak. "In fact, you actually helped me survive." She broke their gaze, looking down at her lap. "My memories of you were the only thing I could hold onto at times." Her voice broke and the tears started flowing. It took all his willpower not to pull her into his arms and he had to sit on his hands to keep from reaching for her.

"But I think that's why it took me so long to see you." Her eyes lifted to his again, the sadness in them heartbreaking. "Because I now associate you with them."

Devastating pain unlike anything he'd ever felt, even losing her the first time, crashed over him like a tsunami, threatening to take him under to the bottom of the cold, dark ocean. Right now, he'd welcome the pain of a bullet or a knife wound over the agony those seven words inflicted on him.

"I'm sorry, Jamie," was all he could choke out.

She shook her head and reached for his arm. He wanted to recoil from her touch because it still sent the same electrical current through his body as it did so many years ago. But this wasn't about him; it was about her. And if she wanted to touch him, by God, he'd let her.

"No, I'm the one who's sorry, Mike. It's wrong. I know it's wrong, but I can't help the way I feel. I am working through it, though. Today helped. Thank you for coming." She smiled, or tried to anyway, but it didn't reach her sad, haunted eyes.

"I'd do anything for you," he rasped. "Anything."

She squeezed his arm slightly, then stood and walked toward the entrance. She turned just as she reached it. "I'd like to see you again sometime if that's okay?"

If that's okay? At this moment, no it wasn't okay. It was far from okay, but being the glutton for punishment he was, of course he agreed. To help her, he'd gladly gut himself. That was the least he owed her, even though she didn't think so. "Yes, of course, Jamie. Anytime."

As she walked away from him, any hopes he'd secretly harbored about a happily ever after with Jamie were crushed. Blown into a million pieces, scattered to the earth. He poured himself a big goddamned glass of scotch, took a healthy gulp and walked back to the bay window. Standing there lost in thought, he wasn't quite sure exactly what he felt in that moment.

Anger? Check.

Bitterness? Check.

Crushing pain? Abso-fucking-lutely.

Self-loathing? Yup. Got a motherfucking Ph.D. in that one.

He was lost in his thoughts when he felt *her* presence. Christ, he was so attuned to her it made him sick. *How much had she heard?* With his luck, probably every crushing humiliating word. She was the last fucking person he needed to deal with right now and she needed to leave before he said something he'd truly regret.

"Not now, Giselle." He tasted the bitter venom in his words. He kept his back to her, taking another big gulp of the liquid gold, washing the bitterness into his already acrid stomach. The burn felt good, it felt right. He deserved that and so much more.

He cringed when her hand touched his shoulder. It felt like heaven, but he needed it so badly to burn like hell instead. She turned him around to face her and the spiteful retort he'd had ready on his forked tongue died a quick death.

If he'd seen sympathy on her face, he'd have let the hateful words fly, but instead he saw empathy in her bright blue eyes. She'd walked a mile in his shoes and in this one brief moment he understood so much more about Giselle than in all their prior encounters. She'd never been this open or this vulnerable.

She said nothing, wrapping her gorgeous limbs around him instead. It was a display of comfort, tenderness ... solidarity. And he found himself wanting nothing more than to cling to the lifeline that she'd so selflessly thrown to him.

So there he stood, in Devon Fallinsworth's living room, hanging on for his very existence to the woman who'd breathed life back into his heart, while mourning the woman who'd shattered it for the second time.

Chapter 53

Damian

They'd been sitting like this for over an hour. He was a mess. He knew it, but he couldn't seem to pull himself out of the black abyss he was relentlessly swirling in. *Analise was safe.* All of the horrific things he'd agonized over didn't happen, and outside of a few bumps and bruises that had already healed, she seemed no worse for the wear. She didn't seem traumatized, but of course she wouldn't. His Analise was a warrior. A survivor.

She'd told him repeatedly he wasn't to blame, but how could she not see that he was? Believing he spoke truth, he'd brought that monster into Dev's home. *He* was one hundred percent to blame, no one else. And he would never forgive himself. How could Analise? How could she even want a mate who practically threw her to the wolves himself, doing nothing to protect her?

"Stop!" she yelled. Straddling his lap, she grabbed his cheeks so hard it almost hurt. *Wow ... she's gotten a lot stronger.* "That's enough, vampire. Do you hear me? It's time to stop your little pity party and come back to me, Damian."

He stared at her, mouth agape. "Damian," she sighed, "yes, you brought Geoffrey into the house, but I don't believe it was under false pretenses. I think he was telling you the truth about Xavier." She sighed, heavily this time. "I didn't know ... I mean, I wasn't sure until today."

"What weren't you sure about?" His gut churned in dread to hear the next words out of her mouth. He knew she'd been holding something back and had been waiting for days for the other shoe to drop and her to tell him all of the horrific things that had *really* happened to her while being held under Xavier's boot.

"I think that Beth is Geoffrey's Moira and kidnapping me was his only recourse to protect her."

His fury ignited. She was *protecting* the vampire who'd kidnapped her? "How can you possibly justify his actions, Analise?" he gritted, his teeth grinding so hard they hurt.

"Well ..." He started to move her from his lap, unable to have this conversation with her. She'd so obviously been brainwashed while she was a prisoner, it now made sense why she would defend a kidnapping sociopath. She clamped her knees hard to his legs, effectively stopping him from removing her.

"Listen to me, dammit. I saw them, in my dream. He took care of her. He protected her. He looked at her the way you look at me. And when I was captive, Geoffrey was the only thing that kept Xavier from killing me, which he wanted to do many times. He protected me and I know that sounds bizarre, given the fact that he put me into that situation, but it's the only thing that makes sense. He needed to get his Moira, Beth, out from under Xavier, and what better way to do that than kidnap a lord's mate and have the cavalry come to the rescue? It makes perfect sense and you know it."

Damian thought on her logic for several beats. And he, unfortunately, had to admit she might be onto something, but right or wrong it still didn't negate the sting he felt at being duped. "What sort of pussy puts another vampire's mate in danger to save his own? That's dishonorable."

She nodded her agreement. "Maybe. But the flip side to that is he could admit he wasn't able to take on Xavier by himself and needed help that only the lords could provide."

"Why wouldn't he just ask me then? I would have gladly brought in the cavalry without putting mine in danger."

"That I don't know. We may never know, but in my gut I know there's a logical explanation. He wouldn't have tried so hard to minimize the fallout otherwise."

He stared at his mate with a newfound appreciation. "How did you get so wise, kitten?" He sweetly kissed her neck and a moan escaped her throat. His dick got hard at the erotic noise and a ravenous need to be inside her body overtook him. He began to disrobe her when she halted his movements.

"I have to tell you something else," she confessed guiltily. And once again, that acid sitting in the pit of his stomach churned with renewed fervor. He swallowed thickly, waiting for a nuclear bomb that would annihilate his world once again.

"What?" He could barely get those four letters out. He wanted to take them back and replace them with ten new letters instead: *don't tell me*.

"When I was prisoner, I had to tell Xavier that I ... I ..." Her eyes were glassy and tears threatened to spill. He wiped a stray that'd escaped.

"What, Analise? You can tell me." True, she could tell him anything; he just couldn't predict how he would react.

"I had to tell him that I didn't love you." Rivers now streamed down her beautiful face, streaking her makeup, and he could feel her genuine shame. Relief hit him so hard; he couldn't help the laugh that escaped him. *That* was her confession? The guilt he'd been feeling left him faster than air from a popped balloon and he suddenly felt lighter than the wind. His mate was sitting safely on his lap and it didn't matter how she got there; it only mattered that was where she was. They were quite the pair, both carrying guilt for circumstances beyond their control.

"Why are you laughing?" she demanded.

"I'm sorry," he replied between chuckles. "I was just expecting you to say something far worse, that's all." He leaned in, kissing her deeply, savoring her delicious taste. One he hadn't had enough of over the last week. "You did what you had to in order to survive, kitten. There's no shame in that." He arched his brows waiting for a response. All she would give him was an agreeable nod. He was so hard now his balls ached.

"Analise," he murmured against her lips, "Christ, I need you so much." This time he didn't need to wait for a response as her lips crashed into his before he'd even finished his sentence. She wound her hands in his hair and ground her silk-covered heat against his hardness. He was so primed he was going to blow in about ten seconds if she kept that up.

She abruptly pulled back. "Take me to our new playroom."

"Wha—? How did you know about that, kitten?" *Fucking Sebastian.*

She simply winked as she climbed off his lap, reached under her dress and removed her light pink panties with a ceremonious drop to the floor. Suddenly he couldn't care less how she'd found out. If the wetness he'd seen on her panties was any indication, she was more than excited to try it out.

He grabbed her and impatiently flashed them there, not wanting to waste another second before worshipping her sinful body. He looked around the room, impressed with what he saw. The black comforter on the king-sized four poster bed was a perfect complement to the deep purple walls and ceiling. The low light sconces on the wall added a dark, dungeon feel to the space. All of the implements he'd requested were perfectly placed, but the piece that drew his eye was the St. Andrew's cross he'd had specially commissioned for her. It was perfect, just like Analise.

He took a black leather chair from the corner of the room and moved it to the center, their gazes burning into each other.

"Strip," he thickly commanded. His cock was so hard it needed immediate relief. He undid his pants, pulling out his throbbing shaft while she watched. She swallowed hard when he began to slowly stroke it. His gums ached and his gut burned with the need to have her sweet blood flowing through him again. He'd been foolish to deny her over the last several days and now his body was paying him back tenfold, every part of him in pain.

Her eyes flicked back to his and she gifted him with a brilliant smile before she slowly unzipped her white strapless sundress. He couldn't take his eyes off her as she slowly let it drop to the floor, her strapless bra quickly joining the dress. His eyes raked over her perfect curves, stopping at her newly bare, hairless pussy.

"Sweet Jesus." His grip tightened and if he didn't stop soon, he would come all over his own stomach. And that was not where he was coming tonight.

"Stand in front of the cross, hands in the air." She readily complied. She was sweet perfection. He wanted to ravage her in every way known to man. Once he had her safely secured, only then did he let himself touch her. He ran his hands and mouth all over her body. Cupping her ample breasts, he leaned down, taking a hardened nipple into his mouth, sucking and licking but careful not to bite yet. He paid equal attention to her other one, relishing in the moans he pulled from her.

He dropped to his knees and ran a long finger through her wetness. She moaned, trying to buck, but he had her tightly bound so she had to remain still and take his ministrations.

"You smell so fucking good. So good," he rasped right before he leaned in and with one long lick tasted heaven. She quivered under his touch. Her taste intoxicated him and it didn't take long before her essence filled his mouth and she was coming apart beneath his tongue, chanting his name, along with God's. *Yah, kitten, I am a God.* Even through her post-orgasmic haze, she laughed.

He didn't want to take her against the hard, unforgiving wood, so he quickly released her, gently rubbing her previously bound wrists and ankles before laying her in the middle of the bed. He ached for her hands and lips and mouth all over him. He'd missed her so damned much.

His clothes joined hers on the floor and he lay on his back, pulling her astride him. She smiled, asking quietly, "Are you sure?"

"I've never been more sure of anything in my life. Touch me, kiss me, make love to me, Analise Lisbeth DiStephano."

"As you wish, my mate," she replied saucily.

As she worshiped him, he soaked in every touch, every bite, every lave, every kiss, every rub, every whisper. He belonged to this woman and she to him and they completed each other in ways neither thought possible. He was whole, he was fulfilled, he was deliriously happy.

"I love you Damian," she breathed right before they went over the edge of rapture together.

"And I you, kitten. And I you."

Epilogue

Five days later....
Rom

He hated this place. He was back in the godforsaken Midwest with its flat plains, fields of corn and *Milwaukee's Best*. Who would drink that swill, he hadn't a clue. Give him the rainy, drizzly weather of the northwest any day of the year. He'd picked that region of the country for a reason ... it matched his somber mood. It felt like everyone here lived perpetually in the merry old Land of Oz. Happy and giddy, skipping down the yellow brick road watching life pass by through their rose-colored glasses. It was nauseatingly annoying.

He was here to strategize with the other lords on the next step to take with their duplicitous captor, Geoffrey. He'd be lying if he said he wasn't slightly impressed with the rogue. It took a lot of balls to face him the way he had.

Damian wanted his head on a stake so he could drive it into the ground right outside his Boston penthouse, warning other vampires what happened when you screwed with his woman. Damian was always one for theatrics. Dev was a little more open to options as long as it resulted in his death when his usefulness wore out.

But the rogue had purpose. And his purpose wouldn't be served by turning him into a pile of burning embers. At least not yet.

Romaric knocked on the door to Devon's estate and was dutifully greeted by his new butler, Hooker. Now what self-respecting vampire lets himself be referred to as *Hooker,* for God's sake? He had half a mind to throw a name book at him and demand he choose a different one on the spot.

"I'm here to see Devon," he said flatly. He refused to utter the vamp's self-proclaimed label.

"Of course, of course, my lord. Lord Devon is having dinner in the shelter with Lord Damian and their mates and asked that you join them when you arrived. I'll show you the way."

Christ. Yes, he was horrible, but he *loathed* the shelter. There was too much agony and pain that hung in the air. It was oppressive and permeated his skin like cigarette smoke, taking days to scrub the stench away. Outside of one time, he'd effectively avoided it for all these months. That was one of the reasons he'd offered to take care of the other human physicians and scientists. Leave the caretaking of these fragile women to someone who actually had a heart and could utter a caring, comforting word. Everyone knew that he couldn't. His had been ripped clean out of his chest over hundreds of years ago and all that remained was a black pit of despair.

"I'll wait." He'd do anything to avoid going over there.

"Oh no, my lord. Lord Devon insisted I bring you right over. I must." *Hooker* looked like he was going to be walked to the stocks if he didn't follow Dev's orders.

For the love of all that's holy. "Fine," he clipped.

A few short minutes later they were across the estate and he was being ushered into the dining room. Their noisy voices were like fingernails on a chalkboard. Jesus, how he detested chatter. The butler announced him and the room quieted. Mercy for small favors.

A gasp and the sound of silverware clattering on a plate brought his attention to the female sitting in the corner of the table between Dev and Damian's mates and his world spun completely off its axis.

Ferocious possessiveness roared through him. Every animal and vampiric instinct he had screamed that the exotically beautiful reddish blonde-haired female with the caramel eyes at the end of the table staring at him was *his*. His mind repeatedly screamed *Mine, Mine, Mine* loudly. So loudly that was all he could now hear, even though he faintly heard someone speaking to him. His vision narrowed to only *her*. He violently wanted to own her. She was *his*. His body thought she was his, his mind thought she was his, but his logic *knew* it could not be so.

Vampires recognize their Moiras instantaneously. There was no doubt, there was room for argument, and there were no second chances. A vampire had *one* true Moira, one true fated destiny in their lifetimes.

And unbeknownst to anyone, he'd already lost his over five centuries earlier.

~ The End ~

Next to books, music is my passion and was my inspiration to tell Damian and Analise's story. I hope you enjoy their playlist and maybe find a new favorite or two!

Kelly

Belonging Playlist

"Chandelier" by Sia
"My Demons" by Starset
"Don't Stop the Music by Rihanna
"S&M" by Rihanna
"Inside the Fire" by Disturbed
"Stay With Me" by Sam Smith
"Broken Pieces" by Apocalyptica
"Familiar Taste of Poison" by Halestorm
"Midnight" by Coldplay
"Fix You" by Coldplay
"Not a Bad Thing" by Justin Timberlake
"Smell of Desire" by Enigma
"Fancy" by Iggy Azalea
"Cantandus," *Mayna Canta*
"Angel" by Massive Attack
"Stranglehold" by Ted Nugent
"Mirrors" by Justin Timberlake
"All of Me" by John Legend
"No Ordinary Love" by Sade
"Nights in White Satin" by Moody Blues
"Bring Me To Life" by Evanescence
"Undivided" by Adelita's Way
"Nothing But a Good Time" by Poison

Upcoming releases:

If you haven't yet read ***Surrendering***, Book 1 in the Regent Vampire Lords series, you can purchase a copy today on Amazon.

Book 3 in the Regent Vampire Lords series, ***Reawakening***, is available now and will feature Romaric's story. Keep reading for a little sneak peek and watch my Facebook or Goodreads pages, or my website, for announcements on the release date!

Also planned for 2015 is a Novella featuring Mike and Giselle's rocky saga and possibly a fourth novel, depending on reader interest.

Please like my Facebook page https://www.facebook.com/pages/KL-Kreig/808927362462053?ref=hl or my website http://www.klkreig.com to keep up-to-date on release dates, cover reveals, etc. I would also love to hear from you, so feel to drop me a message at either place or my email at klkreig@gmail.com.

Keep reading for a snippet from ***Reawakening***.

An unedited snippet from *Reawakening,* Book 3 in the Regent Vampire Lords series, coming Spring 2015.

His hands traveled lightly down her exposed arms. She wanted them to thread underneath her pajama top and palm her aching breasts. She wanted his lips to take her pebbled nipple into his mouth, but he frustratingly kept his touch light, teasing. Hot breath skated along her neck but his mouth never touched her skin.

She didn't want to wake but consciousness beckoned her. *"Just a few more minutes," she pleaded.*

"More," she begged.

This was the first time he'd ever touched her in a dream. After all these years of aching for him, he finally had his hands on her but it was not enough. And why did it feel so right, yet so weirdly wrong, at the same time?

It was *him*, but he'd yet to show his face. It was *him*, but every time she tried to look into his icy blues, they became concealed again. *Gah*! Why was he hiding from her?

Morning rays spilled in around the closed shades and the last images of her erotic dream faded away. She whipped off the covers, her body in agony with unfulfilled need. Her hand snaked down under her panties, finding her pussy completely drenched. She had to relieve some of the pressure that'd built to volcanic proportions. She'd never been so turned on.

And it was just *a dream. Imagine how the real flesh and blood Romaric would feel against your skin, in your body.*

Spreading her moisture, she reached climax in record time and lay panting on sweat soaked sheets. Once wasn't enough and after the second release, she finally felt a small amount of the heaviness subside. If she did happen to see Romaric, she wasn't sure she'd be able to keep from jumping him on the spot. And wouldn't that be embarrassing, throwing yourself at someone who didn't bother to give you the time of day.

Pushing down her disappointment that she hadn't seen him last night, she headed for the shower. Thirty minutes later, hair slightly damp and curly, with a light coat of mascara and some powder to cover her shiny pores, she dressed in jean shorts and a navy blue tank. Slipping on her flip-flops, she opened her bedroom door and froze.

Standing in her doorway—no, more like taking up her *entire* doorway—was Romaric Dietrich.

Romaric, Greek God of sex.

In.

The.

Flesh.

Sweet. Holy. Mother.

With his sexy goatee and light hair so closely cropped to his head that he almost appeared bald, he *was* god-like perfection and scary intimidating all at the same time. The entire package was rounded out with his clear blue penetrating eyes, and shoulders so broad he'd put any NFL linebacker to shame.

And his scrutiny of her now was as, if not more, piercing as that night at dinner seven long days ago. Hungry eyes raked over every inch of her exposed flesh, lingering on the swell of her breasts, before snapping back to hers. She suddenly wished she'd worn wedges, not only to make her taller, but to lengthen her less than model short legs.

Sweet. Holy. Mother. Yes, she was repeating herself, but *Jesus*, it was worth repeating.

"Hello Sarah," he drawled. The deep timbre of his voice echoed in her ears long after he'd stopped talking.

"Uhhhhh ..."

He chuckled and this is the first time she'd seen a hint of a smile on his oh so serious face. She *loved* it. If he would full on smile, she was sure she'd drop to her knees and kiss his feet. Or something else.

Sarah ... stop.

"It's customary to say hello back."

Not knowing what else to do, she complied. "Uh, hello." But it came out choppy and breathless, instead of sexy and confident.

Groan.

To her surprise, he grabbed her hand—her *rubbin' the nubbin'* one—and brought it to his mouth, brushing his lips across her knuckles before inhaling deeply.

A knowing grin spread across his face and she wasn't sure if she should die of mortification on the spot or kneel at his feet, as she'd earlier thought. His smile lit up the entire room, brighter than the sunlight streaming in her now open window.

Oh. My. Gawd.

He was the sexiest damn thing she had ever seen.

"Accompany me to breakfast."

Was that a demand or a question? She wasn't really sure it mattered at the moment because her answer was yes, yes, *hell* yes.

"Sure," she replied nonchalantly. His grin spread even further, knowing she was anything but unaffected by him. Jesus, instead of acting like the grown ass woman she was, she was acting like a crushing schoolgirl who liked a boy, but for some dumb reason didn't want him to know.

Never letting her hand go, he silently led her through the shelter back to the main house and into the smaller of the dining rooms. The table in here could still easily hold twenty guests. Dev really did like the finer things in life.

"Sit." He pulled out a chair and gestured for her to take a seat. Surprisingly, he pulled out the chair right next to hers and sat, but not before scooting it closer to hers. He had nineteen other chairs to choose from but chose the one right next to hers instead.

Suddenly she was very nervous. And kind of pissed off, actually. After seeing him again, she *knew* she hadn't dreamt up their mutual attraction, so why hadn't she heard from him before now? Why didn't he stop by last night? Why hadn't he called her before now? How about a text or a secret note through Dev or Damian? Why hadn't he made even a shred of an attempt to let her know that she wasn't concocting this insane connection in her own sometimes-crazy head?

"How did you sleep?" he asked.

How did she sleep? That was his first question? He hadn't seen her in a week, ignoring this raging sexual inferno between them, and he wanted to talk about how she'd slept? Why not just ask her what she thought of this ungodly hot summer they'd been having or her thoughts on global warming or hey, what do you think of North Korea's nuclear warhead threat?

How did she sleep?

Nancy: because he was with another ho ... I thought I already went over this with you, Sarah.

She turned in her chair to face him, tucking her right leg beneath her left.

"What are you doing?"

"Having breakfast," he replied flatly. All traces of humor had vanished and the insanely intense Romaric had resurfaced.

Kate and Analise had warned her against Romaric. Analise thought he was 'scary as fuck'. Kate just thought he was lonely. Both agreed he was stoic, calm and calculating. Almost unfeeling, like an emotional lever had simply been flipped off.

She observed him for a few moments. As much as she wanted to have sex with the sex god himself—and she *really, really* did—she suddenly didn't want to be added to a very long list of women that came before her. And if she stayed here, she'd have to see him occasionally, and wouldn't that just be awkward. She could just imagine that conversation.

Hello Sarah, how are you today?

Great, are you in town long?

Just tonight I'm afraid.

Oh ... are you interested in maybe ... coming back to my room?

Thank you for the offer, Sarah. I have someone else lined up this evening.

Yah ... that would *so* not work for her. She would get insanely jealous and lash out and probably be asked to immediately leave the premises. Can't have a psycho ex living here, verbally threatening a Vampire Lord.

"I'm not talking about food. I'm talking about what are you doing with *me*?"

"I thought I made that clear."

Uh ... what?

"Breakfast?" she asked.

"No, Sarah. You."

He was so serious she almost laughed. Maybe Giselle learned her tail chasing from Romaric, because he was making no fucking sense whatsoever.

"What the hell are you talking about?"

"I want you, Sarah. I'm not sure how much clearer I need to make it."

His intensity suddenly increased tenfold. His cheekbones became more defined, sharper; his eyes glowed, making them appear almost crystalized; his sinewy body went completely taut and she could see the flex of his muscles underneath the tightness of his stuffy button down shirt.

"But if you need me to spell it out for you, I will."

He pushed his chair back and stood. He was already a good foot taller than her short five foot six frame, but with him looming large over her sitting form, he almost seemed like a daunting mythical warrior that had risen from the ashes. If he suddenly brandished a medieval longsword it wouldn't surprise her in the least.

He gently took her hand in his and pulled her to her feet. His piercing stare was so ripe with longing she almost couldn't catch her breath and the reasons she shouldn't have sex with him vanished like they'd never existed at all. He walked her backward until her back was flush to the dark blue painted wall.

She swallowed hard, not knowing what to expect next, but waiting for it on pins and needles all the same. Romaric's eyes never left hers as his hands came to the wall on either side of her head, caging her in. His feet came on either side of hers and his inner thighs pressed against her outer ones, which allowed him to unashamedly push his rock hard erection into her stomach. She was well and truly trapped and *so* incredibly turned on by his blatant display of ownership over her body that she thought she could possibly climax from this physical contact alone.

"What I want, Sarah—no, what I *crave* more than my next breath—is to bury my aching cock deep inside your hot, tight, soaked pussy and fuck you until your throat is raw from screaming my name. I'm going to fuck you until you've come so many times you think you can't come again, but you will because I will demand it. I'm going to fuck you every way I can until you crave me on a subconscious level and can't live without my cock. Then I'm going to make love to you until you agree to be mine."

Fucking. A. Well ...let's get right to *that, then.*

"Is that clear enough for you now, my beauty?"

Yes. Yes, that was as clear as the Caribbean Sea. But his words had robbed her lungs of air and apparently severed the connection between her brain and mouth, so she could only nod her understanding.

"Good."

She expected him to kiss her next. Christ, she *wanted* him to kiss her next. One would think after a guy verbally fucked you like that, they'd follow it up with a soul-sucking kiss to prove they weren't all talk.

But not Romaric.

He pushed away from the wall, which also pushed him away from her body, and she swore every single nerve ending he'd touched while leaning against her was burning out of control.

Once again, his stony mask snapped into place. He held out his hand to hers, escorting her back to the table, resuming the same positions they'd had before. She was stunned speechless and pinched herself to wake up from this most bizarre dream, but the sting proved she wasn't sleeping.

She dared a sideways glance at Romaric, who was staring at her with open interest.

She felt like a science experiment and she opened her mouth to demand he stop it, when Hooker entered, rolling an entire cart full of food. He always, always went overboard and she felt bad for all the food that went to waste.

"That will be all," Romaric rudely replied when Hooker placed all the items on the table.

Hooker started to leave when Sarah called, "Thank you, Hooker."

His lips turned up and he inclined his head slightly in acknowledgement. He would never say, but she knew he appreciated the kindness. Just because these vampires were lords and all powerful, didn't mean they needed to be assholes. A nice 'please' and 'thank you' went a long way, as far as she was concerned. Maybe that was the Midwest girl in her.

After he was gone, Sarah turned to Romaric, "You didn't need to be so rude, you know."

He set his fork down on his plate, which had been halfway to his mouth filled to the brim with scrambled eggs.

"Rude?" He seemed genuinely confused at her accusation.

"Yes, rude. He works hard cooking and cleaning and doing whatever else it is that Dev demands of him. It's not too much to ask to say thank you for all the work he went to making breakfast."

She turned back to her plate, but her appetite had vanished. Both her physical and sexual one. Romaric may be a hottie but who was she kidding? He was *waaay* out of her league and she was still very much intimidated by him. He may think he wants her now but he would quickly tire of her. She would never fit into his world. Into *this* world. And she'd been naïve to think otherwise.

They were complete opposites.

She had manners. He clearly didn't.

She wanted happily ever after. He just wanted to fuck her brains out.

She was sympathetic and empathetic. He was emotionally closed off.

She had a hair-trigger temper. He was calm, cool and collected.

He intrigued her on so many levels and what she wouldn't give to be able to peel away his protective layers one by one. To *really* get to know the untainted soul she saw hiding underneath his gruff exterior. He put on a very good front to everyone else, but the second she'd looked into his eyes, she knew there was so much more to Romaric Dietrich than he would ever let on to the outside world. She'd seen a deep wound that she'd foolishly wanted to uncover and heal.

But it would never work between them. She was far better off keeping him in her dreams, where he belonged. Where he'd always been.

"I'm not hungry after all."

Placing her napkin on top of her untouched food, she stood and walked toward the door. She didn't make it five steps before running smack into a solid, immovable object, which threw her off balance and she began to fall backward. Strong arms reached out and swept her off her feet before she could hit the ground.

"Where do you think you're going, Sarah?" Romaric said, holding her tightly in his oh so strong arms. She had no choice but to put her own arms around his neck for support.

Okay, so she did, but her momma didn't raise no fool.

"I'm going back to my room," she retorted. She didn't owe him anything, certainly not an explanation. And she'd be damned if he she would give him one.

"I don't think so."

He didn't think so? What?

Me Tarzan.

You Jane.

If his hands were free, he'd probably be pounding his chest with his melon-sized fists trying to convince her of his male worthiness.

"Um, I *think* so, buddy. Let me go." She now used her arms to try fruitlessly pushing out his iron grip hold.

"We've already been through this. You're mine, Sarah. You're not going anywhere."

She stopped her futile efforts and gawked at him in disbelief. *Wow*. He needed a lesson in twenty-first century courting, because he was *soooorely* behind the times.

“I’m *yours*?” She couldn’t have kept the biting sarcasm out of her voice if she’d tried. Which she didn’t.

“Yes.” The very matter-of-fact way he said that word got under her skin.

She laughed. *Really* laughed. She couldn’t help it. This entire thing was so unbelievably ridiculous and she couldn’t wait to gossip to Kate and Analise about how downright preposterous her morning had been.

Me Tarzan, You Jane.

“You’re mine, you’re not going anywhere.”

They’d laugh about it for months and months. She’d just keep his impassioned ‘fucking’ speech out of the story, however. That was for her ears alone and God knows she’d be replaying that twenty times a day like the crushing fool she was.

Romaric was gawking at her like she’d gone to crazy town and maybe she had. She finally got control of her laughter enough to speak.

“I’m not a piece of property that you can just claim, Romaric. And I’m not *yours*. I belong to no one except for myself. Now, kindly put me down. This has been … interesting, but I have a very busy day.”

She didn’t.

At her tirade, a devilish grin ate up his entire face and a terrible sense of foreboding wormed its way into the pit of her stomach.

“Ah, but that’s where you’re wrong, my beauty. You *are* mine and I’ve come to do exactly that. Claim you. For you see, Sarah, *you* are my Destiny. My Fate. *You*, my insolent beauty, are my

Moira, which makes *you One. Hundred. Percent.* Mine."

Oh.

My.

Holy.

God.

Acknowledgements and Thanks!

Wow, I'm writing my acknowledgements for my second novel and it's beyond surreal. Again, how can *thanks* ever adequately express the gratitude I feel for all the help that I've received getting here? It seems inadequate and it really is, but I don't know a better way to express how I feel!

To my readers and fans (Ah! I have FANS?!!!??): **Thank you** for purchasing my book!! I am in love with these characters and I hope you are too! If you like my books, please spread the word! Please leave reviews! Please follow me on social media! The best thing you can do to support an author you love is word of mouth.

To my *girls*: Tara, Kaitlyn, Beth, Sherri, Teresa, Emma, Diane and Amanda...once again a million thanks will never be enough for your honesty, your valued opinions and for helping me through this process. I'm so blessed to have each and every one of you in my life! (Sniffle, sniffle, get the tissue...)

To the bloggers and reviewers who have graciously agreed to both read and plug my book...wow. I never really fully understood the power of social media until I went through this process, so thanks very much for supporting me!

To my husband: Babe, you are my everything, my inspiration, my very heart. I can write about romance because I live it every day with you. Thanks for your undying support when I am literally consumed with my writing. You are turning into quite the chef! Who knew it would just take writing books to get you in the kitchen. (wink). You are my rock and I'm so very glad that you're proud of what I've been able to accomplish, because none of it would have been possible without you.

Thanks to my editor, Alicia, for all of your great comments and suggestions. I have a better story because of your feedback. And finally a special thanks to Yocla Designs for the absolutely ***A MA Z I N G*** job you did on the book cover art ... again! You brought my vision of the story to life and a picture really does say a thousand words through your work.

Finally, I want to shout out to all of the amazing romance authors that gave me the inspiration to try penning my own book and those that have helped support me through this very confusing, very overwhelming process. Some days it felt like too much, and you were always there to answer my stupid questions. Emma and Amanda, I especially thank you for your guidance and patience and our new friendships!

About the Author

Most authors will tell you that writing is all they've ever wanted to do. I guess I'm one of the few that don't fit in that bucket. Writing a book was never on my bucket list until three years ago. On my list was: Climb the Corporate ladder. *Check.* Go to Europe. *Check.* Complete a half marathon. *Check.* Eat chocolate daily. *Double check. Isn't this on everyone's bucket list?* Catch up on two seasons of Games of Thrones in one day. *Painful, but check.* Lose five pounds. *This will never be checked.* And finally, devouring romance books at an alarming pace like the unashamed book addict I am…*Over a thousand checks!*

Living in Nebraska with my soul-mate hubby, I pen my magic world at night, while paying the bills with an actual compensating job in the corporate world during the day. Writing is just an all-consuming passion for now, but, boy, if I could dream...

My other loves include my simply amazing, incredible and talented children, a steamy novel, great friends and family, and a warm ocean breeze gliding over my sun drenched skin with a cocktail in hand.

If you enjoyed this book, please consider leaving a review at Amazon, Barnes and Noble, Goodreads or the many various other on-line places you can purchase ebooks. Even one or two sentences or simply rating the book is helpful. If you're anything like me, you rely on reader reviews to help make your determination on purchasing a great book in the vast sea of available ones. Many THANKS!

Finally, if you would like to learn more about me or message me, please visit the following places:

Facebook: https://www.facebook.com/pages/KL-Kreig/808927362462053?ref=hl

Website: http://klkreig.com

Goodreads author page: https://www.goodreads.com/author/show/9845429.K_L_Kreig

Email: klkreig@gmail.com

Thanks!

Kelly

Made in the USA
Las Vegas, NV
17 January 2022